*The shining splendor of [the] cover of this book refl[ects]
the story inside. Look for [the ... when]
you buy a historical roman[ce that guar-]
antees the very best in quality and reading entertainment.*

WILD DESIRE

Caroline was floundering. She was overly conscious of how dark Luke's eyes really were and how very handsome and masculine he was. He was a man with whom any woman could so very easily fall in love . . . but she was not just any woman. She was Miss Caroline Rowe, she reminded herself desperately, and she didn't cavort with pearl divers and fishermen.

"I asked you once before if you liked what you saw," Luke said softly. "I ask you again, my dear Miss Rowe, because it's yours for the taking."

She drew in her breath. He was outrageous . . . and also more exciting than any man she had ever known.

"You presume too much—" she said, her voice hoarse.

He leaned forward to caress the side of her cheek with his fingers. She shivered, feeling an almost irresistible urge to grasp those caressing fingers and bring them to her mouth. Was she going completely mad?

Wordlessly he pressed his mouth to hers. She stood as still as she could, trying very hard not to respond in the slightest way, because he was crass and undisciplined and the very epitome of bad taste.

But it was too much to expect of anyone. Pressed close to his heart, she succumbed to a wildness in her own nature that she was only just discovering . . .

**PUT SOME PASSION INTO YOUR
LIFE . . . WITH THIS STEAMY SELECTION OF
ZEBRA *LOVEGRAMS*!**

SEA FIRES   (3899, $4.50/$5.50)
by Christine Dorsey
Spirited, impetuous Miranda Chadwick arrives in the untamed New
World prepared for any peril. But when the notorious pirate Gentleman
Jack Blackstone kidnaps her in order to fulfill his secret plans, she can't
help but surrender—to the shameless desires and raging hunger that his
bronzed, lean body and demanding caresses ignite within her!

TEXAS MAGIC   (3898, $4.50/$5.50)
by Wanda Owen
After being ambushed by bandits and saved by a ranchhand, headstrong
Texas belle Bianca Moreno hires her gorgeous rescuer as a protective escort. But Rick Larkin does more than guard her body—he kisses away her
maidenly inhibitions, and teaches her the secrets of wild, reckless love!

SEDUCTIVE CARESS   (3767, $4.50/$5.50)
by Carla Simpson
Determined to find her missing sister, brave beauty Jessamyn Forsythe
disguises herself as a simple working girl and follows her only clues to
Whitechapel's darkest alleys . . . and the disturbingly handsome Inspec-
tor Devlin Burke. Burke, on the trail of a killer, becomes intrigued with
the ebon-haired lass and discovers the secrets of her silken lips and the
hidden promise of her sweet flesh.

SILVER SURRENDER   (3769, $4.50/$5.50)
by Vivian Vaughan
When Mexican beauty Aurelia Mazón saves a handsome stranger from
death, she finds herself on the run from the Federales with the most dangerous man she's ever met. And when Texas Ranger Carson Jarrett steals
her heart with his intimate kisses and seductive caresses, she yields to an
all-consuming passion from which she hopes to never escape!

ENDLESS SEDUCTION   (3793, $4.50/$5.50)
by Rosalyn Alsobrook
Caught in the middle of a dangerous shoot-out, lovely Leona Stegall falls
unconscious and awakens to the gentle touch of a handsome doctor.
When her rescuer's caresses turn passionate, Leona surrenders to his fiery
embrace and savors a night of soaring ecstasy!

*Available wherever paperbacks are sold, or order direct from the
Publisher. Send cover price plus 50¢ per copy for mailing and
handling to Zebra Books, Dept. 3956, 475 Park Avenue South,
New York, N.Y. 10016. Residents of New York and Tennessee
must include sales tax. DO NOT SEND CASH. For a free Zebra/
Pinnacle catalog please write to the above address.*

JEAN INNES

TROPICAL FIRE

ZEBRA BOOKS
KENSINGTON PUBLISHING CORP.

ZEBRA BOOKS

are published by

Kensington Publishing Corp.
475 Park Avenue South
New York, NY 10016

Copyright © 1992 by Jean Saunders

All rights reserved. No part of this book may be repro-
duced in any form or by any means without the prior written consent of the Publisher, excepting brief quotes used
in reviews.

Zebra, the Z logo, and the Lovegram logo are trademarks
of Kensington Publishing Corp.

If you purchased this book without a cover you should be
aware that this book is stolen property. It was reported as
"unsold and destroyed" to the Publisher and neither the
Author nor the Publisher has received any payment for
this "stripped book."

First printing: November, 1992

Printed in the United States of America

Chapter One

They were safely nearing the end of their long voyage now. They had traveled halfway around the world from England, and the horizon was already showing a glimmer of darkness where the vague outlines of Australia lay tantalizingly ahead of them.

Australia, and a new life! Caroline felt the familiar thrill of anticipation every time the name of the unknown continent entered her head. And her father was still enthusing to her and to their dinner companions about the grand new life they would all start there. He was so sure of their bright new beginning, so lovingly and confidently sure that this was to be their golden future. His words helped to allay her natural apprehension, which unsurprisingly mingled with the excitement.

"We'll not fail to prosper there, my love," her father, Sir William Rowe, told her repeatedly. "The country is crying out for information about the rest of the world, and Britain is still filled with curiosity about this relatively unknown land. It's no longer filled only with the wretched convicts we sent there, but also with honest settlers trying to make good.

Just like ourselves, in fact, and this is what I intend to tell the world."

As their traveling companions murmured their approval, Caroline hid a small smile at his comparison with honest settlers. Sir William Rowe had position and status, and their new life was hardly to be compared with the lives of those who still struggled to make a living with their bare hands in such very different and alien surroundings! Despite his sometimes indifferent health, Sir William was a newspaperman of great integrity, and had ambitious plans for creating an entire new world of accurate reporting to counter the garbled reports that Britain often received about Australia and the new Australians.

That was what *they* would be, Caroline reminded herself. New Australians. She couldn't resist commenting on the fact to her father as they continued with their evening meal on board the luxurious *Princess Victoria*.

"I don't think we should forget that we shall be the foreigners," she reminded him. "The Englishmen who have been there for some years will also see us as the interlopers, Father, so I suppose we can expect some opposition if we try to infiltrate too quickly."

It seemed a timely warning, for although Sir William's newspaper reports were noted for their honesty, they weren't always the most tactful. It wouldn't do to antagonize their new compatriots in a strange new land. It still felt odd to Caroline, coming as she did from a gentle English background, but after her mother died, she and her father had both known that London was too full of memories for them to remain. And this had seemed such a golden opportunity . . .

The idle chatter was such a pleasant way to spend these last days and nights before finally reaching their destination. The dining room was filled with genteel folk like themselves, and the hazy smoke from the men's cigars lent an odd sense of stability and continuity to the surroundings. Together, they were still a little part of England, of all that they held dear and familiar . . . and then, in an instant, it seemed, the nightmare began.

A dozen bells clanged out, and crewmen were shouting out orders, summoning the passengers on deck to lash themselves to the rails or anything stable as the sudden violence of a tropical storm enveloped them without any warning. On deck, they would be near at hand to the lifeboats, should the need arise.

Even as the implication of what the crewmen were saying seeped into the stunned minds of the passengers, there was panic. From that moment on, as she struggled with her father to reach the narrow doorway along with a hundred other hysterical passengers, Caroline forgot how it felt to have her stomach remain in its right place.

Dazed with shock, Caroline was herded onto the deck, the screaming wind and rain whipping all around her. A nightmare of confused images confronted her: huge, towering waves blinding the eyes and smothering the decks with spume; the unearthly cracking of timbers which sounded as if the ship were in its death throes; the wild screams of panic from the women passengers and shouts of encouragement from the gentlemen.

And through it all came the futile reassurances from the crew, laced with the constantly repeated warnings for the passengers to tie themselves to the ship's rails by every available means.

"This is madness," Sir William said as they were commanded to remain on deck in readiness for the expected order to abandon ship and to take to the lifeboats. "We'd stand more chance of staying alive in our cabins," he'd shouted in her ear as they both struggled to keep to their feet on the slippery deck. "This way, we're more likely to be thrown overboard than to succeed in jumping into a small boat in these seas."

While he talked, he tied her securely to one of the bulwarks with a loose piece of rope. He then kissed her frozen, rain-soaked cheeks, and went away to help others in distress, promising to return as quickly as possible to get her into one of the fragile boats that would be their only means of survival. She had long since lost sight of him in the crowds, and a stomach-clenching terror gripped her.

"Father, where are you? I can't see you! Please help me. Don't leave me . . ."

Caroline's screams were lost on the wind as the great ship pitched and rolled ever more relentlessly. Without warning the ropes holding her were torn to shreds as if by a giant hand, and the young English girl found herself sliding across the deck that was churning and foaming with the angry wash of the sea. She struck her head against something solid, and was dazed for a few seconds. Then, as she touched her forehead, she felt something sticky and hot, and knew it was her own blood.

Terrified sobs tore at her throat. She had never felt so alone.

"Are you all right, miss?" she heard a voice yell nearby. A crewman was lurching toward her, and she felt a surge of thankfulness.

"I'm well enough," she shrieked. "But my father— Have you seen my fa—"

The query was drowned out as a sodden timber seemed to crash down from nowhere, crushing the crewman instantly.

"Oh, dear God, help me!" Caroline moaned at the appalling sight. There was nothing she could do for the man. The timber would have been far too heavy for her to move, but in any case, there was little doubt that the man was already dead. She turned

8

away from the sickening sight, whimpering like a wounded animal, and tried to crawl away to a corner where she could huddle.

She had always thought herself strong, but these last hours must have tested even the strongest man aboard the *Princess Victoria*. And her father had not been the most robust of men.

She sobbed now, wondering where he had gone. She felt with a growing dread that she was never going to see him again. And where, too, was everyone else on the ship? Now and then she heard shouts above the storm, and an occasional scream, but all seemed comparatively quiet now, as if the hurling ravages of nature were determined to overtake all that mere mortals could accomplish.

The ship had been carrying wealthy, paying passengers, so it hadn't been overcrowded like the terrible convict ships of some years previously, but surely they couldn't all have perished. . . . A feeling of cold dread settled around Caroline's heart at the thought, and she refused to contemplate such a thing. Darkness was beginning to descend over everything now, with the swiftness of that region. As she tried to stand to assess her position, she suddenly realized that the ship was at a stark angle to where it should be, and she had great trouble in holding onto her senses. Then, as if taking pity on her, her own spirit gave up the struggle, and she collapsed in a faint where she lay.

Some time later she opened her eyes to a brilliantly hot sun overhead. She saw instantly that she was no longer on board the *Princess Victoria*. Of the once-mighty ship, there was no sign except for the flotsam drifting about in a deceptively innocent-looking blue sea. She lay in the corner of a small boat, realizing only now that as well as the cut on her head there was an ugly gash in her leg on which the blood had

9

partially congealed.

She couldn't remember it happening, but it throbbed and ached abominably now, and her long skirt was soaked in blood. She gently covered the wound with her skirt to shield it from the burning rays of the sun. She eased up on her aching limbs until she could peer over the side of the small boat into which someone must have thrust her. How she had got into it, she had no idea, nor where any others who may have accompanied her had disappeared.

"I can't bear it," she whispered through parched lips. "Oh, Father, where are you? I want you so much!"

Any companions in the lifeboat were most likely gone to the sharks, she thought, shuddering. The crew on the *Princess Victoria* told their tales with relish of how the razor-toothed sharks basked in these southern waters. The wealthy English passengers had been excited by these tales because there had been no fear of encountering the monsters—then.

The storm had well and truly blown itself out now, and slowly Caroline tried to move a little, wincing as her wounded leg seemed to be stiffening quite alarmingly. The sun was so brilliant overhead it hurt her eyes to try to look at it, and she gauged by its position that it must be nearing midday. Her arms, though covered by the long sleeves of her gown, were beginning to prickle from the heat, and her face and neck were uncomfortable.

It seemed ludicrous now to recall how her maid would fuss and complain if she was out in the sun for too long.

"You'll ruin that lovely complexion, Miss Caroline," Sophie would say sternly, speaking with the intimacy of one who had been in the Rowes' service a long time. "And then you'll be obliged to avoid going out to parties and balls for the season, and you'll miss meeting all them eligible young bachelors your Pa looks out for you!"

"You've got the cheek of the devil, Sophie," Caroline would reply with a laugh. "And since I'm not particularly interested in any of the young bachelors I've seen so far, what does it matter!"

"You'll not be saying that when you're thirty and still on the shelf, you mark my words," Sophie always followed up darkly with a meaningful sniff.

But what did any of it matter now, Caroline thought, her lower lip trembling. Her flesh was soon to be burnt to a blistering hue in this heat, and no one would see it but the fishes. And Sophie, too, would have perished on the *Princess Victoria*. She had no doubt in her mind by now that all hands must have gone, save for those lucky enough to cling to wreckage or escape in lifeboats. The gentry would have been allowed to go first, and she prayed desperately that her father had been one of them.

But it would drive her to madness to dwell on such things. Her own survival must now be her main concern. She gazed around, desperate to see any hint of land, but to her sun-dazzled eyes, there was nothing. She was totally alone on a vast ocean, drifting helplessly in a small craft. She didn't have the remotest idea of how to handle it. She had been born a lady and hadn't had to lift a finger to do anything for herself. All her life someone else had pampered and cherished her, and this treatment, which had seemed so normal to her, now threatened her very existence.

She was aware of utter, gut-wrenching panic, and for a few seconds she was almost ready to throw herself overboard to be devoured by the waiting sharks, if sharks there be. Anything was better than drifting, slowly starving, waiting to die. . . . The breath was so tight in her chest she was already finding it difficult to breathe. Her leg throbbed and stabbed, and finally she sank into the bowels of the lifeboat again,

11

exhaustion and pain once more sending her into blissful oblivion.

Caroline had no idea how long she had been unconscious, but when she awoke with a start, she wondered briefly if she was already hallucinating. She could hear voices in her head. They were men's voices shouting in a guttural foreign tongue, so she knew instantly they weren't the cheery British crew from the *Princess Victoria*.

Just as quickly, Caroline became aware that the voices weren't inside her head at all. They were somewhere out there, on that vast blue ocean, and whoever the voices belonged to, they were her only means of rescue. Hope flared in her heart, and she struggled to grip the side of the boat and pull herself up. She tried desperately to call out, but her throat had dried so much that her voice was little more than a hoarse whisper. Her leg hurt so badly she could hardly move now, and she waved a futile hand, praying that someone would see it and not think that her frail boat was empty.

"Hold to, boys. I think there's somebody inside it after all," she heard a strong male voice say sharply.

They seemed to be quite near. But by then she was past caring. The effort of trying to speak and to move was draining her fast. Her thoughts began to wander and become fuzzy. It would be so much easier now just to give up . . .

Seconds later she was aware that the brightness of the sun was briefly obliterated. She struggled to open her eyes and saw a face looking down at her. It seemed very dark, but perhaps it was only in contrast to the sun creating a halo around it. Was it God, come to claim her? The incongruous thought swept into her head, and even though the vision was awesome and frightening, Caroline couldn't even cry out.

12

"Good God, it's a woman," the voice said, roughly now. And then there were more faces peering down at her, and these were truly black, their faces and torsos glistening with heat and salt spray. She felt a searing fear that she was about to be doomed to something far worse than the sharks, when the first voice spoke again. And now she registered what should have been obvious to her in the beginning. It spoke in English, with a clipped hard accent she knew vaguely to be from the north of her home country.

"Don't be afraid, lass. You're quite safe now. We'll tie your boat onto ours, and one of the boys will come on board yours to steer it. We'll soon have you safe on dry land again."

Caroline's eyes flooded with tears of relief. The man sounded so *normal,* the words so comforting, after the terrors of the night and the realization that she was entirely alone. She tried to voice her thanks, but the words still wouldn't come. She dashed the weak tears away, remembering in a ridiculous burst of memory how her old nurse had always instructed her never to show emotion in front of strangers. The old habits were deeply ingrained inside her, even as she recognized the mad irony of them now. These people were her rescuers, and without them, she would almost certainly have perished.

The boy had leaped into the craft and sat grinning at her now. As her eyes focused on him, she felt hot, shocked color sting her cheeks. She had no idea how old he was. She had never seen black people before, and although she had been taught that they were exactly the same as white people except for the pigment of their skins, she was totally unsure how to speak to him. But even worse than that, she simply didn't know where to look because he was completely naked.

"Does Jojo bother you, lass?" she heard the

13

amused voice of the Englishman say. "Clothes get in the boys' way when they're on pearl-diving trips."

Without thinking, Caroline's eyes traveled down the man's own torso. He, too, was bare to the waist, his body richly tanned by the sun, the fine spread of dark hair trailing down to his midriff and matching the color of the hair on his head. He wore the briefest pair of beige linen knickers Caroline could imagine, and beneath them his legs were long and lean and also very tanned. She blushed wildly, especially when she saw how he was grinning down at her, just as if he was well aware of her unwitting speculation . . .

"I'm sorry. I'm—not offended. Just surprised."

She wasn't sure just how she managed to get the words out, but she sensed that it would be foolish to show how very offended she really was by such a display of masculinity, given that these people were her saviors.

But it couldn't be more of a contrast to the way gentlefolk behaved in Victorian England. Even at the seaside, in those flourishing resorts so favored now by the Queen and Prince Albert, bathing machines were hauled right down to the waters' edge, and gentlemen and ladies bathed quite separately.

But she was quickly realizing that none of the four boys accompanying the man wore anything at all, and they all seemed unconcerned by the fact. And it was her own inhibited and sheltered upbringing that made her so aware of the difference in the male bodies to her own, Caroline thought faintly. But since she had never seen a man's body before, she could hardly prevent herself from being shocked— and curious.

Beneath her veiled eyes, she glanced again at the linen knickers of the tall Englishman. They were well-filled, and she couldn't help wondering . . . She tore her gaze away quickly. Was she going mad? And

14

just what her father would think of such wanton thoughts in the head of a young English lady . . . but since her father had always been a bit of an aristocratic rebel as well as an inquisitive, probing newspaperman, he'd brought her up to be just as curious about everything . . . providing she was discreetly curious as a well-brought-up young lady should be.

"Well, lass? Do you like what you see?" the man asked, smiling broadly now. Before she could think of a withering reply, even if she could have voiced one, he had reached for a leather flask. "Never mind. We'll assess one another at some later date. I suggest you drink some of this before you become totally dehydrated, and then we'll be on our way."

He took the stopper out of the flask and handed it to her. Without arguing, Caroline drank thirstily. Water had never tasted so good, and after a few good gulps, she sputtered as it spilled and ran over her neck and breasts.

"Steady," her rescuer said coolly. "There's plenty more where that came from, and if you drink too quickly, you'll make yourself sick."

He'd hardly got the words out before Caroline knew that was exactly what was about to happen. She just managed to lean over the side of the boat before she retched violently, feeling more humiliated than she ever had in her life as the man calmly handed her a cloth dipped in seawater with which to wipe herself and her gown.

"I'd offer to do it for you," he said, noting how her hands shook with embarrassment and shock, "but I fear I would be unable to keep my hands any steadier than your own."

She saw that he was studying her with undisguised interest, seeing how she pressed the cloth to her gown, where its dampness emphasized the lush curves of her breasts. There was a darkening in his eyes that she didn't fully understand, but from the

15

chattering comments of the grinning boys and his quick reply in their own language, she guessed they must be making some lewd reference to her rounded shape and the way the gown clung to her now. She tilted her chin and spoke as sharply as she could, considering that her throat was again dry and parched from the retching, despite the very welcome water.

"I'm quite ready now, thank you. The sooner I reach Australian soil the better, and I'm sure my father will reward you handsomely for rescuing me."

Even as she said the words, her chin shook with swift shame. She heard herself, so gracious and so condescending. Yet she had no idea if her father had survived the storm or if she would ever see him again. But such a possibility didn't bear thinking about, and she stared stoically at the man who nodded gravely now, his eyes expressionless.

"Then we had best get started," he said. "Though I don't hold out much chance of repayment from an absent father. In any case, I may well prefer my payment in kind, rather than coin."

There was no disguising his meaning now. Even though she had had little contact with gentlemen, save those her father had introduced with care to the house, Caroline couldn't mistake the sudden hot look in the man's eyes and the way his gaze lingered more insolently over her shape now. And she wasn't so innocent that she didn't know about the coupling of a man and a woman.

One of their housemaids had used the term with some relish some months ago when she was describing to Caroline the reason for another's dismissal . . .

"The silly little ninny had upped with her skirts for the butcher's roundsman, right inside the stables when visitors were expected. They could hardly help seein' the coupling that was going on. And that

16

butcher's boy's very well-endowed, if you get my meaning, miss. It must have been a fine sight, with his bare backside all exposed to the skies, and young Polly moaning and groaning under 'im."

Caroline had listened, wide-eyed, knowing she should be firmly putting a stop to this low confidence, but simply too curious to do so. And the girl had added considerably to her education on that early morning.

Coupling . . . She had felt an odd little thrill at hearing the word at first and in realizing just what it implied. It was a word that could be taken romantically or coarsely, but from the way this stranger was looking at her now, she had no illusions as to the way *he* would see it! She felt a sliver of panic, knowing she was completely helpless among these people, and the early euphoria at being rescued was tempered by a new and more desperate fear.

"Can you please just get me ashore?" she said, as imperiously as she could. "I'm beginning to feel quite ill."

To her horror, she realized that her head was starting to feel as if it didn't rightly belong to her anymore. She had been adrift in this small boat too long, hatless in the blazing sun for too long, her wounded leg unattended for too long, the cut on her head throbbing for too long . . .

"Please . . ." she said faintly. She had never fainted in her life before this voyage, and it had already happened twice since the nightmare began. Now she was very much afraid it was about to happen again. She tried desperately to hold on to her senses, and then it seemed as if sea and sun were rushing toward her in a great roaring of sound and stabbing light just before everything went black and she knew no more.

Caroline awoke slowly. The nauseating motion of

the small boat was no longer beneath her. She was lying in a clean bed with fresh-smelling sheets and a soft pillow under her head. Although the room was darkened by the heavy curtains pulled across at the windows, she could see that it was quite large and elegantly and tastefully furnished. Whoever lived here was no pauper. The room was almost as large as her bedroom at home, and at the swift, poignant memory, the stinging tears rushed to her eyes as she knew in her heart that she would never see it again.

She felt so feeble, and she hated to feel that way. The lovely Miss Caroline Rowe, eighteen-year-old daughter of the prominent businessman and newspaper proprietor, Sir William Rowe, could have had all of London at her feet by now, had not the two of them decided to take on this big adventure instead. To travel to Australia, to the other side of the world, and to start a new and exciting life . . .

Caroline felt the weak sobs well up in her throat again. She tried hard to remain calm as the recollection of all that had happened since then rushed back to her mind. It did no good to fret about anything now because there was nothing she could do until she found out exactly where she was and, just as importantly, whose house this was. And at least she was safe and alive.

She vividly recalled the face of the Englishman at that moment. She recalled how he had stared at her, his gaze lingering over her body, and the remembered sensation strangely filled her senses. She shivered, wondering if she would ever see him again. She doubted very much that this place had anything to do with an uncouth fellow who went pearl diving with natives, unless he was an employee of the house owner.

That could be it, she supposed, closing her eyes again, surprised to realize how exhausted she felt. But she couldn't rid her mind of the man's image now, and she was faintly annoyed to think how much she remembered about him. It seemed almost as if he were imprinted in her mind as indelibly as the black ink on her father's newspapers.

He was tall, much taller than the black-skinned boys. His hair was as dark as his eyes, and his skin was tanned to a healthy mahogany by the hot sun. He had a wide, easy smile and an undoubtedly arrogant sense of self-importance that she knew could irritate her very much if she let it. To judge by his coloring and also by the way he conversed so easily with the natives in their own tongue, he had obviously lived here for some time.

She felt a sudden jolt. Natives. For a moment she had no idea what kind of natives they could be, and then she remembered what her father had told her about this new continent of Australia. He had done his research well.

"The native Aborigines have lived there for thousands of years, Caroline. They still consider it their land, and the white man should respect that, though many don't. It's always that way when one race feels itself superior to another. Unfortunately it always causes friction and resentment when outsiders establish claims to land and begin settlements there, even when the original inhabitants have done little to develop their own country."

"But if the outsiders improve the land and make it more cultured, how can these people object? Especially if they help the natives to prosper," Caroline had said in all innocence.

"My dear girl, you have to think in their terms to understand that. Why should they want anything about their land disturbed when it's suited them very well as it is for thousands of years? It was their land first, remember. We're the invaders."

The conversation came back to her now, and it seemed reasonable to suppose that the four young

19

pearl divers along with the Englishman had been some of these Aborigines. But they hadn't been resentful or unfriendly, she had to admit. In fact, they had been far too familiar in their smiles and nudges and gestures.

She became weary of speculation and wished someone would come to explain to her exactly where she was. She also realized she was ravenously hungry and that she probably hadn't eaten for several days. She was wearing an unfamiliar white cambric nightgown, and she didn't want to think how she had been divested of her gown and petticoats and corsets and put into this garment, nor whose it was.

Without thinking, she started to swing her legs over the side of the bed, meaning to go toward the window and assess her surroundings. As she did so, she became aware of the huge bandage on her right leg. It stretched from her ankle to above her knee, but even so, its support was minimal. Her leg buckled at once as she tried to stand on it, and she crashed heavily to the carpeted floor with a cry.

Almost at once the door flew open and a woman came rushing inside.

"My heavens, miss, what are you trying to do? Mr. Luke would tan my hide if he thought I was allowing you to fall about like this. Come on now, let me help you back into bed. You're too weak to try standing on that leg for a few more days yet."

Caroline listened to her as if in a state of shock. The woman was as fair-skinned as herself, though considerably older, and although she sounded far from genteel, the sentiments were obviously kindly meant. But Caroline was more concerned with the implication of her last words. As the woman heaved her back into the bed and tucked the covers around her, she spoke hoarsely.

"Please . . . how long have I been here?"

"It's nearly two weeks since you was picked up out

20

of the sea," the woman said, obviously enjoying the dramatic turn of phrase. "And lucky not to be shark bait, by all accounts. Your guardian angel must have been looking after you that day, miss."

Two weeks! And what of the *Princess Victoria* in all that time? And her father's fate? Nausea threatened to wash over her again and she was cold all over.

"Have you any news of a shipwreck?" Caroline said through lips that were suddenly trembling. She saw the look of alarm on the woman's face and how she started to back away.

"I think I'd better fetch Mr. Luke to discuss all that with you, miss. I don't like the look of you at all. You've gone right pasty-looking, and the doctor said you wasn't to get excited over anything until that leg's mended properly."

She vanished from the room before Caroline could say angrily that it wasn't her leg that was bothering her, although it was truly beginning to ache badly now. It was not knowing anything that preyed on her. Who Mr. Luke was, she neither knew nor cared.

Minutes later a tall, well-built man came striding into the room. And then she knew. She swallowed, feeling as gauche and young as she ever had and at a distinct disadvantage with her dark hair lying loose across the pillow and this man so handsome and elegant now.

The last time she had seen him, he had been stripped to the waist, his body glistening with sea spray and vitality, his limbs exposed to wind and weather. Now he wore clothes of the finest quality: dark trousers, a white shirt, and a maroon silk necktie pinned with a single pearl stud. He folded his arms as he reached her bedside, smiling down at her guardedly.

"Well now, what are we going to do with you?" he said softly. "Do we have to tie you down to keep you

21

safely in bed until that leg's mended, I wonder?"

The memory of that other time she had been tied down, when the powerful *Princess Victoria* had been threshing about like matchwood in a boiling sea, made Caroline flinch.

"Please don't patronize me," she said as strongly as she could, though very aware of the tremble in her voice. "Will you please tell me exactly where I am and who you are?"

He gave an irritating smile. To her further annoyance he pulled up a velvet-covered bedside chair and seated himself. He crossed his legs arrogantly as if he had every intention of staying there all day if he so chose.

"I think you owe me the courtesy of telling me who you are first. I prefer to know the names of my guests."

She felt her mouth drop open.

"This is *your* house?"

Utterly confused now, Caroline tried to remember her manners. "I just thought, seeing you in the fishing boat with the, er, boys, that you must also be a fisherman. If I'm wrong, then of course I apologize."

She knew how stiff she sounded, but it was impossible for her to feel easy with this man, especially when she was so very aware that she was alone in a bedroom with him, which was something never to be tolerated in any decent English household. She would have been compromised at once, her reputation in ruins, and her father and all polite society scandalized.

Somehow, all such proprieties seemed to have no meaning here, and she still didn't know why.

Chapter Two

"My name is Caroline Rowe," she said shortly. "I was traveling on the Princess Victoria from England to Sydney with my father. He was — is — Sir William Rowe, the newspaper magnate."

When he didn't comment on this, she went on.

"You have obviously not been in England for some time. My father is the proprietor of a very reputable newspaper company in London and will be taking over new offices in Sydney to give accurate reports of the new colonies to British readers."

Just saying it in those present terms made it all seem still real. Still a possibility. Still not doomed to tragedy and the fish of the southern seas.

Caroline was nervous and irritated by the man's unblinking stare, and she rushed on. "Why don't you answer? Do you have you news of him at all? Someone must know something of the *Princess Victoria!* A huge steamship can't simply disappear without trace. Now I'm told I've been here two weeks already. There must be some news! Can't you understand how distraught I feel at having lost those weeks?"

Her voice broke at the end and her hand moved

automatically toward him. He caught it and held it fast. Despite her resistance toward him, she felt oddly warmed and comforted by the contact. It was so long since she had felt the warmth of another human being.

"My dear Miss Rowe, I fear I have no good news to tell you. If I appear to be hesitant in discussing it all with you, it's merely because the doctor said you were to remain rested as long as possible with no more agitation than necessary—"

She snatched her hand away. "I'm not a child, and you will have the goodness to tell me immediately what news you have," she said, knowing that anger was the best defense against complete hysteria.

"No, you are definitely not a child," the man said, his mouth curving into a slight smile as she leaned forward tensely in the bed. As she did so, her breasts were pushed hard against the cambric nightgown, their shape as clearly revealed to him as if she were naked.

"Please don't insult me, sir," she said angrily. "If you won't tell me what I need to know, then I demand to see this doctor, whoever he is."

"That won't be necessary. The wreckage of the steamship *Princess Victoria* has been reported scattered over a wide area," he said brutally. "There are rumors that some individuals have been picked up and taken to the mainland, but you'll realize that on the islands we have little chance of true confirmation. Nor of knowing whether your father was among the survivors. I'm sorry I can't tell you more."

Caroline stared at him for a long moment, trying to take in all that he had said. The words were obviously meant to be frank, said in an unemotional manner, but they were still just too cruel to bear.

Without realizing how she came to be there, she was suddenly in the man's arms. They were holding her limp body close to his, and she could feel the

24

rapid beat of his heart against her own. Hers was so erratic, she truly wondered if she were about to die, and coupled with her gasping sobs and strangled breathing, she wouldn't have been at all surprised.

"Hold on fast now, my sweet lass, and just let all the pain and hurt go out of you. You'll feel all the better for it," the man said.

His voice had become gentle, his breath warm against her cheek. He had a very deep, rich voice, and she could sense the vibration of it against her body. His strength seemed to flow into her, and for a while she was completely unaware of her surroundings as she sobbed her heart out in the comforting arms of her rescuer.

Only slowly did she realize what a desperately compromising position she was in now. Whatever the cause of her distress, she was in a strange bedroom in a house she didn't know, apparently on some unknown island somewhere off the coast of Australia. Her hair was loose and unpinned, and she was in a state of undress in the arms of a stranger . . .

As the sobs began to subside and hot embarrassment took over, she swallowed hard and tried to extricate herself from the unrelenting embrace.

"I thank you, sir," she whispered, "but I think now . . ."

She thought he would let her go at once, but one arm still held her close. With the fingers of his other hand, he raised her chin to meet his gaze, and his face was very close to hers. She could see the strength in it now, the firm clefted chin; the maleness of the skin, so much less soft than a woman's, but with its own allure for all that; the straight nose; the wide, sensual mouth; and those devastatingly seductive eyes. She almost wilted again at the power of those eyes and knew she must keep control over her emotions at all costs.

"I think now that if I don't kiss that lusciously trembling mouth I shall go mad," the man said, outrageously teasing. "You wouldn't have it said that you drove a man mad for lust, would you, Miss Caroline Rowe?"

She gasped, never having heard a man speak so in her life before. The men of her acquaintance had been all so correct, as they tried to obtain her father's approval to court his most eligible and lovely daughter. But this man had no such finesse—nor any eye to her dowry, she thought shrewdly. This man was undoubtedly in the habit of taking what he wanted . . . and right at this moment, it was obvious that he wanted *her*.

"How dare you—"

But she should have known how futile it would be to protest, and before she could utter another word, her mouth was covered and silenced. The man's arms were around her body, one hand holding her head tightly, so that there was no way she could avoid his kiss. She experienced a moment of sheer stunned surprise that this should even be happening, and then there was the brief exquisite sensation of being wanted and cherished, and loved. However unreal and unlikely, she was caught and held by the sensation, and after the horrific days that had passed, it was a feeling she simply couldn't resist.

His lips moved against hers, firm and sensual and warm. She hardly knew how or when she began to respond to them, nor when her soft mouth opened slightly, and she felt the soft touch of his tongue against her own and then its gentle movement around her inner cheek. It was something she had never known before, and when the exploration became more intense, she found herself moving with him, her tongue reacting almost against her will, her senses filled with him.

She was still held to him in that fast embrace, and somewhere in the depths of her loins she felt an utter sweetness begin, a strangely new and rhythmic pulsing that took control of her and stunned her. She

26

had no idea what was happening to her body, only that it wasn't in the least repugnant and that somehow *he* was the cause of it. This stranger, who was somehow bringing her back to life from the sea where she had truly believed herself to be in danger of drowning.

This was a kind of drowning too, she thought dazedly, this rush of pleasure to the secret places of her body that he seemed to be awakening so readily . . .

Too late she remembered why and how she was there, and she pushed against him violently, rubbing at her mouth where his kiss had so intoxicated her. Searing shame ran through her that she could have forgotten her father and her situation so appallingly quickly.

"You take advantage of me, sir," she said, her voice shaking again. "Such behavior is hardly worthy of an English gentleman—"

"Are you always so pompous when you're afraid?" he said, his voice husky with a passion she couldn't fail to recognize now. No, not merely passion. She remembered the word he had used. It was *lust*. He *lusted* after her. The ancient word had an uncanny thrill about it, even while she knew it should disgust her. That she should feel even the slightest thrill at his use of it angered her even more.

"How can you expect me to be anything but afraid when everything I loved has been lost to me and I have no idea where I am or who you are?" she said tensely.

"I'm the man who saved you, and as such, you belong to me, lass."

And who was being pompous now? she raged. She sat back in the bed as far from him as she could. She pulled the bedcovers tightly around her, ignoring his amused smile, and glared into his face.

"I belong to no one," she snapped. "I freely acknowledge that I owe you my deepest thanks—"

"And your life."

27

"And my life," she allowed. "But you don't own me, and you never will. And I'd be very obliged if you would please tell me your name and exactly where I am, so that in due course I may instruct my father to reward you handsomely."

Caroline gave him a stare as unblinking as his own, daring him to deny that such an occasion would ever arise. She had to go on believing it. She had to go on hoping that somehow her father would have been rescued and that one day soon they would be together again. She had been rescued, and the man himself had said there were reports of others being saved too, so why not Sir William Rowe? She forced herself to believe that anything was possible. She was the daughter of an optimist, and if ever she needed to follow in his entrepreneurial footsteps, she needed to do it now.

"My name is Luke Garston," he said abruptly. "I hail from a mining town in the north of England—"

"I thought as much," she put in without thinking.

"Does that bother you unduly? Have no fear, Miss Rowe, I quite understand that all London folk think we northerners are born with wool threads hanging from our mouths and with the clatter of the mill machines turning us deaf!"

She stared at him, aware of the sharpness in his voice. She couldn't imagine why, but she knew instantly that here was Luke Garston's vulnerable spot. He was sensitive about his background, though for what possible reason she couldn't imagine. It seemed that here at least, he must have prospered. That much was evident, even from what little she had seen of this fine house, and from the quality of the clothes he wore.

Her brief interest quickly vanished. She had more important things to consider than Luke Garston's Achilles heel.

"It doesn't bother me in the least. I'd have you know that my father was the most liberal of men in his reporting activities, and I believe I'm the same."

She stopped the rush of words, realizing she had referred to father in the past tense, which she was quite determined not to do, and her eyes filled with tears. She dashed them away angrily, not wanting to appear so weak in the presence of this forceful man.

"Will you please tell me exactly where I am and how soon I can get to Sydney? There are people there who will help me, business acquaintances of my father who were expecting us—"

Her voice died away as she saw the way he shook his head decisively, and her stomach dropped at the sudden pitying expression in his eyes.

"Your education has probably not gone far enough in the geography of our wild Southern Hemisphere, Miss Rowe," he commented. "Sydney is not just around the corner from Brundy, and communication between us is nil."

Caroline swallowed. "And what is this place, this Brundy?"

"This is Brundy Island," he confirmed. "We are twenty miles from the mainland off the northeastern tip of Australia, and between us and it is the Barrier Reef, which is where most ships flounder if they're blown off course. I imagine that's what happened to your *Princess Victoria*."

He ignored her sudden flinch and went on ruthlessly. "Sydney is hundreds of miles south of us and as such is totally unknown to most of the people living here on the island."

"But that can't be!" Caroline leapt upright in the bed again, her eyes wide and aghast. "Before our ship even hit the storm, there were signs of land ahead of us. I was sure we were nearing Sydney!"

"What you saw would have been the darkening of the Barrier Reef or possibly the faint outlines of the mountains in the northern interior. It would certainly not have been Sydney. Did anyone ever say as much?"

No, they had not said so, Caroline remembered. Nothing had ever been said about where they were on that fateful evening, and any such announcements as to their location would have been made later, after dinner as usual. The ship, filled with its wealthy passengers, had been making a leisurely voyage across the Pacific Ocean after leaving San Francisco on the American continent, calling at many of the larger islands en route.

By the time the shadowy outlines ahead of them had been sighted, Caroline, like most of the other sea-weary passengers, had just assumed that land meant the end of their voyage. Now, if this man was to be believed, it would seem they had had many more sea miles to travel down the eastern coast of the new country. The *Princess Victoria* had undertaken the adventurous newer route across the Pacific Ocean, avoiding the treacherous southern coast of Africa and the old convict transportation route, and this had been the result. She felt a great wave of nausea sweep over her again, and she fell back on the pillows, breathing heavily.

"My poor sweet lass," Luke Garston said softly. "This will have been a shock for you. Your color has left your face, and I shall send Mrs. Hughes in to attend you while I order some breakfast to be sent up. You need food now to build up your strength."

She gathered up what little strength she had left and shouted at him, "I don't need food! I need to know how soon you can take me to Sydney!"

But even as she watched his elegantly retreating back, noticing the tight-fitting trousers he wore beneath the well-cut jacket, she knew instinctively that Luke Garston had no intention of taking her anywhere. She was his prisoner here on this unknown island called Brundy, and in his own words, she belonged to him.

Her blood ran cold at the thought of it. Charismatic and handsome he might be, but she belonged to no one, not even the man who had rescued her from the sea and who was now claiming her life as his own.

Minutes later the same woman who had attended her before came bustling into the room. This then, was Mrs. Hughes, and presumably the housekeeper of the establishment. Caroline meant to get as much information out of her as she could.

"Now then, dearie, would you like some washing water or one of Doctor's powders to settle you down before your breakfast?" the woman began comfortably enough.

"I suspect I've already had enough of Doctor's powders," Caroline replied crisply. "What I want is information. Mrs. Hughes, can you please tell me who and what Mr. Garston is?"

The woman looked startled for a moment, apparently not having expected this spirited reply. Caroline was clearly expected to be tearful and humble and mightily grateful to her rescuer. She pursed her lips, knowing she was indeed the last, but it was against her nature to be either of the former!

The housekeeper folded her arms serenely over her ample bosom. "You'll be feeling better in a day or so, love," she said soothingly. "Then I'm sure Mr. Luke will tell you everything you need to know —"

"Dear Lord, is it such a secret that you can't even answer a civil question! Can't you understand that I want to know now!" Caroline almost yelled.

Her nurse would have been scandalized to hear her ranting so loudly, but this was no time to be ladylike. Especially when the man of the house had held her close and kissed her in so lustful a fashion and she had felt the beat of his heart merging with her own through her thin nightgown; and when this buxom jailor, or whoever she was, seemed intent on evading her every question.

31

Mrs. Hughes looked a mite nervous at this sudden revival on her patient's part. She spoke more defensively, obviously indignant at this reaction from a guest.

"Mr. Luke is the owner of Brundy Island, miss. You are in the house of a gentleman. He owns Garston Manor and all the smaller houses on the islands. He owns the fishing boats and the pearl-diving equipment, and all the boys work for him and are devoted to him. There's none here will say a word against him, and you're a very lucky young lady that he found you so near to death in that flimsy boat."

Caroline stared, trying to take it all in as the words gathered momentum. The man actually *owned* the island? And no one here would say a word against him? The woman might be speaking out of loyalty to her employer, but to Caroline's heightened senses, it also said very clearly that there would be no one who would help her leave this island if Luke Garston didn't choose to let her go.

She didn't miss the fact that the house was named Garston Manor. Such a very English name in what was obviously a very alien environment only added to the bizarreness of the situation in which she found herself. That it was also a very self-indulgent name to give to his house confirmed her impression of the man himself. Egotistical, self-important, opinionated . . . and her captor. She ran her tongue around her dry lips.

"And what of the doctor?" she managed to say. "Is he owned by Mr. Luke as well?" She couldn't avoid sarcasm.

"That's rather an odd remark to make, if I may say so, miss. No one is owned by Mr. Luke. We choose to live here in this lovely place, and it's our privilege to serve a good man. As for the doctor, well, he came here much as you did, after being shipwrecked some years ago, and has been the island's doctor ever since."

"From choice, I suppose?" Caroline said dryly.

Mrs. Hughes looked at her steadily. "Naturally from choice. Now then, I'll send someone up with that washing water, and your breakfast will be following. We'll leave the decision of the settling powder for the present."

Just as long as it wasn't put in the tea or sprinkled over the food, Caroline couldn't help thinking. Suspicions washed over her. She had been here for a considerable time already, and she was completely unaware of anything that had happened to her during that time.

She felt her face fill with color now. Anything might have happened. Luke Garston could have . . . could have . . . but she wouldn't even think about such a thing. And somehow she didn't think he would be the kind of man who would want an insensible woman in his arms. He would want someone vibrant and alive to his every seductive touch, a woman who would respond with eyes and mouth and body to whatever sweet demands he made of her . . .

Caroline was horrified at the course of her thoughts. She was still innocent about the intimacies between a man and a woman, except for the most peripheral knowledge. Luke Garston was the first man she had come into close contact with, without the benefit of conventional introductions or chaperon.

She hardly knew the man at all, yet she wasn't unaffected by his magnetism. Nor of the fact that however much she protested, she owed him something. In fact, she owed him everything. She would no longer exist if it wasn't for him. Her thoughts teetered on.

It was a huge responsibility he had put on her, and ironically, it made her even more resentful toward him. Suddenly, she was the one who felt vulnerable. She was helpless, totally at the mercy of Luke Garston and the people who apparently lived here in some luxury but from whom there would seem to be no escape. None at all.

A dark-skinned maid appeared with a pitcher of hot washing water which she poured into the china bowl on the bedside table. From the cupboard beneath, the girl brought out towels and washing cloths, and put them alongside the bowl. Until then, she hadn't spoken, and Caroline hadn't the vaguest idea of how to address her. She was aware of the girl's envious glances at her own white skin and slender hands, and reminded herself of how her father would expect her to behave.

"Good morning. My name is Caroline," she said slowly and distinctly. She pointed to her chest. "Me Caroline. That is my name. Do you have a name?"

She made gestures that made her feel idiotic, but suddenly it was very important to her to make a friend in this odd household, and the girl looked somewhere about her own age as far as she could tell. Her facial features were flat and her nose broad, and her hair was a tight scrunch of black curls. In appearance they couldn't have been more different, but at least she might be a kind of substitute for her maid Sophie, of whom Caroline had been extraordinarily fond.

The girl looked at her without saying anything for a moment, and Caroline tried again. She banged her chest.

"I am Caroline. *Caroline.*"

"I know who you are, Miss Rowe," the girl said in slow but perfectly adequate English. "My name is Petal."

Caroline knew she must look a fool, sitting up in bed with her mouth hanging open at the smooth reply. She wasn't sure whether to be more startled or angry at this response. In the end she clamped her lips together quickly as a laugh escaped them. The sound was unexpected to her ears. It seemed a very long time since she had laughed.

"You speak English! And very well," she said, praying that she didn't sound too condescending. The girl gave the slightest semblance of a smile.

"Mr. Luke, he tell me how. And Mrs. Hughes and the others, they help sometimes when I make mistakes."

"The others? Are there other English people living on this island then?" Caroline's interest quickened.

At the sudden light in her eyes and the sharpness of her voice, the girl started to back away a little.

"Mr. Luke, he say I not to tell too much. Mr. Luke is bossman here. He explain to lady."

And this girl was clearly Mr. Luke's adoring slave, Caroline saw swiftly. She wondered what else the girl might be to him. She had a very comely appearance, and she was young and shapely. And Mr. Luke was not the kind of man to live a celibate life. Even on such short acquaintance, that much was perfectly obvious to Caroline.

"All right, Petal," she said casually, knowing that if she was to get anything out of this girl, she had better go slowly. "But just tell me how you got your name. Mr. Luke wouldn't mind that, would he?"

She was annoyed with herself for falling into the pattern of everyone else she had met so far and referring to the man as Mr. Luke. It was far too subservient to her own ears, and the nurtured and pampered Miss Caroline Rowe had not been brought up to be subservient to anyone.

The girl's face held a broad smile now, and she was really very pretty, Caroline saw.

"Mr. Luke, he call me Petal. He say my old name was too long for him. When he saw me for first time, I was gathering flowers for my hair, so he call me Petal."

Caroline had asked for an explanation, and she

had got one, simple and revealing, and conjuring up a swift picture of that meeting. The girl, young, nubile, perhaps in the woods or among whatever vegetation the island boasted, with flowers in her hair; and the man, coming across her and wanting her . . .

Caroline shivered, wishing these erotic fantasies would stop assailing her. She had never had them before, and she didn't want them now. Particularly with regard to the man she was privately starting to think of as her enemy, since he was the one keeping her here, no matter in what kind of luxury.

"You want me for more, lady?" Petal was saying now, and Caroline saw that she was edging toward the door.

"No, I don't want you for more, thank you," she said, falling into the girl's own speech pattern without realizing it.

"Then I fetch breakfast when you ready. When the sun is high, Doctor Sam will come."

Before Caroline could ask for more information on this Doctor Sam, the girl was gone. The frustration was beginning to needle her more and more. Her leg still hurt, and she was afraid to attempt to walk after her last abortive try. There was nothing for it, for the moment, but to accept the conditions and be grateful at least for her existence.

However much it galled her to know it, she admitted that but for Luke Garston, she almost certainly wouldn't even be alive now. It would be far easier, she thought, if he had been older and if she could have related to him in a paternal way, but nothing about him was such. Neither his age nor his persona was that of an elderly guardian. He was young, virile, and more . . . and he disturbed her far more than she liked.

Quickly, she turned her thoughts away from the man. She was determined instead to try to keep the belief alive that her father, too, had been as fortunate, and that he, too, had been rescued. If she had been, then why not Sir William?

She kept the hope buoyed up in her mind and turned her attention to the washing water on the table beside her. She realized for the first time that the day was already hot and she was feeling decidedly uncomfortable, although presumably the sun wasn't yet high in the sky. She unfastened the ties at the neck of the nightgown and slipped it down over her shoulders, feeling the need to be refreshed from neck to waist.

There was fragrant soap and a soft washing cloth, and minutes later she was luxuriating in the freshness of the warm soapy water as she bathed her shoulders and arms and breasts. She had spread the towel in front of her, to save dampening the bedcovers, and she reveled in the sensation of being clean once more.

Not that she was in any way less than dainty already, she realized. And if she had been here for two weeks, then someone else must have been seeing to her needs all this time. She flushed, wondering who it might have been, and presuming, and fervently hoping, that it had been the homely housekeeper.

Without warning, she caught sight of her reflection in the mirror on the wall opposite. She was not normally in this situation, carrying on her morning ablutions while sitting up in bed. Her long dark hair was its habitual morning tangle, before Sophie teased and pinned it into its usual tidy style of curls and topknot. Her shoulders looked soft and warm from her attentions with the washing cloth, and her breasts were firm and glistening as the trickles of soapy water ran over them.

Caroline drew in her breath. She looked like a wanton, so decadent and brazen with the fullness of her breasts so exposed. It occurred to her that she had never seen them in such a way before. Why should she, when the morning washing ritual nor-

37

mally took place in the privacy of the newly installed bathroom adjoining her room in her London home or in the confined washing area of her cabin on board the *Princess Victoria?* She didn't normally see herself reflected in a bedroom mirror, looking as though she waited for a lover. Without thinking, she dropped the washing cloth, and her hands softly palmed her own breasts to feel the hard thrust of the nipples against her skin.

Without warning, there was a brief tap on a door at the side of her room, and it suddenly opened. Already she had registered uneasily that there were three doors leading to this room, and now she gasped in horror as she saw the tall figure of Luke Garston walking toward her.

She snatched up her towel to try to protect herself from his eyes, but it was too late. She knew in a moment that he had seen her naked from the waist up.

"How dare you come in here unannounced!" she stammered, too shocked to feel even anger for the moment.

It was too humiliating that he had witnessed her staring at her own body, her hands unconsciously touching herself, and instinctively wondering how it would feel to have a man's hands touching them. In her fevered mind she knew that he was devil enough to know exactly what her feelings had been.

"I apologize, Miss Rowe," he said with exaggerated courtesy. "It was not my intention to catch you in such a state of undress. From Mrs. Hughes's remarks, I had expected you to be awaiting your breakfast by now and had come to suggest that I would join you if you wish it."

He indicated the table by the window where presumably he would sit and eat while she took her own in the bed. The suggestion did little to pacify Caroline's nerves. She didn't miss the way his eyes had lingered over her shape and, even now, the way he seemed to be mesmerized by the way the towel she pressed against her emphasized the fact that her nipples were still aroused. But it was no longer by awareness of her own body, she thought furiously, as anger spilled over now.

"Do you make a habit of walking into a lady's bedroom without invitation? If this is so, sir, then I suggest your manners have taken a serious turn for the worse, in however long you have been away from England!"

She was breathing heavily, wishing she dared pull her nightgown or a dressing robe around her bare shoulders. But such a movement would have revealed her body to him even more. As it was, she could merely sit still, the towel held over as much of her upper body as it would cover, her shoulders and arms still bared to his gaze. She couldn't even reach to pull the bellpull for help. And if she did, who would come, since he was obviously lord and master here?

"I merely wish to make you welcome, Miss Rowe," he went on coolly. "You and I have plenty of time to get fully acquainted in the foreseeable future, so I shall leave you for the present, if that is what you wish."

"Of course I wish it!" she snapped. "What decent young lady in her right mind would wish to continue her ablutions with a gentleman looking on!"

Even as she said it, the image of it all swept into her mind, and there was something so unimaginably wicked about the scene that she caught her breath. Her imagination simply took hold of her as it had been doing ever since she returned to her senses that morning. Whether or not the faintly hallucinatory illusions were the aftermath of the sedative powders she had been given she didn't know.

But it seemed as if all her imaginative powers were heightened, and she could no longer let go of any thought without seeing the imagery of it in her mind. And what she was seeing now was a picture of herself lying back in a scented washtub, her own hands playing with the glistening soap bubbles on her body, tantalizing the man who was watching her with passion-dark eyes. And the man in question, coming ever nearer to continue what her own hands had begun, was Luke Garston . . .

She flinched as the images faded, and she saw that the object of her fantasies was moving slowly toward her now.

"Are you feeling faint, lass? All this has been a sore trial to you, and I shall leave you now until you're decent, as you call it. Though I confess, I prefer to see you as you were when I came in—"

"A true gentleman would pretend he had seen nothing!" Caroline whipped back at him, and he backed away, his palms held up as if warding off blows.

"It seems to me you've lost your sense of humor along with all your worldly possessions," he said dryly. "But no matter. Once you're back to full health, I've no doubt we shall find much in common. Doctor Sam expects to take the bandage off your leg today, by the way, and you'll be feeling much more comfortable. I shall take pleasure then, in showing you around the house, and when the day cools down, we may take a drive around the rest of my island. You'll want to be familiar with your new surroundings as soon as possible."

"Please don't make it sound as if I'm going to be here forever," she said sharply as he reached the door he'd come through earlier. "I thank you for your hospitality, but as soon as I'm fit I must begin making enquiries as to my father's whereabouts. I trust you can arrange for one of your many boats to take me to the mainland?"

"I do not go to the mainland," Luke Garston said in a clipped voice.

He left the room, and the door clicked shut behind him. Caroline stared at it for a few seconds before she remembered what she was about. She quickly finished dabbing herself dry and slid her arms back into the nightgown, fastening it as tightly as she could, as if to erase the fact that Luke Garston had seen her without it. She was still bewildered by the shortness of his voice and that strange comment he had made.

"I do not go to the mainland."

But she hadn't asked for him to take her, only that he supply the means to take her there. Neither had she expected the sudden sure suspicion to be planted in her mind that there must be some deep reason for his words. For whatever reason, Luke Garston seemed to be as much a prisoner on his own island as she was herself.

Chapter Three

The doctor was due to visit her later that morning. Long before then, Petal had brought her some breakfast on a tray.

Caroline had eyed the food with distaste. It was nicely presented, but the thought of filling herself with the over-large egg and the strange-looking meat when she had taken no exercise at all lately, filled her with horror.

"I know I must have eaten something while I've been here, though I don't remember any of it," she said. "I'll just have the toast and preserve, and you may take the rest away."

Petal stood where she was and placed the tray firmly over Caroline's lap.

"Mr. Luke say you was to eat, miss. I not suppose to leave here 'til you do."

Caroline glared at the girl, who stared insolently back. Finally she bit into the thick toast, managing to finish one slice of it, drank half a cup of the odd-tasting tea, and pushed the rest away.

"Very well. I've done what Mr. Luke said. I've eaten, so now *go!*"

Petal snatched up the tray resentfully. The girl would benefit from some proper training in the service of a lady's maid, Caroline thought keenly. Sophie used to bully her, too, but Sophie had been with her for a long time. They had practically grown up together . . .

"Will you please tell Mrs. Hughes to bring me my clothes and help me to dress?" she said as the girl reached the door. Petal looked at her uneasily.

"I don't know 'bout that. Mr. Luke say—"

"Ask Mrs. Hughes to come here, please. *At once!*"

The girl fled from the room, and Caroline leaned back on the pillows, extraordinarily tired after such a simple exchange. But she was determined now. She was obviously recovering from whatever ailed her, and she wanted to be out of this bed. The sooner she did so, the sooner she could leave Brundy Island. She allowed herself the small superstition of crossing her fingers at the thought.

And although still confined to bed, she finally persuaded Mrs. Hughes to bring her clothes to her and was pleasantly gratified to find them clean and pressed and fresh-smelling. The places where her gown and petticoats had been torn were also neatly mended. If she had never worn mended clothes before, such a fact mattered little now. What mattered most was to be wearing her own things and to be feeling more in control of her own person, in however small a way.

She certainly felt less vulnerable than in her nightclothes. It still galled her that she had had to practically beg for this one favor since she had never had to beg for anything before. She also resented the fact that whenever Luke Garston wasn't around, it seemed as if the housekeeper was set on acting as substitute benefactor and jailor.

But however wildly she resented it, she also knew

that for the present there was no help for it. She
might as well act compliant until she could assess
her position fully and find out what means there
were of getting away from Brundy Island and onto
the Australian mainland, which she was determined
to do.

She had every hope that the doctor might be
able to help her. His name had sounded English
enough, and if so, he must surely be sympathetic
to her cause.

"Dr. Sam Atkinson," she murmured, remembering. "With reasonable luck, you could be my life-
line out of here. You could tell me how to reach
the mainland."

But even as she thought of the huge task of trying to trace what had happened to her father, her
blood chilled. The mainland would be as alien a
place as this island. She knew no one here except
the few people in Luke Garston's employ as of yet,
and she had no idea of how near or far she was
from the unknown continent.

She simply rejected Luke's comment that the
nearest point of land from Brundy was hundreds
of miles away from Sydney, unable to believe it
could still be so far away. Not when she had assumed, along with most other passengers on the
Princess Victoria, that they were almost at the end
of their long voyage when that dark smudge on the
horizon had been sighted.

She wished that she had paid more attention to
her geography lessons, she thought in some frustration. Because it was becoming crystal clear to her
now that she eventually needed to get to Sydney. It
was where her father would make for. If all else
failed in her search for him, she could contact the
newspaper offices already established there, awaiting her father's new leadership. She felt a small
buoyant hope inside.

There were people there who knew Sir William, among them the rough-talking reporter they called Stoneheart Taylor, on account of his ruthless ways of getting information out of his interviewees. Caroline had met him several times in London. She remembered clearly the first time he had fixed his piercing gaze on her, as if he could look right through the elegant gown she wore at the reception they were all attending, right through to the soft womanly flesh beneath.

"So. This is Sir William's lovely daughter, is it? He's kept you hidden for far too long, my dear," he'd said, his normal rough-edged voice softly cloying for the moment.

It had made her shudder. The hand holding her limp one was hard, and the slight pressure of his fingers against her palm made her want to snatch her hand away at once.

"I'm pleased to meet you, sir," she had said icily, her tone belying the words in a way that not even he could fail to understand. He had given a twisted smile.

"Oh, I trust we shall meet often in the future, my dear Miss Rowe," he had said as smooth as a snake.

Caroline had vowed there and then that she would avoid any further contact between them. Even so, she knew his integrity as a newspaperman and his loyalty to his profession. She knew that in these new circumstances he would want to help trace her father. It would be predominately for the glory of the search and reporting it first-hand, of course, and it would also be for the fee he would try to extract from Caroline for his services. She knew his methods only too well . . .

She shuddered, just remembering the oiliness of the man. She rarely felt hate for anyone, but she was revolted by him and by the lack of finesse in everything he did. But at least he was someone she knew, and if anyone would try to ferret out what had happened to Sir William Rowe, Stoneheart Taylor would.

She became lost in her reverie, making desperate and impossible plans, and was startled by a knock on her bedroom door that announced the arrival of the doctor. She sat up eagerly, thankful she had also managed to twist up her hair into a knot at the back of her head, so she didn't appear so young and helpless as before. She wanted to look capable and well and able to leave here at the earliest opportunity.

"Dr. Sam's come to take a look at you, miss, and I shall naturally remain in the room while he makes his examination," Mrs. Hughes said in what was meant to be a comforting tone.

It did nothing to stop the surge of disappointment and panic in Caroline's stomach as she saw the doctor. With Stoneheart Taylor still uppermost in her mind, she suddenly saw a facsimile of the man. It was not truly so, she thought swiftly, for this man was at least smiling and openly friendly. But the doctor was also well past middle age, paunchy and unkempt. He wore a shabby suit that had probably once been tropical white, but was now a dingy gray. He spoke heartily as he approached her bed, and she tried not to flinch at the thought of those pudgy hands touching her.

"Now then, little lady, let's see if we can take that great bandage off your leg today. The cut on your head was only superficial and healed nicely, but it was the leg that gave us the big worry. I daresay you're all of an itch to be out of that bed and using your pins again by now though, eh?"

His words were frank and to the point. Caroline swallowed, knowing her state of health probably owed much to this man. But he couldn't have been more different from the so-correct and elderly consultant who used to come to their house to attend her father and herself whenever anything ailed them. She quickly chided herself for her snobbery, for Doctor Sam's words were kindly and determinedly cheery.

"You're a—a Londoner, aren't you?" she almost croaked, unable to think of another thing to say for the moment.

"That's right, my old china. A Londoner, born and bred. Like yourself, I suspect, from what Luke was telling me about you and your old dad."

Caroline's mouth twitched as he compared the two of them so artlessly. Nobody ever referred to Sir William Rowe as her old dad except the cheeky Cockney maids in the Rowe employ, and it was suddenly so endearingly familiar and so carelessly classless that weak tears filled her eyes.

"You're right. I'm a—I'm from London too," she said. "Perhaps you know of my father—Sir William Rowe?"

She almost held her breath. The weakest tangible link with home would be a godsend now. For someone actually to know the name, even to have read her father's vigorously worded columns in the newspaper . . . She saw the doctor shake his head.

"I ain't been back to the smoke for forty years and ain't never likely to see it again," he said without regret. "The old town did me no favors, so I never saw no reason to take any more interest in its goings-on. We don't ask for such news here, duck. Now then, let's take a look at you."

He approached the bed, passing over her comment lightly, and motioned for her to put her bandaged leg outside the bedcovers. Caroline complied, carefully keeping the rest of herself well-covered. Although fully dressed, she felt idiotic and exposed as she kept her soft gown and the sheets

47

pressed over her lower body and her other leg. The doctor looked at her shrewdly.

"I do have to get at the bandage, girl," he said with exasperated amusement. "I promise you these old hands ain't been in contact with anything catching, and they ain't in the least bit of a lecherous inclination. So if you want me to help you, you're going to have to let me get near you!"

Caroline blushed, embarrassed at how obvious she had been and even more so by the fact that he knew it.

"I'm sorry," she muttered. "Please do what you have to."

She released her tight grip on her clothing and bedding, and felt the cold contact of scissors as he began to cut the top of the bandage away from her leg before starting to unravel the rest. She felt the freedom of being released from it and with it a new anxiety about the use of her leg in the future. It still felt numb and tight and was thinner than its twin, but she could see that the ugly gash had knitted together while being confined.

There had been some kind of a dark poultice covering the wound, which the doctor removed while she averted her eyes. It looked and smelled disgusting, and she didn't care to imagine what kind of herbal or animal curative dressing it might have been. But remembering how badly her leg had throbbed and ached, she now felt an enormous sense of relief and gratitude to this unlikely medical man as he inspected her leg with a professional eye, prodding the soft new flesh gently with an expert finger.

"You'll do," he said at last. "The leg will be weak for a few days yet, and you'll need to exercise it gradually. You can have a trip downstairs today for a start, and I daresay Luke will want to show you over his kingdom very soon."

"Thank you," Caroline said huskily. "I'm—I'm embarrassed to say that I don't have the means to pay you—"

She stopped mid-sentence. She had never had to think about money before, but now she realized that such services would have to be paid for. She should probably suggest that he gave her an account for her father to settle up in due course. Then she heard Doctor Sam's throaty laugh.

"You needn't worry your head about that, duck. Luke takes care of his own, and there's no fee owing."

She didn't care for the way he said it. She wasn't Luke's own, and she didn't want to be beholden to him for anything more than was necessary. But now was obviously not the right time to bridle. She would settle things with Luke Garston later, even to the point of giving him an IOU for all his care and attention. Ladies didn't normally do such things but circumstances had changed things beyond all the normal conventions.

"How did you come to be here, Dr. Sam?" she finally couldn't resist asking, as he began to bundle the soiled bandage and dressing into the battered old bag he had brought with him. "You've been here forty years, you say? That seems like a lifetime to me."

Even as she said it, she had the most appalling suspicion running around in her brain. The doctor would probably be well over seventy years old, so he would have been a young and active medical man forty years ago, probably in the very first years of his profession in London. Why would such a person have wanted to give up all that to come here to the colonies?

The answer came to her immediately. Forty years ago, in the twenties, Australia was virtually only known to Englishmen as the dreaded place at the

49

other end of the world where convicts were sent to rot and die in obscurity. Or, for any in luckier circumstances, to somehow escape from their jailors and to find their island paradise, and to flourish as a practicing medical man under the protection of one Luke Garston . . .

So had Dr. Sam been a convict? And if so, what was behind his association with Luke? And what of Luke Garston himself? He was too young, surely . . . The practice of convict transportation had been thankfully ended some years ago as Caroline very well knew, but these new doubts and suspicions wouldn't leave her mind.

"No more questions now, girlie," Dr. Sam was saying briskly. "We'll have plenty of time to get to know one another, and your man has promised me a good dinner for putting you back on your feet again. We'll be arranging it soon, I'm sure, and meanwhile Mrs. Hughes will take good care of you."

He pattered to the door on his soft-soled shoes. He waved an airy hand to Mrs. Hughes, saying he knew the way out well enough, and he wasn't likely to steal the silver as there was nowhere to hide it, so she was not to bother showing him to the door. Caroline heard her chuckle at his nonsense.

"He's a caution, isn't he, miss? But he's a good doctor, for all his odd ways, and you've cause to be glad about that by all accounts. That leg of yours was in a bad way when Mr. Luke brought you here."

Somehow Caroline had the feeling the woman wasn't just making idle chatter. Somehow she sensed that she just kept talking in order to divert Caroline's thoughts from the one that was uppermost in her mind. But she wouldn't be diverted from it. She wasn't a newspaperman's daughter for nothing, and she knew too much of the history of this land, even if it was only reported news.

"Was Dr. Sam transported to Australia for some reason, Mrs. Hughes?" She didn't dare suggest outright that he might have been a convict. She recognized the awfulness even of mentioning transportation in relation to a man who had probably saved her leg, if not her life. But she still had to know.

The woman tightened her lips. "There are some words we don't care to use in this house, miss. Those days are long gone, thanks be to the Lord and the government men who finally came to their senses. There were far too many folk sent here for such petty crimes. It makes your heart bleed to think of them and what became of them."

"But was Dr. Sam one of them?" Caroline persisted. "It can do no harm to tell me!"

"It can do no good either." Luke Garston's harsh voice said from the doorway.

The doctor hadn't bothered to close the door, and Caroline wondered how much of the conversation between herself and Mrs. Hughes her host had overheard. Her face flushed as he came into the room, his eyes hard and unsmiling. As he did so, Mrs. Hughes unobtrusively left them together, probably thankful to get away from this inquisitive guest.

"I see no reason why I shouldn't be curious about the people I'm obliged to come into contact with, for however short a time," she said hotly.

"You may be curious, but I also see no reason why that curiosity should be satisfied," he said with maddening patience. "As to your being here only a short time, I advise you to think again about that, my dear Miss Rowe. You must accept that Brundy Island is your home from now on."

She gave a small cry of disbelief. "You surely can't mean to keep me here indefinitely!"

51

She felt utter panic as he folded his arms across his chest. The movement seemed so implacable, so much a statement that whatever Luke Garston wanted, Luke Garston got, and there was nothing and no one that could stop it.

"You obviously haven't been listening to me properly, Caroline," he said, his use of her first name hinting at his assumption of ownership of her. "We are twenty miles from anywhere, and the first landfall is not land at all but the Barrier Reef, which is death to large ships as well as small ones. No one from Brundy dares to breach it or cares to try. We are a complete community here. We have everything we could possibly want. The island is fertile, and the seas around us are rich and bountiful. You will be happy here like the rest of us."

She listened, half-dazed, as his voice seemed to mesmerize her by its finality. It spoke of paradise and also of captivity, just as surely as if she were chained to his side.

"But I don't want to stay! I want my father! And I want to go *home.*"

Even as she spoke, she tried to still her trembling lips, remembering that there was no longer a home in England to return to. They had sold up everything in this bright new venture, and although a few of their assets had been sent on to Sydney, most of them had been locked securely in the safe on the steamship *Princess Victoria.*

She felt a wild sob in her throat, recognizing the hopelessness of her position, and with the dawning realization that for the present, at least, she was penniless. She was totally dependent on the goodwill of the man who had rescued her. Luke Garston.

"I'll do what I can to find out what became of him," he was saying roughly now. "There may be a way—"

She looked up at him, hope shining in her eyes. "You will help me?"

He didn't answer for a moment, and then she heard him give a low curse. "When you look at me with those damnably seductive blue eyes, I'd give you the earth if I could. But for the moment I can only give you Brundy. You'll have to be satisfied with that. The only hope is when the trading ship calls. It goes on a roundabout route to the mainland and eventually on to Sydney. I'll send a message with them."

She ignored the complimentary first remarks. She didn't want to hear them anyway. She was only interested in the fact that there was a ship that called at the island and that it went to Sydney.

"You won't need to send any messages. I can go on the trading ship myself," she said joyfully. "I can go to my father's office, and there are people there who will help me."

"No. You will not do that," Luke Garston said. "I wouldn't care to entrust you to the roughnecks on the trading ship. Some of them are little more than barbarians, and I wouldn't vouch for your safety or your honor on board such a vessel."

"And you think I'm safer here, do you?" she said sarcastically, remembering the way he had fastened his hot gaze on her naked breasts and that he had already declared that she was his property. She had been relatively immobile until today, but with the doctor's visit, things had changed, and she was still unsure just how he meant to interpret those words. Whatever happened, she was certainly not prepared to become any man's plaything, and the sooner he understood that, the better.

"You will always be safe with me," Luke said arrogantly. "You owe me your life, and therefore I now have an obligation to you to preserve that life. It means that from now on our two lives are inex-

53

tricably entwined. Fate decreed that we should be brought together, and we can no longer escape one another."

She didn't know whether to be charmed by these words or insulted by them. Besides, she was the one who was the prisoner, not he. She was the one who needed to escape. He had everything he wanted right here. He surely didn't have need of her too.

She averted her eyes from his gaze and returned to her original question, putting the thought of the visiting trading ship to the back of her mind for the present. It was enough for now to know that such a vessel existed.

"You still haven't told me what I want to know. Was Dr. Sam transported to Australia here forty years ago, and if so, for what crime? I think I have a right to know."

She spoke very deliberately, bringing her thoughts right out into the open, so that there was no mistake. She stared into Luke's dark eyes, willing him to tell her.

He stalked toward the bed, and before she could even guess his intentions, he had thrown back the bedcovers and thrust his hands beneath her, lifting her bodily into his arms. He held her very close to him, and she was obliged to put her arms around his neck to keep her balance.

"I think a man's past is his own affair. I also think you talk too much," he said harshly. "And I have a very effective way of stopping that."

He slid one hand around her neck, and as he did so, her feet touched the ground and she was standing for the first time in two weeks. Her legs felt very weak, and she still had to cling to him, a fact that obviously suited him very well as he pressed his mouth to hers, his tongue forcing her lips open and moving seductively inside. It was impossible for Caroline to keep her balance, and she gave a strangled cry in her throat as they both fell heavily back on the bed and she was pinned beneath Luke Garston.

She struggled to break free of him, but it was impossible. He was too strong for her. And even while she struggled, the kiss didn't end. It went on and on, and into Caroline's dazed mind came the thought that no one would come running in answer to her weak cry. It probably hadn't been heard, deadened as it was by the hot pressure of Luke's mouth. But even if it had, she sensed that no one would disturb them. Luke ruled supreme here, and she was a prisoner of his passion . . .

The weight of him was knocking the breath out of her, but she couldn't fail to feel the hardening of his body where it met the core of her own softness. There was plenty of clothing between them, but there might as well have been none as far as Caroline was concerned, in the dawning realization of what was happening. She had never felt such a thing before, but with an instinct older than time and with sensations more exquisite than a serving maid's garbled descriptions could convey, she knew exactly what was occurring now.

Seconds later, Luke raised his head from hers, looking deep into her eyes, and she could only stare up at him, bemused, as these new and sensuously tingling sensations began to flow into her lower body and her limbs.

"You see what you do to me, sweet Caroline? Would you have me go through life without your easing this affliction?"

Without warning, he caught hold of her hand and pushed it down between them to where she could feel the hard thrust of his arousal against his garments. She gasped, awed and afraid, and snatched her hand away quickly. He gave a low

55

laugh and suddenly moved against her in several long slow movements. Without meaning to, she closed her eyes, and she heard that low soft laugh again.

"You see? However much your mind refuses to acknowledge that you and I belong together, your body is telling me differently. You can't deny your body's needs, my sweet lass, and someday soon those needs will be satisfied. But not yet. I'm not so lustful that I can't relish the thought of a little courtship first. And besides, what's the hurry? We have eternity ahead of us, so a few more days of anticipation will only make our joining all the sweeter."

"No gentleman would ever take such advantage of a lady, and I fear you have been away from civilized company for too long, sir," she whispered in outrage, even while her awakening sexuality cried out yes, yes, *yes* . . .

But the saner part of her recognized that she must be half-drugged by her situation to feel such attraction for a man she had only just met. And one who would seem to hold all the cards, she thought despairingly. He obviously thought he could do what he would with her, and she had no say in the matter.

"My name is Luke, and I ask that you use it since we are to be such close and loving companions," he said, enraging her still more by his self-assurance. "And I assure you we can be very civilized on Brundy, as you will soon see. As for not acting the part of a gentleman," he tipped up her chin with one long finger, "if you wish that I would court you in a leisurely fashion, then you're doomed to disappointment, for I have waited too long for you already."

She stared up at him from her disadvantageous position on the bed. She was breathing very heavily now, and despite the tension of the moment, she began to feel ridiculous.

"Please don't speak to me in that obscure fashion, just as if I was destined to come here and be part of your life!"

She felt a surge of anxiety in her heart at her own words, for didn't she herself half believe that what fate decreed mere mortals could never destroy? She pushed the thought aside and went on speaking shrilly. "And I do not wish you to court me at all! I thank you most sincerely for your assistance, but as for anything more — "

He laughed again, but as he leaned upward from her, he ran the same cool finger around the neckline of her gown where the soft flesh was flushed from the unexpected contact and with something more.

"You will soon learn that it's futile to fight me, Caroline, though I confess it's an invigorating challenge to have a spirited wench in my arms rather than the subservient ones at my disposal."

She was even more outraged at that, both by his calling her a *wench* as by the implication that he was no stranger to lust and that there were plenty of other women on this island only too willing to fall into his arms and his bed. Caroline had yet to know of them. So far she had only seen the matronly Mrs. Hughes and the nubile Petal . . . Even as the incongruous name came into her head, she wondered if Luke Garston was in the habit of inviting servants into his bed — and native ones at that. She had never thought herself a racial snob and had the same liberal views as her father on racial equality, but there were some things that were abhorrent to her. Forcing young servant girls to submit to a man's lust was one of them, no matter what their background.

"What particular bee is running around your

57

bonnet now, for God's sake?" Luke Garston said softly. "I swear that your beautiful face is also the most expressive I ever saw, Caroline Rowe. You should learn to hide your disapproval if you want to fit in with your new surroundings—"

She twisted away from him, managing to sit upright on the edge of the bed while he remained there, lounging, as if in full possession of her territory. Angrily she saw that her skirt was still caught beneath him, and she wouldn't permit herself the indignity of tugging at it to free herself.

"How many times must I tell you I do not intend to stay here?" she snapped. "And since Doctor Sam said I may go downstairs today, I would be obliged if I could do so. This bedroom is beginning to stifle me."

She hoped her words were pointed enough for him to realize that he stifled her too. He was much too masterful, too arrogantly self-confident, too charismatic for comfort . . . too much of the man she had always dreamed of finding and never hoped to meet . . . She cut off her meandering thoughts immediately. In another time, another place, perhaps, but not here. Not in captivity. Not on Luke Garston's terms.

"Of course." He stood up at once and held out his arm to assist her. Refusing it, Caroline stood up stiffly and then swayed as her weakened limb threatened to buckle beneath her. She gasped and found herself leaning heavily against Luke once more.

"Steady, my love," he said in a more normal voice than the arrogant one he had used earlier. "You'll feel weak for a while, so if you will allow me, I'll carry you downstairs to the drawing room. Then, if you wish, we can take tea on the terrace overlooking the ocean."

Despite all, Caroline felt a small wash of pleasure at his words. It all sounded so blissfully normal and correct. Downstairs to the drawing room and then tea on the terrace overlooking the ocean. She gave a short nod, suddenly weary of all her resistance, for what other choice did she have? For now, she was no more than a leaf in the wind, doing whatever Luke Garston required of her. But just for now, she vowed weakly.

He lifted her in his arms again as if she was feather-light and walked with purposeful strides to the main door of her bedroom. Outside, she saw that the landing was carpeted, with doors leading off it. A double staircase curved gracefully away from the center of the landing to meet on what appeared to be a spacious reception area below. This was also richly carpeted, and the whole area was adorned with many pieces of heavy furniture and brightly patterned Chinese vases filled with exotic flowers Caroline didn't recognize, but which filled the air with a heavenly scent.

She knew at once that this was a rich man's house, and she regretted some of her scathing remarks earlier. Especially when she remembered how she had first mistaken him for a fisherman, his torso bronzed and glistening in the salt spray, his hair tousled from the tropical winds, his skin tanned by the southern sun.

"Does something about me bother you?" he said now as she bounced gently against him as he carried her carefully down the stairs. She realized she had transferred her gaze from the furnishings to his face and remembered what he had said about her revealing expressions. She tried to make her countenance as bland as possible.

And since he had mentioned it, then yes, something about him bothered her, she thought aggressively. *Everything* about the man bothered her, but in a way she was certainly not going to explain to him!

"Only what you're doing here," she said coolly. "I would have expected someone like yourself to be living in some elegant London establishment, with a gentlemen's club at your disposal, and servants waiting on you hand and foot."

"But I have all that here. Oh, not the gentlemen's club, I grant you, but since gentlemen are not always what they seem, Caroline, I don't consider myself lacking in any respect. And I thank you for the compliment."

"What compliment?" she said resentfully.

"The fact that you consider me worthy of your station. It proves to me that you and I will get along very well, once you accustom yourself to the idea. We're the same kind of people."

"Oh, I hardly think so!" Caroline said as they reached the door of a downstairs room. "For one thing, I do not cavort with naked fishermen." However much she tried not to, she vividly remembered the scene at the time of her rescue. "Nor would any decent gentleman of my acquaintance," she finished hurriedly, anticipating some arch reply.

"But you enjoy fine things," he said. "You like to wear soft underwear and precious jewelry and to live in comfort."

The fact that he seemed well aware of her very personal attire made her suspicious again of just who had helped remove her sodden clothes and get her into the cambric nightgown she had been wearing when she recovered consciousness. Just how intimate was his knowledge of her already . . . ?

But she had no chance to question him, even if it hadn't been far too delicate a matter to do so, because he was opening the door of what was presumably the drawing room and setting her carefully on her feet while his arm still supported her. And as she took a quick, startled look around her, Caroline simply gasped anew at such magnificence. This could surely not be the house of a convict, however reformed . . .

"I trust you will accept now that you are in the house of a gentleman," Luke said, his words and voice quietly understating what was instantly obvious to her.

Chapter Four

Luke offered her his arm. She linked her own inside his, knowing it would be foolish to resist, and
she was held against him as he half-supported her.
Despite her gratitude, all her instincts cried out for
her to be independent and to stand on her own
feet, metaphorically as well as physically. Patience
had never been one of her best virtues, Caroline
thought guiltily, but she knew she had better de-
velóp the trait as quickly as possible now.

He led her through the beautifully appointed
drawing room to the long open windows where a
soft breeze blew the net curtains gently into the
room. The scent of the sea was suddenly strong in
her nostrils. For a moment she rebelled against it,
feeling sick and faint at the memory of those last
terrible hours on the *Princess Victoria* and the
fragile craft in which she had been rescued.

Without thinking, her fingers curled around
Luke Garston's arm, and he glanced down at her.

"You're quite safe now, love," he said quietly,
just as though he could read the spinning thoughts

in her mind. "The sea is our friend as well as our main source of wealth."

"Do the pearls bring such wealth then?" she murmured, remembering Mrs. Hughes's words. She asked the question more for want of something to say than out of real interest. Luke gave an amused laugh.

"They do indeed. And it will be my pleasure to find the most precious pearl of all for you."

"There's no need for that. I would be far too embarrassed to accept it — " she began quickly, and then they were stepping through the long windows onto a wide, marbled terrace. It was shaded by foliage of glossy dark green in which grew brilliant scarlet flowers. For a second, Caroline imagined the dark-skinned Petal fixing one of the flowers in her hair and laughingly turning to Luke for his approval . . .

She willed the image away and looked around her. A wicker table and comfortable wicker lounging chairs awaited them. Above their heads was a slowly circulating fan of plaited leaves on a bamboo frame, which was ingeniously blown by the breeze with just enough movement to keep the scene below blissfully cool.

Below the terrace were lush gardens filled with greenery and more exotic flowers, and beyond them was the sparkling sea. Blue and calm as the heavens now, the water stretched away to the distant horizon until the two merged hazily into one, and it seemed that nothing existed but the infinite sea and sky.

Caroline swallowed.

"Does my paradise please my lady?" Luke said softly.

"It's . . . beautiful," she felt obliged to say, for it could hardly be called anything else. Luke was right. Coupled with the singing of birds in the palm trees and the rich-sounding humming of bees, this place could truly be called paradise, and for those who chose to live here of their own free will, they would surely end their days in perfect harmony with nature and themselves. But Brundy Island hadn't been her choice . . .

He held a chair for her, and she sank into it as the housekeeper came through from the drawing room with a tray.

"Then I'm sure something else will please you. Mrs. Hughes makes superb biscuits, and she knows how an English lady likes her tea," Luke said briskly, again with that uncanny perception that she was about to ask more questions.

There was so much that she needed to know, and not least of all just how Luke Garston himself came to be there. But for now, with an English lady's taste, and ignoring all else, she decided that tea on the terrace was the thing she wanted the most. For the moment, questions could wait.

"You're looking better," he said approvingly when she had relaxed with the steaming cup of tea. It was just as if she was the lady of the house, and she and her husband were enjoying a morning tête-à-tête . . .

"You were right," she said coolly, pushing the thought as far from her mind as she could. "These biscuits are delicious, and I shall tell Mrs. Hughes so."

Luke leaned back in his chair. His hair was slightly ruffled by the breeze, making him look more like he had when she first saw him, spray-washed, darkly handsome, lithe and scantily clothed . . . Her face flushed at her wayward thoughts.

"Why does it bother you when I pay you a compliment?" he said lazily.

"It doesn't! Why should you think so?"

64

"Because you always change the conversation or lower your eyes or clench your hands together," he said, observing her far more accurately than she cared to be. She unclenched her hands at once.

"That's better. Now perhaps you'll really relax," Luke continued.

"You can hardly expect that, when I'm in a completely foreign environment among strangers, and not knowing what's happened to my father!"

"I've already told you where you are. I can do nothing about finding your father at present, but as for being among strangers, that situation can be remedied any time you wish."

She stared, full of resentment at the innuendo. She put her cup down in her saucer with a clatter, ignoring the fact that it was unladylike to do so. Such attention to etiquette seemed of little consequence now.

"I would be grateful if you didn't keep making these obscure suggestions, Mr. Garston. I'm obliged to you for all your help — *very* obliged — of *course* I am. But please, it must go no further. I *wish* it to go no further —"

She was suddenly floundering because of his level, unwavering gaze. She was overly conscious of how dark his eyes really were and how very handsome and masculine he was. He was a man with whom any woman could so very easily fall in love ... but she was not just any woman. She was Miss Caroline Rowe, she reminded herself desperately, daughter of a well-respected gentleman, who didn't cavort with pearl divers and fishermen, no matter how different their onshore lives would seem to be ...

"I asked you once before if you liked what you saw," Luke said softly. "I ask you again, my dear Miss Rowe, because it's yours for the taking."

She drew in her breath. He was outrageous ...

and also more exciting than any man she had ever known. She couldn't deny it, and the blood ran faster in her veins at the dark desire in his eyes. It touched a chord in her that she had never known existed until now.

"You presume too much—" she said, her voice hoarse.

He leaned forward to caress the side of her cheek with his fingers. She shivered, feeling an almost irresistible urge to grasp those caressing fingers and bring them to her mouth. Was she going completely mad?

"I presume everything," Luke stated. "I claim you as mine, Caroline, and be quite sure that I mean to have you, no matter how much you may protest. You're merely wasting time by doing so."

She gasped aloud now as his fingers curled around her chin and held her fast. She pushed his hand away, no longer enchanted. He was impossible and arrogant.

"You cannot claim another person as yours," she said witheringly. "You may claim possessions, but not people."

"I hate to contradict a lady, but you'll soon learn that the ancient superstitions that rule these islands are far stronger than your petty English niceties."

"What ancient superstitions?" Caroline said. "Don't try to frighten me—nor deny that you're as English as I am!"

"I don't deny my origins," he said briefly. "But I also have every respect for an ancient way of life. Each different tribe of Aborigines has its own customs and beliefs, and you'd do well not to scoff at them."

"I've no intention of doing anything of the sort," she snapped, thinking how easily it was to be angered by him. And she remembered how, just moments ago, she was thinking how easy it would be to fall in love with him! She decided that being angry was the safer bet.

"Then respect their belief that a life saved from the sea belongs to the rescuer," he said calmly.

She made a move of disbelief. "You just made that up!"

"Did I? Then ask Jojo or Makepeace or Petal or any of the other natives. They'll confirm what I said. Why do you think everyone is so attentive toward you? You're not just any guest, Miss Rowe. Everyone knows you're my woman."

In a fury, she got to her feet without thinking and almost fell as her weak leg threatened to give way under her. She made to grab at the edge of the table, but Luke was too quick for her. He caught her in his arms, and his breath warmed her cheek, forcing her to look up at him.

"Don't be a little fool," he said savagely. "Do you want to undo all the good Dr. Sam's done for you?"

"I just want to leave here," she retorted. "You can't keep me here against my will!"

"That's exactly what I can do because there's nowhere else for you to go, and the sooner you realize it, the better for us both. I can offer you a life of luxury, and you'll not lack for anything. Nothing at all, my lovely one."

His voice had softened seductively, and the arms holding her were becoming more possessive as he felt her pliant in his embrace. Wordlessly he pressed his mouth to hers. She stood as still as she could, trying very hard not to respond in the slightest way, because he was crass and undisciplined and the very epitome of bad taste.

But it was too much to expect of anyone. Pressed close to his heart and to every pulsating part of his body, she was succumbing to a wildness in her own nature that she was only just discovering, and after a few moments she found that her own arms were holding him, her mouth was responding to his kisses, and the warm sensations flooding through her body were too new and too exquisite to ignore.

Whatever else she would lack in a life with Luke Garston, she knew instinctively it wouldn't be a lack of loving. She sensed that the man was a master in the art, and only the Lord knew how many women he had practiced it on to achieve perfection.

And she was destined to be the next . . . Faintly, as wild and erotic thoughts flitted through her mind, Caroline knew one thing with fierce certainty. If she was destined to be Luke Garston's lover, then she had to be his only one and his last one. She would never share him.

She realized he was finally putting her gently away from him, and that she was the one still clinging on. Burning with embarrassment, she turned away from his knowing eyes.

"Don't," he said softly. "Don't ever be afraid to let me see that wanton look in your eyes, my Caroline. You were made for loving, and only a fool denies his own needs."

She had no idea how to answer such blatant words. No one had ever said such things to her before, and she was honest enough to admit that they excited her as much as they shocked her. She even admitted to herself, however reluctantly, that the raw thrill of his frankness was beginning to outweigh all the rest. She was already coming under his charismatic spell, despite herself. She sat down again, and as he did likewise, she had the strangest feeling that a small crisis had passed.

"Is it true what you said about the ancient superstition?" she said huskily.

"I would never lie to you, Caroline. There are

many things that are taboo subjects in this house, but whatever I choose to tell you will always be the truth."

She could easily scorn his words, but somehow she felt compelled to believe them. Even so, she still had choices. He might consider her his woman, but unless he resorted to rape, she could still deny him what he apparently wanted most of all from her. She shivered again, wondering if she had completely taken leave of her senses, even to be thinking such thoughts.

"What is it you want of me?" she asked him directly.

A sudden look of mischief came into his eyes, lightening an atmosphere that had become as charged as if a violent storm was brewing. And Caroline wished at once that such a comparison hadn't come into her mind.

"I don't think you can be that naive, my sweet. What do you think I want?"

"I asked you the question, and you said you'd never lie to me," she replied promptly. His teasing was infectious. She knew they were playing a reckless game of flirtation that could be just a delightfully meaningless pastime . . . except that on Luke's part, she was sure it was not.

"All right then," he said, far too casually.

She should have been warned, but she wasn't. She still expected the teasing to go on, and her face went a slow shocked red when it didn't. He caught hold of her hands, so that she was held captive between them. He stared into her widening eyes, daring her to look away. She felt the rapid beating of her heart and the wild pulse at her throat.

"I want you in my bed," he said. "I want you there every night for the rest of our lives. I want to wake up in the morning and see your hair spread out on my pillow and see the sleep leaving your

69

eyes as I begin to wake you with my body and know that you're a part of me. I want to be so deep inside you that neither of us knows where one of us ends and the other begins—"

"Dear God, please stop this," Caroline whispered.

"I've only just begun, my darling," Luke went on ruthlessly. "You asked, and I'm answering. And don't pretend that I'm not arousing you. I can see it in your eyes, and you can feel it in all the luscious places I want to be. Can't you, my seductive little sea-witch?"

His eyes were compelling her to be as truthful as himself, and somehow she could be nothing else while he stared into her eyes so unblinkingly. He was a devil in man's clothing, she thought wildly, and as his hands tightened their grip on hers, the words were spilling out of her.

"All right! Yes, yes, *yes,* I do feel something! But only because you're so—so—"

"So honest? I'll wager that none of the milksops you've come into contact with before have aroused you in such a way."

"I would never have allowed them to say such things to me!" she said, trying desperately to hold on to her dignity while being completely shaken by the force of her own reaction to a stranger.

Luke gave a short laugh. "You would never have allowed them to take such liberties, either. But you allowed me. Can you deny that you were kissing me just now?"

"I couldn't help it. I couldn't get away . . ."

"And you never will. Accept that and our future life together will be the best that any two people could ever have, I promise you, Caroline."

"Our life together!" she echoed, dragging up some semblance of common sense. "We don't have a life together. I've already told you, I have to search for my father, and I mean to see that through, with or without your help."

He let go of her hands abruptly. She rubbed at them, aware that they were quite sore from his grip.

"You'll not get very far without it," he said shortly, his mood changing as quickly as hers. Caroline couldn't help feeling relieved. The last few moments had become altogether too intense for her peace of mind, and she still didn't know just how honorable Luke Garston's intentions were.

He called her his woman, and he was obviously already envisaging a life for the two of them here, however impossible that would seem to her. He saw her as a good catch, for certain, Caroline thought bitterly. But he had never mentioned marriage, and it was unthinkable that he could expect a genteel English lady to enter into a liaison without it.

She brought her thoughts up in a kind of panic. What in the good Lord's name was she thinking about, even to contemplate marriage with the man! She bit her lip, wondering just how far she had already come from being the pampered daughter of an English gentleman to be harboring such thoughts.

"Accept the inevitable, Caroline," Luke was saying more gently now. "No one ever leaves Brundy. Why should they, when it's an island paradise? Most people would give their souls to live here."

Her eyes flashed dangerously. "Then most people would be in the grip of the devil to let such an idea even enter their minds! *Are* you the devil, Mr. Garston?"

For a second, he looked startled, and then he laughed.

"There's certainly something of the devil in me when I look at you, my fiery love. What is it

71

about you, I wonder, that brings out the worst in me?"

He was taunting her now, and she felt the telltale flush in her cheeks again. If she brought out the worst in him, she thought wildly, then it was a good thing he had no idea that he brought out something deep and primitive inside her too. Something she had had no idea existed in her ordered life until he had brought it so unerringly to the surface.

"And what is it in *you*," she said, with a small break in her voice, "that cannot understand that I have to know what happened to my father! How can you be so insensitive to think I can simply pretend he never existed? Would you feel the same way about your own father?"

She was instantly aware of the closed look that came over Luke's face. And just as instantly, she knew there was something in his past that he chose to block from his memory. Instinct told her that whatever it was, it hadn't gone away of its own accord. Luke Garston was deliberately keeping his past locked away in his heart—if he had one.

"Of course you want to know what happened to him," he said shortly. "But it must be obvious to you already. There can never be any certainty about it, but common sense must tell you that there could have been no survivors."

"But there was one. There was me. And you told me that small groups had been taken to the mainland. You *said* that."

Their eyes clashed, and for long moments it seemed as if neither would give way. Caroline felt as if she were drowning all over again in the depth of hidden emotion she glimpsed in the man's eyes. Emotion that was too deep and bitter to share with anyone. For one crazy moment, she longed to be the one to comfort him, to chase away all the hurt and bitterness that lay deep within him. But as he continued speaking brutally, she told herself just as quickly what a fool she was being to imagine something that probably wasn't even there.

"You were lucky. And I'm sorry, but a twist of the truth seemed justified at the time. You were in a highly emotional state—"

"Do you mean it was all lies, and that no one was reported found!" she almost screamed. She felt sick and betrayed, and she hated him.

"I merely said there were rumors. The fishermen bring back all kinds of garbled stories, and there's no real way of knowing truth from lies—"

"So you invented it all," she said bitterly.

"Why should I bother to do that?"

"Because you mean to keep me here," she said in a high, choked voice. "You want to make me your slave—"

"If I wanted a slave, I'd find one easily enough. That's not what I want from you, Caroline."

She swallowed the thickening lump in her throat, uncaring of his seductive innuendoes now, because it seemed as if all hope for her father was slowly dying. And she wouldn't believe it. She daren't . . .

"I warn you, I shall find every means possible to get away from here. Until I know for certain about my father's fate, I'll never—I'll never—"

She stopped, hardly knowing what she was trying to say. Never be his woman? Never accept that she was destined to remain here on Brundy Island forever? She was sobbing again and furious with herself for doing so. For feeling so weak when she had always believed herself to be so strong. She took a long, shuddering breath and tilted her chin defiantly, despite the blurring of her eyes.

"You may think you own me," she said in a low voice. "But no one will ever do that, Mr. Garston. I may be helpless to fight you, but whatever you do to me, always remember that you do it against my will."

His voice became caressing again. "Haven't you realized yet that the last thing I want is to fight you? And I'll make a wager that the time will come when nothing I do to you will be against your will, my sweet. You can't hold out forever — and I'd be obliged if you'd stop this ridiculous formality between us. Lovers have no need for it."

She drew in her breath. The man was impossibly uncouth. None of the fine trappings with which he surrounded himself could ever alter that, she thought furiously.

"I'm sure you've discovered that well enough in the past," she said pointedly. "I'm sure there are other ladies on the island eager enough for your favors."

"Don't ever doubt it," he said with a grin. "In fact, in a couple of days, I'll take you around the island. You won't be expected to walk anywhere for a while, naturally."

She stared at him. He was so damned self-assured, she thought, allowing the blasphemy into her mind without even thinking. Where Luke Garston was concerned, none of the usual conventions seemed to matter anymore.

"If you expect me to ride on horseback, I'd rather not. Horses were never my favorite animals," she snapped.

"I do not," he said, still with that maddening grin on his face. "I do own more comfortable vehicles, ma'am."

A few days later, Caroline had determined that she must recover her spirits with all speed, if only to assure this difficult man that she was perfectly well enough to make a journey to the mainland by

74

whatever means were available. She simply didn't believe that a small boat couldn't negotiate any old reef, probably far better than a larger vessel could.

This afternoon, she was seated beside Luke in a luxuriously padded and shaded carriage with open sides to admit the warm island air, and drawn by two plodding mules. She was beginning to learn that nothing moved at a very fast pace on Brundy and nor was there any need for it. From the viewpoint of this lush and admittedly beautiful island, the bustle and noise of London, and of home, had never seemed so far away.

At the unbidden thought, the sheer poignancy of her situation threatened to overwhelm her again, and without warning, her head and shoulders visibly drooped. To her surprise, she felt Luke's hand cover hers.

"Hold on, my brave one," he said in a surprisingly gentle voice. "Dr. Sam will be our first port of call today, providing he's not too busy. I want to show him how fast you're recovering under his good auspices. He'll be happy to see that his patient's thriving, but not if he finds you in low spirits."

"I hardly think he can expect anything else," she murmured, unexpectedly touched at this concern. "Physically, I'm well enough, but nothing's really changed, has it? My father's still missing, and until I find him, I'm totally alone in the world."

She knew it was a mistake as soon as she had said it. The pressure on her hand tightened a little.

"Haven't I already told you that you're never going to be alone again?"

He removed his hand as he steered the mules around a corner on the rough grassy track that served as a road. His words were oddly sincere, and the ready retort stuck in her throat. She didn't want his attentions, but neither did she want to feel

75

so completely adrift in the world. He was the only thing she had to lean on now, and if she was still finding it hard to accept that, she also knew what she owed him.

She had faced up to that in the long lonely hours of the night. Without Luke Garston, she would assuredly be dead. For all that the doctor had done to salvage her leg, she knew she wouldn't have stood a chance on that vast ocean if Luke hadn't come to her rescue.

A sudden shout prevented her from making a fool of herself by blurting out her thanks all over again in an uncharacteristically maudlin way. She looked up to see the ungainly figure of Doctor Sam coming toward them from the bushy trail, a gaggle of young natives following him. There were girls as well as boys, Caroline saw, and all were as naked as the day they were born.

"Try not to show your disapproval," Luke said calmly. "It's traditional that none of them bothers with clothes until they've passed twelve summers."

And on the freedom of the ocean, the pearl divers didn't bother with such accoutrements well after that age, she recalled vividly . . .

"What are these children doing?" she said in confusion.

"Taking lessons. Doc's a great one for teaching them to speak English, and the young 'uns love it. I daresay it's been a botany lesson in the bush today. I've had a hand in teaching them myself, but I don't have his patience."

She managed to avoid his eyes. He'd obviously had enough patience to teach Petal some English, but remembering the girl's wide, welcoming smile and lissome shape, Caroline decided she probably didn't fall into quite the same category as a gauche "young 'un."

"It's good to see you back in the land o' the living, my duck," Dr. Sam greeted her breezily. "No ill effects from the leg, I hope?"

"It's beginning to feel stronger all the time," she said, smiling. It was true. Now that she was able to use it again, it was regaining strength surprisingly quickly, and the long livid scar was already starting to fade. She felt inordinately grateful to this unlikely medical man and tried to tell him so. It was obvious they weren't to be invited into whatever abode he inhabited after all since Luke made no attempt to get out of the carriage. The doctor waved her thanks aside.

"Good God, do you think I'd not have enjoyed tending a lovely young thing like yourself, girl, after dealing with these young rascals most of the time? It was a pleasure."

"But you know I can't repay you, and I'd like to —"

She stopped in embarrassment. How could she ever repay a man for saving her life when she owned nothing? She owed him an enormous debt, and she could never, ever repay it.

"Well, if you really want to repay me and you've a mind to it one afternoon, you can help me teach these young sprogs their letters. God knows I've tried, but all they want to do is learn the names of flowers and trees and birds and suchlike. A fine, educated lady like yourself could be doing them a power of good. What do you say?"

She was taken aback by the suggestion. She looked uneasily at the friendly black faces of the children and found it impossible not to smile back.

"Well, perhaps I could help a little, just for one afternoon," she said slowly. "Just while I'm here, of course."

A small jabber went up from the children then, mostly in their own incomprehensible language, but with a smattering of the English words they knew.

77

"Fine lady . . ."

"Mr. Luke got new pretty lady . . ."

"Fine and pretty . . ."

It was all innocently said, but to Caroline it all seemed to enmesh her still further into the life on this island. These children would have heard of her presence several weeks ago, she realized, and would have been curious to see the new pretty lady Mr. Luke had got . . .

"Come over for supper tonight, Sam," Luke was saying now. "We'll uncork a bottle or two."

The doctor agreed, and all the children waved them on their way as if they were royalty. Maybe it was how they all saw Luke, she thought. If his was the biggest house on the island, and he was the one who had organized the pearl divers into a viable industry, trading with other communities, and putting Brundy Island on the commercial map, then no wonder they would look on him as something of a godlike benefactor. It wasn't the way she *saw* him . . .

"Are you telling me you have wine here?" she said, for want of something to say. As the children's chatter died away, the bush seemed to close around them.

"Of course. The trading ship brings us anything we want, but we also have a special island brew that you'll like. Some even swear that it's a potent aphrodisiac. We'll try some tonight, and you can tell me what you think."

The small, open-sided carriage suddenly lurched over the rutted terrain, and she fell against him with a little cry. He halted the mules and held her close to him for a few minutes.

"I'm sorry. I'm all right," she mumbled. "It was just that I thought I was going to fall out."

She was held close to his chest. Slowly she looked up into his dark, fathomless eyes. She could

78

feel his heartbeat as if it were her own, deep and rhythmic and very fast, as if the contact was affecting him in a way she had not intended. It had been a pure accident that put her into his embrace . . .

"Dear God, but I surely don't have the need for aphrodisiacs when you're in my arms, lass," he said roughly. "I'm not sure how long I can go on pretending—"

"Pretending?" she said, instantly alert. "Do you have news of my father after all? What are you keeping from me?"

He gave a low groan and his arms tightened around her. His breath was hot on her face, and her breasts were flattened against him. She was very aware of every part of him, hard, muscular, with all the arrogant masculinity of a man who badly wanted a woman.

"I'm keeping nothing from you regarding your father. If I knew anything, I would tell you. But it's time you realized he's not the only man on earth. And however dear he was to you, a father cannot give you everything a woman needs."

"And you can?" she said, unconsciously seductive.

She felt his hand slide up the length of her leg until it reached her thigh. Thank goodness it was her *good* leg, the incongruous thought flashed through her mind. She knew she should stop this indignity at once, and yet somehow, she couldn't. Here in the middle of this isolated place with the lush trees and shrubs momentarily isolating them from everything else in the world and only the soft cooing of exotic birds somewhere high above them, they were entirely alone. They were on a small oasis of their own making, and she was suddenly past resisting.

His mouth was covering hers, his tongue caressing her own, and the sweet pleasure of it was fill-

79

ing her senses as his trailing hand moved closer and closer toward its goal. There was no room for any thought of sin in her mind. There was only pleasurable sensation as those cool fingers sought and reached for her, and without even knowing she did so, she arched gently and opened up for him.

Even with his mouth on hers, she experienced Luke's own indrawn breath, as if this intimate contact was all and more than he had expected. There seemed to be a timeless moment, as if all the world was waiting, when suddenly his tongue was forging harder into her mouth. At the same time, she was aware of a sharp sweet pain as his fingers forged inside her, matching the movement, but the small sting was lost in the erotic shock of what was happening.

Just as suddenly, he left her, pulling her skirts tenderly down about her limbs, and she rested her head, trembling against him.

"Forgive me, sweet," he muttered softly against her forehead. "This was surely not the time or place for breaking you, but it will make our joining all the sweeter when it happens."

She didn't understand his words. She didn't even know what he had done to her, only that she felt damp and uncomfortable and suddenly very, very tired.

"Can we go back to the house, please?" she whispered. "I'm not ready to meet people after all, especially not now. I feel . . . unclean."

"It would be best. Mrs. Hughes will prepare a bath for you, and I suggest you have a long soak and a rest before this evening. Perhaps after we've had supper with Dr. Sam, the three of us can play cards if it pleases you. Sam's a fair fiddle player too, and he invariably brings the instrument with him to sing for his supper, as he calls it."

She sensed he was trying to put her at ease. He

said he had broken her, which must mean something very significant. She knew she must be very stupid, but as he turned the mules around, she had to know.

"What did you mean by saying you've broken me? Have you hurt me in some way?"

In her naivety, she presumed that since he had not lain with her, her virginity was still intact. She had certainly not been raped . . . and she mentally cursed the primness of a society that refused a young woman proper education in such matters.

"My sweet innocent, you're as truly mine now as if we had produced a dozen children. Surely you know that? No other man would want a woman who had lost her maidenhead so deliciously."

The shock of it stunned her for a moment. If she had felt betrayed before, then how much more did she feel it now! In a sudden wild rage, she began beating her hands against his chest like a fishwife, uncaring of anything but the need to hurt him as he had hurt her. But it was all to no effect. He sat there like a statue, not even warding off her blows, and she had never felt more trapped. And certainly raped in spirit, if not in body.

Chapter Five

Caroline dressed carefully for supper that evening. She paid as much attention to her appearance as if it were for one of her father's acclaimed London dinners. For a long sweet moment she was swept back into the heady atmosphere of those evenings: the men's newspaper talk, which she was privileged to hear due to her progressive father's indulgence, always excited and enthralled her far more than women's drawing room gossip, whether it was the national or local incidents they discussed so avidly or the worldwide events they conjured up so vividly.

Because of it she was intelligent and knowledgeable far beyond the kind of education most young girls received. And she missed it all so much . . .

She caught her breath, knowing how near were the threatening tears of self-pity once more, and she was determined not to let that happen. She had to prove something to herself, and to Luke Garston. He must see that she was not something to be picked up out of the sea and used in any way he wished. She had been born and bred a lady. He might think that by defiling her he would humiliate her so severely that she would give in to this enforced slavery. But he would soon learn that Caroline Rowe was a slave to no one.

It wasn't for Luke that she wore one of the pretty gowns she had found in the closet of her room, though it had taken great fortitude not to question Petal closely on how they came to be there. It wasn't for Luke that she pinched her cheeks to make them rosy and teased out the tendrils of her glossy dark hair into a becoming frame for her face. It was all for Dr. Sam's benefit. Tonight she was going to wheedle Dr. Sam into telling her the quickest way out of here.

It surely didn't depend totally on the trading ships. If strangers arrived on Brundy Island, then strangers could also leave it. To the daughter of a newspaper magnate, steeped in a background where logic and clear-headed reporting was of prime importance, the tiny sliver of hope helped to buoy up her spirits considerably.

She was also used to the company of men in semibusiness surroundings. As her father's hostess, she had learned to cope with gentlemen's conversation. By the time she went downstairs to the drawing room, where the two Brundy men were smoking in leisurely fashion, she had almost recovered her usual aplomb.

Almost . . . until the sweetly aromatic scent of their cigars practically overwhelmed her with nostalgia. Almost . . . until she saw Luke turn to look at her with that straight, level gaze she was beginning to find so disarming. She ignored the sudden trembling in her limbs and forced herself to look at him just as directly.

"Well, sir? Will I do, or do I have a smudge on

my nose?" she said, her voice a shade higher than she would have liked.

"You'll do very well for me, Miss Rowe," he said gravely, and she shivered slightly, wishing he wouldn't make her every remark a source of intimacy between them. It wasn't fair. She turned to the doctor at once. The crumpled suit hadn't changed, though he looked shaved and a mite more spruced up than before. She supposed it was the only concession he made to polite society.

"Good evening, Dr. Sam," she said.

To her surprise, he got to his feet and ambled toward her. He took her hand in his and raised it to his lips.

"And a far better evening it is now, dear lady, graced by your sweet presence," he said, oozing gallantry so blatantly that she had a job not to laugh out loud. He was a flirtatious old rogue, she thought at once. But she felt an odd kind of affection toward him, too, remembering how he'd led those eager-eyed native children in their lessons.

"And how is the offending limb, my dear?" he enquired when she had seated herself in one of the luxurious armchairs. "Not giving you too much trouble, I hope, though it will be weak for a while yet, I daresay."

"It's not too bad at all, thanks to you," she said, glad to give him a genuine smile for his care, however unorthodox it may have been. "I've decided I shall live," she added lightly.

"Then praise be from us all," he chuckled. "Luke here would have skinned my hide if he'd saved you from a watery grave only to have all my efforts wasted."

"I do realize I owe you both a great deal," she said fervently. "I could never repay either of you—"

84

"Caroline is obsessed with thoughts of payment, Sam," Luke broke in. "I've told her payment doesn't enter into it, but naturally enough, she's still clinging on to the old ways."

"Of course she is. You can't change a lifetime's habits overnight, boy, but I'll wager that in a few weeks from now, the gentle pace of the island will have worked its magic. It does it for all of us."

It dawned on Caroline that they were discussing her as if she weren't there. She leaned forward tensely.

"I'd be very glad if you didn't imply that I'm to be here forever, Dr. Sam. All this talk about clinging to the old ways, as if you've found something special and unusual here, may be charming to you, but it's not to me! I didn't come here by choice, and I shan't remain here through choice. I want to find my father, and then I want to go home — and home will be wherever my father and I choose to settle!"

She was breathing very heavily. She had never intended to blurt out everything like that, but all this talk of magic and the assumption that she would fit into the role of whatever Luke Garston intended for her was suddenly frightening. She felt her eyes blur with tears and realized she was weaker than she thought. She wanted to control her own destiny, not have these two men control it for her.

She saw them now through a haze of cigar smoke and tears, and fumbled for the handkerchief she had tucked into the pocket of her gown. Silently Luke handed her a much larger square of linen. She ignored it for a moment, then, realizing she must have dropped her own somewhere, she accepted his with a bad grace and blew her nose into it noisily.

85

"What are you so afraid of?" he said quietly. "No one's forcing you to do anything you don't want to do. I merely offer you hospitality, and Doc here has patched up your wounds. Is this obvious suspicion of everyone's motives the way young ladies are taught to show their gratitude in England nowadays?"

She sniffed inelegantly, glaring at him above the linen square. He had a fine way of turning the tables on her, she thought irritably. As for not forcing her to his will—she closed her eyes for a second—no, he hadn't exactly forced her into anything, she remembered with a different kind of shiver . . . She thrust the hanky into his hands, and he kept his gaze on her flushed face as he tucked it into his jacket pocket.

"Well then, I'm sorry if I offend you," she said awkwardly at last, finding it all the more ludicrous that she should be apologizing to him, and for no reason at all that she could define. Nor should she be as damnably grateful as he seemed to expect— except that she *was* a guest in his house, and he *had* saved her life. Her feelings were so muddled, she felt as though she could hardly think straight anymore, especially when he looked at her with that direct and seductive gaze.

"You don't offend me," he said softly, his hand closing over hers. "But I'd prefer to see a smiling face to a gloomy one, or poor old Doc will wonder why he's been invited to supper if you go on like this. He sees enough gloom among his patients, so how about cheering us all up with a smile instead?"

"As long as you stop treating me like a naughty child, then I daresay I can manage it."

Even as she spoke as lightly as she could manage now, she couldn't stop her mouth from twitch-

86

ing. And then he was drawing her to her feet as Mrs. Hughes appeared in the room to announce that supper was ready.

The smell of food wafted toward them as soon as they entered the dining room. Once again Caroline was stunned by the opulent way in which this man lived. It could have been one of the best English houses, given the furnishings, the paintings, the servitude of the staff, the food and wine, and the manner in which it was all presented.

"Are you still so surprised by all you see?" he asked, watching her face. She gave up being annoyed that he could read her expression so easily since in this case it hardly mattered.

"What else would you expect? I hardly expected to find such luxury in the middle of nowhere," she answered coolly, when they were all seated at the dining table.

Its rich damask cloth gleamed with cut crystal and silverware, and the immaculate table was further embellished by soft candlelight and bowls of fresh and glazed fruits. Whether intentional or not the entire atmosphere, together with the scent of the exotic flowers inside and outside the house, was undoubtedly sensual.

Caroline was suddenly glad of Dr. Sam's presence. His prosaic and down-to-earth attitude diffused the continually charged atmosphere between herself and Luke Garston. She would have been a fool not to recognize the existence of such tension by now. She was acutely aware of every glance and every brush of his fingertips against hers. Whether she hated him or not, she was made more alive every time he came into a room, she thought suddenly. But the knowledge had the power to frighten her as much as it exalted her. She didn't want to be drawn into his spell, nor have any regrets at leaving the island. Once this interlude was over, it should be relegated to memory.

"You've eaten very little, Caroline," Luke observed, when the two men had partaken heartily. "Mrs. Hughes will be offended if you don't eat, and you could certainly do with a little more flesh on your bones."

She felt her face go hot as his glance ran over her, resting for a long moment on the soft swelling curve of her breasts in the low-necked gown. She was not thin by any means, but maybe her figure didn't quite measure up to the lush brown bodies of the few native girls she had seen, she thought with something that was almost a stab of envy. Angered, she wondered if Luke Garston was comparing her unfavorably to those nubile girls, and she shouldn't care a jot about his opinion.

"I don't care to be too well-covered," she said coolly. "It's always considered rather vulgar in the best society."

She stared at Luke defiantly through the flickering haze of candlelight and heard Dr. Sam give a low chuckle.

"That's put you in your place, m'boy," he said roguishly. "But with a few solid months of Mrs. Hughes's good cooking, young Caroline here will soon fatten up to your liking."

This was too much! Her cheeks blazing now, Caroline turned furiously toward the affable doctor.

"I assure you I've no intention of fattening myself up like some prize cow for Mr. Garston or any other man, sir! And I've too much respect for myself to think of being any man's chattel. As for being here a few months, well, even a few days more would be too long for me!"

The two men said nothing for a few minutes,

and Caroline decided it was time to abandon any idea of subtlety or of trying to get Dr. Sam alone this evening. She might as well make her position quite clear, here and now.

"Will you help me, Dr. Sam?" she said bluntly. "Luke tells me it will be months yet before the trading ship calls at Brundy Island, and I simply can't wait that long. I must find out if my father is still alive, and I can't do it by twiddling my thumbs. Luke says it's too dangerous to take a small boat to the mainland, but you strike me as a man who would be willing to take a gamble. Obviously, my father would reward you handsomely—"

She realized her lips were trembling. The possibilities of finding out what had happened to Sir William Rowe seemed so pitifully small, yet she could never abandon hope until she knew his fate for certain.

"What would I want with rewards, girl?" the doctor said. "I have everything I want here, and I'm as reluctant as Luke to go to the mainland. There's nothing for me there, and the time will soon pass until the trading ship arrives. You'd do better to be patient."

Without intending to, Caroline sprang to her feet, her knuckles white as she pressed her hands on the tablecloth.

"Don't you understand that I *can't* be patient? You may both have chosen this life, but I haven't. I'll never settle here, never!"

"Sit down, for pity's sake," Luke said harshly. "You'll have the servants thinking we're molesting you."

"So you are, mentally at least," she whipped back. "But you're obviously too insensitive to my feelings to see it!"

"What I see is a spoiled brat who's totally un-

89

grateful for the fact that she was half-dead when I rescued her and even more so for the fact that Doc here saved her leg and her sanity."

Caroline gasped at the calm censure in Luke's voice.

"Nobody has ever spoken to me like that before—"

"Then it's about time they did," Luke snapped. "Are you going to sit down and finish your meal like a civilized young woman, or are we all going to end up with indigestion?"

She sat down abruptly since her legs began to feel they would no longer hold her up. He was impossible, she raged! How any woman could ever find him in the least charismatic, she couldn't imagine.

"Anyway, my dear," Doc was saying in a slightly guarded voice now, "I have to admit that I have plenty of reason not to leave the island, and not even for the sake of your lovely self would I risk it."

His words only confirmed some of Caroline's private suspicions about the man. Generous and affable though he was, and obviously skilled in his vocation, he had some secret to hide. And so did Luke, she thought bitterly. Why else would they both be so unwilling to leave their self-imposed exile, even for humanitarian reasons?

"So I'm obliged to stay here until the trading ship arrives then," she said in a dull, hopeless voice.

"Maybe not," Luke answered without expression. "Maybe I'll take you to the mainland myself after all."

Even as hope flared in her heart, Caroline heard Doc's warning words.

"Luke, I think not! There's the reef . . . and

90

other considerations."

Luke shrugged. "If it means getting this irritating female out of my life, then yes, it's wise, old friend. She obviously doesn't care to stay and share our paradise, so I shall put her ashore on the mainland where she wants to be."

"But you'll help me search for my father, surely? You wouldn't take me there and leave me!" She felt renewed panic as he looked at her steadily, a small smile curving his mouth now.

"I do believe the lady wants me by her side after all," he said, so softly and intimately that there might have been just the two of them in the room.

"You know what I want. I want to find my father," Caroline said in frustration. "And I'd be glad if you would stop teasing me. I don't believe you're the kind of man who would just leave me on the mainland. You saved my life, remember? And because of that, we have an obligation to one another. Didn't you say something of the kind?"

She was starting to flounder, wondering just how deeply she was pushing herself into this man's life after all, but knowing no other way of persuading him to do as she wished. But he had already said he'd take her across the Barrier Reef to the mainland. And exhilaration was beginning to flood her veins now. She felt oddly lightheaded, as if she had been through a great battle and had won.

She heard Dr. Sam's low chuckle. "She has you there, boy. I reckon you've met your match in this one."

"That's just what I've been trying to tell Caroline," Luke went on, still in that soft, mesmerizing voice. "We're a perfect match for each other."

"Well, all I want to know is how soon we can leave," she broke in sharply, wanting to get things

91

organized at once. "Tomorrow? The day after?"

"We'll see," was all he would say, to her utter annoyance. And Dr. Sam seemed unusually quiet about the whole scheme. But she dared not push Luke further. He was her lifesaver in more ways than one, and she couldn't antagonize him too much.

"I think none of us is in the mood for cards this evening, but perhaps you'd care to play for us after supper?" he said casually. "Doc will give us a tune on his fiddle, I'm sure, but we both like to hear the pianoforte played."

Caroline complied, if only to keep him agreeable to her wishes. It would all be worth it, to get her own way at last . . . and it never entered her head that there might be more payment expected of her in the sweetly scented hours of the subtropical night . . .

Long after the various types of music had ended and Dr. Sam had gone on his way, the house settled into darkness. Caroline lay sleepless on top of the covers in her own bed. The windows were flung open to let the still-warm evening air infiltrate the room, drenching it with the sensually erotic perfume of the island. The sky was a deep endless blue, dotted with a million dazzling stars, and the huge golden globe of the moon lit her room as light as day.

It was impossible to sleep. Her mind was too filled with the glory that soon, very soon now, she would voyage to the mainland of Australia and her quest for her father would begin. Her normal optimism and buoyancy was fast returning, and she was convinced that God was fashioning her life for her and that He would surely not have let her come this far and survive, without real hope for the future. She pinned all her hopes and her faith on that.

Yet, for all the swirling possibilities that were going around in her head, she was extraordinarily lethargic now. It was a delicious feeling, half-hypnotic, half-dreaming. The lazy thought drifted into her mind that it could be partly due to the island brew they had drunk so pleasurably. It had seemed so innocuous a brew at the supper table, but she seemed to recall a voice telling her at sometime that it was quite potent, and a positive aphrodisiac . . .

By the time she heard the soft click of her door handle, she was in a semisomnolent state. She was lulled by renewed hope for the future and by the thought that whatever was in Luke's past, it couldn't be so bad if he had finally consented to take her to the mainland. And in her newly generous thoughts toward him, she admitted that she didn't want to think too ill of him.

"Caroline," she heard Luke's voice say quietly. "It's time for me to claim my woman."

Her eyes didn't seem to want to open at all. Her lids felt so heavy, so leaden now. She moved her head sideways on the pillow and with effort opened her eyes, and the vague image of someone moving toward her became a reality.

"Luke," she said hoarsely. "You have no right to be here. My reputation—"

He gave a soft laugh. "You're still too indoctrinated in the past, my sweet. Reputations were invented by old men with old ideas. This is the new land of opportunity. Didn't your father tell you that? From all that I've heard about him, I'm damned sure he did."

"My father . . ." she said faintly.

93

"We'll try to find him," he promised her. "Did you really think I would take you to the mainland and abandon you there? You haven't been listening to me properly, Caroline. From now on, you and I belong together."

He was close to the bed now, and for a moment his image blotted out the light from the window. Caroline still struggled to stop her senses from swimming, and as Luke was framed in the window, she was aware of the dark shape he made and of how the moonlight caught the lights in his hair, creating a kind of halo around his head. As if he were an angel when she already thought of him as the devil incarnate.

It was so ludicrous a thought that for a moment she wanted to laugh aloud, but it was something far removed from laughter that was sending such powerfully urgent feelings rippling through her as Luke Garston slowly undid the cord of his dressing robe and turned sideways against the light.

Caroline drew in her breath. Until the lifeboat when Luke and his boys had rescued her, she had never seen a man's naked body before. Then she had averted her eyes quickly from the sight of the native boys, so grinningly aware of her discomfiture and embarrassment. But she couldn't avert her eyes now. She swallowed thickly, aware of the pulsating in her throat and the magnificent animal stature of the man leaning toward her.

"Do I please my lady?" Luke whispered.

"I . . . I don't know . . ."

"Then we must find out," Luke said, and before she could think what he was about to do, he had lifted her nightgown from her pliant body and raised it above her head. Still dazed, without thinking, she lifted her arms with a childlike obedience, and the removed garment rustled, unwanted, to the carpeted floor.

It was Luke then, who drew in his breath.

"Dear God, but you're so beautiful," he said, his voice oddly harsh. "With the moonlight pouring in on you, you're like a lovely statue, carved out of marble. But never as cold as marble, I pray."

He reached out and circled one aroused nipple with his finger. Caroline shivered at his touch, yet her whole body was suddenly heated with a fever she had never known before.

"I'm not really cold," she whispered, as if she needed to explain to him.

"Even so, I intend to warm you in a way that you'll always remember, my darling. Once I've covered you with my body and filled you with myself, you'll never be cold again."

She heard the words as if they were the sweetest music ever to enter her head. She was drowning in the passion he exuded just by his presence. His hands were exploring her, wanting her and knowing her, and by an instinct as sure and primitive as breathing, she discovered she was reaching out for him.

She touched him tentatively at first, awed and very aware of the potent power she held in her palm, and stroked with her fingers. And then, as his gasping words assured her she was doing exactly what he wanted of her, she moved more surely. As he stroked and fondled her, warming every part of her with his hands and his mouth, Caroline patterned his every move.

She was gripped by some kind of wanton fever now, hardly knowing where sensation began and ended, as Luke's demanding, questing tongue sent a flame of desire searing through her.

"Luke," she gasped. "Oh, Luke, please . . ."

She hardly knew what she was begging for, only

that she wanted it so badly and she wanted it now. She couldn't wait, she couldn't bear to wait . . .

Within seconds her whole being was devoured by pleasurable sensation as his body covered hers and he slid inside her, filling her. He half-lifted her from the pillow, gathering her into him, as if he couldn't be close enough to her. She was wrapped around him, so much a part of him that she couldn't have said which of them breathed or gasped or thrust. They were one being, one love . . .

She was transported into a state of new and un-explored rapture, where all her senses were accentuated and sharpened by the pleasure he was giving her. And she gave it all back, and more. She knew it by the murmured words he spoke, some of which were in a language she couldn't understand. As if, even now, while she gave him everything, he was reluctant to reveal his innermost emotions, in the more guarded ways of men . . .

Caroline felt her fingers digging into the taut flesh of his back as the perverse thought flashed through her mind that she wanted all of him. Not merely the body, but the soul as well. She needed to know his thoughts, his needs, his emotions, his deepest fears . . . and she wondered feverishly if she too was some kind of devil, to want to possess another so badly . . .

But then all time for thinking was over. She felt the rush of Luke's seed invade her body and with it came glorious, spreading sensations she had never known before, tingling through her in waves of pleasure. She held him fast as he twisted against her, and then gradually relaxed. The weight of him was still a blanket over her nakedness, a part of him still hers.

"Oh, Luke, I never knew such feelings existed,"

she whispered, still clinging to him. She felt the womanly need for words, to know he cared for her, to hear him say he loved her . . .

"I didn't mean it to happen quite like this," Luke was murmuring against her mouth. "I meant to take things more slowly, but you're too enticing, too beautiful. If I've shocked or hurt you, I'm sorry, but nothing can change the fact that you're truly my woman now, Caroline. We will always belong together."

Her eyes blurred momentarily. What he said was simple and sincere, but his message wasn't the most essential and beautiful one of all. He didn't say he loved her. And with the sudden chill that came from the end of exertion and passion, Caroline shivered, wondering if she was the world's biggest fool after all. For already, and however vehemently she fought against it, she knew she was starting to imagine a life with him.

But there also had to be love, and in her heightened emotional state now, all Caroline imagined that she heard was a note of muted triumph in Luke's voice. And in the words. She was truly his woman now. He had done what he set out to do, and she had been only too willing: the atmosphere, the soft subtropical night, the charisma of the man and the debt she owed him for saving her life, and no doubt the island brew that had so dazed her senses had all contributed to this hour of passion. To her it could have meant so much, while to him it obviously meant nothing more than one more conquest. At the dawning realization, Caroline's humiliation was complete.

She moved restlessly beneath him, and he shifted away from her at once. She clamped her legs together as if by doing so she would obliterate the memory of the violation. She forced herself to

97

think of it in that way, even though it could hardly be called rape. She had been too willing a partner for that . . .

"I'm cold now. Would you cover me, please?" she said in a cracked voice.

For a moment he said nothing. She could hear his breathing, still heavy from the exertions of lovemaking. She could feel her own, tight and short in her throat, as she willed herself not to cry. She wouldn't humiliate herself further by showing him her distress. Such moments were best kept for the privacy of darkness and solitude.

Luke picked up the coverlet from the foot of the bed and covered her tenderly. She was thankful he made no move to help her struggle back into her nightgown. She couldn't have borne that. She closed her eyes, hearing the rustle of cloth as he donned his dressing robe once more. She felt the merest touch of his lips on hers as he leaned over her, and the sweet tang of his body odor was a poignant reminder of all that had occurred.

"Good night, my princess," he said softly. "And I trust your dreams will be happy ones. Until to-morrow then."

He was gone before she risked opening her eyes. She stared straight up at the ceiling and then let her gaze move slowly around the room. Everything was as it was before. The elegant furnishings, the rich carpet, the gentle salt breeze drifting into the room, the moonlight playing on the ruffled drapery at the windows, the scent of flowers . . .

Without warning, Caroline turned her face into her pillow and felt the stinging tears run unchecked down her face. *Everything was as it was before* indeed! *Nothing* was as it had been before, she thought with a wild passion. She was despoiled, ruined, assaulted, ravished, besmirched, defiled . . .

All the ancient words she could drag up into her consciousness to describe the thing that Luke Garston had done to her were as brittle as glass in her mind. Somehow she needed to defend herself in her own thoughts because, guiltily, she knew she had done nothing to resist. And every decent young English lady would have defended her honor to the death.

As the sobs gradually subsided, the more logical side of her began to emerge once more, and Caroline told herself she was being extremely foolish. The thing was done, and there was no undoing it. It was more important, now, to show Luke Garston that it had meant little to her, and that it wasn't going to change anything. She still belonged to herself and to no one else, and her pride was never going to let her succumb to him repeatedly.

She shivered, unable to forget how ecstatic it had been but full of a new determination never to let him dominate her. She scrambled out of bed and into her nightgown, as if symbolically putting a barrier between herself and her violator. Then she slid back into bed and closed her eyes, willing herself not to dream of him or of anything but the hopes of tomorrow when he had promised to take her away from the island in search of her father. That was her only goal. Tomorrow . . .

Caroline awoke to the sound of torrential rain and the sight of Petal rushing to close her windows. There was already a large water stain on the carpet where the wind had blown the rain inside the room, and although it was noticeably cooler than of late, the air was still hot enough to make all the surrounding vegetation steam unpleasantly.

How could it all have changed so drastically, she thought, appalled.

"Lady should have shut windows when storm came," Petal scolded. Caroline scowled back at her, realizing that her head was throbbing and that despite her need to be gone, she was reluctant to leave this warm bed on such a morning.

"Lady didn't know there was a storm," she said shortly.

"You want breakfast in bed?"

Caroline pursed her lips. Normally she would have said no, she didn't want breakfast in bed. That was for old men and invalids. But today she might as well be pampered. It would probably be the last time.

"Yes, please. And then you can help me get a few things ready to take to the mainland. I'm sure Mr. Luke will expect me to take some of the clothes he's kindly provided."

She knew she was talking too fast. As she listened to herself, she knew the reason why. Of course they couldn't leave today. One glance at the ferocious wind whipping through the steaming trees and bushes told her that only a fool would be stupid or reckless enough to take out a small boat in such weather. She felt sick with disappointment. It seemed that even the elements were on Luke's side.

"Where is he?" she said thickly to Petal when the girl didn't answer.

"He gone to help boys secure boats. They don't go to sea for days now, lady."

"What do you mean, *for days?*"

She saw Petal shrug uncaringly, and she had a sudden presentiment of what she was about to hear.

"Storm was due soon. Every year at this time

100

bad storm comes, and no boats go out for fishing or diving. Bad weather lasts maybe few days, maybe few weeks. Mr. Luke say is gods' way to balance good days with bad."

It was clear that Mr. Luke had spun his own kind of philosophy for Petal and that she had taken it all in adoringly. But all Caroline could think of was that he must have known bad weather was imminent and that he knew the trip from Brundy would be delayed. He had betrayed her. And Dr. Sam hadn't said one word against it last night when Luke had said so arrogantly that he himself would take her to the mainland. She understood Dr. Sam's hesitant warning now. But he had said nothing . . .

She threw off the bedcovers in a fury, hardly noticing how Petal moved back nervously at the aggression in her voice, nor the way her own head ached and swam.

"I shall go downstairs for breakfast after all. And as soon as Mr. Luke comes back, you can tell him I want to see him immediately! Do you understand?"

"Mr. Luke no take orders, lady—"

"You *tell* him, do you hear me?" Caroline yelled at the girl, and Petal turned and fled from the room, obviously thinking she was dealing with a madwoman.

Chapter Six

"You lied to me!"

Caroline faced Luke furiously in his study. Since he hadn't deigned to answer her summons, she had been obliged to seek him out, which certainly hadn't sweetened her temper.

He leaned back in his leather chair with such an air of male superiority, she could have thrown something at him.

"Good morning, Caroline," he said evenly.

"Don't 'good morning' me! You knew all the time there would be no chance of leaving Brundy today, and you led me on, letting me think I'd be leaving here today!"

"I'm not aware that I did any such thing," he said, infuriatingly calm. "It was you who put a date on your leaving. I merely said I'd be willing to take you to the mainland myself, instead of waiting for the trading ship. I can't be held responsible for bad weather, and I hardly think you'd care to risk another gamble with Neptune, nor the island gods, nor the ancestral spirits of the natives. None of them would take too kindly to such foolishness."

"Don't try to blind me with myths and legends," she whipped back. "I want to leave this place, and I want to leave *now*. How much plainer do I have to be!"

Luke came around the desk so swiftly that she had no chance to back away. Before she knew what was happening, he had taken her by the shoulders and was shaking her. The shock of it stopped her in mid-sentence.

"And how plain do I have to make it that I'm not risking my life, nor that of my boys for the whims of a spoiled child?" he said harshly. "We'll leave here when the weather eases, and not before."

"And just when is that likely to be?" she asked shrilly. His hands were still cruelly on her shoulders, holding her fast.

"How in damnation am I expected to know that?"

"Since you profess to know everything, I assumed you could gauge it exactly! Isn't this all part of the great seduction plan, to keep me here until I never want to leave? If that was your intention, I'll tell you now that it's failed miserably. I intend to leave here as soon as possible, and I'll be watching the weather every single day until I can do so. Until then, I'd be obliged if you'd respect my wishes and keep your distance."

She was breathing harshly now, knowing she was denying what her heart desired so much. But she needed to do so, if only for her own self-respect and survival. She daren't risk allowing the sweetness of his seduction to control her. Her place was not here and never would be. She had a duty to herself and her father, and she had to see it through.

She felt his fingers digging into the flesh of her

shoulders and refused to flinch in the slightest. Nor did she let her eyes waver as his unfathomable gaze seemed to bore into hers. And then, just as suddenly, he let her go.

"Very well. I promise you I shan't bother you again," he said in an oddly remote voice. "But you have your memories, and I defy you to deny them, Caroline. Last night wasn't a dream."

"I don't care to think about last night," she said stiffly.

He gave a slight smile. "You may be able to control your thoughts, but you can't control your dreams, my darling. I may not be with you in the flesh, but you won't lose the images, I promise you that. And if such images torment you, so be it. Any time you want to change your mind and invite me into your bed, you only have to say the word."

"You're despicable," she whispered, even more shamed at knowing the truth of his words. She clenched her hands together, forcing away the unbidden pictures of herself writhing beneath him in ecstacy, and of the many ways he had pleasured her. . . . Her palms were damp and her mouth dry as she swallowed.

"Am I? For knowing what I want? How many people in this life can say as much? And how many waste a lifetime by not going after what they want? Life's too short and too precious for that, Caroline."

To Caroline, such blunt and logical comments were too much like those of her father for comfort. They filled her with a mixture of approval and annoyance because she didn't want to compare this man with her father in any way at all. Yet they were so alike — both strong, both hardheaded, both the epitome of heady masculine power.

"Well then, since I know exactly what *I* want," she said, deliberately turning the comments to her own advantage, "I trust you won't go back on your promise to take me to the mainland when the weather improves."

"I never go back on a promise. You have my word and my hand on it."

He stretched out his hand to her, and reluctantly she put her own small hand in his. She couldn't ignore the warmth and strength in his clasp, nor could she forget how caressingly those wonderful hands had touched her, bringing her dormant sexual feelings so exquisitely to life.

She gave his hand a brief squeeze and then snatched her own away, but from the knowing look in his eyes, she guessed he was remembering everything too.

She ran her tongue around her lips, knowing that for the present there was no help for it. She must remain on Brundy Island in the damp sticky heat that accompanied the subtropical storm. Just like the one that had wrecked the *Princess Victoria* and sent her toward this strange new life.

"Very well," she murmured. "Then I shall go and find something to do to keep myself amused. You have books in the library, and you won't object if I play the pianoforte when it pleases me?"

"I should be honored. This house is yours for as long as it pleases you, Caroline. You know that."

"Just until the storm breaks," she said, and turned quickly to leave the study before the prospect of beginning another life without Luke Garston in it assumed a yawning emptiness.

It wasn't in her nature to be idle for long. She

realized that life among the hardy natives and the stoic immigrants on the island went on. The only ban was on boats going out to sea. And one glance at the lashing white foam on the heaving pewter gray water was enough to make Caroline fervently appreciate the sense of that. She had no wish to be fish bait.

Dr. Sam called that afternoon, shaking out his canvas hat and dripping water everywhere. He announced that it was Caroline he had come to see. And since Luke was keeping busy in his study and probably out of her way, Caroline thought shrewdly, she was inordinately glad to see him.

"Though you could have warned me about the imminent bad weather," she complained indignantly.

"There was no point, duck," he said, cheerfully unrepentant. "It was just as likely the thing could have veered away from us altogether. I never did see the sense in anticipating trouble until it comes."

All the same, she thought to herself.

"Anyway, I can guess you're a mite fed up at the moment, so I've come to put a proposition to you," he went on.

"What kind of proposition?" she said suspiciously.

"Come over to my house and help me teach the native brats a bit of English. Young Maureen Finnegan comes in once a week, but she's putting such nonsense bits of Irish blarney into their heads now, they're getting confused. It'll do 'em a power of good to have somebody speaking the Queen's English, since you'll have gathered that mine ain't so correct as your own, gel."

He paused for breath, and Caroline said quickly, "A young Irish girl? So there *are* other European

106

folk on the island, then? Luke never mentions them."

"Well, he'd have his reasons, I daresay," he said cagily. "There are a few you wouldn't want to associate with, but there's a small community that's worthy enough."

If Sam was anything to go by, she wondered at the others, and immediately told herself not to be such a snob.

"Should I share the teaching on the same day as this Maureen, then? It might help if we did it together, so I could iron out anything she didn't make too clear."

She was careful not to make herself sound superior, but Doc Sam chuckled.

"My own thoughts exactly. So we'll start today, shall we? Maureen usually arrives when it suits her and her wastrel of a father, and the brats will be there soon."

The immediacy of the plan startled her, but she nodded quickly. It would be good to have a change of scene and breathing space away from Luke.

"Isn't it a bit demeaning to call the children brats?" she felt obliged to ask.

Sam grinned. "Not at all. As it happens, their particular tribal word for children is *bratans,* so they accept the shortened form quite naturally. Don't go trying to overeducate them, gel. They're a simple people, but by that I don't mean simpleminded. They tolerate us well enough as long as we respect the old ways. It's important that we don't overstep the mark."

"I see. And you're a wise old man, aren't you?"

"Maybe just wise enough to use a bit of common sense," he agreed. "You'd better fetch a coat or shawl before we go. My old cart ain't exactly weatherproof, and a brolly would blow inside out as soon as you opened it up."

And she didn't see why she needed to tell anybody where she was going. She wasn't beholden to Luke for every move she made, and the sooner she showed her independence the better. She was suddenly doubly grateful to Dr. Sam for giving her the chance to relieve the boredom.

As it turned out, she found it an unexpectedly invigorating afternoon. The brats were glistening with dampness, their black hair clinging to their heads, the water seeping into Sam's parlor floor, but he seemed neither to notice nor to care. Caroline discovered it was easy enough to ignore the children's naked state and to concentrate on helping them with their English words and pronunciation. It was soon obvious that the freckled-faced Maureen, although keen to "educate" them, lacked any finesse or teaching methods at all, and went off into peals of laughter every time one of the children mispronounced a word or phrase.

"Sure, and they're a real caution, ain't they, miss?" she said, wiping her eyes for the tenth time in as many minutes.

"Maybe, but you're not exactly helping them by laughing at them, are you?" Caroline said mildly.

"Oh, you don't have to take it all so seriously! They love to laugh and to hear my blarney—don't you, brats? They think some of the English words are very funny."

It was obvious they loved Maureen, too, and Caroline knew she couldn't compete. Nor did she want to. Maureen gave them laughter and fun, and Caroline decided that if she herself were able to correct a few mistakes in the time she was

108

there, it would be enough. What did it matter? These moppets were never going to set foot in England or know the finer points of English society, and as long as they made themselves understood to the likes of Luke Garston, it was all they needed. It wasn't snobbery that made her think so, it was sheer common sense.

She told Dr. Sam as much when Maureen had taken them all off to some back region of the cluttered little house where there would be biscuits and lemonade.

"Maybe you're right. But it gave you an afternoon's entertainment, didn't it? And you could be doing a useful job if you cared to come back another afternoon, Caroline."

"Is that what this was all about? Did Luke put you up to it, to make me think I had some calling here that would make me want to stay?" she asked at once.

Sam shook his head and gave a small sigh. "I reckon you must be the most suspicious female that ever lived. Can't you ever take things at face value?"

"And why can't you ever give me a straight answer! But never mind. I enjoyed the afternoon anyway. And while the bad weather lasts, I've no objection to repeating it."

"Good," Sam said. "Now we'd best go and see what those young monkeys are up to. Maureen will be telling 'em all kinds of fancy Irish yarns if I don't keep an eye on her."

Caroline followed him dutifully to the back room, where, true to form, Maureen was filling their heads with some fey Irish nonsense. With their inborn penchant for enjoying myths and magic, Caroline could see the brats were relishing every moment of it.

"How's your sister these days, gel?" Sam asked her casually.

"Oh, she's well enough," Maureen said carelessly. "Still making sheep's eyes at the lord and master of Garston Manor enough to make you want to puke at times though."

At the sound of this new word, half a dozen of the brats began excitedly experimenting with it. By the time Sam had calmed them down and mildly rebuked the girl, Caroline was bursting with curiosity. The lord and master of Garston Manor was obviously Luke . . . but she was more interested in Maureen's sister.

"How old is your sister?" she asked as casually as she could.

"About the same as you, and you're not so different in coloring. Kathleen's got dark hair and blue eyes as well, though they don't flash quite as much as yours," she said cheekily.

"And are there any others in your family?" Caroline said, not quite knowing what to make of this outspoken girl and finding the description of her lovesick sister a little more disturbing than she cared to admit.

"There's only me old Dadda and the dogs. Kathleen keeps house for us all. I daresay you'll meet her sometime. She and Luke have always been thick."

Caroline was definitely beginning to wonder now why she hadn't met her already. When she had questioned Luke about other Europeans living on the island, he had been vague, saying Caroline needed to recover her strength before she need bother her head about socializing too much and that she'd meet them all in good time. But no names had been mentioned, and certainly no one by the name of Kathleen Finnegan. In any other

110

circumstances, wouldn't it have been natural to suggest a meeting with a girl of about her own age?

Now she sensed why perhaps it hadn't happened. Was this Kathleen Luke's paramour possibly? She had no reason to think so except instinct, but her instincts were very strong at that moment. So too, was the sudden stab of jealousy that ran through her, keen as a blade.

She knew she was being ridiculous and oversensitive, and besides, why should she care what Luke Garston did in his spare time? But she couldn't help thinking back to the nights she had gone to bed early, when among the settling sounds of the house she had heard the closing of doors and had had the feeling that people were moving about outside.

What could have been more natural than Luke visiting his ladylove? And she had been naive enough to think his attentions to her were genuine, when all he wanted was someone to feed his vanity. He had saved her, so she belonged to him . . . and her resistance had only made him more determined to claim what he deemed his rightful own. She pushed aside the moments when her resistance had been very low indeed . . .

The brats were preparing to leave the house now, and Maureen went with them, saying she hoped to see Caroline again next week. Even while she agreed, Caroline hoped fervently there wasn't going to be a next week for her on Brundy Island. By then, she prayed the storm would have worn itself out and that Luke would live up to his promise.

When they were alone, Doc Sam suggested a brew of tea before he took her back to Garston Manor.

"Exhausting, ain't they?" he said cheerfully. "But

111

they liven up the place, especially when bad weather sets in."

"How long does it usually last?" Caroline asked.

He shrugged. "Could be hours or days or weeks," he said vaguely, and infuriatingly. "The only sure thing with these tropical storms is that they end as quickly as they begin, and once one is over, you can be reasonably sure of a calm period before another one occurs. The islanders say it's the gods making sure we know who's boss."

"But you don't put much store by such beliefs, surely? Doctors usually scoff at such superstitions," Caroline said skeptically.

"Doctors working in opulent London consulting rooms may do so, my dear, but when you've lived with another culture as long as I have, you begin to tolerate vastly different ideas," he said with what Caroline sensed was rare seriousness.

"And how long would that be?" she asked.

He poured boiling water from an old kettle into a large china teapot and swished it around over the tea leaves in a token gesture to brewing. His old eyes began to twinkle as he placed cups and saucers, a jug of milk, and a dish of sugar onto a tray. He spoke teasingly, but she sensed the underlying warning all the same. "No more questions now, my duck. It's one of the unwritten laws among us here. When we came and why we came is nobody's business but our own. It's not the past that counts, it's what you make of the future that's important. You'd do well to remember that. Now then, let's have our tea in the parlor where we can be cozy."

She knew she'd get no more out of him. It was maddening, especially to the daughter of a newspaperman. From the day she was born, she had been steeped in the investigative process and would

112

dearly have liked to have known this man's background and the background of all the others living here. The few she had met so far were a complete mystery to her. Doc, the Finnegans, Mrs. Hughes . . . and Luke. Especially Luke.

"I suppose escaped convicts could be living on any of the remote islands around the mainland," she said casually.

Sam chuckled, handing her a cup of dark thick tea with a steady hand. From the brief brewing it had had, it was remarkably strong, Caroline observed.

"Now then, you're not going to catch me out like that, gel. If anybody wanted to tell you about themselves, I reckon it's their place to do so and not mine."

She became as teasing as himself. "Well, I'm almost beginning to wonder if you yourself have a criminal background, Dr. Sam! I can't imagine so, since you're so kind and obviously a very clever man in your work, but my father always said that even the best of people are so rarely what they seem. Everyone has something to hide, however innocent it may be."

"Then your father was a very astute man. I'd have liked to have had a good jaw with him," Doc Sam said, still smiling. "And despite all the flannel, that's all you're going to get out of me, young lady! I think you'd better hurry up and finish your tea while there's a small break in the rain, and then I'll get you home. Luke will tan my hide if he thinks you've been abducted or run off."

The very idea of running off was so appealing, she ignored the fact that Sam was very clearly squashing any further discussion of his past. Not that there was anywhere to run to, but a few hours away from Luke's dominating presence while

113

he fretted over the loss of his prized possession might do him a lot of good, she thought with some relish.

"Ready?" Doc Sam said, while her eyes glazed over, imagining the fury that Luke might feel at her escape. Not that it would ever happen, of course. But even such a small and futile dream was enough to lift her spirits.

How pathetic she was becoming, she thought as she drained her cup obediently. But how determined too. She *would* leave this island, and she *would* find her father, whatever the outcome. She swallowed and smiled brightly at the old man, realizing she was becoming remarkably fond of him for all his eccentric ways.

"Ready," she said huskily.

She slipped back into the house unseen. She had been away several hours, and it seemed that no one had missed her. The illusion lasted for all of two minutes as she slid the damp shawl from her shoulders and shivered slightly at the chill of its release. Then Luke came striding out from the drawing room, his face dark with anger.

"Where the blazes have you been? Are you aware that I've been looking everywhere for you?"

She looked at him defiantly. A little devil of mischief made her tilt her chin at him provocatively.

"Do you mean to say you've missed me, then? Was I worth searching for?"

He gave a smothered oath and reached out for her shoulders, shaking her as he'd done before. He exclaimed at the dampness he felt.

"You risk catching your death of cold if you don't get out of those wet things. I expected to find you in the library. What kind of lunatic idea made you go walking about in the rain instead?"

His assumption that she could have been so idiotic made her blue eyes flash. "I have not been walking about in the rain! Do you take me for a complete idiot?" She rushed on, not wanting him to answer that question. "If you must know, I've been with Dr. Sam. He came to see me and suggested I help teach the brats. Since you seemed to think it was a good idea too, I hardly think you've got cause to complain about it!"

She glared at him, shaking off his gripping fingers. They stood stiffly, each defying the other, and then he had the grace to give a short nod.

"I don't complain about it. But you should have told me. The interior of Brundy isn't the place for a young girl to wander about by herself. It may not hold all the perils of the mainland bush, but there are risks, all the same."

"What risks?" she said scornfully. "I can take care of myself. I don't need nursemaiding."

He gave a superior smile. "Tell me that when an aggressive kangaroo sees you blundering about and wants to protect its young. Or when one of the deadly spiders decides you'd make a good supper. Shall I go on? There are other varieties of livestock hidden in the undergrowth—"

"No, thank you," Caroline said quickly.

But she couldn't prevent an involuntary shudder. Anything that crawled, silent and unseen, had always terrified her far more than large animals, and the almost legendary kangaroos she had learned about had always seemed such gentle animals. Luke Garston put a different interpretation on them, and she supposed she should be grateful for his concern, even if he was only protecting what

115

he considered his own property. Namely, Miss Caroline Rowe.

"We'll talk more later. Meanwhile you'd better go upstairs and get out of those wet clothes," Luke said abruptly. "I'll send Petal up to your room with hot water and towels. Do you think you can manage to bathe yourself, or would you care for some assistance?"

Caroline flushed angrily as his languorous gaze ran over her body, which was covered provocatively with the wet fabric of her gown.

"I certainly don't need anyone's assistance," she snapped. Least of all his . . .

"Then I'll see you at supper," Luke said, and turned on his heel.

Caroline went swiftly up the stairs. Her heart was thudding for some inexplicable reason. It was the unexpected encounter, she told herself, making her feel like a guilty schoolgirl sneaking into the house after hours. He had no right to make her feel that way, she thought angrily. Nor to make that veiled suggestion about assisting her with her bath.

Without warning, her imagination took over. The image of herself in the bathtub, leaning back luxuriously while certain hands that knew her well leisurely soaped her willing body, was all too evocative in her mind. Her senses were suddenly alive with the longing for it to be real, for Luke to come to her, not as her captor, but as a lover. Wanting her, not only with lust, but with love.

She reached her bedroom, her heart pounding. She closed it quickly and leaned against it for long moments, her eyes closed. She didn't understand these powerful feelings that assaulted her whenever he came near. Nor the anger and frustration she felt so often. Was this the way love happened?

With all this uncertainty, this agony of not knowing how someone else felt toward her? Was the unthinkable really happening to her?

"I *won't* love him," she said savagely, out loud. "I simply and definitely refuse to let such a thought even enter my head about the high and mighty Mr. Luke Garston!"

But entering her heart might be a different thing altogether, the little devil inside her whispered . . .

She strode to her bed and began stripping off her damp clothes with trembling fingers, wishing she could strip away all her surging emotions as easily. Wishing she could remain cool and bland and sensible with regard to Luke Garston . . . and wondering if such a state could ever occur again. If he had never made love to her, it might just have been possible. But now she knew him with all the intimacy of a lover. She knew how a man wanted a woman, and of a woman's response. . . She knew the ways of lovers.

She stared at her body briefly in her long mirror for a moment before covering her nakedness with her dressing gown, seeing the lush curves of her breasts and remembering the way Luke had caressed them with his hands and his tongue. And remembering all the fire he had brought to her senses.

She so rarely blasphemed, but never had there seemed such a moment for it as now. "Damn you, Luke Garston," she whispered. "Damn you to hell and back."

The knock on her door made her jump. She clutched at the belt of her gown as if to protect herself from Luke's too-knowing eyes. But it was Petal who entered the room, hauling the heavy pails of hot water for the bathtub in Caroline's small adjoining bathroom.

"There's cold water already there, miss," Petal said, obviously put out at having to do this task in the middle of the afternoon when it was normally a morning duty. Her expression clearly said she couldn't see why anybody would want two baths in a day, either.

"Thank you, Petal. And you needn't bother about coming back again with clean towels. I've got some already in my bathroom."

"Yes, miss," the girl said, still in a sulk.

"Petal, do you know somebody called Maureen Finnegan?" Caroline asked suddenly. "She's a bit younger than you and teaches the brats their letters with Dr. Sam."

She saw Petal's expression change. Her eyes glittered for a moment. "I know her. *And* the other one."

The native girl's lips suddenly clamped together as if she didn't intend saying any more. And Caroline knew her instincts were right on two counts. If Petal hadn't actually shared Luke's bed, she had expected to at some time or other and was patently jealous of "the other one" who was obviously Kathleen Finnegan. And that also meant that Kathleen figured somewhere in Luke's life.

"Thank you, Petal. If you'll please get my bath ready now, I can manage by myself," she said coolly, and busied herself with pinning up her hair well away from the nape of her neck while the girl attended to the bath water. Not for the world would she let Petal guess how furious she was at the artless revelation. Not for the world would she admit how upset she was inside to know that Luke apparently consorted with any woman who attracted him.

And it didn't take much imagination to know that any woman at all would be flattered and willing to share his bed. She couldn't blame this inno-cent young native girl, nor an Irish girl far from home who might well crave the company of some-one more her own kind. But she could condemn Luke Garston for adding herself to his list of con-quests. There had been absolutely no need for it at all, as far as she could see. He had no fine feelings for her, and his seduction was merely to satisfy his lust, no more. It was a bitter lesson to learn.

An hour later, mollified by time and calmed by the soothing bath, Caroline had dressed more de-murely for supper than on the previous evening. If tonight had to be a tête-à-tête between herself and Luke, then she had no intention of letting him think she was prettying herself up for him. In a fit of devilment, she scraped her hair into a less be-coming style than usual and took no trouble in pinching her cheeks or her lips to make them more alluringly red.

If he saw her as a little plain mouse and regret-ted his earlier pursual of her, so much the better. Though eyeing herself dispassionately in her mirror once she was ready to go downstairs, even Caro-line could see that no one in their right minds would ever call her a plain little mouse. Still, she was less flamboyant than usual, and serve Luke right if he decided he'd made a mistake in rescuing her.

She descended the carpeted staircase toward the drawing room, where by now she knew it was the habit for them to foregather, and then paused un-certainly as she heard the sound of laughter from below. She recognized Luke's deeply intimate chuckle at once, but she didn't recognize the other

119

voice, only that it was a woman's. Caroline felt her heartbeat quicken. It certainly wasn't Mrs. Hughes's rather raucous voice, nor was it one of the maids.

She hesitated. If they had visitors, then a fine sight she had made herself appear in the least attractive gown in her closet, a silver gray silk that did nothing to lift her coloring, buttoned high into the neck, and with her hair a less than alluring frame to her face. She half-turned to flee back upstairs and repair the damage, but it was too late. Luke must have heard her and was already calling to her from the door of the drawing room.

He appeared in the doorway, and his amused glance took in her changed appearance. It was just as if he knew very well why she was doing this, she fumed, and didn't care a jot. At the brief glimpse of a scarlet gown through the open door of the drawing room, she could guess why. Only a young and very confident woman or a harlot would wear such a color, and either would obviously be of interest to Luke Garston!

"Caroline, my dear," he said, oozing false charm. "I decided it was high time you met one of our neighbors. Come and be introduced to Miss Kathleen Finnegan, who's joining us for supper this evening."

If he'd thrown cold water into her face, Caroline couldn't have felt more humiliated. Not only was she about to meet the woman she strongly suspected was Luke's lover, but she herself was looking a sketch.

"I wasn't expecting company" she said shrilly. "If you'll excuse me, I'd like to change my gown—"

"Nonsense. You look perfectly charming," Luke said, but the smile on his mouth and in his eyes told her he understood her motives only too well. He would know, too, how she would hate being compared to this other woman. As he took her hand, she felt his fingers curl around hers, allowing no quick rush back upstairs, and she had no choice but to enter the drawing room with him, gritting her teeth and holding her head high.

Kathleen Finnegan turned at once, tall and elegant and breathtakingly pretty, and held out a hand to greet Caroline.

"I'm happy to meet you, Miss Rowe," she said in the same husky-soft accent as that of her sister. "I've been hearing all about you from Maureen, and when Luke called to invite me to supper this evening, I couldn't resist it. I do hope it's not inconvenient for you at such short notice."

"Of course not," Caroline murmured. "This is Luke's house, and he must invite whom he pleases."

She was being ungracious, and she knew it. But, galling as it was, she couldn't fault this girl's manners, nor the soft Irish voice that would be so captivating to men.

"You'll be missing the company of young ladies like yourself, I daresay," Kathleen said, with an intuition that took Caroline by surprise. "I'm sorry I don't have your education, Miss Rowe, but if there's anything you'd care to know about the island, I'd always be glad to come by and tell you."

"That's very kind, but I doubt that I'll be here long enough to bother," Caroline said.

She listened to herself with a kind of horror, knowing she was showing herself up in a very bad light, but seemingly unable to stop it. And Luke did nothing to help. He seemed to be positively enjoying this, the *rat*, Caroline seethed.

"Have you lived here long, Miss Finnegan?" she

121

asked sweetly, wondering how much of this woman's family history was dubious and hoping to embarrass her enough to put her at a disadvantage. And if she was acting against her own innate good manners, then perhaps she was just discovering the truth in the old saying "all's fair in love and war," Caroline thought crazily.

"Six years," Kathleen said. "We came from Ireland on the trading ship hoping to make good in Australia. But when we saw Brundy, we fell in love with it and so we stayed. My mother died here, so we wouldn't want to leave it now."

"Oh."

The dignified statement took all the wind from Caroline's sails. So Dadda Finnegan wasn't a convict, and there was nothing suspect in this girl's past. She would obviously make the perfect wife for Luke Garston. And for all that she shouldn't care, the thought was enough to plunge Caroline into total depression.

Chapter Seven

The evening wasn't as much of an ordeal as Caroline might have expected, if only because Kathleen Finnegan was a very natural and outgoing young woman. She didn't have an ounce of coquetry about her, despite the flamboyance of her dress. Caroline's unease at meeting her soon disappeared since she could hardly remain disagreeable in the other woman's guileless company.

"I knew we were going to be friends when Maureen told me how well you both got along together," Kathleen told her. "She has a way with the brats, but I'm sure you'll be more of an educator than my young snip of a sister, Miss Rowe."

"Oh, for goodness' sake, please call me Caroline," she said quickly. "And yes, I'll do my best for the children, but I can't think that I'll be much influence on them in the short time I'll be here."

"Sure, and you're not really thinking of leaving us, are you? This place is truly paradise, far better than smelly old London."

"You've been to London?" Caroline said in surprise.

"Oh, we passed through it when we took the boat from England, and that was enough for Mammy and Dadda. Maureen won't remember the place, but I do well enough. Dirty and foggy, and as far removed from our old farm in Ireland as possible."

"Why did you leave your farm?"

Kathleen shrugged. "When there's no work to be had, there's no food to be put in the children's stomachs. So Dadda decided we should take a chance on Australia. We got a passage on the trading ship, but when it stopped at Brundy, we knew we'd found what we were looking for."

A shadow passed over Kathleen's face at that moment, and Luke squeezed her hand sympathetically.

"It still pains you to recall your Mammy dying here, doesn't it, lass?"

"That it does, and I'd rather leave the subject alone, if you don't mind," the girl said quietly.

"Then we'll have no more talk of it, nor of London, or Caroline will start to look gloomy too. Though how anyone could prefer the London you both describe to Brundy, is beyond me. Now if you were comparing it with my own heather-covered moors and dales of Yorkshire, that would be different."

Teasingly, he turned the conversation neatly away from more depressing ones, and throughout the evening, Caroline found it hard to define the relationship between the other two. She couldn't even guess whether or not Kathleen was angling for Luke's affections. It was either being done in a very subtle way that was very clever, or it was nonexistent.

Luke was obviously fond of her, but he wasn't so overattentive as to arouse Caroline's jealousy,

124

and she found herself breathing a little easier after seeing them together. And then, as she analyzed her own reactions, she decided she must be going completely mad. Since she had no intention of remaining on Brundy Island or getting involved with the man, what did it matter to her whom Luke Garston favored! Yet it *did* . . .

By the time Dadda Finnegan called to take his daughter home, she was very curious to see this man who had fallen in love with the island and stayed on after burying his wife here. The senior Finnegan turned out to be big and brash and full of the blarney, and very like his younger daughter.

"So you're the lovely colleen my Maureen's been bragging over all evening!" he said jovially, "Fair taken with her new friend she was, and telling me she'd have to mind her own p's and q's now there was a real teacher in the offing for the wee brats!"

"Oh, but I'm only temporary, Mr. Finnegan," Caroline said quickly, wondering just how often she was going to have to repeat it.

"Sure, and they all say that," he said easily. "But you'll surely think differently when the island casts its spell on you, me darlin'."

"Not Caroline," Luke said calmly, handing the man a drink of whisky that disappeared down his gullet with lightning speed. "She intends to leave as soon as possible. Once this storm abates I'm taking her to the mainland."

"Is that a fact now?" Dadda Finnegan stared at her. "Well, 'tis still my bet that you'll be back. After bein' saved from the clutches of the sea, you've a kind of obligation to the land here, wouldn't you say?"

"No, I wouldn't, as a matter of fact," Caroline said evenly, wishing they wouldn't all have such

125

similarly dogmatic thoughts. She knew she owed Luke—and Dr. Sam—her life, but that didn't mean she had to pay for it indefinitely with her presence.

She was thankful when the Finnegans finally left. She was starting to feel very tired, and the violent wind and lashing rain were still unabating. They reminded her only too acutely of the storm in which the *Princess Victoria* had foundered. The poignant memory, combined with the heavy air pressure and the accentuated earthy scents of flora and vegetation were making her head throb, and she longed for the comfort of her bed.

"I'll say good night now, Luke," she said as soon as the visitors had gone. "It was an—entertaining evening."

He gave a half-smile. "Kathleen's a charming lass, don't you think?"

"Oh yes. An absolute charmer."

If his words were meant to imply a personal interest in the girl, she couldn't begin to guess and didn't care to try. She made for the stairs, unable to bear the thought of listening to Luke elaborating about the charming Kathleen Finnegan a moment longer. It struck her that he didn't often call Caroline "lass" anymore, that little northern word she had begun to find oddly endearing. In fact, they were too often at daggers drawn lately for him to call her anything at all, she realized.

But he'd used it in regard to Kathleen. Perhaps she'd been wrong after all. Perhaps these two were so secure in their feelings for one another, they didn't need to parade them in front of anyone else.

As she reached the landing above, she glanced downstairs to where Luke was standing in the drawing-room door, watching her go. She couldn't read his expression. She only knew it brought a lump to her throat, for a reason she didn't even dare to contemplate.

But if she could deny her own feelings in the hours of daylight, she could, as he'd suggested, no more stop him infiltrating her dreams than she could fly to the moon. The instant she closed her eyes, his image was there. The instant she drifted into sleep, he was holding her in his arms. His hands were caressing her, his mouth was urgent for her, seeking out all the warm secret places he had been before. And she, no longer prim and demure, but a woman in need of her man, was opening up to receive him, gloriously and wantonly, with a passion and hunger as old as time.

"Dear God, what's happening to me?" she whispered as she awoke dazed for the third time in as many hours of erotic dreaming. She buried her face into the pillow, refusing to believe she could be so wanton, yet knowing, too, that this was the essence of fulfillment and that she was capable of all that a woman could be. Luke Garston had taught her that, even though it had left her empty and wanting.

For the next few days it seemed he had decided not to leave her so much to her own devices. If she said she was going into the library to read, he went with her, showing her some of the many books he had collected. He was quite a scholar, she discovered to her surprise. She was also fascinated by his own writings on the skill of pearl diving, and the careful records he kept of every trip he and his native boys made.

"So it's a proper business then?" she said, for want of making conversation.

"Of course it is. How else do you think I make my living and provide you with such home comforts?"

"But can such riches exist so far from civilization?"

In answer he went across to the desk in the corner of the library and unlocked a drawer. He drew out a long case and brought it over to her.

"I had this made up for a very special person," he said ambiguously and opened the lid.

Caroline gasped at the purity of the pearl necklace the case contained. She was no expert, but her life had been an easy and cosseted one, and she could see at once that the pearls were of the finest quality. And the necklace was intended for a very special person . . .

"Would you like to try it on?" he asked. She shook her head at once. She had no wish to wear something that was designed especially for someone else. She wondered if it was for Kathleen.

"I don't think it was intended for me," she said, her voice oddly husky.

"It was intended for the woman who would become my wife." She saw him finger the largest of the pearls in the very center of the necklace, and he went on absently, as if almost unaware for a moment that she was in the room at all.

"This gem almost cost me my life. There were sharks basking in the area, and my leg became entangled in weeds as I was diving for the oysters. Jojo took his knife to one of the sharks while one of the other boys cut me loose, and they both received vicious gashes as a result. I owe those lads a great deal. So you see why this pearl in particular could only go to a very special woman."

Caroline ran her tongue around lips that were suddenly dry, as if only now had she seen the danger of his occupation.

"Then I suggest you lock it away again and save it for the right occasion," she said crisply.

Suddenly she couldn't bear to look at it any longer. It was too perfect, too pure, and her own association with Luke Garston was too sordid. Even though he hadn't come to her room since that one spectacular night, she hadn't forgotten a single pulsating moment of their lovemaking. She only had to close her eyes, and she was reliving it all again . . .

She heard the case close with a snap, and it was like the end of all her dreams. The necklace, for which he had risked his life, was intended for a very special woman, and she was obviously not the one. For all his insistence that she belonged to him, he had merely been playing with her after all. She had never felt so close to crying.

"Am I permitted to go to my room for a while?" she asked him in a high voice. "I'd like to write some notes to keep everything recorded for the future. When we meet again, my father will want to know everything that's happened to me."

She avoided his eyes. For of course, she could never tell her father all that had happened. Some things were far too personal and private to share with anyone.

He nodded without speaking and she fled upstairs. In the notepad she had found in a drawer, she was keen to record thoughts and feelings as well as everyday occurences. It was the reporting background coming out in her, she thought, and she had been too long at her father's knee when he was building his own empire not to appreciate it. If Queen Victoria had made such diary-keeping fashionable among the young in particular, to Caroline it was a natural instinct.

But how could she put down her innermost feelings when they defied mere words? Some things were too deep to find expression in cold hieroglyphics on paper. Some things were too close to the heart . . . In the end she wrote tersely about the Finnegans' visit that evening and closed the notepad.

Caroline opened her eyes next morning with the feeling that something was different. There was a stillness over everything that she couldn't instantly define. And yet, as she became more fully awake, she was aware of plopping and sizzling and dripping. The sounds seemed to fill the air, and she looked sharply toward the window. Over the brilliant green vegetation and the vividly exotic flowers was a haze that seemed to glaze the plants as if with spun sugar. For a moment she wondered if she was hallucinating, or if she could somehow have been transported back to a London pea-souper fog.

Her senses couldn't take it all in for a moment, and then, as she felt the sticky heat permeating into the room from the slightly open window, she knew. The storm was over. The violence of the wind had gone, and the rain dripping and plopping off leaves and foliage was giving rise to steam. Everything outside was steaming, and as Caroline rushed to the window with her heart pounding, she could see the blue sky and dazzling sunlight above the blanket of steam. The day of her salvation had arrived.

She didn't wait for Petal to bring her fresh washing water or to attend her. She splashed cold water on her face and limbs from the jug in her bathroom and dressed as quickly as she could. All

130

she wanted was to hear Luke say he would honor his promise. That this would be the day she left Brundy Island for the mainland.

She found him in the dining room, already eating breakfast. He glanced up at her with no surprise at seeing her at such an early hour.

"Good morning, Caroline. I trust you slept well?"

"Well enough. But I trust I shall sleep better tonight. I certainly couldn't stay in bed a minute longer once I saw the change in the weather!"

She couldn't quite demand that he take her that very moment. Something held her back from being quite so brash.

"It's a good day for pearl diving. After a storm—"

It was too much to expect her to hold her tongue after this. She felt her face redden furiously.

"Pearl diving! Is that all you can think about? You know you promised—"

She saw the slight smile curving his mouth then.

"You jump in quicker than anybody I've ever known, lass. But, aye, pearl diving is usually pretty much on my mind, seeing that it provides a good living for the native boys and also provides all the creature comforts you've enjoyed while you've been here."

Caroline clamped her lips shut and counted to ten. She could see that he was playing with her now, but she couldn't bear to be teased when this was so all-important to her. Her voice was low and tense as she leaned toward him, involuntarily putting her hand on his shoulder.

"And don't think I don't appreciate everything you've done for me. But for pity's sake, Luke,

131

you know what I want more than anything!"

He caught at her hand and held it against his shoulder. "And you know what I want. But today, you shall have your way. We'll see which of the boys is willing to take a boat out today."

"You mean they won't just do as you say?" She twisted her hand out from under his and moved back a pace. "I thought you had control over everything that goes on on this island."

"Not everything," he retorted. "It's true that I give them employment when the sea and the conditions are right, but they make their own choice. Particularly when it means going to an alien place. Some of them refuse ever to set foot on what they call Big Land. They're steeped in superstition, as you may have discovered."

As she listened, Caroline began to think the nightmare was starting all over again. She had thought it was all so certain, as good as a *fait accompli,* and now Luke was putting all kinds of doubts and obstacles in her mind. She was angered, too, that he hadn't settled all this long before the day for sailing arrived.

"Then isn't it time you got your crew together?" she snapped. "I didn't think you'd go back on a promise, but if necessary I presume you can steer a craft yourself?"

She could hear amusement mixed with impatience in his voice now. "You're more naive than I gave you credit for if you think one man could steer a boat to the mainland through the Barrier Reef and get through unscathed. You may have a death wish, but I do not, so you'll just have to trust me. We'll go when I've got the boys together and the conditions are right."

She all but stamped her foot with frustration. "The conditions are *perfect!*"

132

"So you're a navigational expert now, are you?"

Tears stabbed her eyes at the way everything seemed to be going wrong. But common sense told her that antagonizing this stubborn man was never going to get her anywhere. She held on to her temper and pleaded with him.

"Luke, I really don't mean to be difficult—"

"Good God, woman, it's a bit late for changing your tune now! You're the most infuriating woman I've ever known. But you're also the most seductive and desirable, and if you keep looking at me with those beautiful blue eyes drowned in tears, I'll probably end up swimming to Australia for you."

He spoke so savagely, she wondered if he was complimenting her or merely being sarcastic. Whatever the motive, he suddenly stood up and pushed his chair back to the table, his breakfast finished.

"You'd better eat a good breakfast," he said abruptly. "I'll go and round up some boys, and we'll aim to leave in a hour or so. We need to cross the reef in daylight, or we're done for."

She could have wept for joy then, and she was too choked for words. At last she was going to leave the island, and the search for her father could begin. It was only when Luke had gone and she began to bite into the baked breakfast fish and toasted bread that she began to consider the enormity of the task ahead.

Until that moment, she had been motivated only by the need to ascertain her father's fate, and she had been carried along by the impetus of her mission. But the bright new life she and her father had intended to share in the suburbs of the cultured town of Sydney was one thing. She had never expected to be alone in a hostile and little

133

known part of the continent, many hundreds of miles from her destination.

Now, knowing so little of this so-called Big Land, she wondered with a jolt of fear just how her mission was ever going to be accomplished. The only thing to keep her sane at that moment when all her confidence seemed in danger of ebbing away was the thought that Luke would be with her.

"All right," he said when he returned a short while later. "We go as soon as we're ready. Pack as little as possible in a traveling bag. There's no room for fripperies. You can't take any changes of clothes, so you'll have to make do with what you're wearing."

She had been hovering about anxiously in the drawing room. By then the steam had all evaporated, and the day was as blisteringly blue and golden as on the day she had arrived. She stared at Luke in horror now.

"What! But you can't expect me to wear the same clothes for days on end! It's not decent."

"Decent or not, you'll do as I say, or we don't go. The boat's a reasonable size, but we're not going on a pleasure cruise, and we need to keep clutter to a minimum. We'll be taking food and drink, and a few weapons and gifts. But you won't see the lads bothering with extra baggage."

At that remark, she averted her eyes from his knowing look. But she was struck by the rest of his words.

"Why weapons? And why gifts?" she asked suspiciously.

"We take weapons in case we need to kill anything, either for food or to save our necks," he

134

said shortly. "And gifts to appease the gods if necessary or to bargain with."

Caroline didn't want to ask any more questions. The stark words conjured up far too vividly all the tales she had ever heard about native superstition, of the darker, mysterious, and unknown interior of the Big Land, and the lurking dangers of the bush. And she was suddenly afraid.

"We'll be all right, won't we, Luke?" she asked huskily. "You wouldn't take this on if you weren't sure of that, would you?"

"I've already told you I have no wish to go to the mainland. From now on, we're all in the lap of the gods, and nothing is certain. If you have doubts, say so now. It's not too late to change your mind."

She took a deep, trembling breath. "My father never gave up on searching for the end of a story, and I won't give up on him now. We go."

Luke nodded, his eyes enigmatic. "He'd be proud of you," he said, and whether it was meant as a compliment or whether he thought her as mad as her father, Caroline couldn't tell and didn't care. It was enough that she was about to do something positive at last.

Several hours later, she wondered what all the fuss was about. Caroline had had a surprisingly emotional farewell from Mrs. Hughes, who had obviously taken the visitor to her heart. And Dr. Sam had appeared on the white-bleached sands, accompanied by a small crowd of brats bringing her gifts of flowers. Caroline felt a real tug of affection toward them all. If she allowed it, she knew she could feel a great pang at leaving this idyllic place, but her mission was too important

135

for her to forget it now.

Dr. Sam and the brats waved them goodbye from the small landing stage where Luke's biggest boat was tied up, and she began to suspect he'd been telling her half-truths all this time. The craft looked sleek and fast, equipped with sails and oars, and the crew of five native boys seemed only too keen to share this voyage with Luke and his pretty missy.

By the time they were well away from the island, she was managing—usually—to ignore the nakedness of the boys, since the teeming crystal clear turquoise waters were a constant source of fascination. When she wasn't watching the darting antics of the brilliantly colored fish and the occasional school of dolphins, she concentrated on fixing her eyes ahead to the dark mass of the approaching reef, and beyond it, the great hazy hump of the Big Land.

For some reason she had got into the habit of thinking of it in the native boys' terms. Big Land. It suited the continent and the vastness of what lay ahead. The adventure had truly begun. And despite Luke's orders, she had brought a small bag containing her diary and personal possessions, and a sunshade, which she was more than glad to keep above her head to shield her from the blistering heat.

There was sufficient breeze for the boat to cruise steadily westwards, and as the day wore on, the coral and shingle of the reef became more prominent. Soon the boys would take to the oars and steer it carefully through jagged edges that could tear a craft apart. They began hauling down the sails in preparation for this, and Luke said it was also time to eat if they felt so inclined. He was obviously not hungry himself, but Caroline found her appetite had been increased enormously by the sea voyage.

"Have you been to these parts before?" she asked Jojo as she bit into a slice of one of Mrs. Hughes's fish pies. His dark face broke into a superior smile.

"We come many times. We make good money from pearls, and this good place here," he said, waving vaguely around.

"But isn't it a terrible risk?" she said, appalled that these young boys should dive in such waters.

Jojo shrugged. "Mr. Luke say nothing worth nothing without risk," he said quaintly.

"And what about Mr. Luke?" she said sarcastically. "Does he let you take all the risks while he takes all the profits?"

"Mr. Luke does not," Luke's voice said right behind her. "The boys do nothing that I don't do myself. Do you need proof, my doubting lassie?"

Before she knew what he was about, he had stripped off his shirt, revealing his bronzed torso beneath. He wore the briefest of short trousers, which seemed to be his usual garment on board, and he suddenly dived over the side and into the shimmering water.

Caroline gasped, leaning over the rail to see his dark hair streaming out behind him as he shot downwards to where waving sea grasses seemed to close around him. She saw the gleam of a knife, held between his teeth. For a wild moment she remembered that other time, when he had so nearly drowned, and she realized her heart was pounding in her chest. But the boys were leaning over the rail, too, jabbering excitedly and pointing fingers to where Luke was already prizing something from the rocky depths below.

In no time at all, he was shooting upward

137

again, arms and legs straight as a dart, the knife held tight between his teeth once more. He was like some magnificent erstwhile merman, Caroline thought as he climbed aboard, shaking droplets of water from his hair and body. The boys crowded around him to examine his find. Like them, she found it hard to contain her excitement as she saw the deep gray-blue of the glistening oyster shell in his hand. Luke had told her that a shell such as this could contain a pearl of great value — and just as often, nothing at all.

She caught her breath as the shell was opened, and she saw the beautiful soft sheen of the object it contained. Luke removed it carefully and held it between two fingers for her inspection. Caroline saw its globular translucence in the sunlight, a perfect pearl.

"It's beautiful," she said, a little catch in her breath. But by then the boys were already diving overboard, deep into those crystal depths, returning time and again with one or two oysters, to pile them on deck until the ceremonial opening later.

"We always do it this way," Luke told her. "Then nobody takes priority over the pearls they find."

"Except for you," she reminded him.

"That was done for your benefit, to prove that I take the same risks as my boys," he told her dryly.

"I see. And how long are we staying here while you add to your collection?"

She was suddenly tired of all this hanging about while the boys seemed to be enjoying themselves, whether it was for sport or work.

"We go soon," Luke told her briskly. "All this may seem like a diversion to you, lass, but it's

138

also for insurance purposes."

"What's that supposed to mean?" she said, staring.

"It should be obvious to a woman with a brain as well as beauty. And let's hope it won't be necessary. But if there should be any occasion to bargain, at least we shall have something to bargain with, apart from your lovely self."

Although he spoke casually, there was an underlying seriousness in his voice, and Caroline felt her heart pound sickly now. If he were teasing, she didn't care for it. Nor for the veiled hint that they might meet with some opposition on the mainland. It wasn't the first time he had mentioned dangers, however obscurely, and she was smart enough to accept their existence. But if she dwelt on it too much, she'd be too afraid to go anywhere at all, so instead, she simply blocked it from her mind.

The voyage continued without incident, and once they had negotiated between the jagged coral needles of the reef, the shorter distance between it and the mainland was eaten away. It hadn't seemed so difficult, Caroline thought suspiciously, and both Luke and his boys were obviously expert boatmen to navigate so effortlessly.

"Don't be fooled by the ease with which we got through," Luke said at her elbow, as if he could read her thoughts. "The sea is calm after the storm, and the swell aids our passage. Besides which, the wind helped our aim of reaching the middle section of the reef where it's thinner and closer to the mainland. Another time, things could be very different."

All the same, she noted the lines of strain on his forehead, and for the first time, she appreciated all that he was doing for her. Had she been

139

so very selfish up to now? she thought guiltily. She put her hand on his arm, where faint crystals of salt still remained from the diving.

"Luke, I am grateful," she said quietly. "I know I've been too slow at putting it into words, but I really do appreciate all you've done for me. There's no way I can ever repay you—"

She caught her breath at the way he looked at her then, and if she hadn't thought it so impossible, she'd have said it was the way a man looked at a woman he loved. The look was gone in a moment, and his voice was bantering once more.

"There is, but you obviously think it's too high a price to pay. It's priced above rubies, so they tell me."

Caroline felt her face flush and removed her hand from his arm quickly. "You've already taken that from me," she said in a low voice. "And I'm not sure I can ever forgive you for that."

He slid an arm around her shoulders, letting the boys continue navigating amid shouts of glee and triumph at conquering Old Man Reef.

"But since you belong to me, I considered I had every right, sweet Caroline. Even so, I would not have forced you had you not been a willing partner. Can you honestly deny that you were?"

As the memory of that erotic night of passion swept through her senses, Caroline knew that no, she honestly could not. And if he had truly bewitched her, then she had gone into her enslavement willingly. She couldn't find words to answer him, and she felt her throat thicken as his arm tightened around her, caressing her shoulder and the pulsating curve of her throat.

"You see?" he whispered. "Why let your head deny what your heart is telling you, Caroline? You want me as much as I want you. We belong

140

as surely as the fish belong in the sea."

She shivered at the hypnotic inevitability of his voice, but she was still strong enough to fight against it.

"So do the pearls, but you wrest them from their environment, too, don't you, Luke? You take everything you want without thinking of the consequences."

He looked down at her, his eyes dark and his expression unchanging.

"Why do you fight me?" he said at last. "Why pretend that you weren't sent to Brundy out of all the women in the world to be mine?"

"Is that what you really think?" she said. "Are you so steeped in native ways by now that you can't think for yourself? I was *shipwrecked*, Luke, plain and simple. There was no mystery in that. You didn't conjure me up by some magical means to come into your life!"

She was warming to the sarcasm in her words now. She had to make him see that she didn't believe in magic and destiny, and that there was a logical explanation for everything. The fact that she mentally crossed her fingers when she thought about destiny didn't mean a single thing. It was mere habit, a silly superstition, and one to which sensible people gave little credence.

"So you don't think it strange that of all the passengers on the *Princess Victoria,* you were the only one to be drifting in the direction of Brundy and that I should have been out on the ocean on that particular day? You don't see the significance in that?"

"I do not," she said steadily. "It was mere chance, nothing more. Though, of course, I don't deny that it was the luckiest chance in the world for me—"

141

She realized he was giving her the slow, wide smile that could usually make her heart pause before racing on. Without warning, he turned her into his arms. The boys were all busily watching the dark shape of the mainland taking on more recognizable proportions ahead of them, chattering and pointing excitedly. And as Luke Garston pressed her supple body into his half-clothed masculine one, she could feel the power of it in every hard muscle and sinew.

"You betray your own instincts without even knowing it, my sweet one," he murmured against her lips. She could taste the salt on them, as tangy and potent as an aphrodisiac. "Chance, destiny, magic, they all mean the same things. Ask our native boys about chance and they'll tell you how the ancient spirits can work their magic to bring two people together. Ask them about a shipwreck that blew a woman to an unknown destination and a storm that kept her there against her will, and they'll tell you the gods have no wish for such lovers to be parted. They'll tell you it's written in the stars and the sea, and that there's no defying what's been ordained."

Caroline pushed hard against him, but there was no way she could retreat from his arms. His words frightened her, even while she could feel the pull of their insistence. She had no patience with this talk of magic and ancient spirits, and even less with the thought of pagan gods wielding their influence, and yet, and yet . . . all that he said was true.

She *was* the only survivor from the *Princess Victoria* to have reached Brundy Island, and there had been no true evidence of any others. The man who was holding her *had* become her lover, and she owed him her life. But she only owed him the saving of her body and not her soul, she thought, with one last attempt to retrieve her self-esteem before it dissolved altogether.

"Land ahead!" Jojo suddenly shrieked out, and for a second Luke relaxed his hold on her. She twisted out of his arms and looked toward the bow, where the gray smudge of the hills was revealing itself more clearly now and a narrow curve of silver beach fringed with dense vegetation lay invitingly ahead of them.

But the most extraordinary sight was the way, after all their frantic jabbering, the native boys suddenly kneeled in the boat as if with one accord, genuflecting with outstretched arms and bowed heads. Or was it a need for appeasement from whatever gods they revered for venturing so far abroad? It was a sight that put more fear into Caroline's heart than anything else so far.

Chapter Eight

The closer they got to the mainland, the more Caroline appreciated the natives' phrase for it. She ran a salt-encrusted tongue around her dry lips. Big Land. It was certainly that. The sight of the hugely forbidding interior mountains and the tangle of flowering vines and jungle that encircled the strip of beach was anything but welcoming.

There was no immediate sign of civilization or habitation. No sign of anything but a virgin territory that seemed to stretch into infinity. As the native boys fell into an uneasy silence, the only sounds were the sliding of oars in the water, the flapping of birds' wings at their approach, and the protesting screeches of the angry black cockatoos ranged in funereal procession in the branches of the trees.

Only the brilliant flash of kingfishers darting among the entangled palm trees gave a respite from what appeared to be unrelenting jungle and a totally hostile environment.

"Well? Does it live up to your expectations?" As Luke's voice jarred into Caroline's senses, she forced herself to swallow the lump in her throat.

"I didn't know what to expect. But I thought perhaps a town of sorts . . . or a settlement at least," she said in confusion.

He gave a short laugh. "And haven't I tried to tell you a hundred times about the vagaries of the winds and the seas? Most of this part of the mainland is still uncharted. God knows what we'll find when we go ashore."

She could hear the grim note in his voice and the way the boys had begun muttering amongst themselves. She held her chin high, determined not to lose her resolve now.

"I *hope* we'll find my father! That's the reason we've come, isn't it? And that's the reason we must go on. You promised me that, Luke!"

For a moment she thought he was going to change his mind, even now. That he expected her to go all soft and feminine on him, showing her fear at this alien land ahead of them. That he had always intended turning back, even after negotiating the Barrier Reef. She remembered his own antipathy to the mainland and knew she had to stand firm.

"I'm not in the habit of breaking promises," he said shortly, and she breathed a little easier. Though not much.

For a wild moment she wondered just how big a fool's errand this search really was. How could she, a mere woman, ever hope to track down one possible shipwrecked survivor in this vast wilderness? But most likely, Sir William Rowe hadn't been the only survivor, she thought optimistically.

If there had been a small group of men battling ashore, then they would have stuck together, warding off any dangers that beset them. The need to survive would have been uppermost in all of their minds, and once they reached land. . .

"This is your last chance to change your mind,"

145

he said, seeing the way she looked uncertainly at the encroaching vines and jungle interior. As he spoke, she felt the first scrape of soft sand and shingle beneath the bow of the boat. The native boys leapt out into the crystal-clear shallow water, hauling ropes to bring the boat as high onto the shore as possible and lashing the ropes around the strongest trees.

"Never," she said steadily. "I won't rest until I know what's happened to my father."

"Your devotion does you credit, even if it puts the rest of us at risk."

Luke leapt out of the beached boat as he spoke and held out his arms to lift her down. She got no comfort from being held close to him for a moment. There was only fear at what lay ahead and the inevitability of her quest. It was a compulsion that drove her on.

By now she was hot, dirty, and disheveled, and she resented his putting these doubts into her mind at the eleventh hour. She resented particularly the way he put all the responsibility for the rest of them squarely on her slender shoulders. It was well-deserved, but she didn't need to hear it voiced. She disentangled herself from his arms and glared into his face.

"I'm sure you're more than capable of dealing with any dangers we may meet," she snapped. "You and the boys came well-equipped with guns and knives to ward off any attacking animals, and I know full well that the Aborigines are expert hunters, so we won't lack for food."

He gave a faint smile. "Your trust in us is touching, my sweet. But I suggest we go no farther tonight. The sun is already going down and we'd be wise to bed down here for the night and start out afresh in the morning. We'll make camp near the boat."

It made sense, even though Caroline was impatient to move on. But the thought of encountering darkness in the midst of that jungle ahead was too daunting to ignore. The boys, too, were clearly in favor of staying where they were for the present. And the dying rays of the sun were already spreading a gloriously crimson sheen over the rippling ocean and the protective reef beyond. The daytime heat was dwindling, and nights on this Big Land might well be cool.

"We make fire, boss," Jojo said at once. "And we catch plenty fish for supper."

Several of the boys were already splashing about in the water and scooping up mullet with their bare hands. The shallow bay teemed with fish, and here, at least, they wouldn't go hungry. They had brought bread with them, and on this first night they feasted well. Caroline was lulled into a sense of well-being as they finally settled down for the night around the comforting fire.

She purposefully closed her mind to all the scuttling, whispering, stealthy night sounds of the jungle and the sea. As long as the fire was kept burning and Luke was with her, she needn't be afraid. It was the last thought on her mind before she fell into a fitful sleep.

Breakfast consisted of more fish and bread, and juicy red berries from the abundant bushes nearby. The sun rose early, as did the travelers. Caroline was thankful for their industry. They seemed a mite more businesslike about the proceedings now. If they had shown too much fear and tardiness, and she had had to think for too long about the journey they were undertaking, she might even now have balked from it. As it was, she felt her normal optimism returning as Luke and the boys scratched patterns in the sand to determine their way forward.

"There's reputedly a hill settlement somewhere in this area," he said. "Whether or not it actually exists, we'll have to discover for ourselves, but we'll follow it up. Any settlers would almost certainly have a lookout, and they may have helped ashore any survivors from the shipwreck."

It sounded like a thin lead, but any lead was better than none. "But wouldn't survivors have kept to the coast and tried to make their way south?" Caroline asked doubtfully.

"You'll soon see the answer to that for yourself. There are many bays like this one, but they all give way to giant cliffs that make up much of the coastline. Nobody can travel that way without first going inland over the hills and then into the mountains."

Since she had no way of disproving his words, she had to abide by them. But there was something else nagging at her. "If there was a lookout who might have seen any survivors from the *Princess Victoria*, wouldn't they also have seen our approach in the boat, or our fire?" she asked.

"That's what worries me," Luke said briefly.

"Why? Surely if they were settlers, they'd send someone to greet us?" she said, in all innocence.

"Dear God, what century were you born in, woman? For one thing, the lookout men may have gone to any survivors only to see if they had any money or valuables on them. We've no idea what kind of men they might be. Have you never heard of hard-nosed convicts who'd steal and rape and kill just to gain a crust of bread? Or of hostile tribesmen, suspicious of every white man who dares to set foot on their sacred lands? Have you never heard of headhunters and cannibalism—"

"Stop it!" Caroline said wildly. "Why are you trying to frighten me like this?"

"I'm just trying to make you face reality, which

148

you seem to have a hard time doing," Luke said brutally. "I'm alerting you to the human dangers we might face, as well as the snakes and poisonous spiders, the packs of hungry wild dingoes, and the inland rivers and sun-baked banks populated by crocodiles. Are you still keen to cross such terrain?"

His words sent sheer terror to her heart, but she'd be damned if she was going to let him see how afraid she was.

"I've already said I'm game if you are," she whispered, her voice a mere thread of sound.

She thought she saw a glimpse of respect in his eyes, but it was quickly replaced by something else.

"They always say the English are totally mad, and they're right," he said briefly. "Well then, you'll leave everything behind but what you can physically carry. The boys and I will carry food and water, and we'll get started."

Resentfully, Caroline clambered back aboard the land-listing boat and gathered her belongings together. Luke's mouth twisted as he saw her small traveling bag.

"Is all that really necessary?"

"Certainly it is. Some personal items are essential to a lady," she said defiantly.

Though such niceties seemed silly in the face of the sheer necessities of survival now. The terrain ahead of them, the lower hills, the mountains and jungle and bush seemed frighteningly insurmountable, and she prayed fervently that they were not heading straight for disaster.

Hours later, Caroline was truly wishing they had never begun this nightmare. By then, the silvery beach, on which the soft warm water lapped so invitingly, was far behind them. Before they left it, their departure had been delayed further by the need to pull the boat higher into the shelter of the trees for security. And now the jungle had completely enveloped them. The boys were hacking their way through the impenetrably wild tangles of bush and brambles that tore at faces and limbs, and snatched at Caroline's soft gown until it soon resembled the garb of a hottentot.

She could have wept at the sight of herself, scratched and filthy, her feet sodden from the dank swampy undergrowth where the sun never penetrated and which the dense vegetation kept so stiflingly cloying that it was difficult to breathe or even to think coherently.

All around them were the sounds of the bush— creaking, swaying, crawling, slithering, rumbling— and all of them terrified her. She was afraid to look where she put her feet, afraid to look upward or sideways, or to keep her eyes anywhere but straight ahead to where Jojo's and Luke's glistening strong brown muscles constantly sawed and slashed a path through the jungle.

Ahead of them was the older man, Makepeace, who had once been this way before and had some faint knowledge of the lay of the land. Behind Caroline the last two native boys grumbled and cursed in their own language, and she felt sure they secretly damned her for bringing them here. And she couldn't blame them . . .

When she felt as if she could hardly put another foot in front of her, the men in front of her stopped suddenly, and she almost stumbled into them. Luke turned toward her, but she could see that his body was vibrantly alert.

"We're not alone," he muttered. "Stand quite still and say nothing."

It was beyond her to say anything. She felt faint with terror, and it dawned on her that some instinct had been warning her for some time that this moment was inevitable. She had felt as if eyes were watching every move they made and hadn't dared to calculate whether or not they were human eyes. Were they all about to be stabbed to death with native weapons? Was this the end of all her hopes of ever finding her father alive? Was she instead to be killed and forgotten . . . or even worse, to be eaten by the cannibals Luke had so brutally mentioned?

When she caught sight of the first movement between the trees, she gasped. The boys had all bunched together now, surrounding her, but their presence gave her little comfort. The smell of their fear was so rank that Caroline had a hard job not to pinch her nose, and she thought how ludicrous it was that at such a time such a thing even occurred to her.

"Come out and show yourselves. We come in peace," Luke called out harshly. He repeated the words in a language Caroline didn't understand, echoed by the jabbering boys. The sounds died away, and only the raucous chatter of birds high above remained. That, and the erratic hammering of Caroline's heart.

"Are you too yellow-bellied to show yourselves to travelers?" Luke said more loudly.

At this, there was the sound of guttural laughter, and suddenly the bushes parted. A group of grizzled and bearded men in dirt-encrusted clothing stood in front of them. But they were not hostile natives. With a wild flood of relief, Caroline guessed by their faces that they were Europeans.

"And what stupid bastards trying to find their way through the bush think to call us cowards?" one of the men snarled aggressively. He spoke with an uncultured English accent, but even so, to hear someone speak in their own language was such an overwhelming relief to Caroline that she couldn't think of anything else for the moment. She blurted out what was uppermost in her heart.

"Please, we're searching for my father," she gasped out. "He was lost when the steamship the *Princess Victoria* foundered and sank in a violent storm some weeks ago. Have you any news of him or any other survivors? I'm willing to pay for any information —"

Luke's harsh voice stopped her flow of words. "What my woman means is we *may* have the means to pay for the right kind of information," he said savagely, and she knew at once how stupid she had been.

How could she have forgotten his warning that ex-convicts would steal and rape and kill for the means of their own survival? And the Lord knew what kind of men these raggle-taggles were.

She saw how their avaricious glances met and then raked over her damp body in the soft foulard fabric of the gown that was so torn and revealing now.

"Well now, we just might be of help to you, little lady," a second man said, stroking his beard with a hand whose fingernails oozed filth. Caroline shuddered as she saw the gesture. Just for an instant she imagined those hands touching her, fondling her. She moved closer to Luke and felt his arm circle her shoulders protectively.

"Have you any news at all, man?" he said sharply. "I warn you, we won't take kindly to being given false rumors."

"And how would you know if such rumors be true or false, me fine laddo?" the first one said. "Seems to me the only way you'll find out is to accompany us to the compound and ask around. The blacks may have information of some use to you, and I daresay we could offer you a bit o' hospitality — providing you mean what you say about payin' for it."

The change in attitude to that of slimy servitude was far too obvious to be trusted.

"You'll respect the lady's wishes," Luke said sharply. "We only seek news of her father's whereabouts. We'll have no wish to remain any longer than necessary. We don't have much to spare, but we'll pay for any genuine information."

"And I daresay a bite of food and a drink o' fresh water wouldn't come amiss. And mebbe the lady would like to freshen herself up?" the man said, keener at the renewed mention of payment. His eyes glinted as he gazed at Caroline, and again she felt a shudder of fear run through her.

"I would," she said faintly, and then Luke broke in, both hands on her shoulders as he stood behind her now.

"Just as long as it's clearly understood that this is my woman. Any man who touches her gets my knife in his belly."

The men laughed sinisterly. "Oh aye, 'tis clear enough," one of them grunted. "We'll not interfere with your pleasure—while you're around to enjoy it."

"Boss no be hurt," Jojo snarled suddenly. "If boss or woman be hurt, Jojo kill."

Caroline had no idea how he produced the knife so quickly. One minute it was secure at his waist, and the next it was singing through the air past the leading settler's head, settling vibratingly into the trunk of a tree, a whisper away from the man's ear.

"All right!" the man yelled. "Now, if you want information, you follow us, savvy?"

The settlers turned and blundered off into the bush, and Jojo quickly retrieved his knife, grinning triumphantly at Caroline. Faint with shock, but with a sliver of hope now, she clutched at Luke's arm.

"We must follow them. They must know something or they wouldn't have invited us, would they?"

"Don't be too sure. It may not be as it seems."

"But what could they want from us? We obviously don't have much—" her voice dwindled away as Luke bent down and deliberately kissed her mouth.

"We have what they may want very much. It's probably been months, if not years since they've seen a pretty white woman. You could be the bait, Caroline. Do you still want to take the risk?"

She hesitated. But the settlers might know something. They had hinted as much, and it was the only lead they had . . .

"As long as I have you with me," she said clumsily.

He gave a crooked smile. "So I had to be compared with those louts to get any real response from you, did I?"

"For pity's sake, this is not the time or the place," she said in a cracked voice. "And if we don't go soon, we'll never find those men again."

"Oh, we'll find them. They'll be waiting for us."

He spoke with certainty, and she couldn't help recalling his words. She was the bait. Well, so be it, if it led them to her father.

"Then I'm ready," she said.

As Luke had surmised, the others were waiting a little way into the bush. The track they followed could barely be seen except by those who knew it existed, and it took several more hours before the vegetation opened out into a shallow saucer-shaped plain in the lower hills where a collection of wooden shacks had been constructed. Other men sat idly about, as disheveled as the rest, whittling sticks, chewing at roots, or just wasting away in the sun. There was no sign of any women.

In the center of the sandy compound was a huge fire, and over it was a crudely constructed spit. An enormous wild pig hung from it, slowly turning and roasting, and the succulent aroma made Caroline's mouth fill with saliva. It was many hours now since they had left the boat, and she was near to fainting with exhaustion and thirst, and she realized now that she was also ravenous.

"Stay close to me and don't look at any of them for too long," Luke ordered. "Keep your eyes down as much as possible."

It wasn't hard to obey his commands. The last thing she wanted was to face those leering men with their obscene gestures and remarks. And now she wished they were any other nationality but English because then she wouldn't be able to understand what they were saying.

"Ask them about my father," she said quickly to Luke.

But she was aware of a searing disappointment. It was obvious her father wasn't there, otherwise he would surely have been brought to her. It was all a wild goose chase, and she was close to weeping as she doubted that they had anything to tell her at all.

"What do we know of a ship that sank in a storm a few weeks ago, lads?" the leader asked loudly around the compound.

Several of the men looked up idly. "There was talk in the bush of men coming ashore in small boats," one of them said. "Probably went south, over the mountains."

"But did any of you actually *see* them?" Caroline broke in, unable to keep silent when it was so important to her.

"Caroline, for God's sake," Luke said savagely as several of the men took a new interest at hearing her voice.

155

"Well now, what's it worth to you to learn a bit more?" one of the whittlers said.

"I only want the truth," she snapped. "I don't want to be fobbed off with fairy tales."

She was beyond reason now. She had come so far, and it all seemed like a useless trail that led nowhere. The story of men being seen coming ashore was no more than a fantasy, and this group of gypsies was no more going to help her than walk barefoot to Sydney.

"Gabby!" the leader of the group suddenly bellowed out. "Come out here and show yourself, you old black bastard, and tell the little lady what you saw."

After a few minutes, a wizened black-skinned fellow came reluctantly out of the shade of a clump of nearby trees. He was much blacker and stockier than any of the Brundy natives. He wore a few ragged clothes, and a hunting knife was stuck in a thick rope around his waist. Behind him was a small group of people, as black as himself, who were presumably his family. The old man came slowly forward and sat down cross-legged in front of the visitors. The settlers didn't move, but the man's own people hovered close behind him.

"Gabby see big ship die," he said eventually, with many gestures that were apparently meant to represent a ship going beneath the waves. "Gabby see men in water, go down very fast. Down, down, down, like fishes. Men no breathe in big waves. Men die in sea."

His eyes rolled expressively until only the whites were visible. Caroline had a job not to cry out as the images unfolded in her mind.

"But not all of them, you old fool. What about the brave ones?" the leader encouraged.

"Brave ones try come to Big Land in small boats," the old man went on, his hands moving as

156

if to show the movement of the boats being tossed about in the heaving seas. "Boats get smashed on needles, and then men die."

Luke spoke angrily in Caroline's ear. "These bloody people are so steeped in storytelling, it'll be ages before he gets to the point. And this one's got such a fine sense of drama, there'll be no hurrying him."

"What are these needles?" she asked, ignoring Luke. Without thinking, she sat down abruptly on the sandy soil opposite the Aborigine, creating a kind of intimacy between them. If this strange man was the only means of locating her father, then nothing else mattered.

"Needles out in sea," the man said, fixing his black gaze on her face. "Needles sharp like knives."

He pulled the huge knife from his waist and stabbed it into the ground alongside Caroline. She tried not to flinch.

"Do you mean the reef?" she said with sudden understanding.

" 'Course the old fool means the reef," one of the settlers said coarsely, and she jerked up her head to glower at him.

"Do you mind? I'm having a private conversation with Mr. Gabby, and I'd like to hear what he has to say without interruption, if you please."

It never even struck her how bizarre it all was. The only thing that mattered was hearing the truth. And she could disregard the settlers' crude laughter as she leaned forward to encourage the old man to continue.

"Please, Mr. Gabby. You mentioned the needles. The small boats were smashed on the needles."

For a moment the realization of what she was saying threatened to make her turn turtle and give all this up. For how could anyone have survived and reached the mainland after what she was hearing?

And yet, *she* had survived. She had been rescued, so why not her father? The thought spurred her on.

"Smashed to sand," the man said, crushing one hand against the other in demonstration. He had begun drawing lines in the sand with his knife, presumably to show the coral reef, and Caroline could hardly take her eyes from it.

"But did any of the men get away?" she persisted, her heart thudding fast.

"Some," Gabby said cautiously. "I seen 'em. Then the great silver fish come through water and gobble 'em up!"

She gave a small scream, her hands tight against her mouth at his graphic description, together with his instantly recognizable sand-scrawled outline of a shark.

"Caroline, haven't you heard enough?" Luke's voice was harsh. She shook off his restraining hand.

"I want to hear it all," she said shrilly. The settlers muttered among themselves and one of them kicked out at the old man.

"Come on, you old fool, stop teasing the little lady and tell her the rest of it. You said there was some that got away, even though we never found 'em. You'd better come clean with it now, or you and your young 'uns will get a taste of the whip."

Caroline listened in horror as the old man cringed. These devils would actually do it, she thought. Somehow they had stumbled on the worst kind of settlers. Whether or not they had once been convicts no longer mattered. They clearly had their own need to survive and would show no mercy to any opposition.

"Mr. Gabby, did any of the men get ashore?" she asked, her voice beginning to break now. "Please, I have to know."

He stared at her from those black unfathomable eyes, and she willed him to know the truth and to say it. Eventually he gave a slow nod and began sketching in the sand again.

"We here. Men get to Big Land here. We watch."

He stabbed at the sand some way south of where he said they were now. Caroline supposed it was feasible. She had no idea of the exact spot where the *Princess Victoria* had gone down, nor how the vagaries of wind and turbulent seas would have tossed a small boat off its course.

"Did nobody search for them?" Luke asked now, seeing that Caroline was nearly at the end of her strength. This time she allowed him to help her to her feet, and she clung to him helplessly.

"Aye, we looked, my fine beauty," the leading settler said, scowling. "There may have been rich pickings off 'em, but without the old fool and his sons to guide us, we had little chance."

"Why wouldn't they guide you?" Caroline asked weakly, wondering if all her hopes were destined to be thwarted at every turn.

She was aware of Jojo and their own crew huddling together behind them now, and felt a sudden sinking feeling in the pit of her stomach.

The leading settler gave her the answer she half-suspected. "The blacks won't go into the mountains to the south of us. There's sacred burial grounds up there, see, and if they disturb the spirits of their ancestors, they'll bring the wrath of the gods down on 'em in this life and into the next and on to all the generations of their families. It's all rot, but there ain't no moving 'em."

Caroline glanced around at their own native boys.

"You wouldn't be afraid to take us, would you, Jojo?"

Luke held on tightly to her arm. "Don't be a fool. You can't ask such a thing of any of them. Their beliefs are as solid as those mountains. To them, it's like committing blasphemy to set foot on

159

the sacred burial grounds."

"But somebody had to set foot on them to create them in the first place," Caroline said, thinking that all men were fools if they couldn't apply such logic. "And if they're kept so silent and sacred, what can harm us if we merely go to the area to look for my father?"

"You tell her, Jojo," Luke said wearily.

"Missy no understand," he said, his eyes large. "Not only spirits guard sacred grounds. Guardian tribe keep place pure. This the way of Aborigine. We no need come to Big Land to know such things."

He paused as Gabby got up from the sandy ground with great alacrity for one so old and bent. He stabbed a finger at Caroline and shrieked at her in a crazed manner.

"You go sacred grounds, you die! Gabby speak truth. You listen what your black boy tell you, woman."

He turned and hobbled away to the bushes where his family awaited him. With one accord they turned and were seemingly swallowed up into the dense vegetation. In the small silence that followed, Caroline felt weighed down with hopelessness.

If she was to believe all she had heard, then a small group of survivors from the *Princess Victoria* had got ashore in the direction of the mountainous sacred burial grounds. If they had ventured right into the place, then the tribesmen guarding it would have surely killed them. And if she and Luke and their boys followed them, they would be killed too.

It was both a nightmare and too ludicrous to credit. Yet the fact remained that none of these hardheaded settlers had gone searching for survivors to rob them. That should have told her something. They must have clearly believed in the guardians of the sacred burial grounds and the

160

threat to anyone who ventured there. She shook with fear, but she had already come too far to stop now without finding out what had happened to her father, whatever the outcome.

"We have to go there," she said in a trembling voice to Luke. "I have to know."

"Are you completely out of your senses?" he said harshly. "God knows how much credence we can give to the old man's tale, but even if it were all true, it all happened weeks ago now. Do you think any of the survivors would still be in the same place?"

"I don't *know!*" she almost screamed. "But it's the only place I have to look! There might be some clues there, Luke, and at least it's a place to start!"

She looked in desperation at the settlers, who were contemplating this battle of wills with wide grins. She looked imploringly at the leader.

"Would *you* go there if I asked you to take me?"

He leered at her. "Depends what's in it for me, my luscious one. If you was prepared to be extra-special nice to me, I just might—"

Whatever else he might have said was drowned out by the crack of Luke's fist on his jaw. The man let out a howl of rage and staggered to the ground. At once, the rest of the settlers rushed at Luke, dragging him away from their leader and holding him captive. It all happened so fast Caroline hardly had time to scream, and then Jojo, Makepeace, and the crew were brandishing their own razor-sharp knives and holding them at the settlers' throats.

"What'll we do, Pike?" one of the men yelled out, looking to the leader for direction.

"Let the bastard go," he screeched back. "There are other ways of reckoning with him."

Luke shook them off and motioned to the boys to release the settlers. The man Pike got to his feet, nursing his fast-bruising jaw. None of the mainland

161

Aborigines had come to their defense, and from the settlers' rough treatment of them, Caroline could hardly blame them. This had been their land, and white men had cruelly torn it from them. It was one of the very indignities her father had intended to investigate through his newspaper empire.

The thought strengthened her resolve. "Well, I refuse to be intimidated by these old stories," she said to Luke. "I'll go by myself if I have to, but I mean to look for my father where Gabby told us."

"You won't go anywhere by yourself, you stubborn woman," he snapped. "You'd be damned the minute you stepped out of the compound. If you're foolhardy enough to take the risk, I'll take it with you, but you'd just better start praying that the boys will follow. Even better, pray that I can persuade Gabby or his sons to guide us as far as possible."

Caroline felt her eyes blur with tears. "Thank you, Luke," she whispered.

He shrugged and turned away from her to face the sullen Pike. "You said you were willing to give us food and drink. As we said, we'll pay for what we take, but we're also tired and need a night's rest before we travel on," he said shortly now.

Pike answered tersely, but it was obvious that the thought of payment had a magical effect on him.

"Take whatever victuals and water you need. The blacks will sleep in the open where we can keep an eye on them, but you and your woman can use the end shack for the night."

"Oh, but —"

Luke clamped his hand around her wrist as soon as she opened her mouth to protest. "Agree to it, or you'll undoubtedly find yourself sharing sleeping quarters with Pike," he told her, softly and grimly.

At the unsavory thought, she bit her tongue hard and followed Luke to the fire in the middle of the

162

compound where the roast pig was spitting and sizzling now. Tired of the confrontation with the travelers, some of the settlers were already hacking pieces of meat from one side of the dead animal and stuffing it into their mouths.

Their lack of manners disgusted Caroline, but once Jojo began hacking at the other side of the pig and handing great lumps of it to her and Luke, it was too much to resist doing the same. And never had food tasted so good. As she drank some cool water, Caroline began to feel as if she could face tomorrow after all. But first, there was tonight . . .

Chapter Nine

By the time they went to the quarters allocated to them, it was late in the day. Darkness came swiftly, and with it a surprising chill in the air. The huge fire in the compound was lower now but was clearly kept burning constantly, and its orange glow lit the meager new surroundings in which Caroline found herself. There was little in the way of comfort, just a straw-filled mattress on the floor, a table, one rickety chair, and a few utensils.

Luke lit the candle in the holder that hung on a wall hook, and the flickering light made the place look even shabbier. Caroline grimaced as she poured a little water from the pitcher into something that doubled as a serving and washing bowl. She splashed the cooling water onto her face and neck, dabbing her skin dry with the hem of her skirt, and wondered feverishly just what she had come to.

"I'm sorry it's not quite up to your usual standards," Luke said in sudden amusement at her fastidiousness. She glared at him and then capitulated weakly.

"It'll have to do," she muttered. "I suppose we're lucky to have got even this small lead from the old man."

He spoke harshly. "Don't put too much faith in all you've heard, lass. Aborigines are born story-tellers, and even though your ancient Gabby may have seen something, the tale may have got well embroidered by now."

"Well, he was convincing enough for me!" she said heatedly, not wanting to hear all this.

"Oh, he'll be believing it himself by now. The more a tale is told, the more convincing it becomes, even to the storyteller. All I'm saying is keep an open mind. You may end up being bitterly disappointed if it all comes to nothing."

She faced him, her hands clenched tightly at her sides. "You mean *when* it all comes to nothing, don't you? You don't think we've got a chance in a million of finding out what happened to my father, do you?"

"No, I don't," he said deliberately. "I never did, and you know that well enough."

"Yet you came with me. You brought me to the mainland against all your better instincts. Why?"

He gave a short laugh. "I've asked myself that question a hundred times, lass, and I still don't know the answer. And I'm not going to spend the rest of the night pondering on it. We've got a long day ahead of us tomorrow, so come to bed."

She bridled at once, eyeing the narrow mattress onto which Luke was already easing his long body.

"I'm not going to sleep on that. Not with you!"

"Suit yourself. You can always sleep in the chair, though you'll be as stiff as all hell in the morning. Or you can lie on the floor and risk being bitten by any crawlers that may come visiting during the night. Or you can take your chances outside with

165

the boys. They'll protect you from the settlers as long as they stay awake—"

"All right," Caroline snapped. She couldn't see that the miserable mattress would be much safer from insects than sleeping directly on the floor. As for the rest . . .

"Do you promise to behave yourself, Luke? You won't take advantage of this situation, will you?" she felt obliged to say it.

"Sweetheart, your innocence will be quite safe with me," he mocked her.

She refrained from snapping at him that since he'd already taken her innocence, such words were all a farce. She blew out the candle, and the pungent smoke filled the room. She took a moment to adjust her eyes to the dimness and glanced through the glassless window to where the native boys were sprawled about on the far side of the compound fire. They were already dead to the world, and she'd already discovered that when they slept there was no waking them until they were good and ready.

For another moment she allowed herself to stare at the great expanse of the sky. Had the sky ever seemed so vast as it did here in the Southern Hemisphere? she wondered. It had softened into a rich velvety darkness now, stretching into infinity and dotted with a million shimmering stars. Though she couldn't see the moon, she knew that its constant light was there, lighting half the world and hopefully smiling down benevolently on weary travelers such as her father. She caught her breath as the poignant thought slid into her mind, and she turned away from the window abruptly.

She moved across the room and got down gingerly onto the mattress, allowing Luke to pull the thin coverlet over them both. She kept as far away from him as possible, her arms hugging herself while she kept her body as rigid as possible. She closed her eyes tightly to shut out the awfulness of this place, but at the same time she willed herself not to lose consciousness until she was sure Luke was asleep. Then she just might be able to relax . . .

"How long are you going to resist?"

At the seductiveness of his voice right behind her head, all her nerve ends were alive and jumping instantly. "You promised —"

"As a matter of fact, I didn't, but I'm not talking about making love to you, delightful though I find the idea. We both have a long way to go tomorrow, and I'm wondering just how long you're going to resist relaxing when you're too damn tired to keep your eyes open?"

She knew he was right, and slowly she let herself uncurl, easing herself back a few inches from the perilous edge of the mattress. But in the silence between them all the unspoken fears suddenly welled up inside her.

"Luke, I'm scared."

It was as if the words were wrenched from her against her will. She could no longer hold them back. Her mouth trembled, and without quite knowing how it happened, she had twisted round and was being held tightly against Luke's chest, and the warmth of his body was restoring her scattered senses.

He rocked her to him as if she were a child, and she was more comforted by his wordless strength than she could ever have dreamed.

"Go to sleep now, lass. Things always look better in the morning," he said softly, his arms folding around her and holding her fast.

She knew it was still night, but also that she must have slept, because she was jerked awake by blood-curdlingly loud sounds outside the hut, and she clung dizzily to Luke.

"Dear God, what is it?" she gasped.

"It's nothing to worry about. It's most likely dingoes tearing a wild pig or a kangaroo to pieces in the bush," he said, his voice still heavy with sleep.

"Are you sure?" she persisted. Her hands still clung to him as she still badly needed confirmation that they weren't about to be devoured by wild animals while they slept.

He was becoming more alert now as he felt the frantic beat of her heart next to his as she pressed closer in fear.

"As sure as anybody who's ever heard dingoes. They'll make their kill and then disappear into the bush. They won't come near the fire, and there's nothing for you to fear, my lovely lass."

She still clung to him, her eyes closed in sheer relief at this simple explanation. She had been so terrified, and it was hard to still her rapidly beating heart. Harder still to think she would ever dare to sleep again this night . . .

She became slowly aware that his hands were moving gently over her, along the taut length of her spine and around the soft womanly mounds of her buttocks. The breath was tight in her chest, and she heard him mutter a soft oath.

"You see what you do to me, my love."

Luke's breath was warm against her cheek. She knew instantly what he meant as she felt the thrust of his manhood against her body. She was no stranger to it now, and the little sigh that escaped her lips was as much an acceptance of her destiny as of what was about to happen.

"Have you any idea how much I want you, Caroline?"

"I think I do," she whispered, and somehow she was moving restlessly as his body covered hers, wanting him with a fever that was quickly matching his. Wanting the normality of the surge of passion that flowed between them to counter this hostile and alien environment.

For a while, at least, she could feel warmed and desired. Even if love didn't enter into Luke's scheme of things, it was enough to know that he wanted her more than anything else in the world.

For her, he had done the very thing he had been most set against. He had risked the reef to come to the Big Land. She owed him so much . . .

The crazy, inconsequential phrases whirled about in her head as if to justify the fact that when he lifted the soiled skirt of her gown, she willingly spread herself for him, welcoming him like a wanton into the warm secret place he craved. She was as feverish as he, needing to feel him pulsate inside her, filling her, writhing against her, spilling his life-giving seed into her to her cries of ecstasy . . .

"Oh Luke, Luke . . ." she gasped his name over and over again, and he spoke back to her in that adopted foreign tongue he sometimes used that seemed to obsess him so huskily at such times. As if he were too afraid to let her know in words she could understand what his feelings really were . . . and as always, she was too afraid to ask, to break the spell . . .

He clasped her to him now, holding her tightly in the final thrusts of his passion. And she felt her eyes spurt with tears because it was all so beautiful, and she couldn't bear it if it hadn't meant as much to him as it had to her. If he didn't love her as desperately as she loved him . . .

The shock of her own thoughts was like a dash of cold water in her face. Because, of course, he didn't love her. To Luke Garston, the act of lust was a bonus to be taken whenever he wished from this once so prim-and-proper Englishwoman who had come so unexpectedly into his life. And she . . . with innate honesty, she faced the truth. She loved him, maddening and ruthless and impossible though he was. *She loved him.*

"I'm sorry," he murmured into her hair. "This was never meant to happen, and I truly meant to honor your wishes, Caroline. God knows it doesn't do for me to be alone with you like this. I'll try to arrange things differently from now on. We'll stick to bedding down in the open with the boys, then you won't be such a temptation to me."

She couldn't speak for the tears scalding her eyes. A *temptation?* Was that all she was to him? Clumsily, she pulled down her gown and turned her back on him, huddling her knees into her chest. When she didn't answer, he spoke roughly.

"I don't expect you to forgive me, but from now on, I promise I'll leave you strictly alone unless you say otherwise."

"Do you really think I shall ask for your favors?" she said, muffled, until she realized how deeply her face was turned into the unsavory mattress.

She came up for air, gasping a little as she remembered for a moment the unkempt bodies that might have been sleeping there before her and almost retched at the thought. Without being aware that she did so, she shuddered violently. Misinterpreting this reaction, Luke's voice was stony now.

"I didn't realize just how unwelcome you found

170

my touch. I'll do my best to avoid touching you from now on."

She felt him move as far from her as he could, although to create any distance at all between them was difficult on the narrow mattress. After the trauma of reaching the settlement, the doubts about the old Aborigine's words, and the fright of wakening to the dingoes' cries, Caroline wept silently. She wept for worry over her father's fate, and deep in her heart she wept for the way everything was so different from the way it should be between herself and Luke.

She eventually fell asleep from sheer weariness. She awoke again to the sounds of human life from the compound, and she had to close her eyes from the brilliance of the sunlight in the window. It hurt her eyes to look at it, and she glanced at Luke to see if he was awake.

His dark hair was as tousled as a young boy's, the strong virile mouth relaxed. She could have leaned over him and kissed that mouth so easily: she remembered the warmth and the taste of it so well. She got up quickly from the bed they shared. If she hadn't done so, she knew she'd have found it almost irresistible not to touch the face that was still lost in sleep and suddenly so dear to her. And that would surely have invited trouble.

She gasped as she saw another face grinning at her through the window. It was the man Pike.

"I'd be obliged if you'd respect my privacy," she snapped, her heart thudding at the shock of seeing him there.

His coarse chuckle made her go cold. "Just as you say, little lady. Though if you and your man are thinking of stagin' a repeat performance in daylight, me and my blokes 'ould like a grandstand seat next time."

As his words sank into her brain, Caroline felt a sense of horror creep over her. "You—you don't mean—"

He laughed at her outrage and made a crude gesture with his arm. "Gave us all more'n goosebumps to listen to it," he slurred meaningfully. "Some o' the blokes have gone off in search of Abo women, seein' as there ain't no white women about, 'cepting your own sweet self. And I don't suppose you're thinking of spreadin' your favors about, my pretty?"

"She is not!" As Luke's furious voice sounded right behind her, he pushed her aside, his hand thrusting through the window to grab Pike by the neck. The man bellowed with rage as his head and shoulders were yanked into the shack where Luke brandished his knife at his throat.

"I've warned you before, man. This woman belongs to me, and one more word out of place from you and I'll slit you from ear to ear. And don't think I won't do it."

His voice had dropped to a silky threat that was more meaningful than the loudest roar. Pike's eyes bulged, and he babbled wildly. "All right, all right. Let me go, you bastard, and you've got my word that nobody will bother you or your woman."

"I don't put much store by the word of scum," Luke said coldly, giving the scrawny neck a last painful wrench before letting him go. "But since we've no time to waste on you, we'll be on our way as soon as we've eaten."

"And what about payment?" Pike scowled, rubbing his sore neck. "We don't give nothin' for nothin'. We ain't no charity organization."

"You'll be left some money for your trouble. Though much good it will do you out here."

"Oh, we'll find a use for it," Pike sneered.

"There's traveling whisky traders and mountain men always willin' to do a trade, don't you worry none about that."

Caroline couldn't bear to look at him. She was sickened at knowing the settlers had been well aware of what had gone on in the shack during the night. She wondered just how close they had been. They could have been right outside, listening, gloating, vicariously taking their own pleasure in something that had been private and wonderful, and was now filling her with hot shame and humiliation.

"Let's get away from here, Luke," she said, her mouth trembling. Suddenly, she couldn't look at him either. How must he feel, wondering if these awful men had overheard everything? Knowing that he had apologized to her and that she hadn't openly welcomed his lovemaking? Or would they have guessed what Luke himself didn't seem to guess? That despite everything, it had been a magical experience for her?

She picked up her traveling bag without speaking and walked out into the blazing sunlight. Luke didn't follow her immediately and she walked straight-backed to the fire where their boys were already drinking a strong brew of tea and eating black bread and huge fried eggs.

Jojo looked up and grinned at Caroline's approach, and for a moment her heart stopped. Surely the crew hadn't joined in listening to them last night? Then she saw him pointing at the eggs, his smile as artless as usual.

"They turtle eggs, missy. Taste good," Jojo said. "Gabby's sons bring. You want?"

They might be from different tribes, but there was obviously a camaraderie between the two groups of Aborigines. Caroline saw the young sons of the old man grinning from the shelter of the bush, and she nodded at Jojo now, a wave of relief washing over her. She thought fervently that if Pike and his men were anything to go by, then any one of these friendly blacks were worth a dozen of the so-called civilized white men who had invaded this country.

Luke still hadn't joined her, but now she saw Pike and several of his men coming toward the fire, and Caroline turned to them, holding her chin high.

"We'd prefer to eat alone with our crew," she said imperiously, remembering the lack of manners at supper the previous night. "My—my husband will pay you for what we take, and we shan't bother you again. But we'd like words with Mr. Gabby to ask him to guide us as far as he will."

Pike's mouth twisted. "And who are you to be givin' me orders, my fine madam? This is my place, and I'll say who has words wi' my blacks."

She stared him out fearlessly, despite the way her heart was pounding. But where the devil was Luke? she wondered frantically.

"They can please themselves as to whom they speak with," she snapped. "And I'll ask you not to prevent them guiding us."

He gave an evil smile. "Oh, they'll guide you all right, little lady, I'll see to that," he said, and marched off toward them.

She turned with relief as she saw Luke approach from the shack. But from the look of displeasure on his face, she knew he'd overheard her clash with Pike.

"Well done," he said shortly. "He'll probably be directing them to lead us round in circles now."

"But I'm sure they won't," she said, with less confidence than she felt. "They'll want to help us, I know they will."

"Not if it means going near their sacred burial grounds. Can't you see that we haven't a hope in hell of finding your father alive, Caroline? Face up to it, and let's get out of here while we're still alive and sane."

Her heart sank. He'd never been quite so blunt before. But she couldn't give up now.

"I can't," she said shakily. "I just can't. I have to go on now."

He gave a small nod at the ready tears that had sprung to her eyes and took the dish of eggs and bread that Jojo handed to him. The settlers obviously didn't provide forks, and Caroline had to follow the example of the rest and eat with her fingers, wiping around the dish with her bread. It looked unappetizing but was surprisingly good to eat.

After a heated discussion with Pike, two of Gabby's sons came over to them.

"If we take, we go far as Big Rock, then we go back."

Jojo spoke to him quickly in his own language. The boy seemed to follow much of it, though Caroline guessed it was a different dialect from his own, and he shook his head vigorously.

"Only far as Big Rock. Then we go," he repeated loudly.

"What's this Big Rock?" Luke asked Jojo.

"It where sacred burial grounds begin. These boys afraid go farther. They no enter caves. Nor we," he finished quickly.

"But you wouldn't desert us, Jojo?" Caroline asked.

"We no go sacred grounds," he said doggedly. Makepeace and the others banged their knees and stamped their feet on the dusty ground in assent.

Caroline looked at Luke helplessly. He shrugged.

"Even if your father was ever there, it's unlikely he'd be there now."

"But Jojo spoke of caves. What better place would there be for survivors to recover and rest awhile?"

"And what better place for the rituals of death to be performed for those who desecrate the sacred burial grounds?" Luke said brutally. "Don't underestimate these people, Caroline. Their beliefs go back far beyond those of the white man, and anyone who ventures into their sacred places faces certain death. Jojo knows it, Gabby knows it, and I'm damn sure that Pike knows it."

She listened in a kind of horror. Her father might know something of the ancient Aboriginal customs, she thought, but in a state of shock and desperation, any innocent-looking cave would seem a safe haven to the half-drowned survivors of a shipwreck and not a place of death.

"What are your names?" She turned to Gabby's sons, unable to acknowledge the hopelessness of the situation a minute longer.

"I Vosto. This one Bengie," the older one said.

"Well, Vosto and Bengie, will you guide us as far as you can to where your father thought he saw the white men from the small boat?" she said, as pleasantly as though she were inviting them home to tea on a summer afternoon in London. She saw them glance at one another.

"We show," Vosto said reluctantly. "But we no stay."

By the time they were ready to leave the compound, the sun had risen higher in the sky, blazing down on them and prickling Caroline's skin. She raised her parasol over her head to protect her from the fiercest rays, ignoring the catcalls of the settlers and waiting impatiently while Luke checked yet again that the boys had filled their water bags. Without water, they would get nowhere. Finally they set off due south, heading inland in the direction of the stark, forbidding mountains.

"I hope you've said a prayer or two," Luke commented briefly as they plunged quickly into the dense undergrowth once more.

She flinched. "I have. Maybe you don't believe in the power of prayer, but I do."

"It'll take more than prayers to see us through this jungle," he told her. Soon they heard the hacks of the natives' knives clearing a way. But it was obvious that Vosto and Bengie had come this way before and were surer in their movements than the Brundy crew would have been.

"We have no choice but to trust them," Caroline said after some hours.

By then, Luke was strongly suspecting it was as he had surmised and they were being led around in circles. They had paused for the tenth time to sip some water and take a breather. The soggy ground beneath their feet didn't seem to bother the natives or Luke, but Caroline's town shoes were useless for such terrain and had quickly been reduced to pulp. But she daren't take them off. She never knew what she might be treading on.

"Missy right." Jojo defended the brothers, to her surprise. "We trust, and we soon leave bush. See?"

He pointed far ahead of them. All Caroline could see was what appeared to be a great red dust cloud on the horizon and enormous wind-sculpted rocks that seemed to soar into the sky.

"We'll never reach there," she said in dismay.

"Maybe not so far over mountain," Jojo assured her.

177

Vosto spoke up. "Boy speak true. We take over mountain. Then we go."

"You're going to leave us there?" Caroline asked him. "Is that where the sacred burial grounds are?"

She saw him shrink back. "You no go there! Not safe. You die—"

"All right, we understand," Luke broke in as the man's eyes began to roll expressively. "You just point the way to where the caves are where the Englishmen may have gone, and we'll do the rest. Do you understand? Take us to the place your father thought he saw the men."

It couldn't be too far, Caroline reasoned. The old man Gabby could surely not have come so far . . . but remembering his strange agility and the way all of these people seemed to be so at one with nature, she began to believe anything was possible of them.

"Let's move on," Luke said abruptly. "The sooner this farce is over, the sooner we can get back to civilization again."

Caroline glared at him. It didn't help her self-confidence one bit to have him constantly referring to this mission as foolhardy and farcical. But she bit her tongue and got to her feet. Seconds later she smothered a scream and staggered backward as a huge red spider appeared from nowhere and settled on her ankle.

"Don't move. One bite and you're dead," Luke snapped.

She stood rock-still, her eyes glazing with fear as the thing seemed to hover over her skin and then crawled lazily onward. Before it could disappear into the undergrowth, Makepeace had crushed it with the handle of his knife.

"That's one problem that won't be bothering us

again," Luke said easily, but she still shook from head to foot.

"Were you serious about one bite being lethal?" she asked, her voice thin with shock.

"Perfectly," he said briefly. "Now can we continue?"

Her legs felt so leaden she was quite sure she wouldn't be able to put one foot in front of the other from now on, but if she didn't, they would go on without her. Doggedly, she clutched her traveling bag and tried to ignore the smarting tears in her eyes. She was the world's biggest fool to undertake such a journey, so ill-equipped and helpless. It was no place for a woman.

She felt the ragged sobs in her throat and tried desperately not to let them out. And then she felt the comfort of Luke's arm slide around her for a moment. "Hold on, my darling," he said gently. "We've come this far, and we'll go on until the end."

She was too numbed to answer him. She could only nod and hope that his words weren't too prophetic.

After a while Bengie pointed ahead. "Soon we reach billabong. Woman can wash."

She looked at him vaguely. She was starting to feel lightheaded. They had traversed the bush by now and had entered rocky territory. The sun beat down overhead, and the stony ground was harder on the feet but at least it hid fewer terrors than the tangled thick undergrowth.

"What is this billabong?" she said to Luke.

"It's a water hole. The boy's right. We can rest there and take something to eat, and we can all wash off the grime of the day."

179

She hoped she'd be able to do more than that. If this water hole was free of dangers she would immerse herself totally. The blissful thought raised her spirits at once. Naturally there was no question of removing her dress, but the thought of wading into cool and refreshing water was suddenly as sweet as nectar. She would feel refreshed, and afterward the hot sun would dry her.

And the thought that her father might have come this way too, found the billabong, and also been invigorated, was an added incentive to forge ahead.

An hour later, they saw the sheen of water ahead as blue as the sky, and Caroline could have cried with relief.

"Is it safe to drink?" she gasped, her mouth parched.

"Safe enough," Luke hazarded. "There's unlikely to be any crocs up here polluting it, anyway."

"Don't even mention such things," she said, shivering

"Woman safe in billabong," Vosto assured her. "Bengie and me drink. Then we go."

She stared at him. Her jubilation at finding the water hole had made her forget for a moment that their guides were going to leave them here.

"But how do we know where to go next?" she asked.

Vosto waved vaguely upward to where the biggest rock of all towered above them, red against the sky, majestic, and as old as time.

"Sacred grounds and caves behind rock. We no go." His voice became more vehement and agitated.

"We understand, boy," Luke told him. "You've done your duty, and we'll manage from now on."

She looked at him in dismay. Why was he letting them go so easily? Surely they could have forced

180

the brothers to lead them farther.

As if he followed her thoughts, Luke turned and spoke quietly. "Don't try to make them go against their beliefs. If you do, they'll kill themselves rather than return to their father with their shame. Do you want their deaths on your conscience?"

Staring at the way the brothers were huddled together as they walked now, their shoulders touching as if for moral support, she shook her head. Their age-old beliefs might be incomprehensible to her, but she had to respect their faith. She shook her head in answer to Luke's question.

They walked on quickly toward the billabong, and the whoops of joy from the native boys more than made up for their own silence. Suddenly there was nothing more to say. This place was a turning point in their fortunes. The certainty of it was like a heavy weight on Caroline's head, but while there was the faintest chance of finding her father alive, she wouldn't turn back.

The scent of fresh water was suddenly strong in her nostrils. The Brundy crew didn't wait for instructions as they stripped themselves of belts and weapons, leaving bags and water carriers on the banks before leaping into the clear water.

Caroline guessed that there must be a spring somewhere in the mountains to feed the lake, otherwise the burning sun would surely evaporate it.

And then she wasted no more time on surmising as Luke strode ahead of her. He dumped his own baggage and dipped his hands beneath the water to splash it over his face and neck. Almost immediately he plunged into it to come up shaking his head about like a gleeful spaniel. Caroline laughed, and the sound of her own laughter was one that she hadn't heard for a very long time.

The whole scene was suddenly so blissfully normal . . . if it could be normal to cavort about in a mountain lake with her lover and a group of naked Aborigines.

"What are you waiting for?" Luke called to her.

She stepped forward and walked straight into the water. It wasn't as cold as she had expected, but the difference in temperature between it and the burning air still made her gasp. Her soft gown seemed to float around her, and she began to feel as though the softness of the water soothed her limbs and cleansed her soul. Within minutes she was used to it, and holding her breath she totally immersed herself for several seconds, the way Luke had done. She came up gasping, her hair streaming out behind her.

"Does that feel good?" he grinned, right beside her.

"*So* good, I can't put it into words," she said fervently. "Right now I'd like to stay here forever."

Luke caught hold of her hands, and they dived beneath the water together to come up sputtering and laughing like children at play. Their crew was doing likewise, and their voices echoed around the mountains. But it suddenly struck Caroline that they were the only ones who had immersed themselves. The brothers had only scooped up enough to drink. She felt a sudden suspicion.

"Luke, what's wrong with Vosto and Bengie?" she whispered. She held his hands more tightly as she spoke. He looked back to where the brothers stood watching them now.

"I don't know," he said, cursing himself for not noticing before. He waded toward them, beckoning them.

"Why don't you join us?"

"*No!* Water belong spirits. We go now."

Before any of the glistening bodies in the water

182

could react or say anything more, the two Aborigines had turned and sped away. Immediately the Brundy boys went for the banks and lay there gasping with fear, jabbering in their own language. Luke spoke sharply to them but they were clearly too frightened to waste time speaking in English.

"They say they think the man Pike told them to bring us here if this billabong is the entrance to the sacred grounds. He'd know we couldn't resist bathing in it after the journey, but the brothers wouldn't touch it except to drink, which the spirits accept. The boys say we're doomed now."

Caroline gasped. "But they were so obliging, so helpful—"

"And so bloody terrified of what Pike would do to them or their family if they disobeyed," Luke said grimly.

"So what happens now?" she said, her teeth beginning to chatter despite the heat of the day.

"Now we sit on the bank to dry off, and we have something to eat to fortify ourselves."

"Are you mad? We have to get away from here, Luke! I don't believe any of this nonsense, but I'm not hanging around long enough to find out if ancient spirits or devils exist!" she said, anger beginning to overtake her fear.

She struggled to get out of the water, her long skirt hampering her, her heart racing in her chest. And then it stopped altogether for a long moment as she squinted into the sunlight.

On the high sculpted rock above them a lone figure was staring down at them. He was as black as night, but even from here she could see that his body was painted with scrolls and whorls. He wore a feathered headband and armbands. Apart from that his only clothing was a kind of loincloth in which the gleam of a knife caught the light. He gripped a long spear in one hand and a painted shield in the other.

From somewhere in the depths of her scattered memory, Caroline remembered her father mentioning such garb and decoration worn by the old tribes of Aborigines. It had seemed a quaintly colorful description then, and quite remote from anything in her experience. But this man staring aggressively now at intruders who dared to wallow in the waters of the sacred billabong was the living example of the image, brandishing a killing spear.

Chapter Ten

The lone Aborigine gave a sudden screeching cry. It echoed around the mountains, and within seconds, the seemingly isolated area was swarming with tribesmen. They poured down toward the billabong, screaming and thrusting their spears high in the air. The gestures couldn't be misunderstood. They wanted blood from these strangers, and Caroline was almost petrified with fear. The men, with their fierce, protruding brows and black skins, all bore a pattern of facial cuts and scars, so symmetrical that she could only assume they must be tribal adornments.

"You see?" Luke said harshly. "There would have been no point in running, especially with your sodden skirt to hamper you."

But the Brundy crew was nimbler on their feet, without the impediments of clothes to hinder them. They streaked away from the site, leaving Luke and Caroline to face the circle of black faces surrounding them. She had met hostility before, but never from an enraged mob of natives who obviously believed these two had violated one of their most sacred places.

She ran her tongue around her dry lips as the Aborigines suddenly began a low, unnerving chanting. It was more terrifying than the screeches had been. She clung to Luke. "What are they going to do with us?" she said through chattering teeth.

"Probably make us the next sacrificial offerings to appease the spirits," he said brutally. She gasped, but from the angrily rolling eyes of their captors and their aggressive stance, how could she doubt it?

Luke suddenly raised one hand and snapped out a word she didn't understand. To Caroline's amazement the chanting momentarily stopped. He spoke quickly in the native tongue she recognized as being used on Brundy. It was highly unlikely it would be same tongue as that spoken by these tribesmen, but it might be similar enough to be understood, she thought, feeling a small thread of hope. The men were aggressively watchful and silent now, and she dared not move.

But although Luke used many hand and arm gestures as he spoke, there was no response.

"What did you say to them?" she mumbled when the group continued to glare at them in silence.

"That we come in peace and that we humbly apologize to them and to the spirits of their ancestors for disturbing their solitude. I also asked them if a brave white elder from across the sea has come here seeking rest in recent weeks since he's well-favored and important to us."

If he hadn't been so deadly serious, Caroline might have found such flowery and ridiculous sentiments laughable. But from the set look on Luke's face, she realized he knew these people better than she did, and if this was the kind of presentation they understood, then so be it.

The men were small and stocky in stature, but

both their aggression and their tall plumed head-dresses gave them the illusion of height, so that they seemed to tower over the intruders. At least, it seemed so to Caroline, but then she realized how tall and straight Luke stood and how unblinkingly he stared at them as if to establish some authority.

It was all hopeless, of course, she thought, her spirit plummeting. They were both doomed, and it was only a matter of time before they became the sacrificial offerings. At the thought, she smothered a small cry, and the one who appeared to be the tribal chief transferred his steady gaze from Luke to her.

Luke moved slightly, standing half in front of her to protect her. He spoke again, more loudly this time and at some length. He seemed to be embracing the sky with his arms, and the tribesmen broke into angry squabbling.

"What have you said now?" she said frantically. "I wish I could understand—"

"I'm trying to save your pretty neck. The blood of a young white virgin would be a much-prized sacrifice among such tribes, since they come across it so rarely."

She was near to swooning at his words. He never tried to soften anything for her, she thought angrily. Then she felt his hand squeeze her own as he spoke rapidly to the natives again, pressing his hands first to his own loins and then circling her belly with his palm. The movements were accompanied by gestures she couldn't mistake. She felt the burning color sting her cheeks.

"Why are you doing this, Luke? How could you be so coarse—?" she choked out.

"For pity's sake trust me, and don't confuse things by a show of womanly modesty," he snapped as the shrieking arguments continued. "It's the only thing that might save you. I've told them you're not

187

a virgin and that you already carry my child. These people look on pregnant women as mysterious and revered creatures, so it may just turn the tide."

"And what of you?" she mumbled, her sense of shock and indignation widening as the tribesmen began inching forward as if to inspect her more closely. "Aren't you risking your neck by implying that you've taken what they want from me?"

"Maybe. But I've also told them my God instructed me to plant the seed in you and that they'll risk the wrath of Him if they harm either one of us."

She stared at him. It sounded like blasphemy to her, but she could hardly condemn him for that when their lives might depend on it. Their Aborigine god would obviously not be the same one as theirs, but Caroline knew that belief in the power and wishes of any god, however pagan, was a primeval and universal instinct. Still, she could hardly believe it would save their necks.

"What woman say?"

The slow and guttural words took them both so much by surprise that Caroline could only stare at the tribal chief from whom the words had emerged. And then she couldn't think of anything else but her quest.

"You speak English!" she stuttered. "Oh, *please*, have you seen my father? He's the important white man who came out of the sea—"

"What woman say?" he snarled again. "Is *prinka* in belly?" He reeled off a barrage of words in his own language then, his limited English obviously being quickly exhausted.

Feeling Luke's fingers gripping hers, she could only nod frantically, assuming that in the native tongue *prinka* must mean child.

Without warning, the chief hurled his spear into the ground just inches from Caroline's feet. It vibrated violently for a few seconds and then continued quivering. At this she was too numb with shock and fear to move a muscle or utter a sound. She was sure they were both about to be killed without any more ceremony.

"Don't move," Luke said unnecessarily. "It's a test. If the spear falls to the ground, you lie."

She stared at it as if mesmerized. Of course she lied! There was no child in her belly . . . but even as she thought it, she knew that there *could* be. She had lain with a man twice, and each time his seed had warmed and filled her . . . but this was hardly the time or place to remember those sweet hours, even if these were her last moments, and she recalled hearing somewhere that it eased the passage into the next world to let the mind be filled with good thoughts . . .

She closed her eyes against the terror of those angry black faces and the sight of the quivering weapon that so far still remained upright in the sand. It finally stopped moving, and Caroline dared to open her eyes a fraction. The chief stalked forward to retrieve his spear and stared deep into Caroline's eyes. She shrank back from the stink of him, but she dared not move. If she did, she would fall into the billabong, and that would incense their captors even more.

To her horror, he reached out a stringy hand and prodded her belly. Then he circled it as Luke had done. She felt his probing fingers go lower, and still she dared not move. As the man's mouth opened into a leer, his open lips revealed broken teeth stained dark with juice. Caroline bit her lip until she tasted blood. Then, just as suddenly, he moved away from her.

"Woman with *prinka* come."

She almost fainted with relief. Apparently he believed the lie about the child.

189

The tribe separated to allow them through. There was no question of doing otherwise. She and Luke picked up their baggage and stumbled on, prodded at intervals by the sure-footed tribesmen as they picked their way through the sparse trees and scrub ahead of them. Caroline had supposed the caves and sacred burial grounds would be close by, but it seemed they had been walking for hours by the time they finally stopped, and her feet were blistered and sore.

They eventually entered an encampment, though there was little there in the way of comfort. The red sandy soil beneath their feet was desertlike, but there was considerable vegetation about, making it a kind of oasis in the mountains. The tribesmen's meager shelters were in the form of four sturdy poles supporting a reeded platform above, which held each one's belongings. Some of the shelters had animal skins stretched around the poles to give a semblance of privacy. Cooking fires were smoldering all around the camp, and the stench of fresh raw meat made Caroline pinch her nostrils together. She didn't dare guess what it might be.

But she could see now that the encampment was a small village. There were women and a few children, who all stared resentfully at the newcomers. She ventured a smile at one of the women and was spat on for her trouble. She averted her eyes at once, her heart pounding.

"Luke, I'm so frightened," she stuttered hoarsely.

His grim face was answer enough to her fears. They were marched to the far end of the village, and by that time there was a long trail of natives following them. And then they reached the caves, and Caroline gasped. Were they taking her to her father after all? She felt a surge of hope that almost took her breath away.

"Don't build up your hopes, my love," Luke said,

reading her thoughts as she gasped, a little color coming back to her cheeks. "They're merely showing us their sacred places and warning us off."

The chief of the tribe began shouting to them once more in his own tongue for the benefit of his own people, disdaining now to use the little English he knew. At each climax to his speech, he raised his spear high, and there was an echoing roar from the rest of them. Caroline gave up trying to imagine what might be said and concentrated instead on the weird drawings that adorned the rocky entrances to the caves.

Some were obvious, depicting men slaying animals or women giving birth, and frequently the act of sex in various poses. From the variety of positions displayed, such pastimes would seem to occupy much of the tribe's time. Other drawings were totally incomprehensible to Caroline, but all of them revealed a notable artistic ability. She tried to keep her senses alert to everything, filing the information in her mind objectively. Her father would be so interested in all this for one of his newspaper articles . . .

Her swooning thoughts were jerked back to her present situation as the tribesmen motioned them forward.

"He's not here, my darling. He never came here. You've got to accept that," Luke said harshly as they were prodded forward without further ceremony.

She felt her senses spin again. She had hoped for too much, and it had all come to nothing. And she had put them both in so much danger.

"Luke, I'm sorry," her cracked voice managed to say, and then she almost stopped breathing.

She had no idea how far they had come since leaving the settlers' compound, and all she knew was that Vosto and Bengie had led them to the pass in the mountain where the billabong and the encampment lay. But now they had emerged onto a great barren slab of rock that seemed to be at the very edge of the world. The sheer face of it plunged downward for many hundreds of feet. And beyond it . . .

Caroline caught her breath. Even while she went dizzy with fear, she could see that beyond it was the endlessly shimmering blue of the sea, with the Great Barrier Reef curving protectively around it. Their journey had sent them in a zigzag direction, and they were not so very far from the coast after all. Except that it might as well have been on the other side of the world for all the good it would do them.

"Oh Luke, it seems so near. Will we ever see Brundy again?"

Her own words took her by surprise. Brundy was suddenly the haven she had never thought it, until now.

The leading tribesman motioned Caroline forward. Her teeth chattering and her eyes dilated, she shrank back against Luke. Surely they weren't going to send her spinning over the edge to the chasm below. She sobbed into Luke's chest, hearing him shout angrily to the chief. The man answered in guttural tones, thrusting his spear into the ground with every sentence.

"They want you to see where the revengeful spirits of their ancestors send those who lie. And then—" he hesitated.

"And then what?"

"You're to be kept prisoner until the pregnancy is ended, and the child that is born will be their sacrifice."

"And if no child is born?"

He gripped her cold hands in his, and she knew she was living through a nightmare. This couldn't

192

be happening, and any minute now she would wake up and find herself safely back on the *Princess Victoria,* steadily steaming through calm southern waters toward Sydney.

Her hands were suddenly pulled away from Luke's, and the chief dragged her toward the very brink of the rock. She reeled back, unable to look into the vacuum that opened out before it met the hazy gray-green of the bush and the red sandy desert soil far below. Her legs seemed to turn to lead as she imagined plunging over into certain death.

But she doubted that it would be such a simple death. The tribesmen would want a full revenge on her for lying once they found that she carried no child. Without thinking what she did, her hand went protectively to her belly, imagining for a sweet moment that there really was a child being nurtured there. For her, Caroline now knew it would be a child borne of love and a child she wouldn't even be allowed to hold to her breast. Her heart wrenched at the tragedy of it.

The chief thrust her back toward Luke's arms again, and she shook uncontrollably.

"Luke, I can't bear it," she stuttered against him. "I'm so sorry. It's all my fault, all of it—"

Even in the midst of her terror, she felt a searing guilt for bringing him here. Against all his better instincts, he had done this for her, and now they were both going to be killed. She knew there was no way out.

"Hush, my darling," he soothed her, stroking her ashen face. "I'll find a way to get back to you. I won't be far away, I promise."

She stared at him, her eyes still wide and terrified as she felt a sudden suspicion. And then the tribesmen were pushing them back the way they had come, and she was stumbling on her poor torn feet to try to keep up with them.

"What do you mean? Won't you be with me?"

He looked uneasy. "Caroline, it's not me they want. It's the child — or it's you. They're going to let me go since I've done my part."

She looked at him, aghast as his meaning sank in. "You mean because you made love to me and they think you put a child in me, they're letting you go?"

"For God's sake, don't panic," he said roughly. "Their ways aren't ours, Caroline, and for the time being you'd do well to go along with them. Every tribe has its own rituals and creeds, and this one believes that any man who gives a woman a child is a man of stature. Even a white man."

He spoke with what was supposed to be grim humor, but Caroline was in no mood to be humored. Almost beside herself, she realized she was going to be abandoned, and all he could think about was saving his own neck. How could she ever have trusted him? How could she ever have thought she loved him?

"You unspeakable *swine!* You're going to leave me, aren't you?" she said in a shrill high voice. He gripped her arm tightly as she made to flail against him.

His voice was taut with anger. "Can't you see I've got no choice? They'll escort me well away from the village, but I'll find a way to get you out of this, I promise. Just remember they're not going to do anything to you until they discover the truth."

She knew only too well the implication of his words.

"You mean I'd have at least three months or so before anything shows, is that it? You're quite happy to let them keep me here for *three months!*"

Hysteria made her voice shrill, and she shuddered violently, unable to contemplate even days of inspection by these savages to see whether or not she

194

was carrying a child until the truth of it became evident. And when it did, *she* would be the sacrifice.

As if to stop them from talking further, Luke was dragged away from her and marched ahead with a group of the tribesmen. He stood head and shoulders above them, but he was as helpless as herself to oppose them. She felt sheer panic again. How was he ever going to rescue her from her fate? Not even he could do the impossible.

She suddenly felt as if all her bones were turning to jelly, and she slid to the ground without a sound. She didn't lose consciousness, but it seemed as if all her willpower had gone, and when one of the tribesmen was ordered to pick her up and thrust her over his shoulder as ignominiously as a sack of turnips, it hardly mattered. Nothing mattered anymore. She was going to die anyway.

When she became sensible again, it was dark. So she must have fainted after all, or she had been drugged . . . She hardly cared about that either. All her spirit had gone, and she was lethargic and detached from everything around her. Her father, the storm that had separated them, Luke Garston — all of them were a dream that no longer existed, floating around in her head like wisps of smoke.

She suddenly realized the smoke had a strong smell to it. It was no longer in her imagination, but very real. It came from a cooking fire outside the shelter beneath which she was sprawled, and its stench was making her eyes smart and her throat raw. She smothered a scream as she saw two shining circles come into her blurred vision. She struggled to sit up and realized the circles were eyes. As her own eyes became accustomed to the dimness beneath the shelter, she discovered the eyes belonged to an Aborigine woman who sat back on her haunches, staring unblinkingly at her.

Caroline ventured a weak smile, trying not to stare at the woman's full, drooping breasts, gleaming like ebony in the firelight.

"Will you help me?" she whispered. "I want—I want—my man—"

The thickness in her throat threatened to choke her again, and she forced it down angrily. Had she become such a poor wretch that she couldn't think for herself anymore? But without Luke she felt so helpless, so alone.

The black woman continued to stare, clearly not understanding. Then she got up and went to the fire, spearing a piece of meat and bringing it to the shelter. She pointed to Caroline's belly and then her own, making expanding movements. In an instant, Caroline saw that the woman was also pregnant, her protruding belly taut against the black skin. For some reason, the fact that the men had put her with this woman gave Caroline back some of her spirit. Besides, a woman was far less frightening to deal with than the fearsome men.

"You want me to eat this disgusting stuff in order to make the child big and healthy like yours, I suppose? And while yours will live and grow in the tribe, mine will be slaughtered. Well, thank you very much for your trouble, but I'll starve first!"

She gave a sudden strangled cry as the woman leapt toward her and thrust the lump of meat into her mouth. It burned her mouth, and its taste was acid. Caroline twisted against it, and the hot bloody juices ran down her neck and into her hair. She felt filthy and defiled, but she clamped her lips tightly together. The Lord only knew what kind of animal the woman was trying to make her eat, but she knew she could never accept it. She retched suddenly, and the woman sprang back in alarm, tossing the meat away from her and screaming out

196

a string of words.

Astonished, Caroline had no idea what she had done, but the woman hurried away from the shelter and returned with something that resembled black doughy bread. She motioned to Caroline to eat, who this time took a tiny, careful bite. It was quite sweet-tasting and palatable, and she realized that she was ravenous. Hungrily she tore at the bread and finished every scrap. If she had to live on it for three months, she thought dizzily, then so be it. Anything was better than the half-cooked flesh of some unknown animal.

Later she was brought a drink of water and nothing else. The Aborigine woman who was obviously her guardian motioned her to go to the bushes for her needs and waited for her. Sick to her stomach with humiliation, Caroline complied, but it was gradually dawning on her that at least the two of them were set apart from the rest of the village. Something Luke said had begun to make sense. The two women were both pregnant and were therefore thought to be mysterious and revered creatures. For as long as it lasted . . .

She accepted that he'd had no choice in abandoning her and felt an unbidden longing that the charade could be true, that she did indeed carry his child in her belly. Just as quickly she knew that it was a futile and terrible longing, for the child was doomed to die before it was even born. Poor, sweet baby . . .

The woman was shouting at her now, and she hastily straightened her clothes and came out from the bushes with her head high. She might be revered in the tribe's eyes, Caroline thought angrily, but this woman obviously didn't see her in the same light. She prodded Caroline all the way back to the shelter they were obviously to share.

"There's no need to be so pushy! That's what I'll

call you since I hardly think you'll tell me your name."

She felt a glimmer of devilment as the woman made no response. She stabbed at her chest.

"Me Caroline. *Caroline,*" she repeated loudly. "You Pushy. *Pushy.* You understand?"

The woman shrugged. "Ka," she said, pointing at Caroline. Then she flattened her drooping breasts. "Pu-shy."

"That's right!" Caroline said. "Me Ka. You Pushy."

It was the tiniest victory, and one that no one could share but herself. But it made her feel better. And anything was preferable to dwelling on the fact that she could face certain death at any moment the tribe decided to dismiss her lies.

She lay down on the crude bed of straw and leaves opposite Pushy's, trying to make her mind a blank and willing sleep to come. If she let her thoughts wander, she would find the hopelessness of her situation too much to bear and would rush out into the dark Aborigine night seeking help. And out there in the darkness, there was no help, only the lurking horrors of snakes and spiders and wild beasts . . . and the certain risk of a tribal spear hurled into her neck.

But out there somewhere in the darkness, there was also Luke, and she prayed that he would rescue her soon. However much she raged against him, he was her only hope.

When she awoke, it was daylight, the sun was beating down relentlessly once more, and Luke hadn't come for her. Caroline felt the blackness of despair seeping through her again. She had been so sure he would come stealthily in the night and somehow get her away.

The black woman came into the shelter and thrust a crudely fashioned plate toward her. On it was another disgusting mess of food, together with more of the black doughy bread. Caroline tasted the food gingerly, but it was as inedible as it looked. She spat it out and ate only the bread. The woman shrugged, uncaring, and obviously resentful of having to share her space with this white woman.

"I don't exactly like it here either!" Caroline muttered to her. "I only came here to find my father, but you wouldn't understand about that, would you?"

The black eyes stared back at her unblinkingly. And all through that long, blisteringly hot day, the eyes watched her wherever she went, whether it was into the bushes or tentatively to the cooking pot to see if there was anything faintly more appetizing to eat. She was never left alone.

Late in the day, she was taken to the chief and his attendants for an inspection. To her horror they took turns prodding her belly, and then the chief's hands reached for her breasts. She had already observed how pendulous and swollen with milk were the pregnant black woman's breasts, so in due course hers would be expected to be the same.

They were obviously not as yet, but at least she was fully formed. She felt briefly detached from herself as if watching the scene from a distance, and she was almost hysterical in her relief at having full breasts for the benefit of an Aborigine chief's inspection.

For a moment she closed her eyes as the prodding went on. As yet, she hadn't been made to strip. If once she was, and those scrawny fingers probed further, she knew she would just want to die. There would be no possibility then of closing her eyes to what was happening and pretending it was happening to someone else.

She heard the tribesman grunt, and as he gazed into her face with that impenetrable stare, Caroline was certain he could see right through her. How could he not know this was all a sham? she thought despairingly.

"Woman big," the chief said, his hands making cupping movements to demonstrate his meaning further. "Woman good for *prinka*."

"Thank you," she muttered. She squirmed inside. It wasn't altogether fashionable to be *big* in the way the black meant, but she supposed she must be grateful for it now.

By the time the pregnant woman pushed her back toward their shelter, she began to feel bruised all over and as though she were being treated like an animal. She hated the woman, and it was obvious the woman hated her.

"Why don't you help me escape since you resent me so much?" she said to her. She knew she wouldn't be understood, but a day of unnerving silent stares from the other was beginning to affect her badly now.

She made gestures to herself and the wild bush beyond, and still the woman stared at her without expression. In the end, Caroline gave up. Nothing was going to save her. Once they discovered that she carried no child, they would kill her. And if she were pregnant then the baby would be killed.

With a primitive maternal instinct, she prayed she was not pregnant. Even if it meant her own death would come the sooner, she couldn't bear an innocent child born out of her love for Luke to be so cruelly sacrificed.

With the thought came a renewed bitterness toward Luke. Love? What did he know of love? And what foolishness had possessed to her to mistake the natural coupling of a man and a woman for love? She turned her face into her rank-smelling bed for her second night of captivity and wept into it.

The routine continued. During the days some of the other women came to stare at her. She found their jabbering tongues unnerving and frightening. It became clear that some were openly jealous of her. She couldn't imagine why. Did they honestly think that her presence threatened their status with their menfolk? A couple of days later the reason for their jealousy became obvious.

She had seen the chief and a group of tribesmen go off into the bush, presumably on a hunting trip. There were only the women and children left in the village and a small group of younger men who were intent on gambling around the cooking fires. There was a lot of raucous laughter going on, and Caroline wondered if this might not be a good time to try an escape. But even as she thought it, she rejected the idea.

Where would she go? And what might she encounter? If not some wild animal that would tear her to pieces, then she might run full tilt into the hunting party and they would show her no mercy. She had no real choice but to stay where she was. She languished on her miserable bed all morning until the sun was high overhead and she had no breath left in her from its relentless heat.

The gambling group was getting noisier, and then she realized they were coming her way. Pushy had realized it, too, and was standing guard outside their shelter, her arms folded. She looked ludicrously aggressive, Caroline thought, with the great breasts propped up on her folded arms and the swollen belly beneath. But this was no time for such observation, and she heard Pushy speak rapidly to the gamblers.

There were three young men nearing the shelter

201

now. All had leering faces, and Caroline hunched her knees together as if to minimize her own body and hide it from their lecherous eyes. Then, as if it were boldly written in her father's newspaper headlines, she guessed instantly why they were here.

She had no idea what their punishment might be, but that didn't seem to worry them. In the mysterious code of men, gambling in any culture would seem to be an acceptable way of claiming a prize, Caroline thought bitterly. And from their lewd gestures and the proud evidence of their young naked loins, she was undoubtedly the prize. They were intent on ravishing her and still arguing over who was the victor. Or maybe they were all to take turns, she thought in horror.

Pushy spread her arms wide as if to keep them from entering the crude shelter. The young men laughed, easily putting her to one side, and one of the men dropped to his knees beside Caroline. She smelt him, rank and powerful, and almost gagged.

"Keep away from me!" she shrieked. "I'll kill you before I let you touch me!"

She raked his face with her finger nails, but his howl of rage seemed to be tinged with delight. She had marked him, and that would seem to be some kind of measure of prestige. She felt sickened and terrified, and drew herself in as tightly as possible. One of the others continued to argue with Pushy while the third threw himself down on Caroline and tried to pry open her legs.

Dear God, it was all going to happen here and now while the others watched. The humiliation of it drew wild sobs from her throat. Then she heard women shrieking, and several of them appeared, fighting and flailing at the other two young men, but none came to pull her ravisher off her. Presumably the victor was to be allowed his enjoyment.

She felt him yank up her gown and then the

touch of his fingers on her skin. He pushed her apart roughly, and she heard him muttering in his own language as he paused to gaze at her. Caroline closed her eyes, knowing she could do nothing to stop this now. He had her pinned down, and his slobbering mouth was inching nearer to her. She felt his hot breath and then the tip of his tongue on her breast, and she bit her lips hard, knowing the penetration of his swollen member must surely follow.

A sudden crack of gunshot in the distance made the man jerk up his head and pause for a moment. It was enough to let her twist sideways and scramble away from him, rolling out of the shelter as hard as she could. The Aborigine women had been hovering there, and now they grabbed her and surrounded her, as if to save her. But she knew very well it was to save face for themselves. None of them would want the white woman to savor the pleasures of their own men.

Caroline didn't care about their reasons, though. All she knew was that for the moment she was safe, and she clung, sobbing, to the nearest woman's arms.

"Thank God! I don't want your men. I only want to get away. You must help me. You *must*. Can't you see I'll always be a threat to you as long as I'm here? Please *help* me!"

She might have been talking to the air. The blank faces stared back at her, and the woman to whom she clung shook her off in irritation. But the young men had slunk away now, muttering, and then the women had a kind of consultation among themselves.

When the hunting party returned, it was obvious that the incident was being reported and that the women were maddened by what had so nearly happened. As far as Caroline could see, the young men weren't going to be punished for their "sport," but the concession, if it could be called that, was that from then on there were always other women near the shelter whenever the hunting parties were away from the camp, and the young men never bothered her again. That at least was some comfort, but still the ordeal of captivity went on . . .

Chapter Eleven

The days merged together. It could have been three or six or ten. Apart from the sense of isolation from everything that was normal in her life, Caroline found the boredom of captivity almost intolerable. She wasn't encouraged to join in anything, nor did she want to. She spent hours just lying on her bed, wondering what was to become of her. She knew it was doing her no good at all to be so lethargic, but her senses seemed to have become so dulled that she strongly suspected she was being drugged. And she wasn't even alert enough to care anymore.

She welcomed the hours of darkness when she could at least get some relief from the heat of the day and blot out all that had happened. Most of all, she blotted out all her loving feelings for Luke Garston. She was certain he had abandoned her now. He would never come for her, and she should have known she couldn't trust him.

She concentrated instead on hating him, just as she hated everything here. She hated the way the blacks gathered around the fires every night, indulging in some kind of tribal ritual that excluded the women, until they were too stupefied to do anything but drop with sleep. She hated Pushy, whom she knew now could never be a friend or an ally. And always, when the sun went down, she tried to relax and sleep. For a few hours at least, she could find peace in oblivion.

One night she couldn't have said what awoke her. There were no human sounds to be heard. There was only the crackling of the fires that were kept constantly burning and the nocturnal sounds of the animal life that stalked and flourished in the darkness. She lifted her head cautiously. Across the width of the shelter, she could see the dark hump of Pushy's body, and she could hear her soft heavy breathing. Pushy too, slept like the dead . . .

And then she gasped with terror as a hand was clamped over her mouth. The sound gurgled in her throat, and she could just make out a tall form crouching beside her in the darkness and behind it several others. *Luke* and their own Brundy boys . . . She couldn't even whisper his name because her throat was so dry and his fingers were pressed tightly against her mouth to stop her from uttering a sound. She nodded quickly as she clutched at his arm.

He motioned for her to crawl outside the shelter as if she were making for the bushes, and she did so in fear and trembling. At any moment she expected to hear war cries behind her and for Pushy to raise the alarm. But if the other woman heard anything, she was obviously keeping very silent and protecting her own territorial rights. Caroline was immensely thankful now that their shelter had been kept far apart from the rest of the tribe. It meant that Luke could finally come for her unseen and rescue her. She was too thankful to care about anything else.

206

They sped through the night without saying a word until they were well away from the Aboriginal settlement. She gasped every time her feet touched something unmentionable, whether it was hard, or soft and squashy and protesting, and she dared not think what it might be.

They were fast descending the mountainside, with the boys who had accompanied Luke leading the way. She was sobbing with fatigue, but the fear of pursual was stronger. They didn't stop until they came to what seemed to be a small clearing in the bush, and then Luke pulled her into his arms.

"From now on, woman, unless you want to get yourself killed, you'll do exactly as I say. Do you hear?" he said cruelly against her pounding breath.

She didn't have time to answer before his mouth was crushing down on hers, and for a dizzy moment it felt as if the kiss truly meant something to him, as if he were truly thankful to have her back. When the kiss ended she went limp against him.

"Oh Luke, I was so frightened—"

"So you should have been," he snapped. "You're the most reckless female it's ever been my misfortune to meet, and if it hadn't been for finding Jojo and the others waiting for us some distance away from the camp, I doubt that I'd have bothered coming back for you at all."

She gaped at him in disbelief and growing rage. She was eternally grateful to the Brundy crew for not leaving her to her fate, but it seemed they'd shown more loyalty to her than Luke himself. And she couldn't ignore what he'd said.

"You mean you had no intention of coming back for me, despite what you said when you abandoned me back there?" she sputtered in a fury.

"I had to say something to calm you, even

though I knew it was virtually hopeless. It was only when the boys and I observed what went on every night that we knew there was a chance," he said brutally.

"And what was that?" she said.

By now she was enveloped in a mixture of grief and anger that he really hadn't intended coming back for her. She was too distressed to wonder if he spoke as he did to hide his real feelings. She had vainly hoped he would truly have moved heaven and earth to save her. If her grief were as tangible as if she had suffered a bereavement, her anger made her very bones feel icy cold at this callous treatment.

"The men sat around their fires every night drinking fire juice which I suspected was from fermented berries, but whatever it was, it drugged most of them senseless in a very short time. It didn't take much to overpower the guard who kept watch, and then we were able to come back for you. Fortunately you were kept well away from the rest because of your condition."

Something in his voice made her wary. "You make it all sound too easy. And you say it rendered most of them senseless. But not all of them?"

"Not all. The chief and his aides were too canny to drink as much as the rest, and they challenged us, albeit pretty halfheartedly."

"So just how did you accomplish the rescue?" Caroline demanded. She was sure she was mad to pursue this, but her questioning mind wouldn't let it be. The tribesmen were far too aggressive to let her go without a fight.

She saw Luke's arrogant smile in the moonlight.

"I bartered for you with a small bag of pearls, my sweet. It meant little to me, but when the chief adorns himself with them in the days to come, he'll probably be reminded of the white woman. You'll agree that his fantasies are preferable to the fate he had planned for you."

"You bastard!" Caroline raged. In her frustration she hit his chest. "You have the gall to say you bartered for me with a bag of pearls that meant little to you! I suppose that's all I mean to you as well?"

He gripped her fast, his voice steely. "You've meant a deal of trouble to me, Miss Caroline Rowe, from the day we met. The sooner we come to a decision on our future, the better I'll be pleased."

"*We* have no future! How many times do I have to say it?" she almost screamed at him. "How can you think I would ever want to share my future with you when you constantly humiliate me?"

"It seems to me that I constantly rescue you," he said relentlessly. "How many lives do you owe me now?"

She bit her trembling lips. It was true, damn him, and there was no argument about that. And it was all her fault that they were here in the first place. She went limp again, all the fight gone out of her.

"You're right," she said dully. "You must think me the biggest fool that ever lived. Why you would ever want to share a future with me I can't imagine."

"Can't you?" He laughed softly. "Well, we'll discuss that later. Meanwhile, there's somebody I want you to meet."

She felt her heart leap, and then he shook his head.

"No, not him, Caroline. When will you realize your father is almost certainly dead? But I suppose you never will unless someone other than myself tells you so."

It was so true she had the grace to feel shame-faced for a moment. He had already done so much for her, more than any man could be expected to do for a stranger, and she rewarded him by constantly putting him in danger. And despite everything, she did love him.

"Oh, Luke—" she began, her voice trembling, her eyes suddenly soft.

"Later," he said.

She nodded weakly. Whatever she was about to say was probably best kept to herself anyway. Now was certainly not the time to tell him she loved him more than life and that she would trust him anywhere—though even as the words entered her mind, she knew it was true. All the hate in her heart had dissipated like moondust, and she knew it had only been an illusion. At the time of her captivity, any strong emotion she could concentrate on was preferable to giving up. The hatred had served its purpose. Now there was only love.

She heard a strange clanking sound coming from the bushes, and her heart hammered against her chest as she heard the boys begin jabbering together. She clung to Luke.

"Don't be alarmed. It's only Mad Jack. He's the one I want you to meet."

Whoever Mad Jack was, he didn't sound the most reputable of persons, Caroline thought in some alarm. By now the boys had lit a fire in the middle of the clearing, and the warmth was comforting in the night air. In its light, she saw the bent figure of someone approaching them, someone she would have given a wide berth to in other days.

But these were not those halcyon other days at

home in England. This was here and now, and this old fellow with the creased and wizened face seemed to be in perpetual motion as he danced from one foot to the other.

"So this is your little lady," he wheezed. "It's my pleasure to make your sainted acquaintance, ma'am, and to give you any assistance I can."

Caroline was alerted at once. She could ignore his ragged clothing, the gun over his shoulder with the carcass of some dead animal carelessly hanging beside it, and the assortment of pots and pans he seemed to carry about his person. She could ignore the rank smell of him, in the swift realization that Luke had surely wanted her to meet this man for one purpose only. She found herself clinging tightly to Luke's hand.

"Do you have news of my father, Mr. Jack?" she asked breathlessly.

"Call me Mad," he said easily. "Everybody does."

The wild old mountain man suddenly seemed to dissolve into the ground. In reality, he merely squatted down where he was, crossing his legs as effortlessly as if they had no bones inside them. The pots and pans settled all around him into some kind of clanking protective circle.

"Mr. Mad—"

"Not *Mr.* Mad—just Mad," he instructed. "You ain't deaf, are you, lady?"

"Do you have any news of my father?" Caroline snapped, losing all patience with this irritating little man.

He put his head on one side as if to consider the question. "Well now, I might and I might not. Like I told your man here, such questions take a bit o' pondering on—"

"I don't have time for pondering! My father could be dead, and I need to be sure about what's happened to him."

She bit her lips. It was rare that she put it into words. She knew that the likelihood of her father's surviving all this time was remote, but she still had to hope. She had survived, so there must be a chance for others.

"Tell the lady what you told me, Mad," Luke said sternly.

"You're all in too much of a blasted hurry, beggin' your pardon, I'm sure, me lady," he said in an exaggerated show of humility. "But seein' as I've nothing else to do this evening and that I'm partial to a bit o' cooked meat if you'll oblige me, then I'll tell you all I know."

"The boys will get some food ready soon," Luke said. "Tell her, or you get nothing."

Caroline sank to the ground beside him, too weary to argue any longer, and Mad Jack clearly saw he'd prevaricated enough. Luke joined her, his arm around her shoulders. She leaned against it for support, but she was too tense to relax properly.

"Seems to me there's more English than Abos in the mountains these days," the old man grumbled.

"What do you mean?" Caroline exclaimed.

He shrugged. "I seen 'em, didn't I? Half a dozen of 'em, half-drowned by the looks of 'em and staggering about as if they was crazy with grog or summat."

"Where—and when?" she almost begged.

"Oh, weeks ago now," Mad Jack said vaguely. "I ain't no good with clocks, and the days don't matter none to me. I travel when it suits me, see?"

She didn't see, and she didn't care. She could have hit this odd bird who didn't seem to understand how vitally important it was to her to find out more.

"But these men, Mr.—Mad. Was one of them

tall and distinguished-looking, with gray hair and—"

He burst into a cackling laugh, dragging a grog bottle from his pocket. He took a long slurping drink and gave a loud belch before he replied. "They was all dregs from the sea when I seen 'em, lady! God knows what they might have been in better days, but I'd say they weren't long for this world by the time they reached shore. They was all as crazed as me by then!"

"Caroline, leave it—" Luke began, but she shook him off angrily.

"Where did they go?" she persisted. "In which direction were they heading?"

"Staggering, more like," Mad Jack slurred. He waved vaguely. "South, o' course. Nobody in their right senses would go north into the wilderness— not that they was in their right senses, mind."

He laughed again, as if he'd made a tremendous joke, and took another drink. It wouldn't be long before he was out cold, Caroline thought.

"South? Do you mean toward Sydney?"

She heard Luke sigh, but she couldn't give up now. She was coming to life again with the first real clue as to her father's whereabouts coming from this disreputable person.

"Oh, ah, Sydney, o' course," Mad Jack said comfortably. "That's where all the nobs go, I daresay. Heard about it, I did, but I ain't got no wish to go there, not even on me old faithful."

"Your old faithful?" The smell of cooking was beginning to waft toward them from the cooking fire now, and she could see that Mad Jack's mouth was starting to water.

"Me trusty steed, lady. I'll introduce you in the morning, and if you're in the market for a coupla his friends, I'll be glad to round 'em up for you."

213

Before she could ask him anything more, he had got to his feet with the same agility as he'd dropped down. He ambled unsteadily toward the fire, where the boys were lifting out half-cooked pieces of meat. Mad Jack was determined to get his share. She turned away from him as he shoved the portions into his mouth, disregarding the way they obviously burned him, and held onto Luke's hands.

"Luke, I must go on. I have to—"

Her voice began to dwindle uncertainly. For how could she expect him to go still farther, chasing a dream that wasn't even his dream? And without him, what chance did she have in this unpredictable terrain?

"I'll make a bargain with you," he said quietly. "Mad Jack says there's a village of sorts some distance south from here, where there are a few respectable white farmers. We'll get that far, and if we find no more evidence of your father in that time, either on the way or by word of mouth from the farmers, then we go back. Is it a bargain?"

Her mouth was dry, but it was as much as she could reasonably expect from any man. And she was too exhausted to continue the argument.

"It's a bargain," she murmured. "But just one more question. Where's this horse of Mad Jack's? His trusty steed, as he called it."

Luke gave a short laugh. "You'd better wait until morning to see his trusty steed, my sweet. You've had enough shocks for one night. Sleep now."

Somehow she was lying down, and he was covering her with a blanket. She was near enough to the fire to feel its hazy warmth and to be drowsily conscious of the sounds of voices and the clank of Mad Jack's accoutrements, but none of it mattered. All that mattered was that she was safe

214

again, and the incongruity of the thought didn't even occur to her. The dubious safety in the middle of the Australian bush wasn't the important thing anyway. Safe with Luke was all that mattered. And when he finally came beneath the blanket and she felt the strength and warmth of his body alongside her, she gave a deep sighing breath, as if she were truly home at last.

She awoke to sunlight streaming down on her and the sight of a huge enigmatic beast towering above her, its jaws chomping nonchalantly as it stared at her. She screamed, scrambling to get away from the beast, which she now saw was resting on all fours beside her, and she felt Luke's arms holding her tight.

"Don't be alarmed. It's only Mad Jack's camel."

"What?"

She glowered up at Luke, hearing the laughter in his voice. She had never seen a camel before, though she had heard about them, great awkward-looking beasts that they were. But surely they lived in the desert countries, not here in the Australian bush? As if reading her thoughts, Luke gave her a little shake.

"You're obviously not as educated as you thought, my darling. Camels are excellent animals for surviving in this country, where there are deserts and mountains as well as the bush. They can travel long distances without water, and Mad Jack is adept at rounding them up."

She stared at him in disbelief, and then at the ungainly hump on the camel's back, in front of which was a coarse blanket containing what was presumably more of Mad Jack's paraphernalia.

"You're not trying to tell me we're going to travel

215

on one of those things?" she gasped.

"We are if we want to reach the village in reasonable comfort and speed," he informed her.

Comfort and speed were not the things she would associate with these lumbering animals, Caroline thought seethingly. But she saw the sense in Luke's comment. Anything was better than walking. Her feet were so sore she knew she would never dance on them again. . . . The thought was so unexpected, she felt her throat thicken.

How long was it since she had danced in an elegant ballroom, with the brilliance of crystal chandeliers trying to outshine the glittering ball gowns of the ladies and the gallantry of their escorts? So long ago . . . a lifetime ago . . .

"Caroline? Where have you gone?" she heard Luke say softly. She gave a start, her eyes blurring.

"Home," she said huskily.

His arms folded around her. She leaned against him, wishing she could blot out everything in her life but knowing him. Wishing she had met him in that other lifetime when her life had been well-ordered and the sunny future of Sir William Rowe's daughter had been assured.

She felt the sudden nuzzle of rough skin on her neck and a strange barking sound. She screamed, leaping away from Luke, the nostalgic mood vanishing at once as she saw the camel's face close to hers.

"He's taken to you, lady," she heard another voice say. She got to her feet and saw Mad Jack grinning down at her. "You can't have Roxy though, but I've found you a mate just like him. And there's a couple more for your boys."

"He was up and about before sunup," Luke said, with obvious admiration.

It was a strange world, Caroline thought, when

you admired such an undignified little figure for his prowess in rounding up a couple of camels . . . but her heart sank when Roxy got to his feet and she saw the great size of him.

"I couldn't possibly ride on him," she gasped. "I'd be dizzy and sick."

"You'll soon get used to it, lady," Mad Jack said cheerfully. "If you've ever bin on a ship, then you won't have no trouble. These old fellers ain't called the ships of the desert for nothin'!"

"What's your price, Mad?" Luke interrupted.

"Whatever you got, mate," the man answered. "I can bargain with any damn thing, even one o' your blacks if you want to part with one."

Caroline listened with horror. Surely Luke wouldn't . . .

"I don't bargain with human flesh," he said coldly. "A handful of pearls is my only offer. Take it or leave it, man."

Caroline saw Jack's little eyes gleam. It seemed a pretty good bargain to her when she presumed that camels were roaming wild for anyone to rope. But it must take some skill, she acknowledged, and she certainly wouldn't care to try it. She saw Mad Jack nod. He spat on his palm and the two men slapped hands to seal the bargain.

"Let's eat, and then we'll get started," Luke said to her. She got up carefully, keeping her eyes on the staring camel. But apart from the barking noises he made, he seemed docile enough and she hoped their own steeds were of the same temperament. She could see them now, tethered to a tree, with the crew already loading supplies onto their backs. She smothered her nervousness and moved to the embers of the fire where huge eggs were frying in some of the fat from last night's meat. A pot of water was boiling to make the strange sweet

217

tea that she now knew came from a bush plant that thrived everywhere.

Quickly revived by the meal and the drink, they said goodbye to Mad Jack. He had given them a few instructions on the way to mount the camels, but the boys seemed to know it by instinct. The beasts squatted on the ground in total unconcern, chewing as usual, while the riders climbed on their backs. Then, with one swift movement the camels rose to their full height and began their swaying gait.

Caroline felt dizziness sweep over her as she followed suit. She sat behind Luke, clinging tightly to him, with the hump of the camel supporting her back. Without it, she was certain she'd have fallen straight to the ground. Only the blanket beneath them gave her any kind of stability, but even so, she wondered how she would ever last the distance to the village.

"You do intend to let me breathe, I suppose?" Luke said when they had gone a few hundred yards. "I find your dependence on me quite delightful, sweetheart, but I'd appreciate it if your fingernails didn't dig into my chest."

She released her grip slightly. If she tried very hard, she could just imagine she was on board ship, she thought, but only when she closed her eyes. When she opened them, she was aware how far they were from the sandy ground, and how the camels blundered through the bush without regard at how the trees snatched at her face and scratched her cheeks and arms.

"I don't like this one little bit," she muttered through gritted teeth.

"I can think of better ways of traveling," Luke agreed. "But just remember it was your idea to go on. We could be safely back on Brundy Island now and picking up the threads of our life again."

"And you just remember that I came here to live in Sydney with my father, not on some remote island," she said smartly.

"Oh, I remember. You never let me forget it," Luke said. "But circumstances can change the direction of people's lives, Caroline. You should learn to be more flexible. Take life more easily, like these camels. Nothing hurries them, nor moves them, if they don't want to be moved."

She had no wish to be compared to camels. But by late afternoon, when the heat of the sun and plodding gait of the animals was having a soporific effect on her, she discovered the truth of Luke's words. They came upon a billabong, that strangely quaint name the Aborigines gave to a pool, and Luke had no sooner said they would stop for a drink, than the animals dropped to their knees a short distance from the water and refused to budge.

"They're stubborn devils," he said after they had pulled and tugged on the ropes around the animals' necks to no avail. "We'll just have to tie them up while we have our fill of water. They won't move again until they're good and ready."

They wouldn't budge all day. Jojo and the boys tried shouting, dangling meat in front of their noses and firing off shots at their feet, but nothing moved them. There was nothing for it but to wait patiently, which was more than Caroline could stand.

"Look, there's no point in getting frustrated and upset," Luke pointed out. "The camels are our best means of transport, and we've come much farther today than we would ever have done on foot and more safely too. I suggest we bathe in the billabong and then make camp here for the night. We'll all be fresher in the morning."

"Are you sure this place is safe?" she shuddered. After the experience in the mountains with the Aborigines, she wondered if they were about to be captured all over again.

"We can only hope so," he said, which didn't give her much comfort at all. But the boys had been splashing about in the billabong for some time already without incident, so she was ready to assume that they could do the same. The water looked too cool and inviting to resist, and as she waded into it, she felt its soothing effect on her body. Only then did she realize just how stiff and bruised and jaded she felt after the uncomfortable ride on the camel.

She saw Luke dip his head beneath the water to come up shaking his head like a frisky puppy, and with a sudden recklessness she did the same. The sensation of her damp hair clinging to her skin was almost sensual, and she gave her own head a great shake. Her long hair whirled about her shoulders, and she closed her eyes for a moment, throwing back her head to the sun as if in supplication.

She felt Luke's arms go around her, and her drenched body was pressed close to his.

"Even like this you have the proud look of a Greek goddess," he said, his voice suddenly husky. "Have you any idea what you do to me, my goddess?"

She was only too aware of what was happening to him as his leg gently forced her own apart. It had been so long since they had had time for one another, and she felt the urgency in him now. She glanced around, but the boys had long left the water in search of the evening's meal. She and Luke were alone except for the gently chewing camels.

"What do you feel, my goddess?" he asked, smil-

220

ing into her eyes. He pushed her hand gently down through the water to where the hard evidence of his desire strained against her.

She felt herself blush. They had come together so few times as yet, but desire always seared between them like a pulsating flame. If they lived and loved through a hundred years, every time would be like the first time, she thought wildly. It would always be new and exciting. She knew it in her soul, even though modesty would never let her voice such thoughts . . .

"You shouldn't ask a lady these things," she whispered, knowing that although she spoke the conventional words, her eyes and face must have shown that her desire matched his in every way.

"Then I'll tell you what you feel," he said, his hand covering her own beneath the water. "You feel a man's need for his woman. You feel that a man must have his woman now. And I dare you to deny that you want me as much as I want you, my sweet, when everything about you is telling me otherwise."

His free hand brushed lightly over her breasts, where the nipples were taut against the sodden fabric of her gown. She gasped at the frisson of his touch, suddenly aflame with hunger for him.

"Yes, oh Luke, yes . . ." she whispered.

She hardly remembered how they waded out of the water to the haven of the bush nearby, nor the hasty removal of their clothes, which lay steaming on the bushes in the sun. The only thing that mattered was that Luke's body was covering hers, and minutes later there was the sweet remembered penetration of love as she opened up to receive him.

All thought of modesty was gone as she clung to him now. Hazily she thought that this was the way God had fashioned Adam and Eve, to lie together

221

in the open in His wild and wonderful new world, naked and joined in ecstasy. If it was a blasphemous thought, she dismissed it totally. How could it be so, when human nature demanded that man and woman be joined to produce their future generations?

"You pleasure me greatly, my goddess," she heard Luke say softly as he thrust into her.

"Please, don't call me that," she mumbled, her senses beginning to scatter as the spreading sense of release and ecstasy filled her loins. "I'm no goddess, only your woman . . ."

He bent to kiss her breasts and then gathered her into him as the moment of climax approached. As she felt the hot thrusting rush of his seed, her eyes blurred with tears. She had no idea why she cried then. It was too primeval a moment to analyze, too precious to spoil with words or thoughts . . .

He lay on her, momentarily spent, and she gloried in the weight of him. Her man, for now and all time.

"Do you doubt now that we were meant to be together?" he whispered into her damp tangled hair, just as if he could see into her soul. She shook her head slowly.

"At such moments, I never doubt it," she said honestly.

He was unusually silent, then he rolled away from her.

"Yet, my sweet darling, you still don't give yourself to me totally, do you?"

She stared at him, the mood imperceptibly changing. "Don't I? I should have thought you'd just had ample evidence of that!"

He circled her nipple with his finger, and she gave a small shiver at the contact. He pulled her to her feet and they held each other, still naked, for a few moments.

"Once we've sorted out your problem, then we'll have proper time for each other. Until then, we merely go through the motions, don't we?"

If she had disappointed him in some way, she didn't know how. And she was suddenly angry at his seeming censure. He would have had women before her, perhaps many women, so naturally he would be comparing her and finding her lacking. At such a thought, she was both humiliated and acutely aware and ashamed of her nakedness. Without another word, she scrambled for her clothes, picking off bits of leaf and grass from her limbs at the same time.

"Leave them to dry a bit longer. I'll fetch a blanket for you to cover yourself," Luke said sharply.

"Thank you. You do have some gentlemanly feelings then," she said, her voice muffled.

"When have I ever treated you as less than a lady?" he said before striding off to fetch the blanket on the camel's back for her, completely unperturbed by his own nakedness.

She stared at him in disbelief. He really believed what he said. He'd ravished her and kept her captive—albeit in considerable luxury in his home—he'd bellowed at her and made no secret of the fact that he considered her the epitome of foolish females, and he truly believed he treated her like a lady!

She should be furious with him . . . but for all that, Caroline knew there was an exhilaration inside her whenever he was near. He made her more alive than any man she had ever known. How could she possibly compare the milksop gentlemen who had danced attendance on her at genteel London parties and receptions, with Luke Garston? There was no comparison at all.

As for being treated as a lady . . . She looked inward and knew that to be Luke Garston's woman was preferable in every way to being the finest lady in the land. With him she was all that, and more.

She felt a spark of laughter bubbling up inside her as she saw him striding back toward her now, the rough blanket tossed casually over one shoulder, the only bit of clothing he wore. One day, when she was good and ready and the time was right, she might even tell him what she thought about him . . .

Chapter Twelve

They awoke in each other's arms, still wrapped in the blanket Luke had thrown around them some time during the night. The campfire still smoldered nearby, and the morning sounds of the brilliantly colored birds and the darting cicadas buzzed and vibrated on the still air. It was a beautiful day, blue, golden and sparkling. But, with a kind of sixth sense, Caroline knew instantly that something was wrong.

She lifted her head cautiously, embarrassed to realize she was still naked. She crept out of the blanket and reached for her bone-dry clothing, still draped over a nearby bush. She felt a mite better when she was dressed, and she looked down at Luke's sleeping face. He looked totally relaxed, one naked arm flung out as if still holding her.

For a second, she felt enormously tender toward him, and then the feeling was quickly followed by resentment. Something was definitely wrong. She didn't know what it was, but Luke should be awake, as aware of it as herself. He was supposed to be her protector . . .

"Luke, wake up!"

She knelt down beside him, shaking his arm and speaking the words in a whisper.

She looked fearfully over her shoulder as if some marauding band of natives were about to descend on them at any moment. But there was nothing. No human sound other than that of their own breathing . . . and now she knew what was wrong.

"Luke, the boys have gone," she said in a panic. "There's none of their stuff about, and the camels have gone too. There's only one beast left—"

He threw an arm around her lazily. "Stay calm, Caroline," he said. "I sent them on ahead with a message long before you were awake. They'll be waiting for us at the village."

At his simple explanation, she felt utterly foolish. She sat back on her heels, staring down at him resentfully. For the last few minutes she had been terrified. The sweet lassitude and the comforting sense of security that had filled her ever since their lovemaking last night had disappeared. She was disoriented all over again, her nerves on edge. And the knowledge that they didn't even have the added protection of numbers, should they be attacked, made her doubly angry.

"How could you be so *stupid?*" she raged at Luke. "We could be miles from the village, and we're completely alone. Any fool could see it would have made sense to keep the boys with us!"

"This fool can certainly see you've got all your faculties back," he said, still in that lazy, indulgent voice that infuriated her so.

"Don't patronize me," she snapped. "I don't know this country, and neither do you, from what you've told me. But from everything I've seen so far, it's hostile and dangerous, and you should never have let the boys go."

226

To her fury, her voice began to shake, and Luke finally recognized the degree of her distress. He sat up, pulling her roughly into his arms.

"My darling, I've not been as reckless as you seem to think. Two of the boys took a ride during the night, and they could see the village in the distance. With normal luck, we should reach it easily by nightfall."

Caroline's relief was tempered by suspicion; nor did she like the oblique reference to "normal luck."

"Why was it necessary to send them on ahead? And what message did you send? Was it something about my father?"

Luke didn't answer at once. He reached for his own clothes and shrugged into them.

"Indirectly," he said at last. "The boys are to inform the homesteaders that we're coming and that we'll be keen to barter for a boat to take us back to Brundy Island since our own is too far back along the coast to retrieve it. They'll surely have some kind of craft, living on the coastal plain."

She had learned the newspaperman's adeptness at skipping anything of no relevance and only heard the most important words. She leapt to her feet, staring down at him with her hands clenched tightly at her sides.

"You never meant to take me any farther, did you?" she burst out. "Did you know about this village all the time?"

"I may have heard tell of it," he said, his eyes beginning to glint as diamond-hard as hers. "I promised you we'll make enquiries of the homesteaders, and so we will. But you can't deny that I've always said it's a hopeless cause."

"Even after what the blacks and Mad Jack said about the evidence of survivors from a shipwreck?"

His look was full of pity. "My love, you're clinging at straws. These people will say anything if they think it may be worth their while, especially an old reprobate like Mad Jack. Caroline, your father is dead. Why won't you believe that?"

Her eyes seemed to burn as she glared at him.

"You don't know it for a fact, so don't say it! Don't you know it's bad luck?"

He didn't answer. He shook out the blanket and strode over to the fire to stoke up the embers with a stick. She watched him silently as he squatted beside the fire and took out some dried meat from his traveling bag. A can of water from the billabong to boil it in and another to boil up for tea, and they'd have a breakfast of sorts.

Caroline felt a sudden plunging depression. Of course Luke was right, she thought wearily. Her father was almost certainly dead, and she was just keeping her head in the sand not to accept that fact. And if he wasn't . . . A new thought struck her. If he wasn't dead, then somehow *he* would find *her*. If by some miracle he had somehow reached Sydney, then when the trading ship and other ships called there, Sir William Rowe would be making urgent enquiries about his beloved daughter. He would be just as distraught regarding her fate as she was about his. For some reason, she'd never stopped to consider it from his viewpoint before now. But it gave her thoughts a change of direction. It made her think how he must be feeling, too. They were two strong characters, and somehow, if her father still lived, they would surely find one another.

"I'm hungry," she said, her mood shifting to the practicalities of the moment.

"Good," Luke said, just as briefly. "We'll eat and be on our way, providing we can get the damn camel to move."

They might never have been such passionate lovers, Caroline thought bleakly as they chewed the tough meat in silence and washed it down with the hot sweet tea. They suddenly seemed to be poles apart.

He almost certainly regretted the day he had ever set eyes on Miss Caroline Rowe. And she wished fate had never sent her to him. Perversely she thought doggedly that even the height of ecstasy he brought her to wasn't worth the wretchedness of his coldness. And she had no intention of remembering those hours of passion. She would simply blot them from her mind and determine that they wouldn't happen again.

They had been traveling for a couple of hours on the lumbering camel's back with the sun sweltering down upon them, making Caroline feel faint, when the animal was startled by a huge black snake that slithered across its path. The camel raced forward with an unexpected burst of energy.

Caroline screamed, clinging tightly onto Luke, as much in fear of the reptile as the sudden speed with which the camel had moved, threatening to fling her off into the bush. She was thrown from side to side as they rapidly covered the distance, and she felt so nauseous she was sure she was about to disgrace herself at any moment.

And then, with a great scrambling motion, the camel stumbled over some unseen rocks and fell to its knees, throwing both Luke and Caroline off its back. She felt a bursting pain as her head struck a rock, and for a few sickening moments she saw everything doubled. Two camels, two Lukes, two skies . . . and then she saw nothing but blackness.

She came around slowly to the deafening sound

229

of a gunshot very close by. It made her head rock all over again, and her ears were hurt by the blast. For a few minutes she thought she was truly deafened, and then she became aware of small sounds seeping into her brain again.

So she wasn't deaf, and although she felt bruised all over, she wasn't dead. She opened her eyes a fraction. The images in front of her were still fuzzy and blurred, and she panicked again. But they gradually cleared, and she gave a great sob of relief. She wasn't blind either . . .

"Thank God," she heard Luke's voice say roughly. "You were lying there so still, I was afraid."

She made a great attempt to be humorous. If she hadn't done so, she would have dissolved in a fit of weeping.

"Did you think you were going to get rid of me so easily?" she said huskily.

He gathered her to him, and she winced at the effect on her bruised and battered body. He released his hold and circled her gently in his arms.

"I'm sorry, my darling. Where are you hurt? Do you think you can walk?"

She wanted to laugh then. Walk? She doubted that she'd ever walk again. She couldn't even think of standing, let alone *walk* . . .

"No, I can't walk," she almost snapped. "I need to get my breath back, and then I just want to get back on that camel and get away from this awful, awful place. I want—" without warning, and despite all her efforts, her eyes filled with tears—"I just want to feel safe and to sleep in a proper bed with clean sheets."

She realized he wasn't answering, and she blinked the humiliating tears away.

"What?" she asked. "What is it, Luke?"

"I had to shoot the camel," he said shortly.

She stared at him, uncomprehending for a moment, and then she remembered the sound of the gunshot that had made her momentarily deaf. Such an affliction seemed of little importance now, compared with the enormity of what he was telling her. The camel was their one means of reaching the homesteaders' village in reasonable time. Without it . . . She gave a strangled cry and beat her fists against his chest in sheer frustration.

"Why?"

"Its leg was broken when it fell. There was nothing else I could do. I couldn't let it suffer."

Somehow the shortness of his words told her more than anything else that he, too, didn't minimize their plight. They were isolated again without means of transport, and she doubted that she could walk ten yards, let alone a journey that was going to take all day on camel-back.

"So what do we do now?" she said huskily.

"First of all, we assess your injuries and make you as comfortable as possible."

She followed his instructions and flexed her limbs carefully. As far as she could tell, there were no broken bones or sprains, just bruises and a bump on the back of her head, from which a little blood oozed. Mercifully she had been very lucky.

"What about you?" she said with sudden guilt. She hadn't even thought about Luke being hurt as well. But if he had been, then her own chances would have been nil. The guilt doubled as she realized she was still thinking about her own plight. She had become quite selfish and self-centered, she thought with swift shame, and this good man was constantly putting himself in all kinds of danger because of her.

"I'll survive," he said with a twisted smile.

231

"Don't worry, I'm not going to keel over and die and leave you to the ravages of the bush."

She felt her face go hot. "Am I so transparent?" she said in a small voice.

"Sometimes. But I don't blame you. The bush is no place for a woman."

She didn't even care about the arrogance of his words. She couldn't agree with them more. "You're right about that," she said fervently, and she heard him laugh.

"Well, if I've convinced you of it at last, that must be worth something. Now then, let's take a look at your head."

She gritted her teeth while he touched it gently and then bathed it with water from one of their water bags. She knew instinctively he wouldn't use very much since there was no way of knowing when they would find any more. And once they began to move forward, they had no real sense of direction. They could be walking round in circles until they dropped from sheer exhaustion and dehydration. And no one would ever find them except the dingoes or the snakes.

"Luke," she said, clinging to his arm. "do you think we'll ever be able to find the village by ourselves?"

"What do you take me for? Of course we'll find it. We've come this far, and we're not giving up now."

But she knew he wasn't referring to the search for her father. Their own survival was of imminent importance now. She gave a slow, defeated nod, remembering his conditions about giving up the search if they learned nothing more.

"And if there's no definite news of my father when we get there, we go back to Brundy, is that it?"

"That's it. To a proper bed with clean sheets and the arrival of the trading ship."

She swallowed. "Then you'll still take me to Sydney, after all my foolishness?"

He spoke shortly, his voice saying he regretted ever making contact with the irritating Miss Rowe at all, but that he was just as determined to see it through. She felt a liability and a nuisance, and it wasn't a pleasant feeling.

"I've told you I never break a promise. Meantime, we'll rest here until you feel stronger. There's a clearing just ahead. It will be safer there."

She agreed meekly, assuming he meant that they would be able to see any animal life that might be lurking around. She shuddered, wondering just what madness had made her embark on this journey and more than ready to return to Brundy right now . . .

"Let's not waste any more time. I'll try to walk."

She stood up with his help, but swayed alarmingly for a few seconds.

"No, I said we'll rest a while," Luke told her firmly. "A few hours will make little difference, and if we haven't appeared at the village by sundown, the boys will be alerted and come looking for us."

"But that would mean another night in the open," she said. "Oh, Luke —"

"We're together, and we're alive, and that's all that matters, Caroline. Nothing will harm us, I promise, and we've survived so far. Don't you think if your Divine God had wanted to see us off, He'd have done so by now?"

He was as irreverent as ever, but she found an odd comfort in his words. She leaned heavily on him as they walked slowly to the small clearing, and despite the heat of the day, Luke lit the inevi-

233

table fire to keep any curious wildlife away. She sank down beside it wearily, praying that her aching limbs would recover soon. It promised to be a long day.

"I never satisfied your curiosity about how I came to be on Brundy Island, nor how Doctor Sam arrived there, did I?" Luke said abruptly sometime later.

By then, they lay listlessly with the blanket partially covering them to keep out the fiercest rays of the sun. She turned to look at him.

"Is it truth time at last?"

She spoke mockingly until she saw his compressed lips. "Luke, it doesn't matter. It's your business, and I've no right to pry."

"You've every right."

He didn't elaborate, but she knew very well what he meant. He still considered her his property and that made them obligated to one another. But until now, all the openness had been on only her side.

He knew all there was to know about her . . . which wasn't very much, she thought in some surprise. She had had a very normal childhood and an easy passage into society. Her father's business reputation had assured that. Nothing had ruffled the serenity of her life until the sorrow of her mother's death. And then had come the big decision to go to Australia . . .

But aside from those two tumultuous events in her life, all the rest seemed suddenly very dull. It was certainly nothing to be compared with the life of a man who had made good by pearl diving and owning and managing an entire island! Caroline knew that if she'd ever entertained such thoughts before now, she would have laughed out loud at such nonsense. A sophisticated young lady from the city could be ranked streets above such a fellow! The quick shame of such a thought and the knowledge that it was so misguided made the hot color run up her skin.

"Well? Do you want to know, or don't you?"

She jumped, praying he couldn't read what had just been in her mind. Luke Garston was a man of stature in every way, and if she hadn't been instilled with such self-esteem by sharing her father's business world, she would have been humbled by Luke long before now.

And his reasons for being on Brundy, good or bad, she knew no longer mattered. They made no difference to the essence of the man. But she was obviously not going to get the chance to tell him so, even if she wanted to right now. Which she certainly didn't, she thought, because it would only swell his head even more!

"I'm sure you won't tell me anything until you're ready, and only then as much as you want to!" she answered.

"Damn right," Luke said. "But a man's wife has a right to know how he came to be in a different environment from the one he was born into—"

"I'm not your wife—"

"But you will be. Why do you always fight it? I'd have thought with your proper English background, you'd have wanted to make our relationship respectable once we get back to Brundy," he said, his face breaking into a grin.

She looked at him angrily. "You promised to take me on the trading ship, Luke. I'm holding you to that, and I don't think you're the kind of man to break a promise."

"Well, thank you for that. It's about the first complimentary thing you've said to me," he commented.

The thought spun through Caroline's mind that

she could say plenty more if she chose! She could say he was the most virile, exciting, gloriously handsome, and charismatic man she'd ever met. That he made her feel a woman in every sense of the word, that she was thrilled by his every touch and caress, that she loved him with a wild sweet love that occupied all her waking hours and dreaming nights, and if only his wish to marry her had been for the right reasons, she would have accepted him gladly.

"So, are you prepared to listen, or are you going to sit there with that vacant look on your face all day?" the love of her heart said irritably.

She gave him all her attention then, thankful he was becoming so engrossed in his story that he couldn't sense her reaction or that she had just come very near to throwing her arms around him and telling him how much she loved and wanted him.

"I'm sorry. I'm all attention now," she said softly. "But I can't think that you did anything very terrible."

It was the nearest she had come to saying she believed in him, but Luke seemed to disregard it.

"England and her aides have a very cruel heritage of punishment for petty crimes," he said with sudden bitterness in his voice, so perhaps he had noticed her words after all.

"I told you neither Sam nor myself had any wish to come to the mainland," he said, seeming to go off on a different tack for a moment. "We both had good reason to despise the authorities there. Sam won't mind my telling you of his reasons, as well as my own, since you'll be a part of our life on the island."

She managed to forgo any comment at that, biting her lips to make herself remain silent for once.

"Dr. Sam came to Australia of his own free will, intending to settle there," Luke went on. "He started up a successful practice in Sydney and was devastated when a child he was treating died on the operating table. He couldn't have saved her, but it haunted him for a long while afterward."

"But if it wasn't his fault—"

"Sam couldn't accept that. He'd never lost a patient before, let alone a child. He took to drink, then finally stole drugs to dull his anguish. The theft was discovered, and even though he could have fought the case and claimed the drugs were a necessary medical aid at the time, he gave in to pressure and was sent to prison. He'd been a good doctor, and they all knew it. So much for justice."

Caroline gasped. It all seemed so unfair.

"Luckily for Sam, he had friends who believed in him, and they eventually broke him out and got him onto a ship. When he reached Brundy, he decided to stay, and thank God he did," Luke finished.

"And what about you?" Caroline said when he paused, still imagining the heartache of a dedicated doctor forced to flee from his chosen vocation.

"My reason for being in Australia was nothing like Sam's. I was just a child when I was brought there with my father because he simply refused to leave me behind. My father had been wrongly convicted of a petty crime, and I was of an age when I could be usefully put to work in the care of the authorities here. But by the time we reached Australia, the true culprit had been discovered, and a pardon was awaiting my father."

His voice became bitter. "I'll never understand how they have the gall to issue a *pardon* for a crime someone didn't commit."

"Luke, you don't have to tell me any more," Car-

237

oline said quietly.

"Yes, I do. I have to set the record straight. I never speak about it, and perhaps I should, if only to rid myself of the impotent fury I feel whenever I recall it," he said.

So even a strong man like Luke Garston had his Achilles' heel, Caroline thought. And far from giving her a sense of triumph, she felt an inordinate sense of tenderness toward him.

"So what happened then?"

He gave a heavy shrug. "We intended to begin a new life in farming, only the privations on the ship bringing us from England had taken their toll on my father. We didn't have the same shipboard comfort that you and yours had—"

"Don't censure me for that!" Caroline said swiftly.

"I don't. But the terrible conditions on a convict ship proved too much for my father's heart and lungs, and he died soon after we arrived."

"So you were on your own?" she said, appalled.

"I managed," he said briefly. "But I had no wish to stay in a country that had killed my father. I became an adolescent adventurer, wandering around the islands and finding what work I could, and eventually I discovered Brundy. You know the rest. I also vowed that once I left the mainland, I'd never return."

"And I made you break that vow," she said, knowing now the enormity of his reasons and understanding them. Hadn't it been her love for her own father that had made her agree to accompany him to this godforsaken land? She could sympathize deeply with Luke's own wish never to be reminded of his own terrible time. And especially not to go back to Sydney.

"Luke, I'm so sorry," she said haltingly.

238

"It's not your fault," he said. "And perhaps you did me a favor. Perhaps you made me face up to my dragon. Anyway, we've had enough storytelling for one day. How do you feel now? Shall we go on?"

She started. She had almost forgotten her aches and pains and why they were lying there in the broiling sun beside a campfire. She flexed her limbs carefully. They were bruised but not broken, and she had no wish to lie there and roast until it was dark. Suddenly she yearned for the things she had always taken for granted: properly cooked food served on damask tablecloths; soft, clean sheets and hot soapy water in which to bathe; and the luxury of fresh clothes every day. She felt grubbier than she had ever felt in her life, and she was normally so fastidious.

"I'm well enough to go on," she said huskily. She felt too ashamed and guilty to tell him what was uppermost in her mind now: that she'd give anything to turn a corner and find a boat awaiting them, a boat that would take her straight back to Brundy and the soft luxury of Garston Manor.

But there were no corners to turn, and they still had a long distance to go until they reached the coastal village where she prayed that Jojo and the boys would have already bargained for a boat to take them home. She no longer had any hope of finding her father on her own, and she simply couldn't go on toward Sydney in this terrain. Her only hope was the trading ship that called at Brundy, which would at least take them there with some dignity and a degree of comfort.

"Do you always travel with pearls for insurance?" she said inconsequentially as they began to head south with their belongings slung over their backs.

"I don't normally travel," he reminded her. "But

239

in this instance it seemed like a good idea. I do have some now and then."

"I thank heaven that you do," she said fervently, remembering that but for bartering, she would be in very difficult straits now.

She didn't feel much like talking. She was too conscious of where she put her feet and of every little scuttling sound in the bush. She was frequently startled by the appearance of the indigenous animals, the kangaroos and small bright-eyed koala bears. And by the surprising sight of the long-necked emus striding through the bush and the sounds of the brilliant chattering galahs high in the trees. They all set her nerves on edge and made her clutch wildly at Luke.

"They won't hurt you," he said when a huge red kangaroo, its young in its pouch, appeared out of nowhere to stare at them, then went leaping away from them just as quickly. "They like to hang around civilization for food, so their presence is a good sign."

He said it to encourage her and didn't add that there were thousands more of them in the wild.

"I don't know how much longer I can go on," Caroline said eventually, when it seemed as if they had been walking for hours. She ached all over, and they didn't seem to be getting any nearer to the vague area Luke had pointed out. As yet, she could see no sign of buildings, or farms, nor even the sea, and she was struck with an acute sense of despair, certain they were going to die, and no one would ever find any trace of them. The vultures and the dingoes would get to them long before any rescuers. She felt sobs deep in her throat.

"We'll stop a while," he said at once. "It's getting near to sunset now, and perhaps we should make camp."

The fear spilled over then. "We'll have to spend another night in this terrible place, won't we?" she stammered. "I should never have made you come here. Luke, I've been such a fool—"

She felt him gather her in his arms, and she felt so lifeless she thought he would crush her without even trying.

"Stop it, lass," he said harshly. "We've come this far, and we'll not give up now. Is it such a hardship to spend another night beneath the stars with me?"

He was teasing, trying to coax her out of her attack of nerves, but it wasn't the time. She couldn't be coaxed, and she leaned against him, totally drained of all emotion. She felt his heartbeat against her breasts, strong and alive, and wished she could draw strength from them, but by now she had no reserves left.

A new sound penetrated her senses then, a thudding, rhythmic sound that seemed to vibrate from the very ground beneath them. It terrified and disoriented her, and she wondered briefly if the earth were about to open and gobble them up. She had heard of the catastrophic effects of an earthquake, when people were simply swallowed up as if they were dust and lost forever . . .

"Over here! We're over here, man!"

Half swooning, she heard Luke shout out the words. Jerking up her head from the comfort of his chest, she then registered that the sounds weren't those of an earthquake, after all, but the blessedly normal ones of thundering horses' hooves and that there were even more welcome sounds of men's voices. *English* voices, using English words.

Her heart leapt in her chest with joy and relief. They had been found! They were no longer lost in this terrible place, and she wouldn't have to spend another night in the open, petrified at every tiny

241

movement in the bush.

"Stay calm, my darling. Take some long deep breaths," she heard Luke instruct, and she realized that she was breathing in shallow painful gasps, and her head felt so dizzy it was hard to hold on to reality anymore.

Caroline's first lucid thought was that she had never fainted in her life before this expedition to Australia, and since then she had lost count of the number of times it had happened.

"Hello, my dear," an English voice said from somewhere in the room. A woman's comfortable, country voice. The sound of it was so wonderful and so unexpected it made a lump come to her throat.

She lifted her head slightly. She was lying on a bed that wasn't made of straw and leaves, but one that was raised off the ground and marginally more comfortable than a ship's bunk. There was a clean patchwork coverlet over her and a proper pillow beneath her head. She could have wept.

"Where am I?" she said huskily.

"Why, you're at Nathan's Farm, my dear, and the sooner we get some good cow's milk into you, the better, I'd say. My Frank will be bringing it in fresh anytime now."

"This is your farm?" Caroline said unnecessarily.

"That it is. Me and my man live here with our sons, and our neighbors farm a little ways away. We're homesteaders, dearie."

The word sounded familiar. She struggled to recall where she had heard it, and after a few moments she remembered. Homesteaders were what they called the farmers at the coastal village. The horse riders who had found them must have come from here. They had arrived at their destination.

"My—my—" she began.

"Your husband's eating a hearty meal, and we've been hearing all about your troubles," the woman informed her. "As soon as you feel able, you can have something to eat too. I can bring it to you in bed, or you can come through to the parlor, as you please."

"I'd like to get up. But first of all, please—Mrs. Nathan—could I have some water to wash?"

"Bless you, of course you can, and if you want to wear one of my old dressing gowns for a while, I'll swill out that filthy gown for you, my dear. It must have been such a pretty sight once," she said with a smile.

The woman was buxom and red-faced, and everything of hers would be far too voluminous for Caroline, but none of that mattered. The thought of some hot water to wash herself and the feel of clean clothes was more alluring than anything else. Food could wait. Her own sense of self-esteem and well-being could not.

"You're very kind," she said huskily. "But I should tell you, Luke is not my husband. He's a good friend helping me in my search for my father. Has he told you why we're here?"

"That he has, but first things first. You need food and rest, my dear, but I'm sorry I got things wrong. I assumed from what he said and the fact that you were traveling together . . ." the small frown on her forehead lifted. "But it's no matter, nor any business of mine. I'll just move in here with you tonight, and your man can bunk in with Frank. It'll be a blessed relief for me not to have to listen to his snoring for once!"

She left Caroline without giving her the chance to say anything more. Clearly her brief shock at two unmarried people traveling through the bush together had passed, but she had no intention of letting anything untoward happen under her roof.

Caroline felt a weak smile tremble on her lips. The conventions were still to be followed even here, where a rough and ready Englishwoman still considered respectability important. It was a comforting little bit of England in an alien land. And she was too weary to care what Luke might think about the arrangements . . .

Chapter Thirteen

Luke was talking companionably with the Nathan family by the time Caroline appeared in the farmhouse parlor, dressed in a voluminous dressing gown belonging to Mrs. Nathan. If there was anything designed to hide her femininity completely, that was it, and Luke's amused glance told her so. Caroline thought shrewdly that it was probably better in this conservative company.

By then she felt blissfully revived after a lengthy washdown in the bedroom, rid of the soiled and torn gown, and was feeling considerably more human again. The farmer was as large and red-faced as his wife, but their two young boys looked awkward and tongue-tied at this female vision amongst them, her hair combed and untangled at last.

"Take no notice of those two, my dear," Frank Nathan said easily. "They don't see many strangers, and they'll be off about their farm work once they've greeted our visitor, and you'll not see them again this night."

Caroline said hello and got brief mutterings in

answer. The boys were obviously more at home with the animals and gladly made their escape from the newcomers.

"Have you spoken to these kind people?" Caroline said pointedly to Luke, unable to wait a moment longer. Though she realized that if there had been any news of her father, she would have already heard it. Strangers were obviously rare in these parts, and Luke would have already made enquiries, even if the Brundy boys had not. Somehow, though, the knowledge that there was nothing to tell no longer filled her with the same sense of despair as before. It wasn't that she didn't still miss her father or that she had lost the determination to find out what had happened to him. But, almost against her will, time was starting to fulfil its oft-despised promise of healing painful wounds.

"There's no news, Caroline," Luke said quietly, his eyes cautiously watching her face.

"I suppose I never really expected that there would be," she answered slowly.

"I'm sorry, my dear," Mrs. Nathan said with quick sympathy. "You've come on a hopeless mission, I'm afraid. You'll do far better to do as your man says. Go back to your island, then take the trading ship for Sydney. That's where any information about your father would have been forwarded."

By what means? Caroline wondered. By bush drums or the mad ramblings of a mountain man or wild rumors that led nowhere? But it would have been churlish to put such thoughts into words since these people were being so kind.

Now that they were all here, and the sons gone about their business, Mrs. Nathan bustled about getting the visitors a meal. The parlor table was quickly spread with the most delicious food Caroline had seen in a long time. A great plate of succulent sliced meat was put in front of her, accompanied by small sweet potatoes and root vegetables, and a jug of thick hot gravy spiced with onions. It was a meal such as she hadn't seen since she left England, and her mouth suddenly watered.

"You do justice to that now, love, and you'll soon be feeling a deal better," Mrs. Nathan said. "Go along now, and eat your fill, both of you."

"It all looks wonderful, but what kind of meat is it?" she asked, trying to sound casual.

Frank Nathan chuckled. "Don't you worry none, girl, it's none of your foreign muck. It's good English lamb, and one of our own stock, so you just go ahead and enjoy it."

She felt foolish at having questioned it, but she knew that being English themselves, the homesteaders would understand the Englishwoman's mistrust of anything "foreign." If it were a national failing, Caroline made no apology for it. Later, she learned that the family came from south Dorset, where they had always been farmers and occasional fishermen, but the damp English weather hadn't suited Frank Nathan's chest complaint, and they'd come here primarily for the climate.

"I can't say we're exactly prosperous," Frank commented. "But my health has improved beyond anything we could have hoped for, and that's worth more than money. Besides which, our lads love the free and easy life here, so we're all content. Isn't that so, missus?"

"That's so, my dear," the wife said steadily, and Caroline guessed she'd have agreed with him if he'd suggested going to the North Pole. For a moment, she wished she, too, had been blessed with such an easygoing nature, instead of being very much her father's daughter and needing to question everything. But then she wouldn't have been herself, and it took all sorts to make a world, she thought, resorting to platitudes.

The Nathans wanted to know everything about their sojourn to the mainland—though they weren't told quite everything, Caroline thought. They didn't know how she had lain in Luke's arms and found such pleasure and abandonment at making love in the open beneath the stars.

Being seasoned new Australians now, they had their own opinions about the dangers the strangers had encountered. Especially about the incident that had frightened the camel.

"Snakes don't normally bother people unless they're scared by them," Frank Nathan informed them casually as Caroline still shuddered at the mere memory of the reptile. "If it had bitten you, you could always have done what the tough old bushmen do to get rid of the venom."

"What's that?" Caroline asked, at the same time wishing she wasn't curious enough to know.

"Why, they just press plenty of gunpowder over the bite, set light to it, and blow the poison away. O' course, they blow away a bit o' flesh as well, but that's preferable to dying, ain't it?"

Caroline definitely wished she hadn't asked. She felt faint at the very thought. She could also see that Luke was quite enjoying yarning with these folk. But when she said quickly that she was thankful dinner was long since over, or she'd surely have had no appetite at all, they reverted to more general topics.

"There's a boat available for us tomorrow, Caroline," Luke said at length.

"Unless you'd care to stay longer, of course," Frank said amiably. "Mother would like a bit of female company, wouldn't you, Mother?"

Caroline had already noticed that he always referred to his wife as "Mother." Into her mind for a second, came the unbidden image of the two of them making love in the creaky double bed she was to share with Mrs. Nathan that night. She willed the thought away, not wanting such an unseemly picture to enter her thoughts. She spoke hurriedly.

"It's very generous of you both, but—"

"But we've already been away from home too long, and Caroline will want to get her wardrobe together for traveling to Sydney when the trading ship arrives on Brundy," Luke finished for her. "You know what young ladies are like for titivating themselves, and these last days haven't been pleasant ones for her."

Caroline listened with growing resentment. Perhaps he didn't mean it, but he made her sound like a simpering, flighty young thing who'd embarked on this journey with a sense of adventure and would be longing, now, to get back to the kind of silly, feminine fripperies of the idle rich. She bit her lip. It sounded too much like the old Caroline and like many of her contemporaries back in England . . .

"I understand," Mrs. Nathan said. "Then you and Frank will get your business done, Mr. Garston, and the boat will be ready for you in the morning. Our boys will see to it at sunup."

The business was presumably the exchange of pearls and shells for the cost of the boat. Caroline had no idea what these people would do with them. Mrs. Nathan hardly looked the sort of woman to wear pearls strung around her neck,

249

but presumably they would be used in bartering. People like Mad Jack were probably the go-betweens who scoured such small communities for any goods of value. It was really no different than paying for things with money, she supposed. After another hour's conversation, she stifled a huge yawn with difficulty.

"I'm sorry but I'm desperately tired," she confessed. "My head is beginning to throb, too."

"I've some powders you can take for that nasty bump you took, dearie," the woman said at once. " 'Twill allow you to sleep soundly, and I doubt that you'll hear me come to bed, if you want to go on ahead."

Caroline did. She felt embarrassed at the thought of sleeping in the same bed as the woman, but there was nothing else she could do. When Luke had heard of the arrangement, she could tell by his face that he found it highly amusing, and her pleading eyes begged him not to shock their hostess by revealing how often they'd already shared the same blanket.

She would miss him tonight, but a drink of warm goat's milk and the headache powder had her drifting into sleep almost as soon as her head touched the unfamiliar pillow. She never felt the dip and creak of the bed when Mrs. Nathan joined her a long while later, nor heard the sounds of chesty snoring through the thin wall of the next room where Frank Nathan shared Luke's company.

The next time she awoke, it was with a feeling of well-being and a sense of anticipation. Memory flooded back, and she realized, with a start, how much she looked forward to being back on

Brundy Island again. To see the people she'd grown to know and like so well: the kindly Mrs. Hughes and the jaunty Petal; Dr. Sam and his small band of native children, so eager to learn; Maureen Finnegan; Jojo and the boys, who adored her now.

She felt guilty at the thought of them, knowing she'd put them in danger, too, with her insistence on coming to the Big Land. Yes, she thought, in some surprise. She was eager to return to Brundy now, and the sooner the better. Naturally she intended leaving again on the trading ship, and perhaps to find her own new life in Sydney, whatever the circumstances surrounding her father. But that was an obstacle to overcome when the time came, and there was no sense in anticipating it.

She was alone in the bedroom, and she caught sight of her own gown, washed and pressed and mended, lying over the back of a chair. She caught her breath. Heaven knew how late Mrs. Nathan had gone to bed or how early she had risen in order to get it finished so that Caroline would return home neat and respectable again. She was humbled by such thoughtfulness, and thanked the woman effusively when she went downstairs a while later, washed and dressed.

"It was a pleasure to have your company, dearie," Mrs. Nathan said. "I always wished for daughters, but the Good Lord only saw fit to give me sons. Not that I'm complaining, as it happens, for they're both good boys, but a body sometimes gets lonely for another woman's company."

At the wistfulness in her voice, Caroline was almost tempted to say they could perhaps stay for just one more day, but she quickly resisted the brief temptation.

251

"The bed was so comfortable after being in the bush, and smelled so fragrant. I couldn't quite distinguish the scent," she said instead.

Mrs. Nathan laughed. "That's the mattress stuffing, dearie. We learned the trick from the Aborigines."

Caroline looked at her with some suspicion. Lord knew what kind of stuffing that might be. At her look, the woman laughed more heartily.

"Don't you go worrying none. It's nothing more than packed down gum leaves — eucalyptus to you, I daresay. The Abos say that sleeping on them is a cure for aching joints, though I'm not convinced there's any truth in it. It's probably as much to do with the dry climate that's cleared up my old rheumatics as anything else. Still, you have to try all sorts, don't you?"

Caroline agreed that one did, wondering whether Dr. Sam Atkinson was aware of the supposed treatment! And then Luke came striding into the parlor with Frank Nathan, and both were looking pleased with themselves.

"Good. You're up and ready," Luke greeted her briskly. "We'll have a quick bite of breakfast and be on our way. The boys are loading up the boat, so there's no reason for delay, Caroline."

She smiled ruefully at Mrs. Nathan. Obviously the deal was done, and both men would be anxious to be about their own affairs. Besides, she hadn't really wanted to stay any longer. She was eager to be home, wherever home was. For the moment, she was happy to accept that it was Brundy.

The craft was a fairly substantial one, but far from luxurious. It seemed even flimsier with the

252

thought of negotiating through the barrier reef looming ahead. But Frank Nathan was able to give them specific instructions about dealing with this coastal region, and Caroline realized he didn't come from a sea-faring part of England for nothing. The Dorset coast was far less hazardous than this one, but a Dorset man would be familiar with and respectful of the sea's vagaries.

They made affectionate goodbyes to the couple and resisted making too many overtures to their diffident young sons. Caroline felt a fleeting anxiety for them. They were so isolated here, with no schooling, nor any other young company. It didn't bode well for their social development. But she accepted that there was absolutely nothing she could do about it, and once they reached the shore, she concentrated instead on climbing into the precariously rocking boat. The Brundy crew tried to keep it steady on the swell, and she finally sat down thankfully inside it.

Luke said little for the first part of the voyage. No one did. They all gathered in the bow of the boat, save for Jojo, who steered the rudder according to the bellowed instructions from the bow. Caroline held her breath as she realized how carefully now they were sliding between and over the glittering spikes of coral, their myriad shapes caught by the morning sunlight.

It was hard to believe that coral was a living thing or that something so beautiful could be so deadly. On the voyage to the mainland, she had been too intent on getting there to notice the lovely colors of the coral, but now she absorbed it all. Not just the usual shrimp-pink coral filled these waters, but there was an artist's palette of colors beneath the waves, sometimes ultramarine, glowing violet, or delicate fernlike green.

As Caroline gazed into the translucent turquoise depths at the brilliantly hued fish darting in and out of the underwater coral forest, her fascination temporarily overcame thoughts of danger. If it hadn't been for her damp palms and fast-beating heart each time Luke shouted out a warning to Jojo to steer away from the needle-sharp coral, she could almost have believed there was no danger at all in its deceptive beauty.

"We're through," Luke said at last. "We can all relax now, boys."

Caroline couldn't miss the tension in his voice. He didn't turn from the bow yet, and she could see the sweat running down his bare muscled back above the waistband of his trousers. She had put him through this ordeal, she thought guiltily, and there was no way she could make it up to him. As if following her thoughts, he glanced round at her, and she flushed. There was one way, of course . . .

"Luke, thank God," she said huskily when he made his way back toward her.

"Just keep on thanking Him until we're safely moored," he said grimly.

Caroline ran her tongue around her dry lips. The sun had cracked them, and the flippant thought that soon she would be able to rub nourishing cream into them to soften and heal them only made her feel more guilty.

"I thank Him constantly for overlooking my foolishness and keeping us safe—"

She heard Luke's caustic laugh. "Try thanking the boys instead," he said. "They're the ones who've got us through this damn coral. Without their expertise, we'd have been fish bait."

He didn't add "like your father," but she

254

flinched at the implication. She spoke with dignity.

"Of course I thank them, every one of them."

Jojo looked at her hopefully. "Do we make dives before Brundy?" he asked. "Maybe good pearls near reef."

"It's up to the lady," Luke said. "I've certainly no objection. We don't usually come this far south, but I've heard tell there's a good catch in this area."

He looked at her steadily, and she swallowed dryly. All she wanted was to get back to Brundy. She didn't care for bobbing about in a small boat while they dived for pearls. Nor did she want to prolong this journey home, or to be reminded of that other time when she had been drifting aimlessly in a small boat awaiting death. Her voice was husky.

"I've no objection as long as it doesn't go on too long. I want to get back as soon as possible, Luke."

"I never thought I've live to hear it," he mocked her. "So Brundy has its attractions after all."

"Of course." She wouldn't let him get her ruffled, not now, when the horrors of the Big Land were behind them. Nor acknowledge the sudden gleam in his eyes.

Oh yes, there were many attractions on Brundy Island, and the most charismatic of all was Luke Garston himself. But he already knew that, and she wouldn't give him the satisfaction of showing it now.

"We'll stop for an hour, no more," he ordered a while later when the boys were leaning over the side of the boat and excitedly pointing into the shimmering depths.

The silvery black oysters below were fat and gleaming, but their size didn't necessarily mean they contained the richest pearls. Only by prying them open could that be ascertained. It was all a gamble, but Caroline knew it was a heady gamble that these fearless young boys loved as much as Luke himself.

She watched as they dived overboard. They struck the water cleanly, their bodies as straight as arrows. Luke dived after them, his hair streaming out, as keen as his boys to search for the riches of the sea. Time and again they came up, gasping for breath, to drop their precious catch into the boat for later inspection. This was always a time of excitement, and when it finally came, Caroline was as mesmerized as the rest of them as they delicately performed the opening ritual.

"It's a good catch," Luke declared when the clusters of gleaming pearls lay before them.

"We come here other time?" the man Makepeace said eagerly, but Luke shook his head.

"Perhaps, but I doubt it. It's too far from Brundy, and if a storm should blow up . . ." He left the rest unsaid, but they were all aware of the way a small boat behaved at the mercy of a storm at sea. Even a large, ocean-going vessel, Caroline thought, shivering at the memory.

"But *perhaps*," Jojo said, seizing on that one word. He had the capacity of blotting out all but the things he wanted to hear, Caroline thought with a small smile, and she recognized that trait only too well.

"Perhaps," Luke said. He wrapped up the pearls carefully in a cloth and stowed them safely away in his pack. The shells would also be kept. They, too, had their value.

"Can I keep a shell as a memento?" Caroline asked.

She fingered the delicate creamy-pink mother-of-pearl interior of a shell. Luke shrugged.

"Keep any one you wish."

It would be a memento to remember him by when this adventure was finally over. The thought sped through Caroline's mind as she examined the pile of shells and decided on the one she wanted. Suddenly she faced the fact that this adventure must surely end. She couldn't spend the rest of her days on an idyllic island with strangers.

She owed it to her father to continue the journey they had begun. To find a place for herself in Sydney, in whatever capacity that might be. She had a heritage to continue. It might not be a woman's place to be at the head of a newspaper empire, but the revenues from it would be hers, and it had been her father's dearest dream for them both to live comfortably in Sydney and begin a new life there. Inspired by his enthusiasm, it had been Caroline's dream too.

"Is something wrong, Caroline? Are you feeling queasy? We'll be on the move again now."

"I'm perfectly all right," she said, but her mouth wasn't quite steady. And suddenly she didn't want the oyster shell after all. She didn't want mementoes of a man who might have meant the world to her and whom she was already planning to leave. She had to fulfill her father's dream.

"You don't look all right," he informed her. "You look as pale as death."

"I'm all right, I tell you," she almost snapped. "And you're right about this shell. It's worthless, and it smells of fish. I don't want it after all."

She hurled it into the sea, ignoring Luke's

annoyed exclamation. The shell quickly sank beneath the water and then floated down effortlessly to settle on the sea floor, sending up little puffs of sand around it.

"So my fastidious English lady has reverted to form," Luke commented. "I wondered how long it would take."

"Did you really think a few days in the bush could change the habits of a lifetime?"

"Perhaps I was hoping that a few terrifying experiences would make you grow up and accept that fate had sent you to me."

"To live the life of a native?" she asked skeptically.

While they were arguing, the boat was being steadily steered on its way now, and she realized she had been feeling very queasy indeed while it had been bobbing on the swell.

"I hardly think you can say that about life at Garston Manor," Luke said. "But if it's the social life you crave, then one of the first things we'll do is arrange a dinner and evening occasion to celebrate our safe return to Brundy."

"I wasn't asking for that—"

"But you're going to get it," he retorted.

She stayed silent as the boat moved into more open stretches of water now, the swell around the reef behind them, and the water glassy and crystal clear. She held her lips tightly together and then felt his finger touch them seductively. He spoke softly, in contrast to his earlier brusqueness.

"Stop scowling, lass. Didn't anyone ever tell you your mouth would stay like that one day?"

She felt her eyes blur. It was exactly what her maid Sophie used to say her, with the familiarity of a servant who had known her since she was a small, lisping girl. It was a parent's comment to a child. It was everything from her childhood. And it almost undermined all her careful self-control now. She felt Luke's arms go around her.

"Besides, I've no wish to kiss a scowling mouth. How can you respond to me in the delicious way I know you can, when you're holding yourself so tight and unyielding?"

"I've no intention of responding to you," she said. "And especially not here in front of the boys."

He laughed softly. "Darling Caroline, your eyes give you away. You want me every bit as much as I want you, and the boys wouldn't bother about us."

"I'm not denying it, but please don't do this, Luke. I'm not in the habit of showing my feelings in public."

"Then it must wait until we're in private, hungry though I am for your kisses, love. Last night was sweet torment, having to sleep in the same room as Farmer Nathan and knowing you were only the width of a bedroom wall away."

"It's a good thing I was well chaperoned by Mrs. Nathan then, wasn't it?" she said shortly. "And I certainly wasn't having any such feelings about you!"

"No? I think you lie, Miss Rowe. In any case, I promise that once we're alone again, I shall do my best to revive them."

He was teasing, clearly disbelieving that she could have lain in bed in the next room to him and not dreamed about him. Perhaps in any other circumstances, his assumption would have been true, Caroline thought irritably. But the truth was she had been so sedated by the headache powders Mrs. Nathan had given her, she had

259

slept like the proverbial log of wood. His arrogance made her doubly sharp.

"You needn't bother. Besides, once you're back on your island, I'm sure there will be plenty of other young ladies only too willing to take advantage of your charms. Miss Kathleen Finnegan for one, I suspect. And since I shall only be there until the trading ship calls, it would be a waste of your time to try any more seduction on me."

Luke let her go quite suddenly. "It's of little consequence to me. And Kathleen Finnegan is a very lovely girl. It may be quite a wrench to leave her behind if I decide to escort you to Sydney."

"You *promised!* And a gentleman never goes back on a promise!"

"Are you going to marry me?" he said as if he hadn't even heard her. She stared at him, taken aback by the suddenness of the proposal.

"No, I am not! And I don't know how you can even ask such a thing in public. It just shows how long you've been away from decent civilization!"

The grinning boys had obviously heard the question, but neither that nor her answer perturbed Luke Garston.

"Well, if you want me to accompany you on the trading ship, I assure you that you'd be far less of a temptation to the roughnecks on board if you were my wife. Did you think I proposed to you for any other reason?" he taunted.

"Certainly not for the right reasons," she said bitterly.

Certainly not because he loved her in the way a woman had every right to expect the man she married to love her. To love, honor, and cherish for the rest of her life . . . To worship her with his body—oh, he'd do that all right. Lust was the

260

only word he knew when it came to being close to a woman. Love didn't enter into it, except in moments of passion, when his tenderness was all that she could ever want . . . She drew in her breath, not wanting to allow the treacherous memories of his lovemaking to intrude right now.

"Think about it," Luke said abruptly. He turned away as Jojo gave a shout, pointing ahead to where the welcome dark shape of Brundy lay invitingly ahead. Caroline felt a prickling in her throat. If only the proposal had been said with a real sense of love. If only she dared accept it on Luke's own terms, knowing he didn't love her, but owing him her life.

But for how long would he be satisfied with her as a wife on those terms? Without love, even his passion for her might eventually wane, and he'd go looking for other attractions on his island. He wouldn't need to look very far. There was the lovely Kathleen Finnegan and other white women living there, and the willing native girls like Petal, who would be only too happy to accommodate him.

Caroline shuddered, knowing she couldn't bear to share him with anyone. Knowing that if he came to her after being in some other woman's bed, it would kill her.

They returned to Brundy to a hero's welcome. They had been sighted long before they arrived, and there was a huge crowd awaiting them. News of their mission had long been circulated around the island, and while most had thought the voyage totally reckless, Caroline knew they had all believed in Luke's prowess and in his ability to get them safely back, whatever the outcome of her quest. He was the hero, not she.

Dr. Sam came striding toward them, vociferous in his welcome, and surrounded as ever by his brats. He pumped Luke's hand and clasped Caroline briefly in his arms.

"It's good to see you both home again, safe and well," he exclaimed. "There's many a prayer been said for you both by those who take heed of such things."

It was the nearest he'd come to admitting he'd probably said a prayer or two as well, Caroline thought, smiling. And if most of the young ladies' prayers had been for Luke, how could she begrudge him his welcome home on such a day? This was his island, and they were his people, and she was just the interloper. She saw Mrs. Hughes among the crowd, and seconds later she was clasped to the housekeeper's bosom and felt oddly moved by the gesture.

"I confess I began to wonder if we'd ever see you again, my dear, having heard of the dangers on the mainland. But here you are, looking as pretty as ever and ready for a good hearty meal, I'll wager."

For some reason the thought of a good hearty meal didn't fill Caroline with too much joy. Her insides were still moving from the motion of the boat, and everything she'd eaten so far that day was threatening to reappear.

"Take some deep breaths, girl," Dr. Sam was saying beside her now, and she guessed that her feelings must have shown in her face. She glanced back to where Luke was surrounded by people and did as she was told. For the moment they had all forgotten her, and it was better so. She didn't want to humiliate him or herself by vomiting in public. She forced the nausea down with a huge effort.

"I'm better now," she muttered. "It was the motion of the boat that caused it."

"Probably so," Sam said, running a keen glance over her. "But I'll be wanting to take a good look at you later on to see that you've survived whatever ordeal you've gone through. And to hear all about it, of course."

It occurred to her that no one even asked if there was any news of her father. She had expected people to ask at once, but of course it was obvious they had no news, or Sir William Rowe would have been returning with them. Or she would have been taken on to Sydney. Or they would have flown a flag of triumph, if there had been any good news to report. All these things flitted in and out of her mind as she listened to the congratulations Luke was receiving at having been to the mainland and returned safely. In retrospect, their concern and relief only intensified the risks.

"Can we go back to the house?" she murmured to Mrs. Hughes. "Luke will be the center of attention for some time yet, and I'd simply love a real cup of tea!"

"Then that's just what you'll have as soon as I can get it brewed. Dr. Sam can pass on the message that we've gone on ahead."

Mrs. Hughes spoke firmly, sensing the sudden exhaustion in the girl. Emotionally and physically, Caroline was drained. There were too many similarities to the first time she'd come here, and the memories of that time were still painful. She was glad of Mrs. Hughes's supporting arm as they slowly walked the short distance to Garston Manor, feeling less of a vivacious young woman than a very old lady. She prayed fervently that the eerie feeling would pass.

She had no wish to talk about her experiences, not even to this kindly woman, who must be dying to know all that had happened. She didn't want to talk about the tribe who had captured them and isolated her with the pregnant woman, believing that she, too, was pregnant.

It was hardly seemly for her to admit to such a thing, with all the explanations that must necessarily follow. Remembering the ritual of the spear vibrating on the earth in front of her, Caroline felt faint and dizzy at how near she had come to death. If the spear had fallen . . .

And then being shown the sacrificial mountainside and the plunging valley below . . . Even sitting in comfort in the drawing room of this luxurious house, she was beset by nerves, unable to rid her mind of the images. Secure and safe now, they came flooding back to haunt her.

In her mind, she saw the huge black snake slithering across their path, and heard the crack of her head against the rock, followed by the report of Luke's gun as he killed the camel. She was haunted by thoughts of death, and no matter how she tried, she could no more conjure up loving thoughts of herself and Luke together, than she could will her father's presence back into her life.

"I'm prescribing a sedative for you, Caroline, and a night's undisturbed sleep."

She heard Dr. Sam's voice without even realizing he and Luke had arrived at the house some time after herself and Mrs. Hughes. By then she was shivering as if with cold, even though the sun had set by now and the evening air was still fragrantly warm and pleasant.

She allowed herself to be taken to her room where Mrs. Hughes helped her into her night things, and she accepted the sedative almost eagerly. She wondered briefly if she would need to be drugged for the rest of her life to rid herself of all the bad memories. She drifted into a half-sleep very quickly. It was all so much like the first time she had come here, and yet everything was different. Nothing was ever the same. She was not the same.

She was no longer innocent, nor unaware of the dangers that existed on the mainland of Australia. She wondered why on earth her father had decided to bring them here, instead of remaining at home in England where they would be safe. And where she would never have met Luke Garston. . . .

Chapter Fourteen

The luxury of the house, the pampering attentions from Mrs. Hughes, and the knowledge that nothing could hurt her here, were like balm to Caroline's senses. She spent a blissful couple of days doing absolutely nothing. Then, remembering all the dangers and sacrifices he had made for her, she felt guiltily obliged to talk to Luke about the sleek boat they'd been forced to abandon on the mainland.

"It's been worrying me a lot lately," she said abjectly. "So much happened during our trip that I completely overlooked the fact that I had cost you your best boat. I'm truly sorry about it, and once I get to Sydney, I'll see that you're properly reimbursed somehow. Unless there's any way you can get the boat back, of course."

"I've certainly no intention of trying to retrieve it," he said tersely. "If some other wanderer has found it and made use of it, then good luck to him. And I certainly don't need your father's money."

"Good Lord, I didn't mean to insult you," she said, riled at once. "But it was such a fine boat—"

266

He brushed aside her clumsy apology as if it meant less than nothing to him. "It was no more than wood and canvas. It was far more important that we all returned safely. I can always build another boat, but its loss can't begin to compare with that of a life, so let's hear no more of it."

His words left her feeling annoyed and inadequate. She would far rather he'd lashed out at her for the loss of his craft. But she could also apply his comments keenly to the tragedy of the *Princess Victoria* and the loss of so many lives on board. And since she didn't want to remember that too poignantly, she thought instead how often Luke Garston could irritate — and surprise her.

She'd fully expected him to rail at her for costing him one of his valuable possessions, yet he never had, even though she guessed that that particular boat had been the pride and joy of his fleet. But of course he was right. No amount of possessions could compare with a human life. However much she thought she knew him, he still remained an enigma to her.

Since Luke never referred to the loss of the boat again, she tried to put it out of her mind, but it was harder to forget the trauma of all her experiences on the mainland. She could still wake up in the night in a cold sweat, imagining she could see the terrifying, white-painted faces of the Aborigines staring down at her with stony eyes.

She could still recall far too vividly the scrawny fingers prodding her in the most intimate places; she could still shudder and shrink back, remembering how she had so nearly been raped — such memories were often enough to jolt her awake to find she had been crying in her sleep. And there was no one to turn to at such times. No Luke . . .

Caroline had assumed he would come to her

room at night, demanding that she bend to his will. She had been prepared for it, anticipated it, and to her shame, dreamed about it. And instead, nothing had happened. With a mixture of emotions, she decided it could mean only one thing. He had tired of the chase and turned to more willing partners on his island. To one of the lovely native girls or perhaps to Kathleen Finnegan.

The Irish girl came to call on her one afternoon when she was lazing on the terrace within sight of the glittering sea, a cool drink by her side. Somewhere out there, she was thinking, Luke and his boys had gone pearl diving, and they weren't expected back until sundown. She found herself praying no harm would come to them and chided herself for her foolishness. What seemed terribly dangerous to her was commonplace to them . . .

"It's beautiful, isn't it?" the soft voice with the distinctive accent said close-by.

Caroline started, and Kathleen was immediately apologetic.

"Sure, and I'm sorry for startling you, Caroline! I didn't go in through the house as I know Mrs. Hughes has a rest during the early part of the afternoon, but Petal told me you were out here and I thought you'd have heard me coming."

"It's perfectly all right," she said, forcing a smile to her lips. Truth to tell, she wasn't exactly pleased to see the girl she strongly suspected was in love with Luke Garston. As for his feelings for Kathleen, she still had no idea—and would rather not know, she thought fervently.

"Would you like some lemonade? Petal will bring another glass."

"Thank you, but no. I've really come to ask a favor of you," the girl said, to Caroline's surprise.

"What can I possibly do for you?" she murmured.

"It's me Dadda," she said. "I think he's suffering from a belated bout of homesickness for the old country."

"After all this time?"

Kathleen smiled ruefully. "When people get old, their memories start playing tricks on them, and Dadda's memory is conveniently forgetting the damp and cold and the miserable winters we spent in Ireland. He has a yearning to see the old country once more before he dies."

Guiltily Caroline felt her heart leap. Did this mean that Kathleen was about to take her father on a sentimental journey back to Ireland? And if she did, one hurdle between herself and Luke would be removed. The fact that the thought had even slipped into her mind, infuriated her.

"And do you mean to see that he gets his wish?" she murmured, trying not to sound too eager.

"Glory, no, I do not!" Kathleen exclaimed. "The last thing I want is to go back to the smelly old place, and Maureen neither! We have a good life here, and we love the sunshine. I know that once Dadda gets over this foolishness, he'll be back to his old self again."

"Then what is it you want from me?"

Kathleen became more urgent. "I want you to talk to him like you did the night we came here for a visit, Caroline. You talked about London and the old pea-soupers and the miserable slums your father had been writing about in his newspapers. Well, the part of Ireland where we lived wasn't so very different, full of gypsies and the common folk. I know I sound terribly snobbish, but Dadda seems to have got a very distorted view of it all now. I remember only too well how the gypsies could frighten the lives out of the local children! They were probably harmless enough, but they weren't like us. Do you know what I mean?"

"I do," Caroline said, remembering the hostile natives on the mainland. They were probably harmless, too, at least among their own people, but to her they had presented a terrible threat.

"So if you could only talk to him again," Kathleen went on. "Make him see how foolish it would be to go back and try to recapture a life that doesn't exist anymore, except in his imagination. I know he'd listen to you, Caroline. He thought you were such a lovely girl."

"Did he?" she said. It was an odd request, but she supposed she could see the sense of it from the other girl's point of view. And naturally, Kathleen wouldn't want to leave the island.

"And you definitely don't want to go?" she repeated.

"Of course not. I love it here. And I've a special reason for saying so." She blushed noticeably, and Caroline assumed she referred to Luke and their feelings toward one another. Was it to Kathleen's willing arms that he went every night now? She gave a small sigh, looking away to where the glittering sea was so inviting and could be so treacherous. A bit like Luke Garston himself.

If she had one iota of sense and self-respect, she should forget all this nonsense about him, she told herself. He had merely found her amusing for a while, despite his remarks about fate decreeing that they belonged together. It was no more than a ploy to bend her will to his, and she was probably the one thorn in his flesh who didn't instantly respond to him.

She constantly tried to forget all that had happened between them, even though it was impossible to completely forget the sweetness and the passion, and it shouldn't matter a jot to her if Luke and Kathleen found happiness together. They'd be a good match, and it might do her cause a lot of good if she mentioned as much to Luke himself, to let him see she was quite unconcerned about it. She resolved to think about doing so if the opportunity arose.

Besides, once the trading ship arrived, she herself would be leaving for Sydney, and she would never have to see the two of them together again. Mentally she threw herself into the new resolve. Though, after Luke's tales of the roughnecks on board, she still desperately wanted him to keep his promise to accompany her on the ship.

But once he'd deposited her in Sydney, she would find her way to the newspaper offices. She would be among her father's friends and colleagues and their wives, and they would take care of her. Luke would return to Brundy, and she would make a new life for herself on the mainland among civilization. It was all cut and dried . . . and if it sounded dreadfully sterile, she pushed the uneasy thought out of her mind and gave a small decisive nod to Kathleen Finnegan.

"I'll do what I can," she said. "You'll all be coming to our special evening, of course?"

She wished she hadn't spoken as if it were an evening arranged by Luke and herself. It sounded far too domestic, but to her relief Kathleen seemed not to notice. Caroline mentally stood back for a moment, wondering how she herself could be so concerned at her rival's feelings. And she knew it was because she was determined not to see Kathleen as such. Kathleen was obviously the right one for Luke Garston, not Caroline Rowe. If she thought it

271

often enough, she might even start to believe it.

"Oh yes!" Kathleen said. "I wouldn't miss it for the world. It seems a long while since we had a real social occasion on the island, and this is such a lovely house. People do love coming here when Luke gives a party."

She glanced around, and Caroline imagined she was looking the place over with a possessive eye. And why not? If she and Luke were married, then this house and the lovely grounds would be Kathleen's domain. An unreasoning shaft of jealousy ran through Caroline's body at the thought. To counter it, she smiled determinedly at the other girl. "Perhaps you could tell me something about the other guests who are likely to be invited. Luke doesn't bother me with such details."

Kathleen laughed. "Luke goes his own way, I'm afraid. The longer you know him, the more you'll realize that. I'm still amazed that you persuaded him to take you to the mainland. He wouldn't do that for everyone, Caroline."

She wasn't sure whether or not there was a note of antagonism in the Irish girl's voice. She spoke quickly. "I know, and I'm very grateful, especially as it all came to nothing. But please—tell me about the friends who will be invited. You'll know them all, and I'll know hardly anyone."

It occurred to her now that it would be far more suitable and natural for Kathleen Finnegan to be Luke's hostess on such an evening.

"Well, you know Dr. Sam and Dadda and Maureen and me. Then there are several other English families on the island who usually come to Luke's home at Christmastime. The Dalbys and the Treherberts, and old Colonel Wray. Miss Pringle generally plays the piano and gives us a few songs, and we all join in. It can get a bit melancholy sometimes

272

though, since she has a penchant for nostalgia, and that might not do Dadda any good."

Caroline hadn't thought that the evening was intended to revolve around Dadda Finnegan's feelings and just managed to resist saying so.

"I'm sure we can encourage Miss Pringle to play something lively if it starts going that way," she said.

"Perhaps you'll be able to stop Colonel Wray telling some of his appalling old army stories as well," Kathleen said with a grin. "He can get a wee bit tedious, but he's an old dear just the same."

Caroline wondered if this girl ever had a seriously wrong word to say about anyone. She was so sweet as to be almost sugary. Caroline could only suppose she would suit Luke admirably since she would never oppose anything he said. It sounded deadly dull to Caroline, but she supposed that was how some people liked things.

"Are there any young people among this gathering?" she asked suddenly. The elderly Colonel Wray and the spinster Miss Pringle hardly sounded stimulating company.

"Oh yes. The Dalbys have two young sons and a daughter. Michael Treherbert is a boatbuilder, and a few years older than myself. His sister Jane is Maureen's close friend. Of course, I'm only surmising about these names, and I'm sure there will be others. I haven't been privileged to see Luke's guest list any more than you have, I gather."

Caroline had to say that she had not. And it irked her. She may not personally know any of these people, but it would have been nice to see their names and learn a little about them from Luke himself. So far, all she had gleaned from him was that the evening would be a pleasant surprise and was apparently intended to prove to her that a good

273

social life could still exist, even in this far-flung corner of the world.

She pursed her lips slightly. It could hardly compare with some of the London soirees she had attended with her father! Nor any of the heady, glittering balls and concerts, where royalty was sometimes to be glimpsed. Such days . . . and they were gone forever, Caroline thought, with a swift plunge into gloom. She had appreciated them so little at the time, finding some of the eager young men so boring and the stuffier older ones beyond recall. She hadn't realized she gave such a deep sigh until she caught sight of Kathleen Finnegan's sympathetic glance.

"Poor Caroline. Is it so very awful for you here?"

She flushed, fancying she detected a slight mocking tone in the other girl's voice. As if to say there were plenty of young women who'd give their eye teeth to be ensconced in the household of the most charismatic man for miles around.

"You seem to forget the circumstances surrounding my arrival," she said tartly. "I didn't come of my own free will, and my father is still missing."

Kathleen had the grace to look shame-faced.

"I'm so sorry, Caroline. You must be finding all this party talk very frivolous. Perhaps it would best if it didn't take place."

"Not at all. I wouldn't want to spoil Luke's plans," she said, thinking that Kathleen seemed to take a very proprietorial interest in the affair. It was just as if she had the final say in whether or not the party was canceled. The idea annoyed Caroline more intensely than she would have wished, and she emphasized Luke's name as she spoke.

Kathleen gave a relieved smile. "Good. I suspect you've already discovered that when Luke gets an idea in his head, he'll move heaven and earth to see

274

that he gets his way. And right now he badly wants to give you this party."

Caroline managed not to make any comment. She knew all about Luke Garston's obsessive need to get his own way. She wondered if Kathleen could possibly suspect how he had pursued her ever since he'd rescued her, or if it bothered her at all. It didn't seem to. Either she simply closed her eyes to Luke's amorous escapades, or they had some kind of understanding that said he could do as he pleased as long as their relationship was secure.

Whatever their personal arrangements, they didn't excuse him in Caroline's eyes, nor could she ever condone any of it. Any woman who wanted to share him must be the world's biggest fool. Caroline never would.

"Anyway, I'd better leave you now, Caroline. But you will give a thought to what I asked you, won't you? It would mean a lot to me."

She gave a start. She'd already forgotten Kathleen's purpose in coming here and searched her memory quickly.

"I'll be sure and tell him how miserable England would be compared with the lovely sunshine we're enjoying here," she promised. "I can't vouch for Ireland, since I've never been there, but I'll do my best for you."

"Thank you."

The other girl squeezed Caroline's arm for a moment in an apparent gesture of friendship and then gave a soft laugh and spoke teasingly. "Of course, if Maureen or meself were to get married in the foreseeable future, he'd have Australian grandchildren to look forward to then, and he'd be sure to forget any daft ideas about going back home. Should I consider that, do you think, Caroline!"

"It's certainly a thought," Caroline said woodenly,

hardly knowing what else to say.

For they both knew that Maureen Finnegan wasn't of an age to marry yet, and it was obvious that Kathleen was giving her the broadest hint yet that she had her sights set on somebody. And who else but Luke Garston?

By the time Luke joined her for dinner that evening, she had worked herself up into a fine old scratchy mood.

"Your friend came to see me this afternoon," she said without preamble.

"And a good evening to you too, Miss Rowe," Luke said mildly.

She glared at him. He had all the primitive instincts of a native, as wild and passionate and hungry for his needs as any caveman . . . yet here he was now, dressed immaculately after his day on the pearling boats, pouring her a glass of mulled wine, as elegant as if he dwelled in any London mansion.

"Does nothing ever ruffle you?" she snapped.

She saw his eyes glitter in the familiar way she knew only too well by now. He gave a short laugh and tipped his glass toward her in a complimentary gesture.

"I'd say you know the answer to that very well, my lovely. One glance from those expressive blue eyes of yours, and I'm extremely ruffled, for want of a better word."

"I didn't mean that, and you know it!"

She was angry with him for always getting the better of her. For being in control of his island, for being in control of his life and hers . . . and for not loving her.

She turned her face away so he couldn't see the sudden trembling of her lips and the shadow that

276

passed over her eyes. How could she bear to see him dancing with Kathleen, flirting with Kathleen, and not betray her own feelings?

"Why don't you tell me what you do mean? And which of my friends came here today?" Luke said quietly. He was standing very close to her now, and she breathed in the fresh aroma of soap and bathing oils on his skin, mingled with the faint tang of the sea that he never quite lost. It was a tantalizing mixture, heady and potent . . .

"I'm sorry. Naturally, you have many friends—"

Caroline bit her lip, knowing she was being churlish, and seemingly unable to stop herself. She looked down at her hands, clenched tightly together. He had so many friends while she had none. He had so much while she had nothing. Her breath caught in her throat. Luke heard it, and instantly he was holding her. She swayed against him and remained there mutely for a few moments, unable to think of anything but the joy of being in his arms where she so often ached to be.

"You know quite well that my friends are your friends too. So tell me who came to see you. Was it Doc? You're quite well, I hope?"

Suddenly he moved back from her, holding her arms and looking searchingly into her eyes.

Into Caroline's mind surged the memory of their time on the mainland. With it came the image of the Aborigine chief, lecherously prodding at her belly. A child was clearly sacred in their eyes. Was this what Luke hoped for too, but with very different intentions, thinking it was a way of keeping her here against her wishes? An unmarried Englishwoman with a child was looked on as a pariah in decent society, and even here on this island paradise the European families would surely never sanction such a thing. A hasty marriage would be the only face-saving thing to do. She felt her cheeks stain with angry color as the thoughts raced through her head.

"Dr. Sam was not my visitor today," she said icily. "And I'm perfectly well, thank you. No, it was your friend Kathleen Finnegan who came to call on me."

Luke looked slightly surprised for a moment and then he smiled, releasing her and retrieving his glass of wine.

"Well, it was good of Kathleen to make you feel welcome here, Caroline."

"She took long enough about it," Caroline said without thinking.

"You haven't exactly been sociable yourself, my dear," he said coolly. "Aside from helping Doc with the brats at the school, you've taken little interest in visiting anyone when I've suggested it or in moving far from the house except on your own. People could be forgiven for thinking you were a standoffish English miss who considers the islanders to be beneath her."

"That's unfair! And besides, there seemed little point in getting to know people when I'm not intending to stay," she snapped back.

His answering silence unnerved her. It gave too much expression to his own sense of the inevitability of their meeting and belonging. It might be what she wanted more than anything, but none of it was worth anything unless it was accompanied by love, she thought stubbornly.

"So what was the purpose of Kathleen's visit, or was it exclusively female talk?" he said now.

She felt her hackles rise. "Sometimes, Luke Garston, you can be insufferably patronizing."

"What the devil do you mean by that remark?" he said.

"If you don't even understand what I mean, then

that only underlines what I've said," she retorted.

He poured himself another glass of wine, and Caroline felt a silly little sense of satisfaction at seeing him spill a few drops onto the fine wool carpet.

"Well, I daresay if Kathleen's visit was of any interest to me, I'll get to hear of it sooner or later," he said, as if totally unconcerned. "So I suggest we go into dinner before it's spoiled."

And since the implication seemed to be that he could see Kathleen any time he chose, Caroline was left feeling more restless than before and wishing she'd never started the silly charade at all.

Once they were seated in the dining room and enjoying Mrs. Hughes's delicious chilled fish soup, she looked at him across the table and spoke abruptly.

"Kathleen seemed to think I'd have seen the guest list of everyone who was coming to the party. I think you might have shared the information with me too, but it's no matter. She told me who the likely guests would be, and obviously she'd have more knowledge of them than I would."

As Luke clattered his spoon into his empty dish, she went on nervously.

"Please don't think I'm complaining. It's your house, and your party, and I'm the one uninvited guest after all."

"*I* invited you here."

"Well, hardly in the usual sense," she said, not really knowing why she was in such a petty mood this evening but seemingly unable to stop herself. "I was forced upon you, wasn't I?"

"Not at all. I could have left you drifting in the ocean until you were fish bait. It wouldn't have taken much longer, from the way you looked when I found you."

Caroline shivered. "I'd rather not talk about that,

if you don't mind."

Nor the way he had looked when she first saw him, like some wonderful mythological god, gazing down on her with his torso bronzed and gleaming with seawater, and sunlight creating a golden halo around his magnificent head — no, she didn't want to think about any of that now.

"You were never unwelcome here, Caroline. If you don't know it by now, maybe you should see Dr. Sam for a head examination," he said.

She registered the nuance in his voice. It was oddly rough, as if he really cared . . . but it quickly reverted to normal as Mrs. Hughes entered the dining room with a steaming dish of boiled chicken and vegetables. When she had directed the serving maid in her duties to her satisfaction, they were left alone again, and Luke continued the conversation.

"But you're quite right. I should have shared the guest list for the party with you. We'll go through it after our meal, and I'll explain who some of the people are."

"Kathleen's already done that, but thank you."

He looked at her quizzically. "And that was all she came to say?"

"No," she said shortly. "She wants me to persuade her father that this is truly paradise island and that he doesn't really want to go back to the old country."

For once, she had caught Luke off guard. He looked completely surprised at this news.

"Good God, what's Dadda Finnegan thinking about? His daughters are completely happy here, and they'd be distraught if they had to leave Brundy."

And what about you? Would you be distraught, too, if Kathleen Finnegan went back to Ireland with her Dadda?

280

"And what the devil does she think you can about it, anyway?" He was brusque to the point of rudeness, but this time Caroline ignored it.

She gave a small forced laugh. "Oh, I'm supposed to engage him in conversation and say how wonderful it is here and how enchanting it all is after smoky old London with its pea-soupers and dank winters. I'm supposed to compare London in a way with damp old Ireland and make him see all the benefits of living on beautiful Brundy for the rest of his life. Everything he could ever want is right here."

She tried not to sound sarcastic, but she realized Luke wasn't saying anything now. She looked across the table through the flickering candlelight, straight into his dark eyes. And she caught her breath at the fire and passion she saw there.

"Rehearse your words well, my darling," he said in a voice that was soft and rich with seduction. "Say them often enough, and perhaps you'll come to realize they mean as much to you as I trust they'll mean to Dadda Finnegan."

She knew she had fallen into a trap, but that didn't mean there was no way out of it. Dadda Finnegan had all his family here, and he'd soon remember that this was his real home now. While Caroline . . . She knew that any real hopes of finding her father alive were slipping away now and had been for some time. And although she tried to keep living on hope, it was like walking on a knife's edge all the time.

But if she didn't have her father, she still had his legacy. In Sydney his whole world awaited her. If her father was dead, his newspaper empire belonged to her now, and she wouldn't let him down by staying here on this beautiful island and forgetting all that he stood for. Luke considered that she owed

281

him her life. But she'd had a life before him, and she owed all her loyalty to her father. Luke must be made to see that. If he had any sensitivity at all, then he must.

"If you've quite finished, we'll go into the study and go over the guest list, Caroline," he was saying now, and she realized she had been staring down at her empty plate for some minutes as the thoughts whirled in her head.

"Luke, there's something I must say—"

"It can wait until later, my love."

He rose from the table and came round to her side to ease her chair back for her. She felt his hands on her bare shoulders in the silky evening gown she wore and knew that this man would always have the power to send the blood surging through her veins and that her limbs would always go weak at his touch. The knowledge only made her the more determined to hold on to every bit of self-discipline that she could muster. She knew her own destiny, and it wasn't with Luke Garston. She repeated the words over and over inside her head, and made herself believe them.

It wasn't often that she was invited into Luke's study. It was essentially a man's room, smelling of leather and books and ink. She wasn't altogether comfortable in it because it reminded her far too sharply of her father's old study, from where the same smells emanated, combined with those of Sir William's favorite cigars. She drew in her breath for a moment, imagining the scent of the Havanas drifting around her.

The imagery made her momentarily dizzy until she realized Luke was smoking a cigar too. She forced herself to concentrate on the sheet of paper he handed her from the other side of the oak desk. Seated opposite her, confident and powerful, he looked exactly what he was. He was the king of his empire, however small and contained that empire.

Quickly she looked through the list of names presented to her in Luke's flamboyant handwriting. She recognized most of them from Kathleen Finnegan's visit that afternoon. The Dalbys, Colonel Wray, Michael and Jane Treherbert, and a few others. The girl clearly knew Luke very well, Caroline thought, with a stab of jealousy, choosing to ignore the fact that there would obviously be a limited guest list at any gathering on this island.

There were also names she hadn't heard of before. Most were obviously Europeans, but there was also a family named Sangai.

"Well, ma'am? Does it please you? We're a very cosmopolitan community here, but we all mix very well. Do you have any comments or suggestions?" Luke said in what she took to be a mocking voice.

"How could I since I know hardly any of these people!"

"You will soon, my love. I can't give you the atmosphere of a London street or an English village community, but these people are our neighbors for all that."

"*Your* neighbors, perhaps, but not mine."

She stood up, suddenly stifled by the closeness of the study, and her eyes dared him to deny her words. But as he blew a fragrant haze of blue smoke into the air, she felt faint again, and he seemed to waver in front of her face.

"Are you all right?" Luke's concerned voice seemed to come from a long way away, and Caroline clutched wildly at the back of her leather armchair.

"Yes," she mumbled. "I just felt odd for a moment. It was remembering my father. He had a study very much like this one." She blinked back the threatening tears. "I don't know why it should be such silly little things that remind me and catch me out so often."

She had a job to hold on to her dignity now. The tears brimmed on her lashes, and with a smothered oath, Luke left the sheaf of papers on his desk and came to catch her as she moved limply toward the chair again.

"We'll get out of here" he said roughly.

"No, not for a minute," she whispered, taking a deep, shuddering breath. "I have to get used to these things. I can't let them rule my life, nor allow the scent of leather and ink to reduce me to a sniveling heap. When I go to Father's offices in Sydney, such things will be all around me. I have to accept it."

He looked at her strangely. "For somebody who looks as though a good headwind might blow her away right now, you're a damnably strong woman, Caroline."

From his tone, she knew it wasn't meant to be a compliment. As she regained her composure, she knew very well that he wanted her soft and pliant and warm in his arms, not willful, intent on walking in her father's shoes—even though she knew she could never fill them. For a moment she wished she could forget all about family loyalty, and be all that Luke Garston wanted her to be . . .

She was still held in his arms, but she sensed that his passion was held very much in check. He spoke in a slow, frustrated voice.

"Caroline, I can fight anything but a ghost. And I'd give anything in the world for your father to walk into this room this minute, so that you and I could get on with our own lives instead of being

284

ruled by his. You know that's what you're doing to us, don't you, my darling?"

"I only know I can't think about the rest of my life until I know for certain what's happened to him," she said helplessly.

Rightly or wrongly, it had become a quest that she had to follow through, no matter how long it took. She felt Luke fold her in his arms and then the tears ran down her cheeks as she felt his heartbeats, so close, and so compatible with her own that they became almost one.

"Then I suppose I must bide my time," he said softly in what Caroline knew must be a rare moment of humility.

But she wasn't going to deny the sweetness of this embrace. She leaned her head against him in the oddly intimate, leather-scented study, reveling in such a moment. She was also ruefully certain that it wouldn't last. He'd called her strong, but she was only too aware of the strength of his own feelings and his arrogant masculinity. He was still engaged in a chase he didn't intend to lose. If she had a quest, then so, too, did Luke, and he'd made no secret of the fact that the object of his quest was Caroline Rowe.

Chapter Fifteen

When the night of the party arrived, Caroline knew how much she wanted to enjoy it. It would be a truly social occasion, the like of which she hadn't known since the voyage on the *Princess Victoria*. Such times had been reminiscent of evenings at home in England, with plenty of shipboard entertainment for the pleasure of the paying passengers.

She deliberately pushed aside the sweet nostalgic thoughts. It was time to look forward, not back . . . and for almost the first time since the shipwreck, she found that she was actually looking forward to something. It was a good feeling, she thought, as Petal helped her to dress in the rustling, wine-colored silk gown that had appeared in her closet for her approval.

She no longer questioned the arrival of such things. If Luke wanted to cater to her needs, then for the time being she would let him. That he had such exquisite taste and knew exactly what suited her was by the bye That Mrs. Hughes was so good with her needle and adept at altering and fitting was another piece of good fortune.

And by now, Caroline was beyond totting up everything that she owed him. She could never truly repay him, but there must be some way. And when she reached Sydney and consulted with lawyers there, she had already determined to see that he was well paid for all his kindness and his efforts to help her find her father.

Meanwhile, she stood up with a shimmer of skirts and twirled around for Petal to admire her.

"What do you think? Will I do?" she asked the maid.

The girl clasped her hands together and spoke breathlessly. "Missy look good enough for Mr. Luke to love!"

Caroline smiled slightly. "No, Petal. The English phrase is 'good enough to eat'!"

She shook her head vigorously, clearly finding some of the English vocabulary incomprehensible. "Mr. Luke no want eat Missy. Just to love. And Missy look real good enough—"

"All right, and thank you," Caroline said hastily. "Now just tidy up in here and then I won't need you again this evening."

She didn't want to hear anything more about being good enough for Luke Garston to love. He hadn't wanted to make love to her for some time now, and she had to accept the fact that love, in the purest sense, was farthest from his mind.

With every step of the curving staircase that she descended she reminded herself of the fact and tried very hard not to care.

He greeted her at the foot of the stairs. Kissing her gloved hand with all the gentility of a country squire, he looked her over. She couldn't read his expression. She only knew that she was breathing unevenly and that her hands weren't quite steady. She gave a small, forced laugh.

"Well? Will I do?" she said huskily, repeating the question she had asked Petal. Only this time, it was far more important to know that she looked right for him.

"Not quite," he answered.

Caroline stared, not knowing what to make of this reply. She had expected some compliment, some declaration of how beautiful and desirable she looked, and she hadn't bargained for anything less. She felt ridiculously let down.

"I'm sorry," she muttered, knowing she should be sophisticated enough to rise above this arrogant response, but quite unable to do so.

She felt him squeeze her hand. "Don't be. You already know you're the most desirable woman in the world to me, but you need something else to make the picture complete."

She looked at him, puzzled.

"Come into the drawing room, Caroline. I've something to give you before our guests arrive."

"You've already given me far too much," she protested. "I can't go on taking from you, Luke."

"Don't talk nonsense," he said, and she detected an odd note of tension in his voice. It was as though he had something else on his mind this evening, aside from the party. Something that was very important to him.

She forgot all about surmising what it might be when they reached the drawing room and he closed the door behind them. For the moment they were alone in this beautiful room. It was lit by extra candles for the evening, and the long open French windows led out to a garden festooned by lanterns for the occasion.

The gently lisping sound of the sea was lulling in the distance, and a huge yellow moon looked down

288

upon them. It was another of those tropical nights made for lovers, Caroline thought fleetingly, and deliberately turned her back on the sight, suddenly glad that they were not to be alone for very much longer.

She saw Luke open a drawer in a little side table and take out a long jewel case. He handed it to her.

"For you, Caroline."

She backed away slightly. She had seen the case before and knew what it contained.

"I can't take this. It's far too costly and important to you. I don't forget how you once told me it was for a very special person. Luke, I'm not that person."

She might as well have been talking to the air. He was removing the pearl necklace and draping it over his hand, where it shimmered and curved in sheer perfection.

"It was made for you, my love," he said softly, and before she could find strength to resist, he had looped it around her neck, where it lay cool against her throat. She caught sight of herself in one of the long mirrors in the drawing room, used to such good effect to reflect and enhance every bit of candlelight in the room.

The pearls were in sharp contrast to the deep lustrous color of her gown, and Caroline knew instantly that this was the reason Luke had wished her to wear it tonight. No one could fail to notice the simplicity and the purity of pearls and wine together. Ice and fire . . .

Caroline's fingers reached up to touch the clasp, but he was there before her. Their reflection in the mirror was one of utmost intimacy, yet she felt oddly alienated from him, angry.

"I don't want this," she said raggedly. "You said it was intended for your wife—"

"So it is, but you'll do me the goodness of keeping it on for this evening, Caroline—unless you want to make a scene in front of our guests."

As if he had engineered the moment precisely, which Caroline didn't doubt for a moment, the door opened, and a manservant began ushering in the first arrivals. Caroline forced a smile to her lips as she clasped the welcoming hands of Dr. Sam, followed by the Finnegan family. From then on there was no time to smart over the way Luke had tricked her into wearing the pearl necklace.

But she wouldn't keep it, she vowed. It was made for the woman he would love and cherish all his life, and she still doubted that Luke Garston was yet ready to make such a lifelong commitment. He was still too intent on the chase.

"This is for you and Luke, Caroline," she heard Dr. Sam say. He gave her a huge wink. "Take it medicinally if you must—as long as you enjoy it, my duck."

She laughed at the bottle of homemade wine he handed her. A gift for the hostess was a lovely custom, and Caroline was too feminine not to love such surprises. The Finnegans, too, had come bearing gifts. A jar of sweet honey and a posy of flowers . . .

"You look especially lovely tonight, Caroline," Kathleen said. "Not many women would have the confidence to wear such a dramatic color with a single string of pearls."

Her gaze was on the necklace as she spoke, and she smiled faintly. Suddenly self-conscious, Caroline wondered suspiciously if the other girl knew the significance of it. Perhaps she had once thought to wear it . . . and perhaps she should be wearing it now, she thought, with another stab of unreasonable anger.

For she still didn't know where Luke spent most of his evenings after he said good night to her.

There had been many nights recently when she had heard him return to the house very late. She had heard the creak of floorboards in his room long after she had gone to bed. Trying in vain to sleep, she had to stop herself imagining where he had been, lying with some other woman in his arms . . .

"Caroline, I want you to meet my good friend, Lee Sangai," Luke was saying at her elbow now, and she turned in some relief from Kathleen's too-knowing eyes to greet the newcomers.

The evening was full of surprises, and the family Sangai was one more. Caroline had assumed them to be some kind of Eastern European family or perhaps even Aborigines, since Luke was blind to any kind of class distinction. At least she approved of that much in him.

But it was something of a shock to be introduced to the three small, neat figures dressed immaculately in their native garb and bowing deeply toward her. The identical young girls, their sleek hair black and glossy with health, were embellished with pearl and diamanté combs, their brilliant kingfisher blue kimonos gracing their slight shapes. The father was resplendent in a garment of similar style, but nonetheless a man for all that.

"You're Japanese!" Caroline exclaimed, and blushed furiously at her own bad manners.

In her head she immediately recalled her old nanny's stern intonings. *An English lady never makes a bold statement in public, especially regarding another race, and never shows surprise. Always remember discretion and decorum in all things, Caroline . . .*

Even as she remembered the old schoolroom teachings, she thought how ridiculous it all seemed in these circumstances, especially as these nice

291

young girls and their father were taking no offense whatsoever.

"How very astute of you, Miss Rowe," father Sangai said affably. "May I introduce my daughters, Sangai Kim and Sangai Yoko."

The girls bowed once more, and as Caroline found herself automatically bowing in return, she caught the look in Luke's laughing eyes.

"We are so happy to meet you, Miss Rowe," the girls said in chorus. "We hear so much about you from Mr. Luke."

She was completely enchanted by them, and also by the softness of their voices. They were obviously twins, and Luke was clearly enjoying the fact that she found them so delightful. Together they produced a beautifully wrapped parcel and handed it to her.

"For you, Miss Rowe, as a welcome to Brundy," Sangai Kim said shyly.

Caroline opened it carefully. Inside the wrappings was a bowl of delicate porcelain, and on it was painted an intricate spray of bright red flowers with black Japanese characters alongside it.

"It's exquisite," Caroline breathed. "But there was really no need—"

"It is the custom, Miss Rowe," father Sangai said solemnly. "My daughters work many hours to decorate the dish."

"You did this?" Caroline said in astonishment, fingering the fine brushstrokes.

"Would you like to know what it says?" Sangai Yoko asked.

Caroline looked bemused for a moment, and then Luke came to her rescue.

"The pretty black marks aren't just there for decoration, Caroline. They spell out a personal message."

"Well, I guessed as much," she said quickly,

292

knowing that she hadn't done any such thing. How was an English lady expected to know that such hieroglyphics, however attractive, were Japanese writing? She smiled warmly at Yoko, ignoring Luke, and silently seething that he hadn't forewarned her about this charming family and their customs.

"Please tell me what it says, Miss Sangai."

"It says that we wish you and Mr. Luke much health and happiness."

"Well, that's very sweet of you both," Caroline said evenly, though feeling more than a little annoyed that their names had been coupled so obviously.

She began to harbor a great suspicion about this party, and wondered just how Luke had worded the invitations she had never seen. The gifts and the pearl necklace in any civilized society would all point to a betrothal party. She turned on him swiftly, but he was already greeting a large group of people who had all arrived together.

From then on there was no time to talk to him alone. She was surrounded by well-wishers and guests, her arms filled with gifts, small and large. Her suspicion was becoming a reality as she was wished much luck and welcomed to the island by people she had never met before tonight.

But she tried not to let it ruin her evening since all these people were so very pleasant and hospitable. The ambience couldn't have been better. And Mrs. Hughes had prepared a veritable feast of hors d'oeuvres to help the evening pass very smoothly. Miss Pringle was persuaded to play the piano several times, and since the old remembered English ditties were the favorites, most of them joined in the singing. The lady made a point of seeking Caroline out when she had exhausted her repertoire.

"It's such a thrill to meet you, Miss Rowe," she said. "We haven't had news of England for such a

293

long time, and it's so good to know of the current situation there."

"Well, I'm glad you think so, though I don't really feel I've told you anything very significant," she said honestly. "It seems so long ago now since I left."

With a start, she realized it was true. The seasons had moved on, even though it had been spring when she left England and was still summer here. Summer seemed to be endless . . . but of course, the world was topsy-turvy in this hemisphere, and what was summer here would be winter in England by now. It wasn't easy to comprehend.

"I always say the past is best forgotten," the crusty Colonel Wray said, helping himself to another glass of the best port wine. "Though I could entertain you with some good old army stories that would curdle your blood, if you've a mind to 'em, ladies—"

"Thank you, no," said Miss Pringle quickly, clearly having heard them all before. "I'm sure Miss Rowe doesn't want to hear any of your unsavory tales either."

"Talking of England." Dadda Finnegan was suddenly at Caroline's side before she could protest that this was really Luke's party, not hers. "My girl says you promised to tell me what the old place was like when you left it, my dear. Shall we find a corner together?"

It hadn't been what Caroline especially wanted to do, but she was grateful to the old Irishman now for giving her time to sit quietly. He whispered that he'd thought she might need rescuing from Pringle and Wray, who usually got into an argument when they were together for very long. Caroline was amused.

Pringle and Wray were two old expatriates, enjoying their arguments as much as most people enjoyed harmony. As far as Caroline was concerned, everyone was friendly toward her, and delightful company, and she had always been charmed by a bit of eccentricity. Dadda himself could certainly qualify for that title . . .

And it all helped to take her mind away from the nagging thought that Luke had inveigled her into this for his own ends. Giving her the pearl necklace had seemed to put the seal on his intentions, but once people had seen her wearing it, she could hardly tear it from her throat. She wondered if he would even have the audacity to make a formal announcement of their engagement. He would never expect her to deny it in public. And she wondered savagely just how he was going to react when she did so.

"We had a terrible winter last year," she told Dadda Finnegan truthfully. "There were pea-souper fogs that took one's breath away, and many old people didn't survive them. My own father suffered badly from wheezing."

She bit her lip for a moment, remembering the nights her father had relied on hot steam and coal tar preparations to ease his congestion, and she had listened to his harsh racking with dread. It had been one more reason to come to warmer climes.

"It's a good thing winter doesn't last all year round," Dadda Finnegan was saying.

"Oh yes, but then we had a drenching wet spring with gales so fierce they blew the tiles from the rooftops and stung one's eyes whenever one stepped outside the front door—"

She realized he had begun to laugh as she exaggerated. Besides, knowing the ferocity of the gales and tropical storms that occurred around Brundy's shores, there was nothing new in what she was telling him. She gave him a wry smile. "You know why Kathleen wanted me to talk to you, don't you?" she said bluntly. "Her heart's in Brundy, and she truly believes yours is, too, if only you could see it, Dadda Finnegan."

"Are you talking about me or about yourself, me darlin'?" he said shrewdly.

"Why, you, of course!"

She looked away. Across the room Kathleen was deep in conversation with Luke. They looked so close, she thought, with a catch in her throat. He, dressed in darkly elegant evening attire, and she in salmon pink silk. They had known one another for so long and complemented each other so well.

As she watched, a tall young man joined them, and to her surprise she saw Kathleen link her hand through his arm. Caroline felt her mouth open slightly and heard Dadda Finnegan's chuckle.

"I think you can forget my old nonsense about wanting to return to the old country. It was just an old man gettin' maudlin for a while, and my girl took it too much to heart. But now the two of them have come to their senses, it looks as though she'll have plenty on her mind from now on. Still, if it meant I had the loveliest colleen in the room sitting with me for a wee while, it was all worth it."

Caroline felt her heart lurch for a moment as she took in what he was saying. And then she saw how happy Kathleen looked, and tried to swallow her jealousy.

"That's Michael Treherbert with her and Luke, isn't it?" Caroline murmured, ignoring the flowery compliment as she noted how Michael Treherbert and Kathleen Finnegan managed to look so cozy together. Kathleen was obviously the kind of girl who brought out the protective instinct in every eligible man she met.

"So it is, and a good, wholesome couple they

296

make, wouldn't you say?"

"Oh, yes, of course. She and Luke look very good together," she said, making herself say the words.

"I wasn't thinking of Luke, me darlin'. No, 'tis the other one I've a fancy for my son-in-law," Dadda said with a chuckle.

If it was sheer lunacy to feel such uninhibited joy at Dadda Finnegan's words, she just couldn't help it.

Before her whirling thoughts could let her dare to wonder if there was any substance in Dadda Finnegan's blarney, she was drawn once again into the general body of the party and persuaded to eat some of Mrs. Hughes's delicacies and drink more of the wine that flowed so freely.

By the time the eating and drinking were almost done, Caroline began to feel quite lightheaded and as relaxed as if she had known these people all her life. And when she saw Luke look across the room to meet her eyes, it was as though there was no one else in the room but the two of them. There was an inevitability about the way he deliberately made his way toward her, taking her hand and drawing her over to where Kathleen and Michael were still deep in conversation.

But all of them were shadowy, watercolor figures, and the only reality was Luke's hand holding hers, his other arm firmly around her waist. As if at a pre-arranged signal, someone banged a glass on a table for silence, and then Luke began to speak.

"My good friends, you'll be thankful to hear I don't intend to make a speech. I just want to thank you all for coming this evening. And firstly, I have Dadda Finnegan's approval to make a special announcement, which will come as no surprise to most of us. So will you please raise your glasses to the betrothal of Michael and Kathleen?"

Caroline blinked in surprise. But seeing the way the other guests looked so approving and how Dadda raised his glass high, she guessed this had been coming for a long time. Apart from the couple concerned, he and Luke were probably two of the few people aware of tonight's announcement. Neither had breathed a word of it—and she had been wrong about Kathleen.

Someone had placed a glass in her hand, and she drank deeply, not sure whether or not to be furious with Luke for not warning her and wondering if she had been wrong about everything else as well. But as the hubbub died down, Luke held up his hand to speak again.

"The second reason for welcoming you all this evening is to propose a toast to my own special and unpredictable lady, Miss Caroline Rowe. You may or may not expect an announcement soon, but in any case, two in one evening is one too many for any gathering. Besides, the outcome of our acquaintance very much depends on the lady's whims."

She realized he was teasing her and that everyone was enjoying the teasing. It didn't seem to matter too much to them. They had their excitement with the prospect of a wedding in their midst, and suddenly Michael and Kathleen were the couple of the evening. They were islanders and part of the community, while Caroline was still the outsider.

She drained her glass of wine and turned to put it on the mantel. For once she wished the room wasn't so full of mirrors. She couldn't escape Luke's eyes, no matter where she looked, and he still held her captive.

"Why did you do that?" she said in a low, angry voice. "You made me look foolish, as if I'm a flighty young thing who doesn't know her own mind."

"Well, do you? Can you tell me with certainty that you'll never be my wife? Can you really look into your heart and say it in all honesty?"

She glanced around, but as so often happened, they were momentarily isolated in a roomful of people.

"No," she said slowly. "But nor can I say that I'll never return to England or that pigs won't fly."

"I doubt the last, and I hope you'll never want the former. But thank you for still giving me hope, my darling."

He sounded too sincere for comfort, and she looked at him sharply. But then someone else was claiming his attention, and the moment was quickly gone.

She knew she was quite mad to feel so hopelessly let down. But what had she expected? Had she really thought Luke would have announced their engagement in front of all his friends and risked her denouncing him? And what if he had done so . . . ? She had been perfectly ready to say that she had no intention of marrying him and that no man was ever going to force her into marriage.

Even as she thought it, though, she knew she never would have replied thus. If Luke had announced their engagement, she would have been the one surrounded by well-wishers now, as intoxicated as if she'd drunk a magnum of champagne because she would have gotten her heart's desire.

Instead she found herself joining in the excitement surrounding Kathleen Finnegan, feeling that once more Luke had managed to find a way to snub her for her refusal to play his game. The one face-saving grace was that none of the others here would be aware of it, only Caroline herself. And only she knew how much it hurt.

* * *

She confronted him after all the partygoers had departed. It was very late, and Luke was pouring himself another glass of brandy, though by then she guessed he'd had more than enough already.

"I suppose you thought that was an amusing little game to play this evening," she said, her voice high.

"What game?" he asked. "I didn't think you enjoyed games, my sweet. You take life so very seriously."

"Sometimes you disgust me. You play around with peoples' lives and think it very clever. You obviously knew long ago that Michael and Kathleen intended to announce their engagement tonight. They should have been receiving gifts, not me!"

"Their turn will come. And as it happens, I wasn't aware of it until they told me, and they wanted it done without the fuss of their own formal party. I'm sorry if you think I played some kind of game with you."

"What else would you call it when you implied so clumsily that it was only a matter of time before you'd be announcing *our* engagement as well?"

"That's not a game to me, and it was just a simple statement of fact. Naturally I realized I'd be putting you in an impossible position if I coupled our names together without your consent."

"Dear God, but it's a little late for a burst of conscience, isn't it?" Caroline said. "The islanders think me little more than a tease now."

"Does that bother you so much?" Luke asked. He came toward her, and she knew he was going to kiss her. She could smell the spirits on his breath, and she didn't want to be kissed like this.

"Of course it bothers me. I'm not that kind of woman, and I've always despised those who are."

He suddenly reached out and pulled her into his arms, and she had no chance to resist. She was held tightly against his chest, and she could hardly breathe, let alone have the capacity to struggle.

"Then what kind of woman are you, my sweet? Are you the kind who would dare all for love?" His voice was thick, but for the moment she couldn't tell whether it was made so by drink or by passion.

"Yes," she whispered. "I would dare anything for love, but I think that's a word you know little about."

Luke laughed harshly. "Then it shows how little you know about *me*, doesn't it, sweetheart? I would willingly risk everything for love. Wouldn't you say that makes us two of a kind?"

"Perhaps."

She was finding it increasingly difficult to breathe now as his arms seemed to hold her in a vicelike grip. Her breasts were flattened against him, and she felt faint beads of perspiration on her forehead. The room was so hot, and the whole evening had been a more emotional experience than she had expected. And if only things had been different, she might have expected it to end seductively and intimately. She closed her eyes against the intensity of Luke's gaze and felt his lips brush against hers. His voice was husky now, and she shivered at its tone.

"We've been apart for too long, my Caroline, and it's a situation that has to end. Since you believe in honesty so much, do you deny that you want me to make love to you?"

The words of denial trembled on her lips. No, she didn't want it. She couldn't bear it. Because if it happened, all the passion and the longing for him would flare into life once more, and she was trying so hard to keep them under control.

Kathleen Finnegan might not be the love of his life, but Caroline still didn't know for certain that she herself was either. Sweet talk came easily to Luke Garston, yet he had never told her that he loved her, and she was too afraid to ask. She cyni-

301

cally believed that a man would say anything in the heat of passion, and love could too easily be mistaken for lust.

"Do you want me, Caroline?" Luke's voice said softly. She felt his knee move gently between her legs, and she was very aware of her own trembling. She hadn't even noticed that his arms had slackened their grip and that she was the one clinging to him now. One of his hands had moved to her bodice and was slowly caressing her breast beneath the silken fabric. She drew a deep, shuddering breath and answered him with all honesty.

"Yes," she said huskily in return. "Yes, I do want you, Luke."

He kissed her more deeply this time. She felt his questing tongue roam around the sensitive flesh inside her mouth before it met her own.

"Then no one will disturb us, my darling. The doors are locked and the servants have gone to bed. And if you have a wish for fantasy, it will be all the more erotic, imagining that the company is still here."

She stared at him uncomprehendingly for a moment and then rich color filled her cheeks.

"You don't mean here, in this room—"

He laughed softly. "My sweet English rose, what else would I mean? There's no need for bedsheets and darkness. I thought you'd already discovered that beneath the stars on the mainland."

But here? In this elegant drawing room where an hour ago people had been talking and laughing and eating their fill? Caroline's eyes glinted as unwittingly she imagined the open-mouthed shock on the well-bred faces of Pringle and Wray, and the chuckling, vicarious enjoyment of Dadda Finnegan, watching two people make uninhibited love on the thickly tufted carpet. The room was still intimately lit by candlelight, and the mirrors all around the

302

room reflected the two people still standing in each others' arms.

Even as the thoughts whirled in her mind so erotically, Luke began to remove his dark jacket and neckcloth and then waited, watching her with a challenge in his eyes. He spoke softly.

"We'll take it in turns until there's nothing between us but your pearl necklace. I'll allow you to keep that on, my darling."

"That's very generous of you," she said faintly.

She felt as if she were mesmerized by those eyes. She turned her back to him, knowing he would unfasten the hooks of her gown and feeling his lips caress her skin with every inch of flesh that was uncovered. She shivered, suddenly reckless about what was going to happen. She knew she was intoxicated by the wine and the evening, but most of all by the man. The man she loved . . .

When all the fastenings were undone, she let the rich silk gown slither to the floor and stepped out of it in a flurry of petticoats. She turned to face Luke, feeling her breathing quicken as his hands went to the fastenings of his trousers. He paused.

"No. You do it," he said slowly.

She hesitated, but before she could voice a refusal, he had caught her hands and placed them where the evidence of his desire was all too prominent now. He gave an amused laugh as she fumbled with the buttons.

"For God's sake, hurry, Caroline, or I shall surely bust my breeches."

She felt laughter gurgling up inside her and wondered if it was appropriate to laugh. But she had already learned that making love with Luke could be a glorious romp, as well as being seductive and sensual, and suddenly she was furiously helping him out of his breeches, and he was lifting her remaining garments high above her head. Everything else followed speedily until they sank to the thick carpet together, rolling unashamedly into its deep musty pile.

"Do you see what I see, my little witch?" he said softly as his hands reached up to unpin the glorious weight of her hair.

"What do you see?" she murmured as his mouth nibbled at her ears, her lips, and then moved lower to the peaks of her breasts. She moved sensuously beneath him, already anticipating the moments when there would be no more separation between them, when their bodies would become fused as one. His heat would be her heat, his skin sliding rhythmically against hers, his body a part of hers . . .

"Look all around you," he said in a wickedly seductive voice. "And tell me if you don't see the most voluptuous pair in all Christendom, doing exactly what nature intended for them."

She glanced around the room, where their reflections were doubled and trebled, and more . . . two abandoned lovers, his fingers entwined in her hair, her body already starting to writhe beneath his as the weight of him and the scent of him awoke within her all the wanton passion of which she was so capable.

"Oh, Luke—" she began, the words of love brimming on her lips despite herself.

"Do you want to talk or to make love? It's been too long since I had you beneath me, Caroline, and I can't hold back much longer."

"Then don't," she whispered. "Don't wait another second . . ."

She felt him plunge into her, filling her, and she exalted in the feeling. He moved exquisitely slowly for a few moments, and her senses reeled. But the need for fulfillment was in them both, and without conscious thought, Caroline wrapped her arms more tightly around him, erotically raking his back with her fingernails.

As if it were the spur he needed, Luke began to ride her more urgently, until the moment of climax claimed them both simultaneously and she cried out wildly as he spilled into her.

When he was spent, he lay on her, breathing heavily, while she wondered bemusedly at their wantonness and knowing that none of it mattered. Nothing in the world mattered but the feelings between a man and a woman, and who was she to say whether or not what he gave her was love? It felt like love. On her part it *was* love . . .

Subtly, Luke moved away from her and pulled on his breeches, handing her her petticoats and gown. The time for confession had gone, if it had ever existed.

"Cover yourself and go to bed, my love," Luke said quietly. "Tomorrow will be soon enough for talking."

Chapter Sixteen

Caroline wasn't sure how she was going to face him the next morning. She awoke with a terrible headache and a feeling that somehow she had not gotten the better of him last night. As usual he had had his own way. The party, the shock announcement of Michael and Kathleen's engagement, wearing his pearls . . . and the lovemaking.

She moved restlessly in her bed, alarmed to discover she was wearing nothing but the pearls Luke had given her. She had crept upstairs, as stealthily as a cat that had been out on the rooftops, and with the same mixture of excitement and guilt. As if at any moment, bedroom doors would fly open, candlelight would stream out onto the corridors, and outraged servants would brand her for being the wanton hussy that she was . . .

Such fears had been nonsense. The servants slept on the floor above, and no one would disturb herself and Luke on this particular floor during the hours of darkness unless they were summoned by a bell. And there were no other house guests.

Caroline remembered now that Luke had escorted her to her door, but that she had insisted on entering her room alone. As if it mattered, after all they had done to one another in the torrid atmosphere of the drawing room! Her face was scorched with color now as she remembered all of it.

There was a brief knock on her door, and the next minute Petal came inside. The maid looked around the room with her sharply enquiring eyes, noting the way the clothes were scattered about on the floor and how quickly Caroline snuggled back under the sheets.

Petal picked up the lovely wine-colored gown and shook out its folds before draping it over her arm and looking down at Caroline with a grin.

"Missy like washing water now? Or Missy want tea in bed?"

"Missy does not," Caroline said crossly. "Missy is not ill, thank you."

She sat up quickly, completely forgetting that she was naked. She saw Petal's eyes widen at the sight of the milky white breasts and throat that showed such obvious evidence of kissing, and her eyes widened still more at the evocative sight of the pearls still around Caroline's neck.

"I take gown for washing and bring hot water," the girl said.

She almost fled from the room, and Caroline knew she still had difficulty in looking at such white skin without a feverish curiosity. Before she came back, Caroline had donned her undergarments and chosen a high-necked voile day gown, to hide the telltale marks of Luke's lovemaking. She hadn't removed the pearl necklace, telling herself she still wore it for safety's sake until she could return it to Luke, but she decided to tuck it inside the collar of the blue day gown.

"Is Mr. Luke downstairs yet?" she asked Petal casually as she attended to her washing ritual.

"He long gone," the girl said. "Everybody go to see ship. Only Mrs. Hughes, she say I must stay for Missy."

"What ship? Do you mean the trading ship?" Caroline spun round.

"That right. Ship come during night. She early, and Mr. Luke go see captain. Everybody go see what on board—"

"Help me to dress—quickly!"

She had already flung the towel aside, suddenly frantic. What if Luke had seized this opportunity to see the trading ship on its way before she had a chance to board it? What if he had intended to keep her here all along and while she slept conducted his business with the captain and then sent the ship on to Sydney, with no further chance of her reaching the mainland town for many months?

The wildest ideas raged through her. She had no idea how long such business transactions took, but she wouldn't put anything past Mr. Conniving Luke Garston.

Petal spoke huffily, clearly taking offense at Caroline's tone. "No hurry, Missy. Ship stay two days, always. Sailors like Brundy girls. You understand?"

She gave a broad wink, and to Caroline's sensitive feelings it meant only one thing. The maid was only too aware of what went on between Luke and his house guest, and was identifying the activities of the sailors and the island girls with them both. Caroline's voice was shrill with humiliation. "I don't care to understand. Will you please help me to dress, girl? I have to see the ship's captain myself."

And she didn't need Luke Garston to make the arrangements for her. She was quite capable of speaking to a gentleman sea captain and arranging her own passage to Sydney.

Petal sulked in silence as she helped Caroline

into her day clothes and only perked up when told that Caroline didn't want any breakfast and wouldn't need the girl's services for the rest of the day.

As soon as she stepped outside into the broiling sunlight and raised her parasol above her head, Caroline realized that most of Brundy had flocked to the coast that day.

Long before she reached the long harbor, she discovered it had turned into a kind of bazaar, with stalls that must have been hastily erected during the early hours displaying silks and goods of every description. The captain and his crew clearly did a magnificent trade wherever they put into port, if this was anything to go by.

She caught sight of Dr. Sam fingering some glassware and cheerfully haggling with the man in charge of the stall. She struggled to reach him through the crowds, bidding a quick good-morning to various people she knew.

"Dr. Sam, do you know how I can recognize the captain? Will he still be on board, do you think?"

The doctor turned, raising his battered straw hat to her in greeting.

"Good morning, Caroline. And a fine one it is for bartering. Now tell me, which of these tumblers do you think is fine enough to hold a man's whisky?"

She had no patience with his nonsense and gave no more than a cursory glance at the display of glassware. She pointed at one set without thinking.

"Those, I'm sure."

"Do you really think so? I'd have said they were more suitable for sherry drinking, myself, and that's no more a man's drink than lemonade."

"Dr. Sam! I want to see the captain. Can you

309

point him out to me or tell me where I can find him, *please!*"

At last he seemed to understand her urgency, and looked at her sorrowfully. "So you're still thinking of leaving us, are you? We all thought you'd given up that idea by now. And speaking personally, I'd hoped—still, it's no business of mine, gel. Anyway, the last time I saw Captain Ellis, he was heading for the drinking tavern on the waterfront with Luke. But you can't go in there, my duck. It's no place for a lady—"

But she was already weaving in and out of the melee and hurrying toward the end of the harbor to the seedy little tavern. The only ladies who frequented it were those of dubious morals, but Caroline had no thought for such things now. Her only need was to speak to the captain, and quickly. And her need wasn't lessened by hearing that he and Luke were probably drinking together by now. And hatching up all kinds of plans to thwart her, she thought savagely, quite unable to think sensibly about this meeting at all.

She drew breath as she neared the place. Its doors were flung wide to let in every bit of air, but its long balcony was overhung with a fringed bamboo shade to keep out the worst dazzle of the sun. Tables and chairs were grouped closely together, and all were full. Caroline's heart sank at the sight of the sailors with their well-weathered garb and swarthy faces. The sounds of their raucous laughter made her pause a moment.

Then she saw Luke. He and an older man were talking earnestly together. The man wore once-smart dark clothes which were well-creased now; a battered peaked cap topped his head. This, then, was the captain of the trading ship.

"Well now, just take a look at what's here, me laddos," one of the sailors said throatily, suddenly

310

catching sight of Caroline. "Things are looking up on old Brundy Island if this is a sample of the goods on offer."

Luke couldn't fail to hear lecherous comments, and his face darkened angrily as he saw her. With a muttered word to the captain, he strode out of the tavern and caught hold of her arm roughly.

"What in God's name are you doing here? Don't you see the effect you're having on these men? It's months since they've seen a decent white woman."

"I want to talk with the captain," she said defiantly. "And you're not going to stop me!"

"Why should I? But not here, unless you want to risk being assaulted. Any woman who frequents this tavern is fair game to the sailors. I did warn you about them."

She shuddered, backing away as she saw the sense of his words. He still kept a tight hold on her arm, though.

"Well then, please ask the captain to come out here," she said imperiously. "I'm not going back to the house until I've arranged to be taken to Sydney."

"And you didn't trust me enough to do that for you?"

She flushed. "Are you telling me that's what you've been doing?"

She heard Luke give a heavy sigh. "No, I'm not telling you that because I'm sure you wouldn't believe me."

He turned away from her, looking back toward the captain, who was watching them with interest now.

"Captain Ellis, can you spare us a few minutes?"

The man drained his tankard and came toward them. "I've things to do on board anyway," he said in a rasping voice that implied many years of shouting at a shipboard crew. "I'll walk along wi' the two of you since I'm sure the little lady won't be wanting to stay near these blackguards for too long. It's a pleasure to make your acquaintance, ma'am."

He smiled amiably enough, showing broken and discolored teeth, but he was the type of swarthy seagoing man of huge girth who knew exactly how to keep a wayward crew under control. They walked away from the tavern, and she tried not to notice the catcalls that followed them.

"Was there anything special you wanted, man?" the captain said, a little impatiently as he side-stepped a group of his men and some giggling native girls. "I thought we'd concluded your special business until you bring your goods for sale on board tomorrow morning."

"So we have, but the lady wanted to ask something of you," Luke said evenly. "Go ahead, Caroline."

"Will you take me as a passenger to Sydney, Captain Ellis?" she said in a rush. "It's very important that I get there as soon as possible. Perhaps Mr. Garston has told you of my circumstances—"

He gave a laugh as raucous as that of his men. "You're behind the times, little lady. Your man has already arranged passage for the two of you when we set sail. I daresay he wanted to surprise you by getting it all arranged before you were even awake this morning. Never fear. When we leave on the evening tide tomorrow, you'll be safely on board. And in a couple of weeks' time, you'll be in Sydney."

"So you're coming after all!"

Having seen Ellis's crew, she couldn't be more happy at the thought of having Luke's company and protection throughout the voyage to Sydney.

"Where else would I choose to be, since it produces such pleasure in you, my dear?" Luke grinned. He winked at the captain. "I wasn't sure whether or not I cared to be away from the island myself, captain, but one has to indulge the fair sex at times, and in the circumstances—"

"Naturally." Captain Ellis winked back. "And who could blame you, my dear sir!"

They had reached the ship now, and the captain tipped his cap to Caroline.

"Until tomorrow evening then, ma'am. And may I congratulate you both."

Her heart had seemed to stop for a few seconds at what she saw as Luke's outrageously patronizing remark, and then it raced on erratically. She wondered if she'd heard the captain's last words correctly, but Luke was still holding on to her very tightly and leading her skillfully through the crowds on the harbor. As soon as she could draw breath, she turned on him.

"Just what did Captain Ellis mean by that last remark? Why should he be congratulating us both?" she demanded. "And will you *please* stop hustling me about!"

She refused to walk any farther until he explained. She stood perfectly still and shook off his restraining hand. She was immediately jostled by the group of sailors and young island girls who had caught up with them, all obviously intent on making the most of their brief time together.

When they were clear of them, Luke shrugged. "What else should he mean but my good fortune in escorting a lovely young lady to Sydney, and yours in having been rescued from a watery grave? Captain Ellis and myself are old acquaintances, so I saw no reason not to tell him how we met and the reason you want to get to Sydney with all speed. I take it you have no objection to that?"

313

"It would be too late now if I did," she said.

"I also asked if he'd heard anything about the *Princess Victoria*, but there have been no reports of any survivors. You know, you really do have to learn to trust people and not question everybody's motives all the time, my sweet," he went on, starting to walk away from her.

As she didn't want to be crushed by the ever-increasing crowds eager to see what wares the trading ship had brought to the island from the Orient and the European ports of call, she followed him.

She was embarrassed to hear he'd asked about the fate of the *Princess Victoria*. It had been thoughtful of him, and she acknowledged that much. Not that it was likely they'd know anything, the cynical part of her argued, since the trading ship had come from the Orient and the Western world, and wouldn't have touched these waters before now. Still, the thought had been there . . .

She walked stiffly behind Luke, keeping her gaze on his broad, arrogant back, aware of a nagging feeling. He had sounded plausible enough, and more important than pondering over nuances and innuendoes was the thought that she was soon to leave for Sydney.

It was not without a definite pang, she realized to her own annoyance, as she knew she would be leaving this island paradise forever. Once she reached Sydney, she would be immersed in her father's world again, among friends who had come to Australia before them, knowing she would be welcomed, housed, and sheltered until she could find her own feet again. She would be leaving behind all these new friends, though she would have Luke Garston's company a few weeks longer. As she caught up with him quickly, without thinking, she put her hand on his arm.

"Luke, I haven't thanked you properly," she said

314

awkwardly. "I know you didn't really want to go to the mainland again, and this will obviously be a much longer voyage than the last one."

"If you want to thank me properly, you'll return to Brundy with me once your futile mission is over," he said.

She dropped her hand from his arm at once. "You know I can't do that."

"Why can't you? You have no ties to keep you there."

The implication of his words was brutal to her ears. He was so sure she would find no trace of her father. Or, if she did, it would be the news she was desperate not to hear.

"I'm grateful for your company on the voyage," she said distantly. "And I want you to come to the newspaper office with me as soon as we reach Sydney. My father's colleagues will reimburse you for everything you've done for me. There will be plenty of resources there for that."

"I've already told you I don't want your damn money."

He was savage, clearly hating to hear a woman discuss such things. An arrogant male, Caroline thought again, so much the hunter and provider, he dismissed her as one of the weaker sex. It infuriated her. And he'd soon discover his mistake when he saw how revered she was in her father's world, as his sole successor.

She swallowed, for in that assumption, she, too, was giving up all chance of finding her father alive. In her heart, she knew the chances now were so very slim. And yet, quite logically, here on this isolated island it was unlikely that news of any survivors from the doomed ship would have reached her, so she had to keep the hope alive. She had to.

They suddenly came face-to-face with Kathleen and Maureen Finnegan, and Caroline flushed, remembering how she had linked the older girl with Luke in her mind.

"Kathleen's bought some cream-colored silk for her wedding gown," Maureen said excitedly. "And meself and Michael's sister Jane are to be her attendants. What color do you think I should wear, Caroline?"

"Oh, something bright, I should think, to suit your personality," Caroline said, making a great effort to sound interested though she would be far away from there when the wedding between Kathleen Finnegan and Michael Treherbert took place.

"You'll be included in the guest list, of course, Caroline," Kathleen said warmly.

"Thank you," she murmured, her tongue sticking to the roof of her mouth a little. She told herself it was because of the heat, but it was more to do with the fact that she wouldn't be at the wedding, and she didn't know how to tell these people that she was to leave so soon. They had all been such good friends in the short time she had known them.

She'd thought it was common knowledge that she intended leaving on the trading vessel, but she realized now that such discussions had been kept to very few people. And those that had heard her say it obviously now believed she had settled down here and had no thoughts of leaving. They had coupled her with Luke in a way she wasn't altogether happy about. She wasn't his wife, but she lived in his house. Of course, it was impossible for her to stay!

However free and easy the lives of these people had become, it wasn't the way things were done in England. Guiltily Caroline knew how little she had considered those so-correct English ways whenever she had been stricken by the fever of passion . . .

She willed Luke not to say anything about her

leaving to the Finnegan girls, not wanting an argument to ensue. For once he seemed to be in tune with her thoughts. Reluctantly she supposed he would have to say something eventually. His friends would be hurt and surprised if he, too, left on the trading ship without any warning, but at least he'd be coming back. He belonged here.

Once they said goodbye to the girls and left the harbor and its colorful displays behind them, she was glad of the quiet solitude in the lanes leading to the house. The island had never seemed so beautiful now that she was about to leave it, she thought. Its lush golden bounties were dramatic and perfect, and in spite of everything, she was going to miss it all so much. She took a deep breath.

"Thank you for saying nothing to the Finnegan girls, Luke. I'd rather not have any fuss when I leave. I certainly don't want a party."

She stopped abruptly, knowing that if he suggested any such thing, it would all be too emotional for her to bear.

"I wasn't going to mention it to them. But if you really want to sneak away like a thief in the night, I suggest you pack everything you need with the assistance of Mrs. Hughes, rather than Petal, or it will be all over the island in no time. I must warn you, though, it's usual for most of them to turn out to see the ship leave. We won't be able to get away without people knowing. And Dr. Sam was well aware of your intention of leaving."

"I know, and I'd like to say goodbye to him properly, anyway. I presume you'll want to see a few people too." She realized anew that her arrival in his life had put him to a great deal of trouble.

"I'll arrange for Dr. Sam to come to dinner tonight. He and Mrs. Hughes know that your time here was only temporary, even if everyone else seems to see you as a permanent resident by now."

She looked at him sharply. Again, there was a little note in his voice she didn't quite understand. As if he had some secret of his own he wasn't telling her. She dismissed the thought as they came up to the house, and she went straight to the housekeeper's room to inform her of her imminent departure.

"I'll be sorry indeed to see you go, miss," the lady said sadly. "It's been a pleasure to look after you, and you've brought a rare bit of sunshine to the house."

"There's always plenty of that here without my adding to it," Caroline said, touched by the sentiment.

"Ah, but you've brought a joy to Mr. Luke's heart as well, though it's not my place to say so."

"He'll be accompanying me to Sydney, Mrs. Hughes," she said briskly. "Just for my safety, you understand, and then he'll be back when the trading ship makes its return journey."

"And you won't, my dear?"

"I'm afraid not."

She then enlisted the housekeeper's aid in packing her belongings. Everything she owned had been provided by Luke, but she had no option but to take it all with her if she wasn't to appear as some bit of flotsam pulled out of the sea.

For a moment, the image of how she must have looked when he first saw her flashed into her mind. Unkempt, filthy, dehydrated, nearly hallucinating . . . That wonderful first sight of him sprang up unbidden: ringed by a golden halo of sunlight around his tousled dark head, his bare, sun-bronzed torso glistened with seawater. A magnificent Greek god, come to claim her for his own . . .

* * *

Luke had told her he'd take their luggage down to the ship later that evening. She would dress normally tomorrow and take a casual walk to the harbor with Luke in the evening, as if they, too, were going to wave goodbye to the transient sailors. At that point, however, she and Luke would go on board, and they would be part of that floating cargo bound for Sydney . . .

A sudden thrill surged through her. Whatever the circumstances and however sad she was to leave this paradise, the next stage of her journey was about to begin. It was the continuation of the voyage she and Sir William Rowe had embarked upon all those months ago, and it was fitting that it should be properly completed. Something stronger than herself insisted that her mission had to come full circle.

"Would you please see that Luke has this, Mrs. Hughes?" she said evenly, handing the long slim case to the housekeeper. "It belongs to him, not to me."

The woman took it without comment, not understanding the significance of the jewel case. It was the one thing Caroline couldn't, in all conscience, take with her. The pearl necklace belonged to the woman Luke would make his wife, and it had only been loaned to her for that one beautiful evening.

"I understand the good doctor is joining you for dinner this evening, miss," the housekeeper said when everything was finally done. "Would you like me to prepare anything special?"

Caroline shook her head. "I'm sure it will all be wonderful, Mrs. Hughes, so I'll leave it entirely up to you," she said huskily, knowing she would hardly be able to taste any of it. She seemed to have lost her appetite lately.

What was wrong with her? she asked herself. She

319

had lived for this day, and now that it was almost here, she was suddenly afraid. It was yet another leap into the unknown . . . and she, who had braved the Big Land and its dangers, was unable to understand her own turbulent emotions.

It wasn't as if she were losing Luke immediately. They had several more weeks together on board ship, and then however long he agreed to stay in Sydney. Maybe they could even see something of the town together . . .

She listened to herself as she extended the time she was to have with him, knowing that once it was over there would be a void in her life as deep and empty as the one left by her father—perhaps more so. In the natural order of things, a father was expected to die before his daughter while two lovers were to share all their lives together.

She smothered a small sob. Just how foolish was she being in rejecting the man she loved so much? She knew she only had to say the word and she could have all this forever. He had made it plain he wanted to marry her. In his eyes, he already owned her for saving her life. It would be the Aborigine philosophy, too, so simple and uncomplicated. But it wasn't hers.

She had been brought up in an intelligent world of thinking men who dealt in facts, not dreams. She was no simpering female, dazzled by the prospect of marriage to a man who could sweep all her inhibitions aside by his erotic lovemaking. Her clear-sightedness was part of the legacy her father had left her, and she wouldn't give in to Luke Garston's emotional blackmail to get what he wanted. She recognized that she was his ultimate challenge. He had taken her most precious gift, and she could never hide her passion for him, but she could still stubbornly refuse him this. She wouldn't marry him without love.

320

She made polite conversation to Dr. Sam at dinner that evening, all too aware that this was the last time she would eat supper in this house. She was too emotionally caught up in her own thoughts to do justice to the meal, and apologized to Mrs. Hughes for her lack of interest in the food.

"You'll be thinking too much about tomorrow, my dear," Dr. Sam said. "It's understandable enough, though you want to pay attention to your health, my dear. You're looking a mite pinched in the face lately."

"I've had a lot to think about," she said ruefully. "It's hardly any wonder, is it?"

"Some sea air will do you good. They say an ocean voyage clears the soul, though I can't say it did a lot of good for the poor beggars who came to this unknown land under the King's orders. I'll look forward to hearing Luke's descriptions of Sydney town when he returns. It was a desolate place when the first fleet arrived there."

"It will be very different now," Caroline said confidently. "My father's newspaper colleagues sent us frequent reports of how the place had been cleaned up and of the fine houses that were being built."

"Oh yes. For those who can afford it, there will always be fine houses."

"You don't begrudge them their good fortune, do you Doc?" Luke asked.

"I do not, and nor do I envy them their town life. I much prefer the good clean salt air of the island, and you wouldn't catch me going back there."

Once the meal was over, Dr. Sam didn't linger.

"You'll both want to have a good night's sleep, and besides, I'll see you at the harbor tomorrow night. You're quite sure this is the way you want it, without letting everyone know in advance?"

"Quite sure," Luke said firmly.

"Then you'll permit an old man the privilege of kissing a pretty girl, I hope," the doctor said.

Caroline hugged him. Her eyes were quite moist. He had done so much for her, and saying goodbye to him was almost like losing a surrogate father.

"I'll never forget you," she said huskily.

"I should just think not, my gel! There's not many like meself around, thanks be to God, I daresay!"

She was thankful when he left. She felt exhausted and drained, and thankful, too, that Luke didn't prolong the evening any longer. She needed to sleep, to blot out from her mind everything but the stupendous thought that this time tomorrow night she would be on her way to Sydney, and, God willing, to definite news of her father.

Luke had business to discuss with Captain Ellis the following morning and had left the house early. When Caroline arose, she told herself she was going to make the most of the day. It was a hot, still morning that seemed to be watching and waiting, and took no account of the vagaries of mere humans. And the house was suddenly stifling her.

"Mrs. Hughes, I'm going to take a walk," she said. "Don't worry if I'm away for a couple of hours. I just want to take a last look around."

She avoided the housekeeper's eyes. This solitary walk was to be her private goodbye to the island, and they both knew it. She had known unbelievable happiness here, and only her compulsion to reach Sydney was strong enough to take her away. She opened her parasol and walked briskly from the house, not wanting to think too deeply about what Luke had said, that he couldn't fight with ghosts . . . and neither could she. Not until she knew what ghosts she had to fight.

She slowed down once she was away from the house. The dense vegetation soon obscured her from civilization. A person could be enveloped very quickly here, completely alone with nature. And yet, there was never any sense of terror as there had been on the mainland.

She heard a sudden high giggle, followed by a man's deep voice and throbbing laughter, and she moved quickly on. Most of the ship's crew would probably be somewhere on the island, and she had no wish to meet any of them. But they would undoubtedly have found their own soft targets by now. And she didn't want to imagine what those mingled voices implied in the tangled undergrowth of the bushes.

She came to a high ridge from where she could look down at some of the houses that were reminiscent of European dwellings. The sounds of children's chatter rose somewhere away to her left, followed by Maureen Finnegan's admonition to keep to the pathways and not to wander off. Clearly another nature lesson was underway for the brats.

Caroline gave a deep sigh. Yes, she would miss them all, but at least she wasn't losing everything this island had come to mean to her. Luke was keeping his promise to deliver her safely to Sydney, and he hadn't left her life yet. This calmed her nerves whenever she thought of the new voyage she was about to undertake. She didn't want to examine the reason for that too closely, however.

"I thought it was you I saw on the ridge, Caroline. Are you thinking about changing your mind, my dear?"

She saw Dr. Sam coming toward her, red-faced and puffing from the exertion of climbing the ridge. He fanned himself briskly with a broad-leafed tree branch for a few minutes while he caught his breath.

"No, I haven't changed my mind, Dr. Sam. I just wanted to take a last look around to keep the memory alive."

"I doubt that you'll lose it so easily, gel. Brundy Island will always mean something special to you, I'm thinking," he said shrewdly.

She was ready to bridle, but then capitulated. "Is it so obvious?" she said wistfully.

He grinned. "It's a mystery to me why two stubborn young people can't see what's right beneath their noses. But you'll tell me to mind my own business, I daresay. Now then, shall I walk back to the house with you? There's a fair few of them sailors up to no good in the woods, and besides, I've no objection to having a second goodbye hug from my favorite gel."

He was so kind in his own rough way. As they went carefully back down the track, Caroline was glad he couldn't know how touched she was, nor see the moistness in her eyes. But with his doctor's intuition, he probably guessed it all the same.

dozer. He turned himself quickly with a broad-
tacked tree branch for a few minutes while he

Chapter Seventeen

There were hugs and tears from Mrs. Hughes
before they left the house that evening, though she,
too, would go with the throngs down to the harbor to see the ship depart for Sydney. It was a ritual everyone followed.

Caroline and Luke strolled among the crowds on
the teeming harbor as if their only intention was
to see the boat on its way. Her heart beat wildly,
knowing how different it was all going to be for
them, and feeling increasingly awkward at the deception she insisted of Luke.

"I know there was very little time to let everyone
know about our departure, but what about your
boys?" Caroline said as she saw some of the Aborigines racing about and cheering as the flags were
being hauled up ready for sailing. "Won't they be
upset to know you've left them like this?"

"They already know," Luke said shortly. "Naturally I couldn't leave them high and dry. They've
been handsomely paid from the proceeds of the
pearls and oysters we got near the reef and are
quite capable of continuing the work without me

until I return. We got an exceptional harvest on the reef, and Captain Ellis is a fair man when it comes to trading, so the boys are not too displeased with their rewards from the trip."

And if the boys knew what was happening, there were probably many more people who knew by now. As if proof were needed, Caroline saw some of their recent party guests bearing down on them.

"So soon after we meet, we have to say goodbye then, Miss Rowe. Good luck to you, my girl," the crusty Colonel Wray bellowed. "I hope you find your father safe and well."

"Thank you so much. I hope so, too," she said, her throat closing at the unexpectedness of the remark.

"Take this, my dear." His companion, Miss Pringle, thrust a cloth-covered parcel into her hand. "It's a fruit cake. Heaven knows what kind of food you'll be served on a trading ship, but this will at least give you sustenance, and you'll know it has been baked with care."

"That's very kind of you!" Caroline said, not knowing whether to hug this prim little woman or not. Miss Pringle saved her the decision by stepping back a pace and nodding briskly.

But they were subjected to more good wishes and plenty of hugs from the Dalbys and even from the enigmatic Sangai family. The effusiveness of the Finnegan girls was almost unbearable to Caroline and was everything she had wanted to avoid as they had all made her feel so welcome. It was idiotic to feel like a rat deserting a sinking ship, but there it was . . .

She turned blindly to Luke. "Can we go on board now, Luke? I don't think I can cope with much more of this."

"And you're leaving us too, my friend?" the

colonel said, turning to Luke, clearly not prepared to let them go. "But only temporarily, I trust."

"Of course. This is my home, and I'll be back when the trader turns around, never fear."

But Caroline would not. She would never see these people and this lovely place again. Tears stung her eyes, and without waiting for Luke, she turned to clamber up the gangplank with unsteady steps. She felt a crewman's hand assisting her and gave him a watery smile of thanks. If he had not aided her, she felt she would surely have gone straight over the side into the crystal waters.

"Keep smiling," Luke said in her ear a moment later. "This is your choice, remember?"

She took some deep breaths, but by the time they reached a vantage point on the main deck, his words had put a new resolve into her. He was right. This was her choice and something she had to do. It was foolish indeed to give way to serious doubts now.

They leaned over the rail to wave at all the on-lookers. It was barely dusk yet, but the tropical night would come with dramatic suddenness. The beautiful blood red sunset now spreading its rays across the expanse of ocean ahead of them would soon be no more than a memory.

"Oh, Luke, this *is* going to turn out all right, isn't it? I have to keep believing that or I'll have nothing."

Her mouth trembled even while she tried to keep the smile on her face, and she kept waving to her friends as the ship began to slide out of the harbor, its sails billowing in the welcoming southern headwind.

She felt his arms close around her. "Whatever else happens, you'll always have me, lass," he said quietly.

327

She was embarrassed to think the islanders would misconstrue the intimate way they must appear now. But people were already too far away to be seen clearly, already taking on miniature proportions as the ship headed away from shore. And the night was swiftly and surely beginning to close in on them.

Luke told her they would sail a central channel between the longitude of Brundy Island and the Barrier Reef until they were south of the treacherous coral. From then on they would steer within sight of the eastern mainland until they reached Sydney. She gave a shiver, knowing that whatever she found there, she would have to accept it.

"You're cold," Luke said, misunderstanding. "It's time we went below. Captain Ellis has arranged that we should eat alone this evening, but we'll join him for our meals from tomorrow onward, if we wish it."

"That's very generous of him," she murmured, somewhat relieved that she and Luke wouldn't be totally isolated from humanity. It would have made their association seem far too intimate.

She had already discovered that this ship had none of the luxury of the *Princess Victoria*. It was essentially a working vessel with limited accommodation, apart from that available for the captain and crew. She had been told that it was rare for a voyage to continue without a few paying passengers en route, but at this stage of this particular voyage, there were only two, herself and Luke.

Caroline followed him below. She hadn't seen her cabin yet, but Luke had kept his word and brought their belongings to the ship on the previous evening, assuring her that everything was safely stowed.

328

She hadn't seen Captain Ellis either, apart from a perfunctory salute to her when she boarded, and he was clearly busy with his navigations now. It didn't matter. It gave her a chance to settle in and accustom herself to this next part of her life.

Luke opened a cabin door and stood aside for her to enter. The cabin wasn't terribly small, though it seemed so to Caroline after her luxurious room at Garston Manor. It was dimly lit by a candle contained in a thick glass holder, for safety's sake. It contained two bunks, a fixed table and two chairs, a chest of drawers, and several closets.

Caroline wrinkled her nose at the musty smell and grimaced at the hard-looking pillows and the serviceable patchwork coverlets on the bunks. The bedding was clean, but there was little else she could say for it. The thick green glass of the porthole was grimy and scratched. It was obvious that passengers were not the first priority of this vessel.

"I'm sorry it doesn't live up to your expectations, Caroline," Luke said, watching her face.

"It'll do," she said, swallowing her disappointment. "I didn't expect first class."

But perhaps she had expected something more than this. The cabin was hot and airless, and she couldn't forget Luke's warnings about the lusty crew. Remembering the sights and sounds of them with the native girls on the island, she could believe it all.

To hide her dismay and unease, she threw open one of the wall closets, as if the sight of her own clothes would give her reassurance. Quickly she fingered the soft silks and voiles of her gowns. Someone had hung them tidily and arranged her shoes and parasols just as neatly, but she was glad to see that her undergarments were still in their boxes.

She opened a second closet and stood perfectly still, aware of the drumming of her heart.

"These are your clothes," she said tightly at last.

She turned to Luke, the anger flashing in her eyes overtaking every other emotion. He stood arrogantly, folding his arms across his chest. He looked back at her with a challenging gleam in his eyes.

"Where else should they be, but in the same cabin as that of my wife?"

"I'm not your wife—" She stopped, feeling the slow sick surge of her heart as her sixth sense told her exactly what he was going to say before he said it.

"But everyone on board this ship believes that you are, my sweet, from the captain down to the lowliest deckhand. It was the safest way for you to travel. Because you pose as my wife, no one will dare molest you. This way, you're perfectly safe."

She stared at him, more enraged than she could have believed at this deception. "Don't you mean I'm safe from everyone but *you?*"

Luke spoke coolly. "Haven't you noticed that there are two bunks? Your chastity is quite safe unless you choose to invite me to share your bunk, Caroline." His face broke into a mocking smile. "In fact, I'm willing to wager that long before this journey is out, you'll have done so."

"Then you're even more arrogant than I supposed, to think so!" she snapped. "I've no intention of letting this situation continue. I shall inform the captain immediately that I want another cabin."

For how could she ever hold on to her self-control if he tried to seduce her? She hadn't managed it in the luxury of his home, nor beneath the stars in the wilds of the bush . . . She licked her dry lips. She must simply throw herself on the mercy of the captain and denounce Luke—but even as she thought it, doubts were assailing her.

Captain Ellis and Luke were old acquaintances, and he'd never believe her wild tale. He'd merely think she was a nervous, highly strung bride, afraid of the physical side of marriage. As a normal man, thinking of them as recently wed, he'd naturally assume they would take every opportunity offered by the narrow confines of one bunk and that the other would be unused. She saw now how neatly Luke had blocked the way to her demanding another cabin.

"I think not, my sweet," Luke said softly as if he read her mind. "A hysterical bride afraid of the marriage bed will only draw sniggers from the crew. Is that what you want? Or are you going to announce openly that we're not married and take your chances with the men? They'll have a few choice names for such a lady, and nobody lifts a finger to help a woman who's fair game for all."

If he made it sound as bad as possible to shock her into submission, she knew only too well the truth of his words. Aghast, she realized it would be disastrous to let the truth be known now, when the crew would be well aware of the cabin arrangements. If they discovered she was unmarried after all, she would be branded as a whore, and, just as Luke suggested, fair game for all.

"You managed all this very well, didn't you?" she said bitterly. "How long have you had it planned?"

Whatever he might have answered was lost as they heard a tap on the door. When Luke opened it, Captain Ellis came inside with a tray holding a bottle of red wine and two glasses. He put the tray on the table.

331

"Welcome aboard, Mr. Garston, and ma'am. I'm sorry I can't offer you better accommodation for your wedding trip, but if there's anything you require, just ask. The crew has orders not to bother you unless you request their service. One of my men will be happy to act as steward for you and will be bringing you a meal in a little while. After that, no one will disturb you this night. Meanwhile, please take this wine with my compliments, and may I wish you every happiness in your life together."

He was flowery in the way of a man unused to making formal speeches, and Caroline's cheeks burned, knowing it was beyond her to make a scene now. Besides, Luke had his arm firmly around her by now, and the captain was backing out of the cabin as if eager to get away from two people who would naturally want to be alone.

She turned on Luke again when the man had gone. "I hope you're proud of yourself! You've involved me in your deception now—"

She couldn't say anything more because Luke's mouth was hard on hers, pressing it into submission with his kiss. She fought to be free of him, her face scorched with rage.

"Please don't think I'm going to fall into your arms just because we're obliged to share this cabin for several weeks! Nor that I shan't think of some way of changing the situation! I can be as devious as yourself if I have to!"

He lounged on one of the bunks, smiling up at her taut figure, her voice full of bravado, her hands clenched tightly at her sides. He seemed to fill the other side of the cabin, and she despised herself for the frisson of raw excitement that ran through her despite herself.

"And how will you do that, my ingenious little

332

wife? Captain Ellis knows me too well to think I would mistreat a woman, so it would be a waste of time to protest on that score. Besides, a man has a right to treat his wife any way he chooses."

"A man with any sensitivity in his soul does not!" she said, outraged by this arrogance. "And I am not your wife!"

"Not yet," Luke said calmly. "So just how do you propose to change the arrangements, my darling?"

"I haven't decided yet," Caroline said, her lips setting in a mutinous line. A glimmer of an idea was stirring in her head, but she had no intention of telling him, for he'd surely find some means to thwart it.

Meanwhile, for this evening at least, she had no choice but to share this cabin with Luke Garston. As she felt the soft movement of the sea beneath their vessel, she knew it was going to be the hardest thing in the world to do. When it came down to the primitive need of a man for a woman, it was hard to refuse him anything.

A man known simply as Barnes brought their meal to the cabin. By then Caroline had stopped speaking to Luke and was lying on her bunk, staring up at the brown-painted ceiling. She moved too quickly when Barnes knocked on the door requesting admittance, and her head spun. There was no reason for it other than temper, she told herself. Her sea legs were good, and she realized she was suddenly hungry. The energy generated by the conflict between herself and Luke had the odd effect of also rousing her appetite. But better the appetite for food than any other kind, she thought grimly.

333

"It's nobbut cold cuts this evening, sir and ma'am," Barnes said in a broader, but vaguely similar accent to Luke's own. "I'll do me best to please ye, so feel free to call on me anytime. Will ye be wanting hot tea later?"

"Yes please—"

"No thanks, man, we'll make do with the captain's wine," Luke forestalled her.

Barnes looked at Caroline doubtfully. She gave a brief nod. Now that she thought about it, she didn't really feel like hot tea anyway. "The wine will do fine, thank you, Barnes, but I'd like some fresh fruit, if you have any. Strawberries, for preference."

"Aye, I believe we do. I'll bring them directly, and if you leave the empty tray outside your door when you've done, I'll see to it later."

Caroline was already lifting the cloth from the tray and eyeing the cold meats, bread, and pickles with some anticipation. Luke had begun to pour the wine and handed her a brimming glass. He raised his own to her.

"To our voyage, Caroline. And may it be a happy and fulfilling one, lass, and the end result be all that your heart desires," he said evenly.

She gave a small nod, refusing to feel choked by the sudden sincerity in his voice. If only she could believe that he wanted her for love and not merely for the conquest. Love would make all the difference.

She sipped the dark, heady wine, and if she doubted the wisdom of drinking any of it on an empty stomach, she quickly abandoned the thought. What was done was done, and there was no turning back now. Tonight there was every justification in taking all the comfort and relaxation the wine could give her. She drank more deeply

334

and picked up her fork to eat.

"What is this?" she said suspiciously, pushing the meat around her plate a little after the first mouthful.

"Wild boar, I suspect. You've no religious or moral objections to eating pig's meat, have you?"

"Not at all. But I do like to know what I'm eating. This meat is so salty I can hardly detect the taste."

"You've been on board ship before, Caroline, and should know that meat has to be kept well-salted to keep it moderately fresh on a voyage. Drink some more wine to allay the salt taste. The captain has obligingly sent us a vintage that's pleasantly dry. As paying passengers we'll get anything we like, as long as they have it on board."

He spoke as if they were dining at one of the best restaurants in London, Caroline thought irritably. As if nothing concerned him at all — and why should it when he always got his own way!

But when the man Barnes brought the bowl of strawberries a few minutes later, she smiled sweetly at him, with the result that the man told his shipmates he thought the pearler had got himself a real cracker of a lass for a wife.

"I didn't know you liked strawberries so much. We could have had them often if you'd requested them," he remarked. "They grow in abundance on the island."

"Yes, I've seen them," she said, without any more comment. She finished her main course and bit into one of the succulent berries, feeling the tangy juice trickle down her throat. She rarely ate too many of them, but tonight she felt reckless enough to have her fill.

She hardly realized how much wine they were drinking as Luke kept refilling her glass until she

335

saw that the bottle was almost empty. By then she was extraordinarily tired, yet she knew she had to keep her senses alert until she was safely in her own bunk.

"I trust you'll do me the courtesy of leaving me alone to undress," she said pointedly when the meal was over.

"If you think it necessary, my love, though I've already seen everything there is to see of your luscious body."

"I don't need you to remind me," she said shakily, the cabin starting to look decidedly hazy now. "I'd just like you to leave me for ten minutes when you put the tray outside, please. You owe me that much respect, since you've taken away all my privacy."

She bit her lip, hating this situation. She was desperate not to show how uneasy she was that the cabin bunks were only a yard apart. She would only have to stretch out her hand to touch him . . . and it would be the same for Luke. Knowing him for the passionate and single-minded man he was, how could she trust him not to take advantage of her?

"I'll take a stroll on deck," he said abruptly. "And you should know by now that you have nothing to fear from me, lass. I only want what's best for you."

"The best for me being you, is that it?"

He gave a crooked smile. "I'm glad you see the sense of it at last."

"I don't! I was merely—Oh, what's the use?" she ended wearily, slumping onto her bunk as her legs began to feel decidedly wobbly.

She wished desperately that Petal was here to unfasten her gown since she was sure she could never manage the back buttons herself. But her pride was never going to let her ask Luke to do it for her. Not when those treacherous hands would undoubtedly find their way around to her breasts . . . and she would be lost.

Caroline closed her eyes for a moment, wishing that the cabin didn't feel so unsteady and knowing it had been a mistake to drink so much wine. It may have relaxed her, but it also deadened her senses, and she needed to keep all her faculties tonight. Tomorrow, things would be different.

She realized Luke hadn't yet left the cabin, and she felt his fingers behind her back and then the loosening of her gown as he unbuttoned it. She was numb, awaiting the inevitable and wondering how it was that a man had all the power in the world while a woman was so helpless. She felt his hands move around her body as the gown loosened and then the tips of his fingers beneath her chin as he cupped her face. And then his mouth moved against hers in a kiss more gentle than she could ever have believed.

"If we had met in another time and place, my lass, I would make the world come right for you."

She opened her eyes slowly, and his own dark eyes were looking deep into hers, too close for her to read their expression properly. But she could feel the beat of his heart and knew how much he wanted her. And the words were almost torn from her that she wanted him too . . . so much . . .

"I won't disturb you again this night, Caroline. You'll manage the rest of your undressing yourself, and it's more than my flesh and blood can stand to watch you. I'll stay on deck for a while, so get yourself to bed and sleep well, my bonnie lass."

He kissed her again, with a touch as light as a summer breeze on her lips, and then he went out of the cabin quietly. Leaving her with brimming eyes. Leaving her unfulfilled, leaving her longing for him and unable to find the words to tell him so.

She never heard him return. She undressed with fumbling fingers and slid into the hard and unfamiliar bunk. She pulled the coverlet up to her ears and turned her face away from Luke's side of the cabin, falling into a deep, dreamless sleep almost as soon as her head touched the pillow.

She awoke to an appalling headache and sunlight streaming in through the grimy porthole. The smell of hot bacon filled the air. Luke would have requested it for breakfast, and opening her eyes a chink as she turned round in the bunk, she could see him already eating. The smell of the food almost made her retch.

"Good morning," he said with a smile. "I tried not to disturb you, but Barnes will bring you some breakfast whenever you wish."

"I don't want anything," she muttered. Gingerly she put up her hands to her face and felt the telltale lumps she had expected. Her face felt as though it were on fire. She moved the coverlet slowly away from her cheeks, and Luke dropped his fork onto his plate with a clatter.

"Good God, what's the matter with you, Caroline? Your face is as swollen and blotchy as if you've been brawling."

"Is it?" she said huskily. "I certainly feel battered, and I itch like fury. Oh, you don't suppose it could be the chickenpox! Some of the brats were suffering from it a week or so ago, and I may have caught it!"

"And it could be smallpox," he snapped. "I'm going to see Captain Ellis at once. There must

338

surely be a ship's doctor on board—"

"Oh, but I don't want a doctor!"

"Don't be ridiculous. Stay right where you are and keep calm."

He went out of the cabin, banging the door shut behind him. Caroline winced. In fact, apart from her throbbing head, she was perfectly calm, and he was the one suddenly in a state of alarm. Smallpox, indeed. She hid a thin smile, thinking that naturally Luke would be concerned for the captain and crew to go chasing off for the doctor so expediently. But then, so he should. Everyone knew how catastrophic an epidemic of smallpox could be on board ship. It was horrifically contagious, even more than the chickenpox.

Guiltily, she snuggled back beneath the coverlet, wishing the smell of bacon would go away and doing her best to ignore it. Her stomach seemed to be turning somersaults this morning, and she was already regretting drinking so much wine last night and eating such a hearty meal.

A short while later, Luke returned with a man looking no more like a reputable doctor than Dr. Sam Atkinson. Caroline's London doctor had been an impeccably correct Harley Street man, and she was nervous at meeting the keenly observant eyes of this stranger, short, stocky, and gnomelike. He wore shabby, crumpled clothes, and clearly did double service as a crewman.

"This is Dr. Moore, Caroline. He'll take a look at you before we say anything to alarm the captain. I've already told him you're indisposed with a considerable rash."

She could hear the agitation in his voice. He obviously thought there might be something badly wrong, Caroline thought, and the concern he showed was unexpected and touching. She could

339

almost believe in it.

"I'd like to talk to the doctor alone, Luke," she said thickly.

"That's not a good idea. I want to hear what he has to say," he said at once.

The man looked down at Caroline's pleading eyes, and then at Luke. "Your wife is in safe hands with me, sir, and I prefer to see my patients alone. If you'd be good enough to step outside? While you're waiting, perhaps you could organize a supply of fresh drinking water. The lady needs plenty of fluids."

Luke hesitated, but the doctor simply folded his hands across his chest and refused to do anything more until Luke left the cabin with an oath. Then the man spoke curtly. "Now then, young woman. I've discovered what you had to eat and drink last night, and I've asked Mr. Garston if you've been in contact with anyone infectious. He says you mentioned some native children with the chickenpox. Is that what you think is wrong with you?"

He looked at her shrewdly, one hand on her pulse and the other on her heated forehead.

"It could be," she said cautiously. "I'm sure it's not the smallpox, though, doctor."

"I think we both know that it's not, don't we, ma'am?"

Caroline swallowed. "What do you mean?"

"Have you had this kind of attack before? The same kind of swelling and itching that comes on conveniently, whenever you feel the need to be away from society for a while or when you're attacked by a fit of nerves?"

"Are you implying that I somehow managed to induce my own illness! I'm not a witch! And besides, why would I want to do such a thing!"

"Why indeed?" he said shortly. "Anyhow, you're

340

not suffering from the smallpox or the chickenpox. What you're suffering from is an overindulgence in something that doesn't agree with you. And since I suspect you would have discovered such an allergy long before now, I suggest that you knew very well the effect of too many strawberries on your system. Or perhaps you simply forgot the allergy in the excitement of a sea voyage. In either case, it's certainly unfortunate for a new bride who would naturally want to look her best."

Caroline's eyes filled with weak tears at this lecture. How stupid she had been to think she could fool a doctor, even such a shabby one as this. She felt humiliated and ashamed. And then she was taken aback by the softening of the man's voice. "Was the thought of the marriage bed so very objectionable to you, my dear young woman, that you had to resort to this for a brief respite?"

He patted her hand, and even though she knew it was wrong, she was ready to clutch at any straw.

"You're right," she said humbly. "Would it be so wrong of you to help me? It's the thought of being on board this ship with so many knowing eyes that has upset me. I'm sure I shall be quite all right when we reach Sydney, and—and of course, I don't want to keep my husband at bay forever! But I'm a very modest person, you see, doctor."

She lowered her eyes as if she were truly a blushing new bride.

"Then what do you suggest?" he said after a moment.

She looked at him hopefully. "If you would just pretend that I do have the chickenpox and that it would be best for my—my husband to sleep in another cabin. It would mean so much to me, and it would give me time to settle my nerves. I know I shouldn't ask it of you . . ."

341

She left the words in the air, wondering if he could be persuaded to go against his medical ethics. Presumably he must have some . . .

"Do you think any doctor would be party to such a story?" Dr. Moore said sternly. As her heart sank, Caroline saw his face relax into a puckish smile. "Very well, you may play your charade for a little while longer, and it shall be our secret. To all intents and purposes, you have the chickenpox, and I shall recommend that your husband move into another cabin for two weeks. By that time, we shall be almost in Sydney, and from then on I hope you'll feel ready to begin married life properly."

"Oh, thank you," she almost gasped. She was elated to think her little subterfuge had been so successful. Luke wouldn't go against the doctor's orders, and she would have this cabin to herself for the next two weeks. She had won this particular battle.

"I advise you to keep yourself covered when your husband or the steward calls on you," Dr. Moore said. "The blotches won't last forever, and you'll have none of the telltale blistering of the chickenpox. Mr. Garston isn't a stupid man and will probably know the symptoms of the illness well enough. Besides which, I've no wish to be thought a fool for diagnosing the wrong thing, even though in the early stages, there's little to tell between them."

"I'll remember," she said swiftly.

"Then I'll allow him in for a short visit and inform him of my findings. I'm sure he'll want to sit with you sometimes, but I'll advise against all physical contact for the time being. I'll call on you again tomorrow morning."

"Thank you, Dr. Moore."

She was grateful for the way he was entering into her little deception; it was only a small one, after all. It didn't compare in deceit with the stupendous trick Luke Garston had played on her, pretending to the ship's company that she was his wife. Any guilt on Caroline's part faded away at the thought.

It just served him right that all his plans had gone awry, she thought triumphantly—even if she were cutting off her nose to spite her face . . . and even if her head did ache abominably from drinking too much wine, and even if the uncomfortable allergy from eating too many strawberries wasn't the happiest way to endure a sea voyage in the musty confines of her cabin.

The man Barnes came to the cabin a short while later with a large pitcher of fresh water.

"Your husband's seeing the captain wi' the doctor, ma'am. Praise be that 'tis only the chickenpox and nowt worse."

"Aren't you afraid of catching it, Barnes?" she said weakly, knowing she must keep up the pretense with everyone.

The man shrugged. "It's all right for me to attend ye, ma'am. I've had the damn spots meself, so I'm not likely to catch 'em again. Is there anything else you're wanting now? Some breakfast, I daresay?"

The smell of the congealing bacon drifted into her nostrils again, and she gritted her teeth. "Just some toast, thank you. But please take Mr. Garston's food away. He's to have another cabin while I'm ill, so his clothes will also need to be removed."

She was suddenly exhausted. She had done nothing to use up any energy, but the allergic reaction to the strawberries and the strain of lying were doing as much to make her feel faint as any real illness.

"You just leave it all to me, ma'am, and don't fret yourself," she heard Barnes say as if from a long distance away. "I'll bring you some toast directly and a nice brew of tea to warm you."

She was already burning up, but she couldn't be bothered to say so. All she wanted was to close her eyes and to blot out everything else but the fact that this ship was taking her steadily southward to her destination.

icing how the hot liquid scalded her lips. She replaced the cup on the tray as dutifully as a child.

Chapter Eighteen

She must have slept for some hours, for when she awoke she discovered a tray of dry toast and butter on the table, and a pot of cold tea. Barnes must have come and gone, and hadn't wanted to waken her. She felt cold now whereas before she had been so hot.

She shivered, wondering if she had been very foolish in eating so many strawberries after all and if she was really going to suffer for it. Her throat felt swollen and sore, and her head ached. She wondered fearfully if she would go into some kind of shock reaction and do herself some real harm. She had no idea, but the sense of panic was made all the more real by the fact that she felt so very much alone.

And she knew she had no one but herself to blame for that! It was what she had wanted, and now she had to put up with it. But there weren't even any books or newspapers in the cabin, even if she had felt like reading, and she had only her own company to while away the long hours between mealtimes.

But where was Luke! Why hadn't he come to see her? She felt alternately frustrated and angry, and very near to tears as she bit into the cold toast, aware that her stomach was rumbling and calling out for food. The cabin was dim, and she saw that someone had put a kind of curtain up at the porthole to stop the light from hurting her eyes or waking her. It would have been Barnes presumably.

The cabin door suddenly opened, and her heart lurched as Luke came inside, closing the door behind him and leaning against it.

"So, my bride is suffering from a child's malady, I understand," he said softly.

She looked at him uneasily, unsure whether or not there was a mocking note in his voice. If he didn't believe her or if the doctor had told him the truth in confidence . . .

"I'm sorry," she croaked.

"Nobody chooses to be ill, do they?" he said, more briskly. "So let's just be thankful it doesn't appear to, be too serious. The doctor says that plenty of fluids and rest will soon put you right. So I'm going to move into the cabin next door, but I'll be close enough if you need anything in the night. You only have to knock on the partition wall between us and I shall hear you."

He smiled slightly, and she suspected he might have said something far more suggestive if he hadn't believed she was ill. Only a partition wall between them . . . but it might as well have been an ocean.

She watched silently as he removed all his belongings, feeling oddly as if he were leaving her life. It wasn't what she wanted at all, she thought bleakly. And she was the biggest fool for not taking all that this man offered.

346

"Luke," she said huskily when he was ready to leave her cabin. "I'm truly sorry."

"I've already told you not to feel guilty at being ill. It's not your fault. Blame it on those wretched brats," he said, trying to make her smile. But she shook her head, trying not to wince as it hurt.

"No, you don't understand. I'm sorry for all of it. For needing to be rescued. For coming into your life and disrupting it so badly. For persuading you and the boys to go to the mainland and putting your lives in danger. And for—for all of this."

She felt the weak tears fill her eyes. He came across the cabin in several long strides, and he sat on the edge of the narrow bunk, disregarding any thought of infection. He took her hands in his and spoke roughly. "How many times do I have to say that you belong to me? All this was destined for us, lass. Why else would you have come halfway across the world and ended up in my arms?"

It hurt to cry and to feel her throat closing up, and she swallowed thickly. She was vulnerable now, and she knew it, but she knew instinctively that he wouldn't try to force himself on her physically now.

"You can't still want to marry me after all the ways I've frustrated you and irritated you," she said in that same husky voice.

She heard him give a deep sigh. "Dear God, woman, how many times do I have to ask you before you say yes?"

When she didn't answer, he looked at her more sharply. "Caroline?"

She spoke slowly and painfully as if the words were dragged out of her against her will. As if some things were stronger than her own will . . .

"More than anything else in the world I want to find my father alive and well in Sydney. But if

347

that should not be the case, then I fully intended to settle into his world there. It was what he wanted."

"But?" Luke said as she paused.

Her voice shook now. "But I realize it's not what *I* want. I'm not my father, and I can never be what he was. His world is a man's world, and I would probably end up being an embarrassment or marrying one of his colleagues in order to become respectable and fit in."

"And that would be a terrible waste," Luke said gravely.

"It would," she whispered. She felt his fingers grip hers more tightly.

"So are you telling me that if you find out once and for all that your father didn't survive the shipwreck, you'll marry me?"

He spoke brutally, and she guessed that he wasn't underestimating the burden she was putting on them both. She made no secret of the fact that he'd be getting second best because, for her, it would be a face-saving way of leaving Sydney again with dignity.

"Do you accept those conditions?" she prevaricated faintly, still wondering, though, if his male pride would make him refuse and not knowing how she was going to react if he did. She was no longer even sure who was proposing to whom, and the tension in the cloying little cabin was razor-sharp.

"Of course I bloody well accept," he said. He bent low over the bed to catch her in his arms and kiss her savagely. "And if I have to bear the indignity of whatever ails you to seal the bargain properly, then so be it."

He stood up quickly, towering over her, and the enormity of what she'd done washed over her.

He'd put it all in its shameful perspective when he called it a bargain.

If her father was alive and well in Sydney, then Luke could leave for Brundy whenever he wished. If not, then she had given her word to marry him.

She would take the next best option, going back to Brundy where she would have a comfortable life among good people. She need never worry about anything again. And she couldn't explain why, instead of being filled with joy at the thought, she felt as miserable as if she had just sold her soul to the devil.

As Luke reached the door, he turned to her. "As a matter of fact, I had chickenpox myself as a child, so I doubt that I'll catch it again. There was no real reason for me to move out of here, except that the doctor seemed to think you wished it, and that came as no surprise to me. But I trust you'll have no objections to my sharing mealtimes with you. It's going to be a long, dreary journey with no company for the next week or so."

"Of course I won't mind," she mumbled.

"Naturally it would be best if neither of us shared the captain's table now, in case the crew get nervous about an infectious disease being on board. But there's not much likelihood of my catching it, is there, my sweet?"

And if that wasn't telling her he half-suspected exactly what had brought on her sudden illness, she didn't know what was. But in any case, it hadn't occurred to her that he might have had the illness himself and therefore be immune to it. She knew nothing of his childhood years, except what he had told her — of the brutality meted out to his father and his own orphanhood in a strange country. No wonder he had gone wild for a time.

"I think not," Caroline whispered. "Please don't

desert me forever. I shall look forward to sharing a meal with you this evening. And Luke," she made an effort to sound more sociable, "perhaps you'd care to tell me something about Yorkshire."

He was abrupt, as if he were tiring of the little game they played. "Perhaps. We'll have little else to do to while away the hours on board. For now I'll ask Barnes to bring you some fresh tea, and see you again later."

And then he was gone, and Caroline lay back on the hard pillow, completely drained.

The day passed drearily, and the only person she saw was Barnes. He came at various intervals to bring her fresh water and enquire if she needed anything. She resented the fact that Luke was keeping away from her so much, but she wouldn't confess everything and beg him to stay. It would be too galling. Besides, the blotches wouldn't go down for several days yet. She knew that of old. The illusion of a real illness would remain.

Luke arrived at suppertime, and she greeted him with almost pathetic eagerness. She was half-sitting on her bunk, having brushed her hair and sprinkled it with rose water to revive its springiness. She had patted her limbs and body with some of the refreshing liquid and tidied herself as she awaited him. He didn't miss the freshness of her appearance.

"So my bride awaits me with some pleasure, I fancy," he said softly.

She flinched, knowing she had best not appear too pleased to see him. "It's been a long, lonely day," she complained. "I've seen no one but Barnes, and there's been nothing to do but stare up at the ceiling or try to sleep."

350

"And my lady would prefer to make better use of her time in bed?"

She felt her blood run faster at the implication, and as it did so, her neck and facial blotches itched and became more pronounced.

"I can hardly think about such things just now!"

"Of course not. You're ill, and I'm a bastard for daring to make such lewd suggestions to my suffering bride."

Caroline gasped. He was not usually so crude, and she eyed him warily, aware that he was in an odd mood this evening. She wished Barnes would bring their meal, so they would have something with which to occupy themselves.

"You said you were going to tell me about Yorkshire," she said desperately.

"I didn't say so. You asked, that's all."

She stared at his calm face. He was so handsome and suddenly so remote, so granite-faced and unattainable. She ran her tongue around her swollen lips.

"What have I done to anger you so much?"

"I'm not angry. I just can't see the point in discussing a place you're never likely to see, and I prefer not to think about it any more than I need."

At once she realized she was stirring up all the memories of his happy childhood. Of the time before the deportation of his father had sent them both to the other side of the world, far from home.

"Forgive me. I didn't think," she said awkwardly.

The tension in his face relaxed a little. "It's no matter. Perhaps it would be good to talk about it. Where's the sense in remembering the bitterness of more recent times if you can't relive the good memories, too?"

Those words could apply only too well to her own situation, Caroline thought keenly. And in her saner moments, she knew it was far more sensible to cherish the good memories than to let the bad ones fester.

"So tell me about Yorkshire," she said quietly, lying back on her pillow.

"In a single evening? You might as well describe the continent of Australia as being a barren land filled with kangaroos and galahs, and think you know it all."

He gave a small shrug as she waited. "Yorkshire's very different, though I suppose there's a small similarity if you stretch your imagination far enough."

"I'll try," she said, and he gave a slight smile.

"The wild, empty moors are what I remember the most, with their great secret pockets and hollows where a wee lad could hide for hours on end and weave magic tales of his own. Of course, the moors could be treacherous as well as beautiful, depending on the time of year and the weather. When it snowed, they resembled great sugar mountains and valleys, and when the mist descended, it was like no place on earth. Ghosts and monsters could leap out of every dip in the hills. But in the spring and summer when the sun shone and they were clothed in purple heather and yellow furze, it was an enchanted fairyland."

Caroline was astonished by the sudden poetic lilt in his voice. She knew at once that he was seeing it all through a child's eyes. The ghosts and monsters and fairies of a small boy's childhood were all being relived in the man's imagination. And she wasn't sure whether or not she should have encouraged them to return.

"And the towns? What of the towns?" she said,

352

hardly wanting to break into this, but she could see how far away he'd gone from her now. And she wanted him back . . .

He gave a short laugh. "Oh aye, the towns. They told a different story, lass. They were dominated by great woolen and cloth mills filled with workers who hardly saw the light of day as they worked for their masters. Not everybody worked for the mills, of course, but most of them did. Whole families were beholden to the wool masters, and many of them died young from chest diseases when the wool and cotton fibers got down into their lungs. Whole towns hung beneath a pall of gray smoke from the mills for weeks on end, and that did them no good either."

"So it wasn't all good?" she ventured to say.

His eyes slowly focused on her again. "It was home," he said simply, and the very flatness of his voice gave a wealth of meaning to the few brief words.

Caroline wished she'd never asked for these reminiscences, but as Luke went on speaking, it seemed as if he couldn't let it alone now.

"We lived somewhere between the two, in a stone-built house on the edge of the moors. There was all the wildness of nature and the great expanse of sky on one side of us, and the smoke and pall of the town on the other. As a child, I hated that smoke. I thought it was the devil rising up to get me. I knew that if the smoke ever reached our house, I'd be dissolved into it."

He gave a short laugh. "I haven't thought about that for years, nor admitted my foolish childhood fears to anyone."

Caroline was embarrassed now. "I'm sorry if I've stirred up too many memories, Luke."

"That's what memories are for, lass," he said

more briskly. "You bring them out on the bad days and remember the good times you once had. Or you enjoy what you have now and compare it with the cold and damp of those other days. I thought you said something of the same to Dadda Finnegan."

"Yes, I did." She nodded, thankful to turn the conversation. "In any case, the news that Kathleen and Michael Treherbert are going to be married changed everything for him. You might have warned me about that!"

"Why? It was their surprise, and besides, it did me good to see that look of relief in your eyes."

The teasing note had returned to his voice, and Caroline looked at him suspiciously. "Why should I have looked relieved?"

He leaned forward and kissed her fiery cheek. "Because, my love, you thought the lovely Kathleen and myself were getting far too intimate. You may not have wanted me for yourself, but as sure as hellfire, you didn't want anyone else to have me!"

His arrogance made her gasp. And she was all the more indignant because it was true. Sometimes he could see right through her, she thought furiously. Though he hadn't got it quite right. She did want him for herself . . . but on her terms. She wanted his love.

"I wish Barnes would bring the food," she complained, changing the subject completely.

"Are you hungry? I'd have thought food was the last thing you wanted. The chickenpox fever usually keeps such appetites at bay. But if you wish, I'll let Barnes know we're ready for our meal."

"I do wish it," she muttered

She didn't care for the way he seemed to know about the progress of the illness. He'd be aware that the itching and blotchiness should turn to blisters in a few days. When that didn't happen, and her own swollen face merely subsided back to normality, he'd know it hadn't been chickenpox after all. There'd be no reason for him not to move back into their supposedly nuptial cabin.

He left her pondering uneasily, and she sipped at the cool water Barnes had brought her, hearing her stomach rumble. Her appetite was healthy enough tonight, she thought keenly.

Ten minutes later, he and Barnes came to the cabin together, and the man enquired after her health.

"I'm feeling a little better, thank you, Barnes," she said, feeling enormously guilty at deceiving the crewman who was taking such proprietorial care of her.

He put the cloth-covered tray on the table, and Luke told him tersely that he'd see to it all himself. Caroline felt her mouth water as she smelled hot beef and vegetables, and she watched as Luke lifted the covers from the plates. And then she stared in disbelief.

"Dr. Moore advised light meals for you for the next few days, so enjoy your poached egg, my sweet," he said.

He cut into the rich piece of beef on his plate, and the succulent juices ran out of it. Caroline could almost taste it as he put the piece into his mouth, followed by wholesome boiled potatoes and carrots.

"How can you sit there and eat that in front of me?" she sputtered. She sat upright in the bunk and glared at him. The sight of the plain poached egg on its bed of dry toast was an insult to her taste buds.

"Would you rather I ate in my cabin? I thought

you wanted some company."

"I do! But I also want some proper food, not this invalid's fare!" she raged.

"But, my sweet lass, you *are* an invalid, remember? You can't expect to recover from an illness in a matter of hours, and you need pampering. What kind of a husband would I be if I didn't see that Dr. Moore's instructions were carried out?"

As she watched him eat, she was filled with deep resentment. He obviously enjoyed the meal and seemed quite oblivious to her discomfiture. Savagely she wished she dared tell him that she wasn't ill at all, at least, not in the way he meant!

Apart from the slight pain of the rash, she was perfectly well. She wished she had the nerve to snap at him that she, too, had had the chickenpox as a small child and was as immune to it as himself! And that it was more the sight of that good red meat disappearing down Luke Garston's gullet that was making her feel weak now!

But such a confession would be to defeat all her carefully laid plans, and after a few moments when Luke said nothing at all, she slowly began eating the egg as she didn't want the growling of her own stomach to keep her awake all night.

She played around with the egg and toast, and eventually began to force it down, but Luke had finished his meal even before she had. She swallowed her last mouthful with a small shudder. She had never been particularly fond of eggs, and this had been a very large one with a stronger flavor than usual.

"I didn't know hens could lay eggs that big," she muttered, thinking privately that she felt very sorry for the hen that had to produce such a monster, but too well-mannered to say so.

Luke laughed. "That egg came from no hen, my

lady. It was an ostrich egg. You needed nourishment after a day of virtual fasting."

She gasped, almost retching. She hated eating anything of which she didn't know the origin beforehand. She clamped her lips together after taking a great gulp of water to rid herself of the taste and the thought.

"No wonder it tasted so strong," she snapped. "Please let Barnes know that I don't want any more eggs. I'd rather starve."

He was still grinning, seeing the sparks in her eyes. She guessed he'd be thinking that illness or no illness, it didn't take much to revive her temper. She lay back on the pillow again, remembering she was supposed to be ill.

"Well, to make you feel a good deal better and to counter the taste of the egg, I suggested you have a special treat for dessert," Luke said coolly. "Barnes handpicked them for you from the storeroom in the galley. I think he's got a shine for you, my sweet."

He sounded far too indulgent for comfort, and Caroline was suspicious. She sat up cautiously as Luke removed the cloth covering the dessert bowl and handed it to her. It contained the largest, most succulent and luscious-looking strawberries she had ever seen. There were at least a dozen of them, and as their sweet, fresh scent rose to her nose, Caroline felt her throat close up in protest.

"I don't want these," she said huskily. "I can't — I can't eat them."

"But you love them, my dear. Didn't you previously eat half of my share as well as your own? Besides, you can't hurt Barnes's feelings after his efforts. You must eat every single one, especially when you've had such a miserable egg supper."

She picked up one of the berries between her

thumb and forefinger, feeling the rich red juice ooze onto her skin. It was true that she did love them, but she dare not risk aggravating the allergy further. She had no idea how dangerous it might be. Perhaps if she just ate one, it would do her no harm, and it might satisfy the monster sitting beside her. She could then pretend to feel faint and push the dish away . . .

She put the fruit to her lips, her teeth biting into the pulp, and the juice ran down the back of her throat. The sensation was almost sensual since for her it was truly forbidden fruit.

Without realizing it, her eyes closed, the way a child's eyes closed at taking any bitter medicine, but this wasn't bitter at all . . .

Suddenly the fruit was wrenched out of her mouth, and her eyes flew open. Luke was looking at her with a mixture of rage and despair.

"My God, but I didn't realize how far you'd go to keep me away from you," he said savagely. "I've seen a strawberry allergy before, and I suspected as much, even before I discovered the truth. But I didn't realize I was so abhorrent to you that you'd risk becoming seriously ill just to keep me out of your bed. Well, you needn't have any more fears on that score, my dear. I shan't trouble you again until we're truly man and wife. I've got your promise on that, and I've no intention of letting you forget it."

As he ranted on, she looked at him dumbly, her thoughts whirling. "You seem to have conveniently forgotten that I said I'd marry you only if I had positive proof that my father was dead," she said through shivering lips. "The fact that I felt as good as blackmailed into it doesn't concern you, I suppose. Nor that I hope and pray it will never be necessary! The last thing in the world I want is to be married to you!"

They glowered at one another, two strangers who might never have shared the most intimate acts of a man and woman. Who might never have lain in the open beneath the stars and made wild, abandoned love as free as nature intended; nor writhed passionately on the thick carpet of Garston Manor, where so recently they had decorously entertained their guests, and later watched their erotic reflections in a dozen mirrors as if they were their own voyeurs . . .

Luke was breathing heavily as he rose to his feet and covered the entire tray with the cloth.

"But I have every intention of holding you to your promise, even if your motive in making it was to take the best option left to you. It makes little difference to me. I want you, and I mean to have you."

She looked at him sickly, wondering if this cold, aloof man had an ounce of tenderness and sensitivity in him. She had seen that side of him so often, but right now it was hard to think it ever existed.

"I'll ask Barnes to bring you something a little more substantial since you seem to have recovered your appetite. I'll leave you to tell him why you didn't fancy his strawberries tonight. And I trust that you'll be well enough tomorrow to allay the captain's fears that he might have an epidemic on board his ship."

"How did you know?" she said dully. "You *did* know, didn't you?"

"You should remember how thin the cabin walls are, my sweet. I overheard the way you wheedled the doctor into betraying his better judgment. So, in future, don't accuse me of trickery without remembering your own."

Caroline's face flamed anew as he left the cabin with the tray, leaving her staring at the brown walls and feeling totally humiliated. He was impossible, she raged, but her anger was enhanced by the knowledge that she had brought all this on herself. It had seemed such a clever trick at the time, knowing of old what the strawberries would do to her. Now it seemed childish and pathetic.

When Barnes arrived a little later with a plate of beef and vegetables, her appetite had already waned, but she knew better than to tell him so. She smiled at him weakly. "I'm sorry I had to return the strawberries after your kindness, Barnes, but it seems possible now that I don't have the chickenpox after all. It may just be a bad reaction to the fruit, so I'd best avoid them in future."

"That's good news, ma'am, and don't you go fretting yourself over returning the strawbs. The crew will make short work of them. Will Mr. Garston want his things brought back in here for tonight now?"

"I think not," she said quickly. "I'm so restless with the itching, and I daresay the swellings may take quite a few days to subside, so we'll leave things as they are for now."

Caroline felt a little hot at telling a steward such intimate details, but it was better that than having him speculate on the peculiarities of a new bride who didn't seem to want her husband at her side.

As it was, she saw Barnes shrug as he went out, clearly thinking it was a fine way to begin married life. But if there had been any semblance of truth in her pretense of embarrassment on board ship, it was certainly intensified now that Luke had told her the cabin walls were so thin he'd heard every word she and the doctor said.

He'd given her a little more ammunition to fire if he once suggested returning to her cabin. No lover with an ounce of sensitivity would want his lovemaking overheard by sniggering sailors on board a trading ship, especially one as passionate as Luke Garston.

Her next visitor was Captain Ellis himself. She was overcome with embarrassment anew at her charade. It had been done for Luke's benefit only, and she had completely overlooked the captain's worry about the threat of infection to the whole crew. She didn't miss the slight stiffness in his voice as he enquired after her health.

"I'm feeling much better, Captain," she said humbly. "I can't apologize enough for causing such alarm. I should have remembered how an excess of strawberries has affected me before, but in the excitement of everything . . ." Her voice fell away at his shrewd glance.

"It does seem surprising that you forgot if you've reacted badly to the fruit on previous occasions, ma'am."

"But not since I was very young," she said hastily. "Much as I love them, I've always avoided eating too many strawberries ever since."

She bit her lip, feeling as though she were sinking into even deeper waters by her explanation. She saw the captain give a half-smile as she pulled the bedcovers even higher around her neck—as if she wanted to slide down in the bunk and be out of sight of every pair of accusing eyes.

"Well, you'll surely remember it in future since it will obviously spoil a very special voyage for you. But Mr. Garston is an understanding gentleman, and you can rest assured you'll have every attention until we reach Sydney."

And she guessed that Mr. Garston would be paying handsomely for the exclusive services of one of his crew, Caroline thought guiltily. She was causing endless trouble . . .

"I'm very grateful, Captain," she murmured.

"Good. Then when you feel well enough, I hope the two of you will be able to join me for supper, as planned."

"That would be very nice," Caroline said.

In fact, once she was alone again, she thought how wonderful it would be to get out of this stifling cabin. Long periods of solitude didn't altogether suit her, and by the time she saw Luke again, much later in that tiresome day, she had begun to feel as though the brown walls were closing in on her. By then she was fretful and ready to snap.

"So how is my sweet wife feeling now?" he taunted.

"Very bored and aching abominably from the hardness of this bunk!" she said feelingly.

"There's something we can do about that," Luke said. "Get out of it for a few minutes."

She had no idea what he thought he could do, but since she had already felt the benefit of walking around the cabin a few times for a minimal amount of exercise, she did as she was told. The atmosphere was too close for her to bother putting on a dressing robe. Besides, it hardly seemed necessary. Her cambric nightgown buttoned high up her neck, and even if it hadn't covered her completely, Luke had already seen everything there was to see of her.

She watched silently as he stripped her bunk with all the expertise of a manservant, shaking out the thin mattress to rid it of as many lumps as possible. Then he stripped the other bunk and placed that mattress over her own, giving it double the bulk.

"I think your ladyship will find that a bit more comfortable," he said. "It should ease any aches for the remainder of the voyage."

She looked at him stupidly. "Does this mean you intend to remain in the cabin next door until we reach Sydney?"

"Isn't that what you wanted? Surely the little game you played was with that in mind? And I've no wish to play the tyrannical husband, insisting on his rights, my dear. As I said, I'm happy enough to leave you well alone for now. Once I claim my prize and we're legitimately wed, it will be a very different matter, I promise you."

Caroline clenched her hands. "You know what you're doing, don't you? You're wishing my father dead, just so you can get your own selfish way."

He looked at her steadily. "I've never wished a man dead in my life. But I truly believe your father has perished and that you and I were destined long ago to share our future. And if you weren't so damnably pigheaded, woman, you'd believe it, too.

He made no attempt to touch her. They stood the width of the cabin apart, both of them breathing heavily as the tension in the confined space rose. She felt the swellings on her neck itch and throb as the blood surged through her veins, and her breasts were strained taut against her nightgown as she folded her arms around herself.

Suddenly she wanted so desperately to feel his hands caressing her. She wanted his mouth on hers, his body covering hers, feeling the warmth, the tenderness, the power of his lovemaking . . . She wanted all of him so badly.

363

He indicated the newly made bunk. "Enjoy your solitude, Caroline. It's not going to last forever."

He brushed past her, and seconds later she was alone.

Chapter Nineteen

The rest of the voyage to Sydney passed without incident, but true to his word, Luke didn't return to her cabin. Whatever the captain and crew thought about it, Caroline didn't dare surmise. In any case, unless Barnes or the doctor were complete blabbermouths, it was unlikely that any of them knew about the unusual sleeping arrangements of their passengers.

Caroline thought fervently that it was probably better that they didn't know since she was now a woman sleeping alone among a lusty male crew. But should any of them think of trying anything untoward towards Caroline, Luke was only a partition wall away.

She was very aware of that fact. Whenever he returned to his own cabin, she could hear the creaks of his bunk and closets, and once the very sound of his breathing penetrated through to her. Sometimes she found herself holding her breath, listening for the sounds that brought him near. And always she chided herself for being such a fool.

As the journey progressed, her nerves became heightened. She had agreed to an impossible situation now. If her father was proved beyond all reasonable supposition to be dead, then she would honor her promise and marry Luke Garston. If, by some miracle, her father were still alive, she would lose all that was dearest to her heart — unless she threw away all her pride and agreed to marry Luke anyway.

But how could she even consider such a thing after all his trickery? Her own seemed of little significance, compared with the way he had pursued her and compromised her.

Once she was pronounced officially well enough to go up on deck, Caroline was so thankful to breathe in the fresh sea air that she abandoned all pretense of being ill. They had already left the Great Barrier Reef far behind them and were in clear open water, steering a shoreward course now. The great mass of the mainland could clearly be seen to the starboard side of the ship, and her heart beat all the faster at the sight of the great protective mountains and the golden beaches that were inaccessible from anything but the sea.

Dolphins frequently cruised alongside the ship in schools leaping and frolicking in the translucent waters. The occasional fin of a shark was glimpsed, reminding Caroline that not all sea creatures were lovable. Shiny gray gulls and more flamboyantly hued birds flew above them as they neared the land and were noisy escorts.

"Not much longer, Caroline," Luke said beside her as they leaned on the ship's rail together. "And I mean to hold you to your promise."

She flushed. "I find that a crass remark under the circumstances," she said stiffly. "If I have to marry you, it will mean that I've given up all hope

366

of finding my father alive, and I shall be in mourning."

She heard his smothered oath. "You offend me, too, my sweet," he said in an unusually vicious voice. "You don't *have* to marry me in the way you imply. We made a bargain, and I expect you to honor it—"

"Honor! I find that a strange word to use, coming from you! You're nothing but a trickster."

"And what are you, my poor little invalid wife?" he mocked. "You seem to have made a remarkable recovery, and once this pointless voyage is over and done with, I trust you'll soon recover from your mourning period and we can continue to live our own lives."

Her eyes stung with tears. For some reason, he was being unaccountably cruel this morning. And whatever else she thought about him, he was not normally cruel.

"Why do you say such things?" she said passionately. "If you had ever loved your father as I love mine—"

She stopped, for of course he had loved his father. He had suffered mentally and physically because of the injustice done to his own father, and she bit her lip at her own thoughtless remark. She put her hand on his arm, feeling it tense and hard.

"I'm sorry," she said quietly. "But you goad me into saying these things, Luke."

He said nothing for a moment and then he put his arm around her shoulders, and she automatically leaned her head against him. They must look, for all the world, like a normal, loving couple, she thought fleetingly.

"We seem to have the knack of goading each other," he commented. "But when you finally admit that we both want the same thing, perhaps the goading can end."

She looked up at him, seeing the darkness of his eyes and the mouth she loved so much. The mouth that had kissed and caressed every part of her and brought all her dormant sensuality to life. She knew the potency and the power in him, and she shivered, even though the sun beat down on them from an endless blue sky.

Did they both want the same thing? Caroline wondered. He wanted her as his possession and his right. A life for a life, he called it. It was a cold, calculating way for a man to want a woman — while she only ached for his love . . .

After it became evident that the ship had been sailing gradually nearer to the coast for some time, the captain joined his two passengers to tell them they would reach Sydney by the end of the day.

Excitement and dread mingled in Caroline's mind now. She couldn't bear to leave the ship's rail, as the seascape unfolded to give way to the land. Her eyes strained, and she wished she were a clairvoyant and able to see beyond the buildings already taking shape in the distance. She wished she knew what lay ahead, whether it be joy or sadness . . .

Gradually they left the great open mass of sea and entered a huge, protective waterway, busy with sailing ships and smaller craft of every description. This, then, was Sydney harbor. Caroline was stunned by its sheer size and couldn't imagine the thrill of that first discovery fleet landing here. It would have been nothing but scrub and bush then, she supposed, but now, as they neared a wharf, the buildings of a town came into focus.

"It appears to be a properly constructed town," Caroline said, for want of something to say.

Because her lips were so dry, she was finding it hard to speak at all. This could have been such a very different arrival with her father, aboard the *Princess Victoria,* ready and eager to begin their new life.

"Aye, and all built by the sweat and tears of convict labor," Luke said harshly.

Caroline glanced at him, realizing that he, too, would be remembering other times and perhaps in particular how he had rebelled against any visit to the mainland ever since those days, until she entered his life.

But there was no time to start apologizing now. And what was the use? They were here, and they had to see their mission through. And already the ship's crew was busily going about their business, ready for tying up at the wharf. Not for a trading vessel the majesty of a Tilbury dockside — if such a thing even existed here, Caroline thought with a wry smile. This was a young country, at least in white man's terms, with few of the privileges she had once known.

"I'll go below and check that Barnes has packed all our belongings," Luke said tersely. "As soon as we get ashore, I'll see about hiring a vehicle to take us to our destination. You do have an address, I suppose?"

"Of course," she was stung into replying. "The newspaper office is already well-established here, but I wouldn't expect an — an islander like yourself to know that."

They were playing a tit-for-tat game again, Caroline thought, and she didn't want that. She needed his strength, for whatever was to come.

"I'm sorry, Luke. That was an unnecessary remark," she said quietly, and she followed him below into her now-pristine cabin. Barnes had obviously done his work, and her boxes were all packed and ready to be taken on deck.

Luke took her into his arms and kissed her lightly on the cheek. It was the first time he had kissed her in days, and her eyes blurred a little at the tenderness in his touch.

"You've no need to apologize to me, lass. What would I want to know of city news? I've everything I need on Brundy Island — or I will have when I take you home again."

She looked at him helplessly. He was so sure . . . and his certainty meant confirmation of her father's death. Common sense had told her long ago that it had to be so, but common sense didn't take account of emotions, and her emotions still refused to let go of the tiniest sliver of hope.

But today, at last, she would know for sure . . . or as sure as it was possible to be. Whatever she discovered now at the newspaper offices, she would accept it. She made that vow to herself, knowing that she couldn't live the rest of her life in this kind of limbo.

Captain Ellis and his crew bade them farewell at the wharfside. Since Luke and Caroline were assumed to be married, there were no plans for a return voyage in four days' time when the trading vessel left Sydney. That would be left until the last minute, whether Luke returned to Brundy alone or with Caroline. She didn't want to contemplate either of those things. It was enough to be here, to be setting foot in this town where she and her father had had such high hopes of happiness. She felt Luke's hand curl around hers as they went ashore, and her footsteps faltered a little.

"It will be an emotional time for you, my love. Take it slowly and get your land legs back."

But they both knew it wasn't just the reaction from the motion of the ship that made her stomach feel as if it were turning somersaults. There was so much at stake. There was her whole life . . .

She waited with their boxes while Luke organized a driver and modest carriage to take them to the address of the newspaper offices. The driver, unshaven, in shabby clothes and a wide hat pulled well down over his eyes to keep out the sun, looked at them both with interest.

"New 'ere, are you, mate?" he said to Luke. "Looking for a job, mebbe? If you and the lady wife are thinkin' of settlin' down in our fair city, you could do a lot worse, especially now the place is more respectable like—"

"Just take us to Greenwall Street, man," Luke said tersely. "We have business there."

The man shrugged, seeing there was to be no conversation here. Caroline knew they must look far too fine and well turned out to be arriving on a trading vessel, but she soon lost interest in what the man thought and looked around her with more interest as they left the wharf area and rode up into the town.

Sydney had clearly grown and prospered since the gruesome convict days. Streets were laid out quite uniformly, and there were some fine red-brick buildings among the older, stone-built and wooden ones. She wouldn't have minded a commentary from the driver, but Luke had apparently silenced him now, and she had to be content with absorbing the general atmosphere of the town.

At least the people out and about looked perfectly normal, she thought. She hardly knew what she had expected, but after their experiences in the bush and the terror of the Aborigines, it was a relief to see ladies and gentlemen in carriages or on foot, conversing amicably. It wasn't London, but it wasn't the back of beyond either.

"This is Greenwall Street," the driver grunted eventually, halting his horse outside one of the red-brick buildings. "Is this 'ere the place you wanted?"

"This is it," Luke said, noting the polished plate outside the buildings proclaiming it the offices of the *New Sydney Reporter.* "Please bring the boxes and put them inside the building while the lady and I make ourselves known."

He helped Caroline alight, and she had a job to stop trembling. If it hadn't been for Luke's supporting arm, she was sure she never would have gotten inside the building without collapsing. Her heart beat like a drum, and she stood leaning against the wall without speaking while the driver stacked their boxes inside the cool foyer and Luke paid him off.

The young man behind the desk looked at them suspiciously. "This ain't a hotel, sir."

Caroline moved forward. "Can I see someone in authority, please?" she said huskily. "My name is—"

"Good God, by all that's holy, it's Caroline!"

She jumped as she heard a rough English voice, and a tall, hard-faced man appeared on the stairs, a sheaf of papers in his hands. The well-remembered smells of ink and newsprint emanated from him, and for a moment Caroline felt faint, imagining herself back in the familiar past when she had visited her father in the old London offices.

"Stoneheart Taylor!" she almost croaked, almost

372

wild with relief at seeing one face that she knew, however much she had disliked the man in the past.

Taylor thrust the papers on the reception desk and strode across the foyer to take hold of her by the shoulders. He placed an effusive kiss on her cheek and stood back to look at her in disbelief.

"Good God, Caroline, we thought you were long perished along with the rest of 'em. I thought I was seeing a ghost, but it's still your lovely self, a bit peakier than of old, but every bit as desirable as ever. You're a sight for sore eyes and no mistake, gel!"

She flinched as his hot eyes roamed over her in his usual lecherous manner. Stoneheart Taylor had always had a dubious reputation among the ladies, and she hadn't forgotten the way she had often had occasion to freeze him herself. Here in this new country, she suddenly realized how vulnerable she would have been.

"Stoneheart," she felt ridiculous at using the nickname, but she'd never known him by anything else, "what news is there of my father?"

Taylor looked uncomfortable. He glanced at Luke, clearly wondering who he could be.

"You'd best come up to the newsroom," he said gruffly. "You and your, er, companion. They'll all be as tickled to see you as I am. Or nearly so. You know I always had an extra special fondness for you, don't you, Caro?"

Caroline felt hot with embarrassment at his clumsy, if mild, attempt to establish intimacy between them. Or it could just be a way of diverting her thoughts from what was uppermost in her mind. Without thinking, she thrust her arm through Luke's. "Stoneheart, this is Mr. Luke Garston, my husband."

She squeezed Luke's arm slightly as she spoke praying that he wouldn't show any surprise or denounce her there and then. It was her one defense against this odious man who was eyeing her so appreciatively, and Luke rose to the occasion magnificently. He held out his hand, and Taylor automatically put his ink-stained fingers into Luke's for a brief moment.

"I'm glad to meet a colleague of Sir William's," Luke said coolly, putting the man in his place without effort. "Now if you could show my wife and myself to the newsroom, we'd be grateful. We've traveled a long way, and we're anxious for news."

As she listened to him, Caroline realized that in getting herself out of one awkward position, she had put herself into another one. How could she throw herself on the mercy and companionship of any of the company wives now, when she was supposed to be married to the man practically holding her up as they ascended the stairs of the building to the newsroom? Her silly defense against Stoneheart Taylor threatened to cost her dear.

But all such thoughts left her mind as they entered a long room that seemed to be filled with people. The strong and distinctive smells of newspaper production were intensified here as were the clatter of machines and the noise of the reporters so familiar and poignant to Caroline.

The men in the room merely glanced at the newcomers at first. There were a few puzzled stares and finally recognition from several of the old London staff. After whispers rippled around the room, everyone fell silent.

Taylor finally said, "I can see you all think you're seeing a ghost, just as I did. But she's not a ghost. She's very much alive and well, and to those of you who haven't guessed yet, she's truly Miss Caroline Rowe, the daughter of our . . . benefactor."

Caroline didn't miss the slight hesitation before he used the word. But before she could force her dry lips to move, an elderly man came forward, dashing the tears from his old eyes. He wore the dark sleeve protectors of the chief editor, and had been her father's right-hand man.

"Miss Caroline, we thought you were dead, and me and my good lady have mourned you this long time."

"Mr. Watson," Caroline said, choked, as she took his hands in hers. "It's so good to see you."

"You're to come and visit with us, my dear," the old man said at once. "Mrs. Watson will insist on it."

"We'll see," she murmured, but her heart was sinking fast. Why would Watson offer her hospitality if her own father was alive and established in Sydney?

She was sure, too, of a new embarrassment among the staff as Taylor spoke to one and another. The newsroom was already reverting to its usual noisy state as if to reestablish business and normality in the wake of this very abnormal arrival. Her thoughts were in utter confusion, and she said the first thing that came into her head, still clinging to Luke for support. "Mr. Watson, this is my—my husband, Mr. Luke Garston," she said, knowing the charade must continue.

The old man shook Luke's hand vigorously. "It's good to know Miss Caroline's happy and settled, sir. And speaking as someone who's known her since babyhood, I can tell you you've a fine young woman here," he said. "The invitation to stay at my home extends to yourself as well, naturally."

"Thank you," Luke said gravely, "but we've come here for an express purpose. Caroline is desperate for news of her father. We've heard nothing of him since the *Princess Victoria* went down. You must know the circumstances, of course."

The man said nothing for a moment, and Caroline could see his jaw working.

"Yes, we know the circumstances," he said sadly. "Won't you come into my office where it's more private?"

He led the way toward a tiny office, where he closed the door and bade them both sit down. Before he did so, he bellowed out an order for some strong sweet tea to be brought to the office. Caroline couldn't even smile, remembering how Watson had been famed in the London offices for his partiality for strong sweet tea, but she guessed that wasn't his only purpose for ordering it now.

"Is my father dead, Mr. Watson?" she said through lips that felt suddenly stiff and swollen. It was also hard to breathe in this claustrophobic little room.

The door opened almost at once, and a tray containing three cups of tea was brought in. The strong aroma drifted into her nostrils, but she couldn't touch a cup until she knew the truth. The moment was finally here.

"I am very sorry, my dear girl but your father is dead." Watson said in a voice deep with sorrow. He had been a colleague of Sir William Rowe for many years, and his own grief was clearly etched on his dry, creased features.

Caroline drew in her breath sharply. "Are you certain?" she cried out, too stunned by the stark statement even to cry.

Watson placed a cup of tea into her shaking hands. Unthinkingly, she drank deeply, hardly noticing how the hot liquid scalded her lips. She replaced the cup on the tray as dutifully as a child, her eyes wide with pain as she watched the old man search in a filing cabinet. Silently he handed her a newspaper dated weeks ago.

Prominently on the front page was a sketch of Caroline's father and, beneath it, another of the once-proud ship, the *Princess Victoria*. The headline seemed to scream out at her: DEATH OF NEWSPAPER MAGNATE CONFIRMED.

She quickly skimmed the first paragraphs of the report.

"The entire staff of the *New Sydney Reporter* is in mourning today for the loss of its London owner, Sir William Rowe, whose death from drowning is officially confirmed.

"Sir William was voyaging to Sydney on the *Princess Victoria* with his daughter, Miss Caroline Rowe, when the ship went down in a violent storm off the northeastern coast of the continent.

"Some badly mutilated bodies were washed up on nearby beaches, and it has been confirmed that one of them was that of Sir William. There has been no news of Miss Rowe, and no survivors of the wreck have been reported."

The report went on to praise the energy and business acumen of her father and to detail his life, but she couldn't read any more.

"How was it confirmed?" she asked Watson through chattering teeth.

"A team of government men was sent to investigate, my dear, and from personal and medical evidence about the man's person, it was clear that it was indeed your father. I'm so very sorry to give you this news, Caroline."

She closed her eyes, fighting not to scream or faint or behave in any way of which her father

377

would disapprove. He'd brought her up in a man's world, in which there was little room for sentiment, but the effort was too much for her, and somehow she found herself weeping helplessly in Luke's arms. They had come so far, and she had kept the flame of hope alive for so long, and it had all come to nothing.

"I'll leave you both alone for a while," she heard Watson say quietly. "No one will disturb you here."

He hesitated and then spoke to Luke above Caroline's head. "I'll arrange with my wife for you both to stay with us for as long as you wish, Mr. Garston. There will be certain legalities to discuss with the company lawyer, of course. But I can assure you that when Sir William's remains were brought back to Sydney he was given a proper burial. I'm sure Caroline will want to visit her father's grave . . .."

Caroline jerked up her head. *"Yes,* of course I will," she choked out. "I'll never truly accept it until I see for myself."

She leaned heavily against Luke again, and Luke shook his head at the editor, willing Watson to do as he said and leave them alone.

"Caroline, you have to accept it now," he said tenderly after a few minutes when the weeping didn't abate.

"I know," she said, muffled against him. "And I know I should have accepted it long ago. You told me so a thousand times, but it doesn't make it any easier to bear."

"I'm not crowing over you, my lass," he said softly. "I wish with all my heart the outcome could have been different."

"Do you?" she said bitterly. "But then you'd have no hold over me to make me marry you,

378

would you? You've won, Luke, and I've no strength to fight you anymore."

She heard his expressive oath.

"I want no woman to marry me on those terms," he said harshly. "If it helps to heal your pain in any way, I absolve you from your promise here and now, Caroline."

She felt his heartbeat, as rapid as her own, and lifted her head slowly to look into his eyes, knowing that hers were diamond-studded with tears.

Without warning, the door of the little office burst open, and Stoneheart Taylor came inside.

"I'm sorry to intrude, but I need some papers urgently," he said, not missing the way Caroline and Luke clung together. He gave a twisted smile as he foraged in a drawer and slammed it shut. "I'm sorry about your father, but at least you've got somebody to comfort you in your grief, Caro. There's no point in mourning forever, I always say—"

"Get out of here, you unfeeling swine, before I break your neck," Luke said savagely while Caroline simply turned her head away from the man's uncouth gaze.

But having seen that their solitude was broken, Watson came hurrying back to the office a moment later. "My apologies for Taylor's appearance," he said. "He really did need those papers urgently, and I'd forgotten that they were in my office."

"It's all right, Mr. Watson," Caroline said, extricating herself from Luke's arms. "It's time Luke and I were leaving, anyway."

She paused, for where would they go? They were in a strange town, in a strange country, and they knew no one but a few of the men in this office and their families. Suddenly Caroline knew she couldn't bear to listen to their platitudes and sympathies, however sincerely meant.

"I'll write down my address for you, and arrange for someone to take you there—" Watson began.

She broke in awkwardly. "Mr. Watson, I'd like to call on you and your wife, but if you don't mind, I think we would prefer to stay in a hotel. Please understand."

She glanced at Luke for support. As if he read her mind, he finished for her. "My wife is naturally very upset, even though we fully expected to hear this news," he said steadily. "I think she would rather not be with too many people at present, and I'm sure you can appreciate that. Perhaps we can call on you and your wife tomorrow evening instead?"

"Of course, my dear sir!"

Was there the tiniest bit of relief in Watson's voice? Caroline wondered. There probably was. Sir William's death was old news to them all now, and to have it revived by a grieving daughter wouldn't make for the happiest of visits, however well meaning the invitation.

She managed a weak smile at the man. "I need to know where my father is buried, Mr. Watson. I should like to go there as soon as possible."

It was all still a horrible dream, Caroline thought faintly. It wasn't happening. There should be rejoicing, hugs and kisses, and a joyful reunion. . . She blinked dazedly at the piece of paper on which Watson had written the address and then Luke took it and tucked it into his pocket.

They walked out of the newspaper offices soberly, and much of the noisy chatter died away. It was a respectful silence as Caroline would have expected. But once they were downstairs, with their belongings loaded onto a carriage and with instructions for the driver to take them to a respectable hotel, Luke all but exploded.

"God, but it was almost like a wake back there! All this is not helping you, Caroline."

"Don't tell me what will help me and what won't!" she said tightly. "I don't want to think or to analyze anything. I just want to see my father's grave and pay my respects to Mr. and Mrs. Watson and a few more of my father's friends. I owe that much to his memory. And if Watson would like to have a firsthand account of what happened on the *Princess Victoria,* I shall give it to him."

As he said nothing, she took a deep, shuddering breath. "Then I just want to get back to Brundy as quickly as the trading ship will take me. I have to live my life somewhere, and it might as well be there as anywhere. Like you, I've no love for the mainland now."

"And what do you propose to do there?" he said coldly.

She was almost timid in her reply. "I made a promise, and I never go back on a promise. I thought that was one of your own rules."

"So," he said at last. "You've decided to make the best of a bad job and marry me, is that it? I'm the lesser of two evils, the first one being a life here in this miserable convict-built town where I suspect the lecherous Taylor fellow would be forever hounding you."

"Something like that," she mumbled, knowing how far it was from the truth but too numbed by this day to say so.

"Then I accept."

The carriage pulled to a halt, and Caroline saw that they were outside the portals of a fairly grand hotel. And despite Luke's derisive comment, there was nothing miserable about the town of Sydney

381

anymore. Convict-built it may have been, but there was luxury for those with money to pay for it, and as a porter came out of the hotel to take in their boxes, she guessed that this place was as plush and comfortable as anything London could provide.

She waited while Luke registered their arrival at the reception desk and then followed him up the sweeping carpet-covered stairs to a long corridor. The porter opened a door and handed Luke the key, and when Caroline stepped inside, her eyes were immediately drawn to the huge window. Beyond it was a magnificent view of the harbor and its environs which took her breath away.

Luke was right behind her, and the porter had left as silently as he had come. All their boxes had been placed in the room since Luke had told the man they would do their own unpacking. They were alone, and she realized it was a marital bedroom.

"Luke, we're not married yet," she said unsteadily.

"To all intents and purposes we are," he replied. "You saw to that, my sweet. Your newspaper people think we're man and wife, and so does the crew of the trading vessel. If word should leak out that we've deceived all those good people, it would do your reputation no good at all, especially as you're so intent on reliving your experiences through the *New Sydney Reporter*."

She stepped back from him a little. This wasn't the time for seduction, when she felt so cold that she was sure her face must be deathly white. Surely Luke must understand her feelings. Because of today's news, she was newly in mourning. To her, the death of her father was today, *now*, and not all those long weeks ago.

382

"No, my darling, I don't mean to ravish you," she heard him say softly, as expressions of grief illuminated her mobile face. "Give me credit for some sensitivity. But tonight of all nights, I didn't think you'd want to be alone, and a hotel bed can be a very lonely place."

She felt ashamed of her suspicions at once. "You're right," she said huskily. "Just as long as you honor my feelings, Luke. Because I can't—I couldn't—"

He placed his hands very gently on her shoulders, as if he knew very well how fragile she felt. As if he sensed that she might break from too much pressure.

"My sweet lass, do you think I don't know how it feels to lose a dearly loved parent? I've been this way before you, and I know you need the time for grieving. But you're strong, and in your heart you've already faced this day. You've been prepared for it for a long while, haven't you? The truth now, Caroline."

She nodded numbly. But however much one was prepared for it, one was never truly ready to say that final goodbye. She swallowed back the lump in her throat.

"So tonight we'll comfort one another," continued her caring counselor. "Tomorrow morning we'll visit your father's grave. In the evening we'll visit the Watsons, and on the day after that . . ."

As he paused, she looked up at him enquiringly. His hands tightened imperceptibly on her shoulders. She could feel the heat of his fingers through her thin gown and sensed a sudden tension in him.

"On the day after that?" she said huskily.

"I suggest we find a preacher to marry us," he said calmly. "The sooner the deed is done and

383

you're my legal wife, the sooner all this pretense will be over. No one will be any the wiser after that, and the Brundy folk will simply believe we wanted to be married on the mainland without any fuss."

Her throat had tightened again, so much so that she could hardly speak. It all sounded so clinical, so much a chore that had to be attended to.

"Is this what you really want?" she finally asked.

"It is."

"Then I agree," she whispered, knowing it was as far from a loving proposal as possible. But as he released her and went about unpacking his boxes, she knew it was as much as she could expect. They had struck this bargain, and for their own reasons, they were both intent on seeing it through.

Chapter Twenty

Caroline spent a restless night. She didn't feel as if she had slept at all, though she knew she must have if only because of the number of times she started so fitfully, half moaning, half crying. And always, she felt Luke's comforting arms wrap around her, keeping her warm, keeping her safe. There was no sexuality in his embrace, just caring, loving companionship, and it was what she needed so badly.

By the time the daylight streamed in through the curtained window, she felt exhausted, yet considerably calmer. It was as if, in some strange way, the night had exorcised all the futile, painful hopes that her father had survived, when in the heart and soul of her, she always knew that he had not.

She turned her head to find Luke still sleeping beside her, his arms still imprisoning her. He must have spent a sleepless night, too, she thought guiltily, for every time she awoke, he was there, always ready to soothe and murmur comforting words and to try to instill her with his strength. She watched him now, his face relaxed in sleep, his breathing deep and rhythmic, and she loved him so much.

He moved suddenly as if aware of her gaze. Before she could turn away, his dark eyes opened, and for a long moment he looked at her steadily.

"Have you returned from whatever hell you've been in, my darling?" he said softly.

She gave a small sigh, and without thinking, she nestled back into him, where she had lain all night.

"I think so," she whispered. "There's just this one last journey to make this morning and perhaps then all the ghosts will rest easily."

He leaned over her and kissed her, a gentle kiss that was no more than a sweet promise for the future. Then, as if unable to bear the proximity of her a moment longer, so soft and pliant, her hair in wild abandonment across the pillow, he turned away and leapt out of bed. He had scorned wearing any night attire, since Sydney was so hot. And through half-closed eyes, Caroline watched the animal grace of him as he went to the adjoining bathroom the hotel proudly boasted, and marveled that this powerful man could be so vulnerable in his dogged determination to have her for his own at all costs.

Instantly then she remembered her promise to marry him tomorrow. Her eyes shone with a mixture of tears and joy, recalling the bargain they had struck. In her soul she knew her father would have approved of Luke Garston. He was exactly the kind of man Sir William would have wanted for her, and as she knelt by his graveside, she would at last have the relief of telling him so.

She still lay among the tumble of bedclothes that spoke of her nocturnal restlessness and knew that a small miracle was taking place. It was as though the very sadness of yesterday's news was starting to heal the pain of uncertainty at last. It was a good feeling. She sensed when Luke came back into the room as she lay with her eyes closed again, thanking God for her sanity.

"Have you changed your mind about tomorrow?" Luke's voice said, half-serious, half-jocular. "Because if so, I warn you that I shall merely abduct you and tell the preacher to marry us by force if need be."

She managed a smile then. If only he knew there would never be a need for force. She knew she only wanted to belong to Luke, now and forever.

"There won't be any need for that," she said huskily. "I never go back on a promise, any more than you do."

For an instant, she felt afraid. She remembered the time when he said he absolved her from her promise . . . and surely he wasn't going to revert to that now? But to her relief, he smiled with satisfaction.

"All right. Then I suggest you get dressed and we go down for breakfast. Otherwise the management may start to wonder why we're spending so much time in our room."

Caroline got up at once. Now that everything was settled between them, she felt a strange embarrassment that almost amounted to shyness. Tomorrow they would be married, and all the pleasure they had shared would be legally theirs to enjoy from that day until eternity. The thrill of anticipation ran through her, and she quickly dashed it away, remembering the main reason for their journey here. And especially today's sad visit.

After she had washed, she dressed in the sober, pewter gray dress she had brought with her just in case. She was glad now that she'd done so. She wouldn't have wanted to visit her father in a frivolous summer frock, and yet, it was the way Sir William had always loved to see her, in light, fresh-looking garments. *My little ray of sunshine* . . . The sweet, remembered phrase he had so often used swept through her mind, taking her off guard and causing her to catch her breath between her teeth.

"Hold on, my love. The ordeal will soon be over," Luke said quietly, seeing her change of expression.

But he didn't understand. It wasn't an ordeal to visit her father's grave—at least, not in the way he seemed to think. It was a necessary conclusion to everything. The final goodbye. Until it was done, it was still unfinished.

"I'm all right," she muttered. "I just want to get it over with."

Her father would approve of that. *Look forward, my darling girl, not back,* he would have said. The ghost of his voice was strong in her head, guiding her through this day, and she felt oddly comforted by it.

As soon as they had taken breakfast in the hotel dining room, Luke arranged with the receptionist to order a carriage for their convenience for the whole day. It was clear from the respectful way in which his requests were attended to that Mr. Luke Garston was considered a client of some standing. And why not? Caroline thought. A man who virtually owned an entire island was a man of importance. The hotel people may not

388

know that, but Luke's air of wealth and authority was impossible to mistake.

She hid a small smile, remembering that she herself had mistaken him for a humble fisherman that first bewildering day. She couldn't think how, when there was nothing humble about him at all . . .

"What's amusing you, lass?" Luke said as the vehicle rumbled through the Sydney streets. They were quickly out of the built-up, populated area and into what was still virtually the edge of the bush, where the cemetery was situated.

"I was just wondering how I could ever have taken you for a fisherman."

"Why not?" he said. "It's what I am. The harvest from the sea has provided me with a good living, and there's no shame in it."

"Oh, but I didn't mean that!" she said hastily. "I meant . . ." she floundered.

How could she say, here in this swaying carriage with the driver dutifully yelling out the pitifully few points of interest now, that Luke was so much more than a mere fisherman? That he was everything and more that she had ever wanted in a man and in a husband?

"Let me guess. You mean that a landowner has so much more to offer than a fisherman, even one with the more regal title of pearl diver."

"I didn't mean that at all. Why do you twist my words?" she said hotly.

"Because they're true, my darling. You have a habit of closing your eyes to the truth, despite your insistence on honesty. You've proved that in recent weeks, otherwise we may not have had to have made this journey."

She stared at him resentfully. "I'm sorry I made you come here."

389

"You didn't make me. I came because I had no intention of letting a foolish woman travel unchaperoned on a trading vessel."

"And that was the only reason?"

Why don't you say it was because you love me and couldn't bear to let me out of your sight since you think you own me, body and soul?

Luke shrugged. "I wanted to see this through as much as you did. Your obsession was becoming unhealthy, Caroline, and though I'm naturally sorry for your distress, I thank God that it's finally over."

She turned away from him, her mouth set in a tight line. Obsession was the word he had used before. It was ugly and unfair to use it when she only did what any loving daughter would have done. She felt his hand close over hers.

"Face it, Caroline—"

"I *am* facing it. I'm here, aren't I? I've come to say goodbye," she said, her voice choked. "Now leave me alone. I don't want to talk anymore."

Luke removed his hand, and they traveled in silence until the driver called out that they were nearing the burial grounds. Caroline's heart beat sickeningly while Luke consulted the paper Watson had given him. As well as giving directions to this place, he had put a cross where Sir William had been buried. There was already a wooden marker there, he'd told Luke quietly, to be replaced by a headstone once the earth had properly settled. The company had agreed on that.

"Here you are, folks," the driver said, jerking the horse to a stop in a flurry of red dust. "Take as long as you like. I'm at your disposal all day."

And he obviously expected to be handsomely paid for the service. But Caroline wasted no more time on such thoughts, already shielding her eyes

390

from the sun and following Luke over the rough dry ground. It could have been a somber place, except for the thickets of trees surrounding it and the myriad of brilliantly colored birds singing in the branches. Somehow they gave a feeling of life to this place of death and sorrow.

"There it is, my love," Luke said, pointing.

She saw the wooden marker with her father's name burnt into it. She went forward alone, and Luke let her go, knowing she had to do this alone. She'd brought no flowers, she thought frantically, as if it were of desperate importance. Nothing to mark that she'd been here. Nothing but her love and her memories as she knelt on the dry earth and touched the carved name, uncaring whether or not her fine gown was soiled.

Her eyes were blinded by tears as she accepted without question now that this was the final proof. And she silently remembered all that the man who lay beneath this red earth had meant to her. Her beloved father had given her life. He'd given her the prospect of a wonderful future in this new land, and he'd perished because of it. She owed it to him to stay, to continue his dream . . .

"But it wasn't my dream, Father," she whispered, her fingers still caressing the letters of his name. "And I know you also hoped I'd find a good man to take care of me. It was what you always wanted for me, and now that I've found him, you do understand why I'm turning my back on your dream to follow my own, don't you?"

A small breeze rustled through the leaves of the gum trees nearby like a soft sigh of contentment. In that moment it was as potent to Caroline's receptive ears as if her father were giving her his blessing.

"Caroline," she heard Luke's voice say gently from somewhere behind her, and she nodded, not looking at him yet.

She stood up carefully, brushing the leaves and earth from her skirt. She whispered a last good-bye and bent to kiss the name on the marker. Then she turned, squaring her shoulders, and held out her hands to Luke. He took them, looking deep into her eyes as she took a shuddering breath.

"I'm ready," she said slowly. "It's done. Can we get away from here now—*please?*

It was as if she were suddenly done with death and morbid thoughts. She needed to be among the living again, to face the future—whatever that future held. She would never forget her father, but it was time to go on.

Luke led her to where the carriage driver lounged against the vehicle, contemplating contentedly the distant hills.

"Where now, folks?" he said laconically.

Caroline drew a deep breath. "You can take us back to Sydney and show us around the town, if you wish. I'd very much like to see where the first fleet landed."

The man shrugged. Such things were obviously of little interest to him.

"As you wish, ma'am, but there ain't much to see on The Rocks now. They've torn down the old shacks and replaced 'em with a few finer buildings, but that's all. The Rocks is what they call the place where the soldiers and convicts landed. I reckon we should all just be thankful we weren't around at the time."

Luke squeezed her hand as they climbed in the back of the carriage and the driver turned the horse away from the silent cemetery. Caroline

392

kept her eyes straight ahead, hearing Luke's whispered words.

"No prizes for guessing from which group he descended!"

She managed not to comment that if his father hadn't gotten his pardon, Luke, too, would have been the son of a convict . . . but she could hardly say so. And already her interest had waned. The trip out to the cemetery had taken considerable time, and she was feeling tired and drained.

"Perhaps we should forget the sightseeing after all," she murmured to Luke. "I think I'd prefer to go back to the hotel and rest, if you don't mind."

"Of course I don't mind. Driver, take us back to the hotel instead, please. I shall still want your services, but then we shan't require you again until this evening."

"As you like, sir." It made little difference to him since the gent was paying handsomely for the whole day.

Once back in their room, Caroline was glad to remove the stained gray dress, reminding her as it did of this sad day. With a small sigh of relief, she got right into bed in her undergarments.

"I don't know why I should feel quite so worn out," she said. "I'm sorry, Luke."

He spoke roughly, the way he did when he wanted to hide his own feelings. She knew that well enough by now.

"There's no need to apologize to me, lass. You've had a bad couple of days, and I wouldn't have expected anything less. Get some rest while I see to some business matters."

"What business can you possibly have here?"

she asked, staring, and he gave a faint smile.

"I have to arrange a wedding, in case you've forgotten. Then I'll go to the newspaper office to find the whereabouts of the company lawyer and arrange a meeting with him. It can't be avoided, Caroline."

"I know," she murmured, enormously thankful that Luke was taking all this worry from her shoulders.

"I suggest that we meet with the lawyer in two days' time," he went on. "Any business can be conducted legally with your married name by then. On the following day we'll set sail back to Brundy, so I also need to see Captain Ellis to arrange our passage. It's not the most luxurious of vessels, but no other has any reason to call at the island."

She heard his voice as if in a dream now, already drifting into sleep out of sheer exhaustion. It didn't matter what kind of ship they traveled on, as long as they were together. Hadn't they drifted on the ocean in a pearling boat? And successfully navigated through the Barrier Reef in his finest craft? Hadn't they come through so many kinds of privations and dangers together as if some kind of guardian angel was watching over them? She felt a strange sense of lethargy, akin to well-being, as if nothing could harm them now that they had come so far unscathed. She felt the touch of his lips on her flushed cheek.

"I'll be back in good time for the evening meal," he said. "Meanwhile, just rest, my darling."

She didn't need telling. She hardly heard him leave the room. She was already halfway in that dream world where everything was rose-colored and serene. The shocks of the past two days receded as if her mind had simply closed against them, and she was somewhere on a sunlit day in England with the sweet melodic sounds of country church bells ringing in her ears.

She saw herself as if in a watercolor painting, soft, ethereal, wearing a floaty white gown and a gossamer veil, holding a fragrant summer bouquet. There were two men accompanying her, one tall, broad, and powerful . . . the other, older, distinguished, but just as dear . . . Luke and her father . . . and in her dream she saw her father place her hand in Luke's, trusting her to his care.

She awoke suddenly, wondering what had startled her, and then realized there was a persistent knocking on her bedroom door. She was resentful at being woken from the dream, wanting to return to that blissful state where the past had merged with the present and she was with the two men she loved best in all the world. She threw on a dressing robe over her petticoats and went to answer the door. A buxom maid stood there holding a tray.

"I'm sorry if you were still sleeping, ma'am, but the gentleman said I was to waken you at three o'clock in the afternoon and bring you some tea and biscuits, as you'd surely be hungry by now."

Caroline looked at the maid stupidly. Three o'clock in the afternoon? But it had barely been noon when Luke had left her, and she couldn't believe she had been sleeping so long.

"It can't be three o'clock!" she said.

The woman shifted the heavy tray slightly, and Caroline stood aside at once to let her in.

"It is, ma'am. Didn't you hear the church bells chime? The hotel's built so close to the church, they sometimes keep guests awake, though not usually during the afternoon."

So that was why the sound of church bells had seemed so very real in her dreaming state . . .

"Will there be anything else, ma'am?" the woman said.

"No—well, yes. I'd like some toast and jam, if it's not too much trouble," she said, aware that her stomach was rumbling with hunger.

"No trouble at all, ma'am."

Caroline appreciated the reassuring presence of another female. It had been a long time since she had had any female company.

"Don't go for a minute," she said. "What's your name? Are you from England?"

She assessed the woman to be in her late forties, and was filled with curiosity as to how she came to be half a world away from home.

"That I am. I'm from London, ma'am, and me name's Gertrude," she said, clearly pleased to be asked.

"What brought you to Australia?"

Even as she asked the question, she wondered if it was going to cause embarrassment. The woman could well be the daughter or granddaughter of a convict. To her relief, Gertrude smiled.

"I took the government's five-pound passage in the thirties, ma'am."

Caroline searched her memory, sensing that as a newspaperman's daughter, she should know what this meant, but she didn't.

"I'm sorry, but I don't know what that means," she said, apologetically. Gertrude obligingly explained further.

"More than twenty years back, the British government was offering a five-pound passage to Australia to young single women of good character wanting work, see? I had a few savings left me by an employer, so I scraped the fare together and took a chance."

"That was very brave of you!" Caroline said, though her admiration was mixed. How foolhardy it might have been, coming to a wild land known for its convict population and the worst of British society.

"Best thing I ever did," Gertrude said proudly. "I got hitched on the boat coming over, and after a coupla years taking any odd jobs that was going, me and my old man got set up nicely once they built this here hotel. He's the head porter now. You saw him when you arrived, I daresay."

"Well, good for you," Caroline said. "And are you happy here? Or do you still miss London?"

"Nah, I don't miss that old place at all," Gertrude replied with some force. "Dirty, smoky old town it was—leastways the part where I lived with me old mum. When she died, well, there was nothing to stay there for and nothing to go back for now. Me and Ted are quite content. Mind, I was lucky to get hitched before I arrived here and not have to face the old harridans of the Ladies' Committee."

"Who were they?" This was a world of which Caroline knew nothing.

"They was set up to get jobs for the single girls when they got here and to make sure that those who hadn't been able to pay their five-pound passage money had it deducted from their employers to pay back the government. A right keen mob of shrews they was too, by all accounts. But they couldn't touch me 'cos I'd already paid, and by then I was a respectable married woman, see?"

Caroline saw. And wondered how much the incentive of just being married had contributed to her being so content with her Ted. Still, it had obviously worked out all right in the end.

When the maid had gone, she continued to think about her. Their circumstances were different but in one respect they were the same. Neither had anything to go back to London for. Gertrude and her Ted had made a new and satisfying life for themselves, and Caroline must do the same. Life never stood still for anyone. It moved on, and if one had any sense, one moved on with it.

At least they both had had choices, not like those poor wretches, the convicts, however petty or huge their crimes. They had simply been deported, and many had died in the terrible conditions of the convict ships. Caroline shuddered, thanking the powers that be that she hadn't been born under such an unlucky star.

Luke returned while she was still waiting for her toast and jam. She greeted him more effusively than he expected, and he looked at her warily.

"I never quite know what mood you're going to be in lately," he said. "May I take it that this one is going to last a while?"

She brushed aside his faint sarcasm, guiltily knowing the truth of his words. "If you must know, I've been thinking how fortunate I am, after all, and that my father wouldn't have wanted me to spend the rest of my life being miserable."

"Well, thank the Lord for that. I hope, however, that your meeting with Cedric Whitely isn't going to depress you again."

"Who's Cedric Whitely?"

"The company lawyer. I found him without too much difficulty, and he holds a copy of your father's will, Caroline." He sat beside her, taking her hands between his own. "Apparently it was deposited here when the arrangements were made for your voyage to Australia."

Caroline felt coldness seep over her, where minutes before she had been so buoyant and warm. Luke went on.

"Your father gave instructions that if anything happened to him, the business was to continue exactly as before. The will was only to be opened in your presence, or, if that was not possible, not before six months after his death. It's almost as if he had some kind of premonition."

Her heart was thudding again. She didn't want to hear any of this, but she knew she had to listen. And she had to go to the lawyer's chambers the day after tomorrow and hear the ghost of her father declaring his wishes through that legal document.

"It never ends, does it?" she said, her lips shivering. "Just as you think you've come to terms with it, something else comes and hits you in the face."

"It ends on Thursday evening, my love. No matter what happens before then, at six o'clock in the evening, we board the trading ship for Brundy, and this time neither of us is ever coming back to the mainland."

"Can you be sure of that? Can you be sure my father hasn't made some order for me to stay here and rule his empire, thinking he was providing security for my future?" she said passionately.

He spoke more harshly now. "If he has, you can simply revoke it. You don't need the money from his business, and I'm sure as hell not leaving you behind. As your husband, I've every right to say where you'll live."

"But you're not my husband, are you?" she

399

said slowly, her eyes large and dark with pain as they gazed into his.

The arrival of the maid with Caroline's toast and jam prevented the conversation progressing any further. But the atmosphere in the room practically crackled as though in the grip of a lightning storm. The unanswered question seemed to hover between them, and later, the maid reported to her husband below stairs that the couple in the best bedroom certainly looked like no honeymoon couple she had ever seen . . .

They dressed with care for the evening visit to the Watsons', remembering that they were already supposed to be married and conscious that the people they were to meet had known Caroline and her father well in days gone by. Though perhaps not that well on her account, she remembered. Theirs had only been a social acquaintance, with none of the intimacies of old friends, and for that she was relieved and grateful. Mrs. Watson was hardly going to probe too deeply into the circumstances of her and Luke's meeting.

But in that assumption, she was wrong. They arrived at the Watsons' modest house after they had eaten dinner at the hotel, and the gray-haired lady ushered them in with mingled cries of delight and tears.

"We truly thought you were gone, Caroline, my dear. It's a miracle you survived, to say nothing of your actually reaching Sydney after all this time. And in such fortunate circumstances too! You must tell us everything about your whirlwind romance with your handsome husband!"

Caroline avoided Luke's eyes. This was obviously going to be harder than she thought. She felt Luke's hand curl around hers as they sat together on the chintz-covered sofa.

"Oh, but you can't expect to hear everything, ma'am," he said, with some teasing in his voice. "Suffice it to be said that after I was lucky enough to rescue Caroline from the sea, we formed an immediate attachment for one another and realized we wanted to spend the rest of our lives together. I knew from the first that I wanted Caroline for my wife and that it was fate that brought us together."

He was so *false,* she fumed as she sat there with a fond smile on her lips. In his reasoning, what he'd known from the first was that he *owned* her, but these honest folk now clearly thought their marriage was a fairy tale come true.

"But how fortunate that you did find her, Mr. Garston! So do you live in the northeast of the continent?" Mrs. Watson couldn't let it rest there. "In the vicinity of where the *Princess Victoria* went down, perhaps?"

Caroline felt a shudder run through her. She had thought about reporting the violent storm and the wreck of the ship for the company and the newspaper readers' benefit—indeed, it was her duty to do so, to put the records straight. She was certain, now, that she was the only one who could. But she knew she must be as detached as she could and tell it all with a reporter's voice, or the temptation would return to simply blot it all from her mind, the way she had tried to do these past few months.

"We don't live on the mainland, ma'am," she heard Luke say, "but on a small island east of the Barrier Reef. We're on the trading route, which is how we came to be here now, courtesy of Captain

Ellis, who calls regularly at Brundy Island with supplies and to buy our produce."

"Is that so?" Watson said, sensing that there might be another story here, but Luke quickly squashed the idea that Brundy was in any way interesting to newspaper readers.

"It's merely a calling point, sir, and gives the crew a breathing space for a few days before the last leg of their voyage to Sydney. We have little there of interest."

Caroline wondered that he didn't comment that some of his pearls were probably gracing the lovely necks of the socialites in this town, but it was clear that he intended to underplay his own vocation in every way. She doubted that he was ashamed of being a pearl diver, because nothing shamed Luke, but he had no wish to bring his own past or present life to anyone's notice, nor to bring his role in her rescue to prominence. At this, Caroline rebelled.

She reached for his hand, which had temporarily left hers, and brought it to her cheek with all the loving tenderness of a young bride. If she caught a small mocking look in his eyes, it was quickly hidden.

"What my dear husband isn't saying is that if it weren't for him, I certainly wouldn't be here," she said huskily. "I've no idea how long I'd been drifting in a small boat before he found me, but I was near to exhaustion and dehydration, and I know I owe Luke my life."

She looked directly into his eyes as she spoke. The look might have seemed fond to the onlookers, but it told him exactly what she thought of him. She owed him her life, and she knew he intended to extract every ounce of it from her for the rest of her days. And that was emotional blackmail.

"Would it be too painful for you to recall all that you remember of that day for the readers, Caroline?" Watson reverted to his professional voice as if the conversation was in danger of becoming too sentimental.

His wife spoke quickly. "My dear, can't that wait until Caroline goes into the office? She's had such a harrowing time, finding out about Sir William."

"It's all right, really. I expected to be asked, and I've no objection to telling you this evening, if you wish," she said. It would get it over and done with, and she knew this man to be as trustworthy a newspaperman as any she had ever known. How much better than to have Stoneheart Taylor writing down her memories and elaborating on every morbid moment. Sir William would have trusted Watson to present the story in the best possible manner, and so would she.

So, over cups of coffee and glasses of port, she painfully began to relate that terrible time when the tropical storm had struck without warning . . . of the hysterical shrieks of the passengers and the screams of the crew to tie themselves to bulwarks or anything else that they could . . . of seeing strong men crushed before her eyes . . . of the terrible noise and the drowning invoked by the sheer weight of foaming water rushing over the decks . . . of losing sight of her father and being certain she was never going to survive this terrible ordeal . . . of not knowing how she came to be in a lifeboat, hurt and bleeding and entirely alone on a vast ocean beneath a blisteringly hot sun . . . of hearing voices, sure that she must be near to death and hallucinating. And then the fearsome sight of a golden-haloed apparition above her that had turned out to be Luke . . .

"Steady, my lovely lass," Luke murmured, his hand holding her trembling ones very tightly now. "Take it slowly now. Breathe deeply and try to stay calm. It's all over now and you're perfectly safe."

Somehow she willed the terrifying images out of her mind, seeing Watson furiously writing down all that she was saying, while trying to extract as gently as he could any more information about seeing the great ship flounder. But there was nothing. She had lost consciousness before the ship finally went beneath the waves, and she could only relate her own experiences until that moment.

"I'm sorry," she said thinly. "Does it help at all?"

Watson gave her a warm smile, his own face white from listening to such a tale. "Of course it does, my dear girl. At least we know for certain now what caused the ship to go down. It ties up many loose ends, and I hope the telling hasn't been too great an ordeal for you."

She spoke slowly. "In a way, I'm glad I've told it. I haven't spoken of it for so long, but it was always festering in my mind, and perhaps now I can put it all in the past, where it belongs."

She wasn't sure for whose benefit she said the words, but when she and Luke returned to the hotel, Luke took her gently in his arms.

"I was proud of you tonight, my lass," he said softly. "It was an ordeal for you to relive the storm, and you came through it magnificently. You faced the telling as stoically as you've faced everything since that terrible day — even me."

"You do agree that you've been something of

404

an ogre for me to face then?" she said tremulously.

He gave a short laugh. "Perhaps. But after tomorrow, I trust I'll be an ogre no more, merely a husband, my sweet. Now I suggest that we get some sleep, for we've a busy day ahead of us, and tomorrow night our marriage will truly begin."

He left her to undress alone and slide into the bed they would apparently share chastely tonight. He was doing the noble thing, Caroline thought, in a suddenly perverse and bitter mood, and honoring her feelings.

But she couldn't sleep with the sound of his even breathing alongside her and the warmth of his body only a touch away . . . and all she wanted was for him to crush her to him, and love her, *love* her . . . and to exorcise the ghosts of the past forever.

Chapter Twenty-one

Luke had ordered a carriage to call for them the following morning. Although he had lived on the mainland and the Sydney environs in former times, he professed to recall little of it. But he had obviously done some homework on the area, for they were taken a long way out of Sydney to a small backwoods town and to an austere brick-built house.

A dulled nameplate on the wall stated that it was the home and offices of a justice of the peace. Caroline wondered just how much business such a man did, living so far from civilization. But there was no time to ponder on it now.

She began to think it was the saddest day of her life, instead of what should have been the happiest one. There were no church bells ringing out in triumph, no choirboys singing, no friends and family to congratulate and applaud them on their glorious day. There was only the feeling that there was something shameful in this marriage, conducted by the justice Luke had unearthed, with only his own staff as witnesses to proclaim them legally married.

"It's better this way," he'd said. "We want no fuss and no suspicion that Miss Caroline Rowe was married after she arrived in Sydney. Especially since her story will shortly be told in the *New Sydney Reporter*, encouraging curiosity and gossip. It's best for us to get away from the town for the ceremony. You do see that, don't you, Caroline? It's for your own sake."

"Yes, I see that," she said dully. But she also saw it as a hole-and-corner marriage and could have wept at the brevity of it, with a stony-faced housekeeper and grizzled gardener standing alongside them, both clearly waiting to get back to their duties.

She felt the coldness of the wedding ring as Luke slid it onto her finger. At his request, she had worn it ever since the trading vessel had left Brundy, and it had been both a mockery and a lie to her then. It seemed no less a mockery now, when she and Luke made their vows and were legally pronounced man and wife. It was still so unreal . . . and all the joy she should have felt in pledging her life to this man had vanished. No matter how desperately she tried, she couldn't bring it back.

"We'll spend the afternoon taking a look around the countryside," Luke said as calmly as if they were prospecting for land on which to build. "With a stretch of the imagination, we can think of ourselves as enjoying a Sunday afternoon drive around Hyde Park."

"It has to be a very wide stretch of the imagination," Caroline muttered, seeing nothing of the pleasure in London's lovely park in these surroundings.

True, the magnificent and lonely sandy beaches were glorious. But the land itself was hot and dry and dusty, and away from the coastal environs meant that they were soon enveloped in great tracts of wilderness, encroached by dense vegetation. In the far inland distance there were always the cruel, blue-hazed mountains ranged against the endless blue sky. To Caroline, it was still an inhospitable land, and one whose insatiable greed for inhabitants had taken her father from her.

"I'm surprised you want to show all this to me," she remarked. "I thought you hated the mainland."

"So I do. Perhaps I just want to remind you of all that we have on Brundy, so you won't be too regretful or nostalgic at leaving all this."

"Why should I? There's nothing here for me, anymore than there is for you. And I really think I've had enough of sitting in this carriage for one day."

She was getting hot and cross, and her head was beginning to throb. If he expected a willing bed partner tonight, he was going the wrong way about it, she thought feelingly. The carriage lurched over every bump and gully in the uneven track, and she thought she would be black and blue by the time they returned to Sydney. The motion of the vehicle was not doing her stomach any good either.

"Just as you wish," Luke said. "The trip has served its purpose anyway."

They reached the hotel again in the late afternoon. By then she felt utterly depressed. It was hardly the way a new bride should feel, but it was impossible to lift herself out of her depression, and from his silence, she sensed that much of it had been transmitted to Luke. But after a short rest, the headache cleared, and she felt more able

408

to dress for dinner. For some reason she felt unaccountably nervous at dining with her new husband.

"Will I do?" she said huskily, twirling around in the champagne-colored gown that seemed appropriate for tonight's celebratory meal. Though, not even the hotel staff could share in what should have been a wonderful celebration, she thought mournfully. The marriage date had to be kept private.

She wasn't even looking for compliments from this stern-faced man who seemed to have so little to say to her now. Either Luke was keeping all his feelings in check, she thought, or he simply didn't have any. Perhaps now that he had gotten everything he wanted, he could afford to be uncaring. There was no longer any need to woo her.

She turned away before he could answer, facing her own hurt eyes in the dressing-table mirror and aware of the lump that rose to her throat. She lowered her gaze, not wanting to see her own reflection and the fool that she thought herself for ever agreeing to this marriage.

The next moment she felt the coolness of something being placed against her throat, and her eyes flew open to see Luke fastening the rope of pearls. These were the pearls that were meant for someone special . . . for his wife.

"So you brought them with you," she said, choked. "Were you so sure of me?"

"Haven't I told you so a thousand times?" he replied. "There was never any doubt that one day you'd legally belong to me and that you'd be the recipient of my gift."

She didn't want it. She wished she dared to tear it from her throat. It was the symbol of his power. It had been created before he knew of her existence, and it was no more special to her than a trinket bought at a cheap bazaar. Without the true sentiment that should lay behind it, its worth meant nothing.

"I want you to wear it always, Caroline. It shows the world that you're mine."

He bent to kiss the nape of her neck as he spoke, and the touch of his mouth on her skin seemed to ignite all her dormant feelings. Just as if a flame had been suddenly rekindled inside her, all the old longings for him returned in an instant. She could only keep that longing at bay for so long, and the time of her resistance had run out.

Without thinking, she turned into his arms. He pulled her to him, and they swayed together, locked in an embrace that stunned all sense of reason.

All that was coherent in her mind was that she was here in the arms of the man she loved and that he wanted and desired her. She belonged to him for always now, and no one could take him away from her. If she was his, then by the same token, he was hers, and the sweet simplicity of it was more heady than wine . . .

"Be careful, my darling," she heard Luke's mocking voice murmur against her mouth. "From such a passionate response I could almost imagine you're happy in our new arrangement. It would be a miracle if the newly wed Garstons actually discovered they loved each other, wouldn't it?"

She drew in her breath in pain at the taunt. How could he demean these precious moments . . . ? But then, why should he not? when she obviously still meant no more than a prize to him. A prize he'd paid dearly for, all the same. She tried to force a light laugh to her lips, but she felt that it sounded more like a sob.

"There's no fear of that, dear husband. As you said, our *arrangement* suits us both admirably, doesn't it? You've acquired a wife as you always said you would, and I don't have to stay in Sydney alone and I have the security of marriage."

She felt utterly depressed as she said the words. They didn't reflect a single part of her being. But her pride would never let her admit that she'd married him only because she loved him so wildly, when he made it no secret that he'd merely won a wager. He'd wanted her and he'd gotten her, and though the tears shone on her lashes, she blinked them back angrily, determined that he wouldn't see them.

"Well then," he spoke more coolly now, releasing her. "I think the successful Garstons should go down to the dining room for dinner. Your gown is the color of champagne, and champagne is what we'll drink tonight, my sweet wife. There may not be romantic love between us, but I still expect the satisfaction of making love to a woman who can be as abandoned as a wanton when the mood takes her. And that's the woman I want in my arms tonight."

He took her arm, holding it so hard she thought it would be bruised by the time they descended the hotel stairs. As if he were almost afraid she would turn and run at the crudity of his words. Despite the irony of there being no romantic love between them, at least on his part, his words only served to heighten her need of him, to start the blood coursing faster in her veins and the singing joy begin, because tonight there would be no separation of mind or body.

They lingered over dinner, as if each was savoring what was to come. The night was mellow and warm, the ambience in their dining alcove soft and

411

seductive. The food hardly mattered. As their glances met across the candlelit table, they saw the reflection of desire mirrored in each others' eyes. It soared like a flame in Caroline, heating her blood, firing her passion. Her mouth was dry, and she drank deeply of the expensive champagne Luke ordered, but she knew her head was spinning with a far greater intoxication than mere wine could induce.

As her fingers curled around the champagne glass, the light glinted on the wedding ring she now wore with pleasure rather than shame. The circumstances didn't matter, she thought passionately. He's *mine,* and tonight will see the culmination of our love . . .

"Shall we retire? Are you ready?" Luke said finally, when it seemed expedient enough for them to leave the dining room without seeming in undue haste.

"I'm quite ready," she murmured, her voice giving a special meaning to the words for his ears only. She saw him give a half-smile, this Greek god of a man who was now her husband. She knew she was tipsy from champagne, but that she didn't need it to be abandoned in their lovemaking. As if she needed champagne for that! But if he thought so, then so be it, she thought hazily. A lady never acted in an abandoned way . . . but a man wanted a warm-blooded woman for a wife, not a paragon of virtue.

In their room, she swayed a little, hoping she wouldn't disgrace herself after all. But it was only the effort of climbing the stairs and the beautiful gown that suddenly seemed far too tight for her. It would be a relief to be out if it. She reached behind her for the fastenings with trembling fingers, and Luke stayed them at once.

"Let me," he said softly.

She turned away from him and felt his hands caress her spine with each hook that was released. He kissed every inch of flesh that was revealed to him, and every new touch heightened her aching longing for him. She wanted him to be a part of her so much . . .

He continued to undress her while she stood perfectly still. Only her rapid breathing and her flushed skin told how she was affected by the sweet torture of his deliberate attentions. The dress slid to the ground, a rustle of satin and silk, followed by the petticoats and the chemise, and each time Luke paused to kiss and fondle a new area of her body until she could have wept with her needs.

"Now you, my darling," he instructed. "Or have you forgotten how to deal with a man's clothing?"

"I've not forgotten a thing," she said huskily, "though I would have you know you're the only man I've ever—I've ever—"

She was very aware of the eroticism of the moment. She was entirely naked now, and the soft warm breezes of the night blew in from the half-open window, whispering seductively over her heated flesh. The curtains weren't drawn, but their room was several floors up, and no one could see them.

They hadn't lit the lamp, but the room was sensually lit by moonlight, sculpting the peaks and hollows of her perfect body. And while she fumbled with Luke's clothing, she couldn't be unaware of the potency of his desire. He was helping her now, obviously as impatient to lie with her as she was with him. The knowledge excited her senses almost to fever pitch.

Without warning, he lifted her in his arms and

carried her to the bed. Almost with one movement, his body covered hers, gently easing her apart with his limbs. His mouth roamed over her, teasing her breasts with his caresses, and she almost drowned in erotic pleasure.

"I've waited too long for you, my lass," he said hoarsely. "From tonight onward, my sweet temptress, you'll be truly mine at last."

In her innocence, she believed he was professing his love, his married love for her . . . He pinned her arms to the pillow and forged inside her waiting softness. She was warm and ready for him. As he thrust into her, she panted beneath him, writhing in pleasure and waiting for the moment of sweet release to come. But then she realized his movements had slowed to a longer, more gentle seduction, and in the soft moonlight, she could see his eyes glittering.

"No, not yet, my dearest. I haven't taken my full pleasure of you yet."

Swiftly, still as one, he rolled them both over until she straddled him. Her hair fell about them both, and he twined it in his fingers, pulling her down onto him. The tips of her breasts brushed his chest, sending a tinglingly erotic thrill deep within her. She was almost startled to realize she felt no shame, no embarrassment, as she watched his hands begin to caress her. She felt how he filled her now, and it was pleasure upon pleasure . . .

"Ride me, sweetheart," Luke's hoarse voice said. "You have me now, so take your wifely enjoyment."

This was a different Luke, she thought faintly, but he was none the less dear to her. She thought she already knew his lovemaking intimately, but he instructed her to take the initiative now. She moved against him, tentatively at first, and then with more abandon as she realized that he was moving with her, in an exquisitely pulsating rhythm.

Her neck and back were arched as she pressed her hands against his strong muscled shoulders. Her eyes were closed in ecstasy, the breath in her throat coming faster with each thrust. She was fevered with passion as Luke's hands cupped her breasts and his lips tantalized her nipples. She could hear his own breathing quicken, and when she finally felt the hot gush of his seed inside her, ripples of pleasure throbbed through her loins, bringing her to newly exquisite heights. Her eyes filled with the sweet tears of fulfillment, so that she gasped out his name . . .

His passion was spent, and as he gathered her into him, he became aware of the dampness of her face against his and her ragged breathing. They lay entwined, but side by side now, and she felt him become strangely still. Slowly he spoke into her ear.

"Why do you cry? Dear God, Caroline, do I disgust you so much? Is it so very objectionable for you to lie with me now? I never thought you were the kind of woman to pretend a passion you didn't feel. Or am I to suppose that all those other times that we've been together, it was all a sham? Have you been playing some devious game of your own all this time?"

Her face was streaked with tears now. Couldn't he see that because of the intensely intimate pleasure he gave her, it was passion itself that made her cry? She assumed that a man would know this by instinct.

It had nothing to do with disgust! It was the same emotional reaction anyone got from a beautiful painting or a poignant piece of music, but the sensual emotions produced from lovemaking were intensified a hundredfold. His assumption that she was shallow enough to have pretended all this time bruised her beyond words.

"Is that really what you think of me?" she said thickly, too hurt to say anything else for the moment.

She heard him give a smothered oath, and he moved swiftly away from her, so that they no longer touched. She was so cold and upset at what he had said that they might as well have been an ocean apart.

"I no longer know what to think, except that you should try to sleep," he said harshly.

She slid quickly out of bed and got into her nightgown with shaking hands since the sight of her own naked body was suddenly shaming. He desired her, but she was certain now that he didn't love her. The effects of the champagne had dissipated, and she was chilled. As she lay back rigidly in the bed, well away from Luke's side of it, she heard him give another savage oath as he donned his clothes again and went out of the bedroom into the night.

She never knew when he came back. It must have been very late because she lay awake for a long time, crying over the mess they were making of their lives, until exhaustion overcame her and she finally slept.

The next morning, Luke said shortly that it might be best to consider that their marriage began from this day. He never retracted last night's remarks, nor apologized for them, and Caroline was too proud to comment.

416

She had no wish to remember how hurt and up-set she had felt, and because she was concentrating on fighting down the nausea of the morning, she nodded distantly. "I'd much prefer it if it was never mentioned again."

To be truthful, she couldn't even remember too much about it now. She knew that a simple, loving answer to his queries might have overcome all the misunderstanding and the way they seemed to have grown apart so suddenly. It was pride which kept her from being honest.

"We have things to discuss before we see the lawyer," he said before they went downstairs for breakfast. He was brisk now and displayed no emotion. "Naturally your father will have left everything to you, and you must decide what you intend to do about it."

"What do you mean?"

He spoke patiently, as if to a child. "There will be annual dividends from the newspaper business, Caroline. There will be money to disperse among the employees as their needs increase. You can't avoid it, my dear."

"But I know nothing about such things!" she said, aghast at the burden the legacy would put on her. It would all have been much simpler if she'd decided to stay on in Sydney, but all that was changed now. She was married to Luke Garston, and her home was far away from here.

"I suggest we ask the lawyer for advice. There will be a company accountant and auditor, and if they're reliable people, you can probably put every-thing in their hands and arrange for the dividends to be delivered to Brundy once a year. We may en-list the help of Captain Ellis for the purpose, and I can vouch for his honesty."

She listened as if in a dream. And suddenly she

417

knew she didn't want this. She didn't want her father's empire, nor his money, nor this legacy. It was too much to bear.

"Do we need this money?" she said huskily. "Would it make a great difference to you if we have the annual dividends, Luke?"

His face was thunderous. "I didn't marry you for your fortune. I thought at least you knew that."

She flinched. "I no longer know why you married me. I don't know *you* anymore! But I want to say that I didn't marry you for money either."

"Well, it certainly wasn't for love," he retorted. "But if it pleases you to hear me say it, then I don't want your damn legacy. It means nothing to me."

"Then I've got some ideas of my own about it," she said. She felt hollow inside; her heart breaking at how far they were drifting apart.

But before she could elaborate on the thoughts that had come to her, the wretched bile rose in her mouth. She was obliged to dash unceremoniously for the wash basin and lean over it while she retched. There was no help for it but to cover it with a towel and leave it for the unfortunate Gertrude to take away.

Caroline did not tell Luke her plans for her inheritance since he made no further reference to it and neither did she. Later that day they sat side by side in the lawyer's somber chamber. Caroline registered every minute detail: the dark-paneled walls, the leather chairs and oak desk, the fussy little lawyer with the monocle, his dark suit and polished black shoes. She thought he looked more like an undertaker, and immediately wished the

418

comparison hadn't entered her mind.

He shook both their hands solemnly. In the same breath he expressed his regrets on the death of Sir William, and his pleasure at seeing her safe and well. It was clear he was a man who didn't waste words or time.

"Shall we get right down to business, Mrs. Garston and sir? I doubt that either of you wish to prolong this meeting."

Caroline nodded, starting a little at hearing her married name. But she was entitled to it now, of course. She belonged to Luke Garston, body and soul.

She pushed the memory away. This was neither the time nor place to dwell on such things, when Cedric Whitely was unfolding a long document tied with a red ribbon. This then, was the last will and testament of Sir William Rowe. Caroline swallowed thickly, then felt Luke's hand grip hers. Rather than pulling away, she took some comfort from it.

She heard the legal voice drone on. It was all very clear. Everything was left to Caroline except for some personal legacies to certain long-standing employees. Among them was a generous sum to Watson and the wish that the man be put in charge of the Sydney venture until such time as he retired and appointed someone of his own choosing to succeed him. Caroline was glad to hear it since it saved her the need to request something of the same.

"So I suspect there's little untoward in the bequests, Mrs. Garston. And I presume you and your husband will be taking up residence in our fair town in order to conduct your business affairs?"

She took a deep breath. "No, we will not, Mr.

Whitely. And although everything is very clear, I have far more business to discuss before we leave."

The man's eyes widened. Clearly he had been expecting the husband to discuss business matters and had not anticipated such a firm reaction from a woman, especially such a pretty one as this. He cleared his throat, glancing at the husband.

"What can I do for you, Mr. Garston?"

Caroline spoke quickly, taking her hand away from Luke's as she did so. "Excuse me, sir, but it's I and not my husband who is the beneficiary of my father's will, and I've already made my decision on what I wish to do with my inheritance. Also, my requests must be put into operation with all speed since my husband and I leave Sydney tomorrow."

She didn't look at Luke as the lawyer sat back in his chair. Things moved slowly in the legal profession, and it was easy to see he wasn't pleased by this young woman who seemingly wanted everything done at once. He looked at Caroline disapprovingly, awaiting her remarks.

"I've decided that I want none of the dividends from the business," she said clearly. "My father wished to make a success of the newspaper here in Sydney, and I want a good proportion of the money earned to be ploughed back into it. That's aside from any provisions for annual increases for the staff, naturally."

"But, my dear young lady—" the lawyer began, appalled at the rejection of a comfortable future for herself.

"I want more than that," she went on doggedly. "I want his fortune and any dividends left over to be put to a useful purpose. First of all, I want a monument erected in my father's memory. Next, there will be a school in his name, a hospital, and a library. In other words, I wish that periodically a new building of importance be named after Sir William Rowe in perpetuity or as long as the *New Sydney Reporter* exists. Perhaps at some time in the future I shall come to see for myself that the work has been carried out, but in any case, I intend to instruct Captain Ellis to contact you annually to bring me detailed reports."

The lawyer was openly gaping now at this forceful young woman and clearly wondering if her husband was completely mad to agree to such a thing. But if the husband was already well-heeled, he was presumably willing to indulge the pretty wife . . . Cedric Whitely mentally washed his hands of them both, and folded his arms across his chest.

"Are you quite determined on this?" he asked in a final effort. "You do realize what you're giving up, Mrs. Garston? And, er, this is your sole decision?"

"I assure you that it's my sole decision, sir. And I think I'm gaining far more than I'm losing," she said quietly. "My father never knew Sydney, but he longed to make it his home. In this way he'll never be forgotten, even though the people who benefit will never know him. I know he would approve."

Whitely cleared his throat again. He was not a man for sentiment, but he grudgingly admired the young woman, even though he thought it foolhardy in the extreme to throw away a fortune.

"You understand that it will take time to draw up the proper papers," he began.

Luke spoke up now, having sat silently all this time as he listened to Caroline's demands. By now she was sitting back in her chair, her eyes huge in her pale face.

"We don't have time, man. We leave Sydney tomorrow evening, so everything my wife requests must be made legally water-tight by then."

"But that's impossible!" the man spluttered.

"Nothing's impossible," Luke said calmly. "I would venture to think that my wife is now one of your most valuable clients. Therefore you can drop everything else and get the documents ready for signing and witnessing by tomorrow morning. Otherwise we shall be obliged to find another lawyer to deal with our business."

"That won't be necessary, Mr. Garston," the man said stiffly after barely a pause. "If you will call here at noon tomorrow, I will see that everything is ready for you."

"Thank you, Mr. Whitely," Caroline said. "Until tomorrow then." She gave him her hand, outwardly cool and dignified, betraying none of her churning feelings inside. And thankful beyond words that Luke was authoritative enough to take over the final details for her.

When they got outside the lawyer's chambers, he took her straight to a nearby tearoom for some much-needed refreshment. When the brew was set in front of them, he looked at her oddly.

"You constantly surprise me, Mrs. Garston," he said.

She felt her face flush at the name, and she spoke quickly. "I suppose you think I should have discussed it all with you first and that it's wrong for a woman to be so independent—"

She stopped, as his hand reached across the table and covered hers. "You surprise me by your thoughtfulness and common sense, when I've seen so much of your stubbornness in the past," he said dryly. "As for your independence, I had nothing but admiration for you in standing up to the lawyer as you did. I was also very proud of you for your decisions, and I know your father would have been proud of you too."

She felt a prickling in her neck at this unexpected praise. He was obviously sincere, and as so often happened, all her antagonism toward him disappeared in the wealth of her love for him.

"Oh, Luke, that's the best thing you could have said to me," she said huskily. "Thank you. Oh, I wish you could have known him."

He turned her hand over and raised her palm to his lips. "If I could speak to him today, I'd say what a fine job he'd done in raising his daughter. But since I don't want to puff you up too much, my sweet, I think that's enough to satisfy your vain little heart for today."

But she saw that he was only teasing, his eyes warm, and Caroline could only bless the fact that the dark clouds between them seemed to have passed — temporarily, at least. For now, it was enough.

The following evening they were back on the trading ship, and it was a repetition of all that had gone before: the welcome aboard from Captain Ellis and the crew; being ushered into the same cabin by Barnes; the image of Sydney and the harbor, receding and ghostly now as the evening mist rose, shrouding buildings and coastline alike in an unearthly atmosphere; the sudden chill whenever Caroline thought of where her fortunes had taken her . . .

"I can hardly believe we're actually on our way back," Caroline commented.

There were still times when she felt completely disoriented. Times when she tried to block everything from her mind and other times when the pain of it all came searing back until she felt over-come with grief for the end of all her father's bright dreams.

She and Luke leaned over the ship's rail now, and she knew she was saying a last goodbye to a life that was destined never to be.

"You're cold," Luke said. "And it's time we went below for the evening meal. Captain Ellis will be interested to know what we made of Sydney."

The captain was already aware of the sadness of her mission and had awkwardly offered his regrets. That had been one of the oddest times, knowing she should be mourning, yet somehow staying stony-faced and dry-eyed. But in truth, she accepted that she had done her true grieving a long while ago. Yet that, in itself, produced a weird sense of guilt in her, so that she almost welcomed the crying times as a penance for being alive while her father and all those other passengers on the *Princess Victoria* had perished.

Chapter Twenty-two

They joined the captain in his cabin for the evening meal as they were invited to do every evening now on the detour back to Brundy Island.

"Did you find the town interesting, Mrs. Garston?" Captain Ellis said amiably as they were served their salted pork and potatoes. "Naturally this wouldn't have been the happiest of visits, but were you able to take in any of the sights?"

"Oh yes," she replied. Privately she thought that apart from the magnificent natural harbor, there were few sights she would have wanted to have seen again.

Sydney was still a comparatively young town. It hadn't yet mellowed with the centuries-old ambience that London boasted. In fairness Caroline knew it was quite unreasonable to compare the two places. In a hundred years from now she had no doubt that Sydney would be just as thriving a metropolis and probably an elegant mecca for visitors. But for her, without her father, it had been a town without sparkle.

"I think my wife enjoyed our visit to the country area more than the town itself," Luke said.

She knew what he referred to so obliquely. In the surrounding country area was where they had found the old justice and became legally married . . .

"It all had its good points," she agreed. "Though some of it I would rather forget."

"Of course," Captain Ellis said, completely misunderstanding. "It was where your father was buried, I understand. It cannot have been easy for you."

She lowered her eyes. Now that the marriage was a *fait accompli,* she felt an increasing sense of tension between herself and Luke. Tonight they would share the cabin as man and wife, and when they returned to Brundy, it would be to let everyone know that they were married. From then on, she would be mistress of Garston Manor, and she wondered just how many tongues would wag because of the decision to be married so far from home.

Luke was so much a part of his island, and he had denied his friends the right to celebrate his nuptials with him. The thought was enough to make her uneasy, and surely Luke must have considered it too. She broached the subject when they returned to their cabin that night. It was very late by then, and they had lingered on deck for a last-minute breather. They had watched the darkening, mesmerizing water scud past the ship's bow, lit by moonlight and warmed by a summer breeze.

It was as if neither of them had wanted to make the first move to descend to what should be a love nest. And the more it occurred to her, the more certain Caroline was that he must be regret-

426

ting the hasty decision to be wed to a woman who had always been a challenge to him and perhaps would never be anything more. All her nerves were on edge, wondering if he was going to take her in his arms that night or if he would spurn her in a kind of revenge for all she had put him through since their meeting.

"Luke," she said as soon as they had closed the cabin door behind them. "How will everyone on the island react to our marriage? Will it be very difficult for you?"

"Why in God's name should be it be?" he said shortly. "I don't have to account to anyone for my movements."

"I'm sure you don't," she said feelingly. "But, well, no one expected me to return with you, for one thing. Especially not as your *wife*."

` He gave her an odd smile, shrugging his powerful shoulders as he began to remove his jacket and then the rest of his clothes in readiness for the night. She was suddenly filled with a deep, dark suspicion.

"Did *you* expect it?" she demanded. "Did you think all along that this was what would happen?"

She tried to remain detached as he stripped off all his clothes without embarrassment, but it was more than she could do to resist watching him. The powerful physique, the broad hair-sprinkled chest, the flat belly and the proud source of potency beneath. She felt her heart begin a slow pounding, remembering the times that source had thrust into her, sometimes in fast, furiously released passion; sometimes in languorously sensual forgings that had aroused such exquisitely erotic sensations in her . . .

She watched as he slid into the far bunk while

427

she still stood rigidly, her hands tightly at her sides, not yet daring to fumble with her own clothing for fear he would see how badly he disturbed her. She had every right to be disturbed. She was his wife . . . but a sure instinct told her there was to be no loving that night, that somehow they had grown too far apart for no reason she could define. It was a subtle parting that left her bewildered and upset. And she still waited for the answer to her question.

"In case you think you'll be done out of a party to celebrate a marriage, my dear, let me assure you it's all been arranged," he said calmly.

"You're talking in riddles," she said, feeling anger well up in her now. "How could you have let anyone know we were returning or that we'd be wanting to celebrate a marriage!"

"It was all arranged before we left Brundy, my sweet," he said, to her absolute disbelief. "I had a wager with Dr. Sam on it, but I was confident I'd be the winner. By the time we were underway to Sydney, he and Mrs. Hughes would have got their heads together and provisionally arranged a celebration party for two weeks after we return. The whole island will know we're married by now and that it was our wish to do it quietly in Sydney, with or without your father's presence."

She was almost speechless—almost. Her breath escaped in a furious gasp.

"How *dare* you," she said tightly. "So you intended all the time to marry me while we were in Sydney? You knew I'd have no option but to return with you."

"That's right."

"And what if my father had been there, alive and well? Did you have a wager on his life too? And do you really think I'd have accepted mar-

428

riage to you if I'd had the chance to stay there with him?"

Her voice was brittle with hurt, and she didn't want to think too deeply about her own questions. All the love she felt for this man was in danger of vanishing in the wake of this betrayal. How *could* he? she thought wildly. He'd accused her of being obsessed with her father's survival, but he'd been just as obsessed with owning her. And he had won.

"Caroline, go to bed," he said, as if tiring of this late-night discussion. "Since you're so upset, I won't bother you with my attentions tonight, so you may rest easy on that score."

And what if she was desperate to be bothered by his attentions, as he so delicately put it? she raged. What of *her* needs, wishes, desires . . . She was a mixture of frustrated emotions, and he seemed to understand none of it. Where was the rapport and sweet understanding between them now?

She turned away from him, finding the lump in her throat almost too hard to swallow. If only they had met in another time, another place, in circumstances that were more normal and less traumatic. What then? Would Luke Garston still have wanted her if they had met in the social circle of her father's world? Would he even have been there?

With sudden insight, she knew that he would not. He would have scorned such falseness, where sycophants tried to curry favor with her father and his friends. Luke would always be the man he was, uniquely proud of the world he'd built for himself out of nothing, and just as proud of his ability to wrest pearls from the sea.

She had removed her gown and most of her

429

undergarments now, and her fingers touched the coolness of the pearls around her throat. She reached for the fastening and felt Luke's hands there before her. She had been so absorbed in her own misery, she hadn't even heard him move out of the bunk.

"Let me do that," he said quietly. Against her back, she could feel the touch of his body, and as she felt the weight of the necklace leave her throat, she was twisted against him.

"At least I'll have a good-night kiss from my unwilling wife," he said roughly, and then she felt his mouth on hers, and the masculine texture of his skin tingled against her softness.

When the kiss ended, he held her tightly against him for a moment, and she felt their heartbeats merge into one. It was too much for her. She needed him so much, and this was no night for modesty . . .

"Why do you call me an unwilling wife?" she said huskily. "A wife's duty is to love, honor, and obey her husband, and I made a vow to do just that."

He said nothing for a moment, and then he gave a short, harsh laugh.

"I thank you for reminding me of your duties, Caroline. I shall take that as an invitation, and it seems I win another wager. Didn't I say you'd be inviting me into your bed before the end of our voyage?"

She raged at the way he was intent on turning everything into a gamble. And then the anger melted away as he lifted her bodily and placed her on his own narrow bunk, as if he wanted to prove to her once and for all that she was his possession and that he could do with her what he liked.

There was no room on the bunk for two people to lie side by side. There was only one way . . .

There was no finesse in his lovemaking that night. There was only pulsating excitement, accompanied by crudely muttered words that, far from shocking her, seemed to add to its eroticism. He treated her as if she was an unwilling wife . . . a chattel . . . yet none of it shocked her. It was all part of the night and of the man he was, wild and powerful, and *hers*. Whatever else he was, he belonged to her now and always would . . .

She felt the hot surge of his seed and then the sudden slump of his body on hers. And the soft tears on her cheeks mingled with the sweat of exertion on his.

"Thank you, my sweet, for doing your duty so beautifully," she heard him say, and she slowly opened her eyes. In the dim light of the cabin, she couldn't see his expression, but his words had hurt her beyond measure. Couldn't he see . . . didn't he *know* . . . that duty had nothing to do with the enormity of her love for him?

The words trembled on her lips, even though she would be the one to say them first, when she had waited so long to hear him confess his love for her. But a man didn't need to love in order to perform the act, she thought bitterly. He only needed a woman on whom to unleash his lust . . .

But before she could speak, Luke had moved away from her and was lifting her in his arms again, this time to dump her unceremoniously on her own bunk.

"I think we'll call that your duty done for the rest of the voyage," he said coldly. "I've no wish to make you cry every time I inflict my passion

431

on you, and perhaps by the time we return to civilization, you'll have learned to control your feelings."

"Are all men such fools?" Caroline said in a sudden rage. "A woman's tears at such a time have nothing to do with pain or dislike. They're an emotional release at the height of desire. You must be blind if you can't see that."

"Then you do admit that your desire, at least, is genuine?" he said in a mocking voice.

She saw no point in denying it. "You know very well that it is. I'm not made of wood!"

"Indeed you're not, my lovely wife," he said, his voice still oozing the sensuality she had come to know so well.

But she had no intention of trying to explain it further. If she did, she just might admit that, to her, desire and love were intermingled. Instead, she turned her back on him in her own bunk, huddling into a ball beneath the covers, and began to wonder just how difficult her life ahead was going to be after all.

He was true to his word, and he didn't touch her again for the entire voyage. In the company of the captain or crew, he was the devoted, attentive husband. But in their cabin, it seemed he could turn off the devotion as easily as turning off a tap. Caroline was bewildered and upset, but she stoically refused to show it.

She was more than thankful when the shadowy outline of Brundy Island came into view on one brilliantly sunlit morning. Whatever the future held, it was here, and not in the increasingly unsavory bowels of a trading ship. She freely admitted it was hardly the best place to spend a

432

honeymoon, however farcical the word seemed to her. But at least she had experienced no trouble from the crew, and remembering their attentions to the island girls, she knew she had Luke to thank for that.

The arrival of a ship drew its usual mass of people to the quayside, and the trading ship was quickly recognized. Word had obviously spread that Luke and his bride were coming home. Before they even alighted onto dry land, Caroline could see the familiar faces of Dr. Sam and Mrs. Hughes; the Finnegan family; the colonel; the pearling boys; the group of children in Doc Sam's school, and many more. It was a grand homecoming, and she felt sudden shame at the way she and Luke were deceiving them all. For this was so much less than a marriage made in heaven . . .

But she had no time for dwelling on gloomy thoughts. She was clasped in so many arms and submitted to so many kisses that she was almost dizzy. Meanwhile, their bags were being taken off the ship and transported up to the house while Captain Ellis bade them good luck and prepared for a quick departure. This was no more than a courtesy docking for the convenience of the well-liked couple from Brundy.

They were escorted to Garston Manor in a great hullabaloo of noise.

"It's good to have you back home, miss — I should say, Mrs. Garston!" Mrs. Hughes said, beaming. "I knew all along that you and Mr. Luke were made for each other, if you'll pardon the impertinence."

"And the good lady has been planning your party night all this while, gel," Doc Sam put in.

"I'm so glad you'll be here to see my wedding, Caroline," Kathleen Finnegan said as they parted.

433

"I was wondering if you'd agree to be my attendant along with Maureen. Please say you will."

"It would be a pleasure," Caroline said huskily, not missing the way Kathleen's hand was clasped in that of her young man. Theirs was truly a love match, she thought enviously.

As the crowds thinned out and they approached the grounds of the house, Jojo managed to make himself heard amid all the excitement.

"We wanted you back, boss. We find new grounds near reef with plenty good pickings. Big pearls there for sure."

Caroline saw how Luke's interest was caught at once. It was far more interesting to him than a wedding party, she thought in some vexation. But she was beginning to feel so exhausted and drained, she thought guiltily, that everything was going to irritate her until she got some proper sleep in a proper bed.

"Have you investigated the area thoroughly, Jojo?"

"Sure, boss. Only bad thing was sharks. Real big fellas there, boss. Maybe sharks like pearls too, eh, missus?" he added to Caroline.

It was a feeble joke, but enough to make her heart miss a beat for a moment. It was surely madness to dive for pearls in shark-infested waters, when there was the whole vast ocean in which to seek out the gems.

"Luke, must you go there?"

She might as well have been talking to herself. Luke was already asking Jojo all sorts of questions about the reef area where the big pearls were to be found, and Makepeace and the rest of the crew spoke excitedly of the find. There was no doubt that Luke would have to see for himself at the earliest opportunity.

434

When they were finally alone in their room and changing into fresh clothes before eating a welcomed home-cooked meal, he smiled briefly.

"I've you to thank for this find, Caroline. It appears to be in the reef area where we left the mainland. The pearls were good quality there, and Jojo assures me they're even better a little to the north."

"But if it's in shark-infested waters, it's surely not worth risking your life!"

"Your concern is touching, my dear, but I assure you we risk our lives every time we dive for pearls. It's a risk we choose to take, and we've always returned safely."

So far . . . but she couldn't say the words that trembled on her lips, and she knew she would never be able to deter him from his task. He reveled in the thrill of danger and in gathering the treasures of the sea that would ultimately result in the pleasure of countless women. And the woman he had married obviously wasn't woman enough to make him turn away from his chosen life.

"When will you go?" she said in a muffled voice. Next week . . . next month . . . sometime after their party . . . as far in the future as possible, she begged silently.

"Tomorrow," he told her, and she looked at him, aghast.

"But you can't! Not so soon, Luke. We've only just returned home—"

"And I've been away from my work for too long. Would you have me sit around the house like a drone, my sweet? It's not my way. I've an urge to see these rich pickings, and you might reflect on the fact that the next time the trading ship calls at Brundy, I should be doing some spectacular bargaining with Captain Ellis. I shall

435

shower you with even more gifts to please you."

She wouldn't respond to his mocking words. She didn't want more gifts, however rich they might be. All of them would be worthless without his love.

"I shall worry about you," she said instead. "About the crew, too, until I see you all return safely."

"You've no need to fear that. Besides, I've everything to return for, haven't I?"

The words should have meant everything to her, and yet they meant nothing. It was an enigmatic reply, if only because of his still-mocking tone. As if he wanted to leave her in no doubt that this marriage was no more than a sham and so much less than all that a marriage should be.

"Shall we go downstairs?" he went on coolly. "Mrs. Hughes will probably have prepared a feast in the short time we've been home, and I, for one, intend to do it justice."

He was true to his words, but Caroline could only pick at her food. It was deliciously prepared, her favorite chicken stew, but her taste for food had gone. All she could think about was that tomorrow Luke would be facing danger again and that he didn't even want her love as a talisman before he left.

They slept in the same large bed that night, but whatever might or might not have transpired between them, Caroline was beset by weariness after the events of the past weeks. She was struck, too, by the aftereffects of motion sickness: the room seemed to swim about unless she lay perfectly still and forcibly willed away the unpleasant sensations.

When she awoke, she stretched out her hand without thinking, but instead of touching Luke's cheek, there was only the cold pillow beside her. She lay her head in the dent where his had rested, missing him so much. Unbidden, an image of Kathleen Finnegan and Michael Treherbert came to her mind. How different their morning awakenings would be from hers and Luke's . . . how different their warm, love-filled nights . . .

And since she knew so well the sensuous pleasure of Luke's lovemaking, it was all the more poignant and painful to Caroline that he no longer seemed to want her, except for his own male gratification.

She heard Petal come into their room, greeting her as noisily as usual.

"Why Mr. Luke gone pearling today, missus? Why he leave you already?" she said indignantly. Caroline forced a smile and prepared to get up, trying not to wince at her spinning head.

"He hasn't left me already, you goose—"

"He not here, is he?"

Caroline laughed at her simple logic, told her to fetch her washing water, and then help her to dress. It promised to be a long, anxious day, and she wondered just what she was going to do with it.

In the end, it passed quite quickly. The house felt too cloying for her to stay indoors, and she went out walking, reacquainting herself with the island and with its inhabitants. Inevitably, she found herself at Dr. Sam's door. He welcomed her inside, immediately pouring her a tankard of suspiciously dark-looking brew.

"It's harmless, gel, but it'll buck you up a bit. A sea voyage didn't do you too much good, did it? Though you'll still be sad at learning of your father's fate, I daresay."

"I should have known all along, shouldn't I? I was being very foolish and short-sighted, but no matter how often Luke told me so, I wouldn't believe him."

She looked down at her hands, feeling restless and out of sorts. She was resentful too. Luke should be here with her today, not gallivanting the Lord knew where in all sorts of danger. They should be visiting people together as a loving couple celebrating their marriage.

"He does love you, you know," Doc Sam said matter-of-factly.

She flushed. "I doubt that very much. He loves owning me as he loves to own everything around him."

"You're wrong, but I don't suppose you'll believe me anymore than you'll believe him."

"I won't believe him because he's never told me!"

Dr. Sam laughed. "Good God, woman, there's more ways than words for a man to tell a woman he loves her. I wouldn't have thought you needed to be told that!"

She pursed her lips. It was hardly the accepted way for a man to be talking to a lady, even if he was a doctor, but she let that pass. Nothing on Brundy Island was done in the accepted way, especially by Dr. Sam!

"A woman needs to hear the words," she said tightly. She coughed a little over Doc Sam's brew and pulled a face at its bitter taste.

"Is there anything you want to tell me?" he said casually.

"Not especially. I just came to visit, that's all—"

"No symptoms of a delicate nature to report?"

"Of course not," she said, blushing furiously.

But she paused all the same. Those increasingly frequent attacks of nausea must mean something, though the Lord knew she'd had enough to cope with lately to induce them. And she had been far too distressed to pay too much attention to the irregularity of her cycle.

"Come and see me any time you think you need advice, my dear," Dr. Sam said, more professionally. "A healthy young woman like yourself usually does so quite early in her married life."

Caroline blushed again. He was referring to a child, of course. And for a moment she let herself dream. A child born out of love between herself and Luke would be so wonderful . . . as long as it was love and not mere lust. Even so, it would be just as welcome, she thought fiercely.

"I'll remember," she mumbled as she rose to go, not wanting to feel the doctor's knowing eyes inspecting her too thoroughly. "I'll see you soon, Dr. Sam. You're coming to our party, of course?"

"I wouldn't miss it for the world," he promised as she took her leave.

Caroline discovered that the party truly had been well-arranged before they returned from Sydney. Celebration, however, seemed far from Luke's mind during the next days. He was wrapped up in investigating the new diving sites his boys had found, and overjoyed with the results. The talk was all of the outstanding pearls they were finding and the shimmering mother-of-pearl in which they nestled.

Long into each night, he was in consultation with his crew or closeted in his study detailing and cataloging the pearls, making ready for the next visit from the trading ship. Since it would be months away, though Caroline felt a growing suspicion about the time Luke spent doing this now and finally deduced that he was avoiding her company for as long as possible.

She was bitterly resentful about it, but she had too much pride to ask why he rarely came to their bed until he thought she was asleep. And she never let him know that she lay awake beside him, willing herself not to throw herself into his arms and beg for his love.

But on the night of the party, things would surely be different, she thought hopefully. All their friends would be there, and the newlyweds would be expected to wear their love like a banner. Luke had far too much masculine pride to allow anyone to think there was anything amiss in their relationship. She pinned all her hopes on that special night, still a week away.

Meanwhile the empty days went on, and no matter how she filled them with visiting friends and trekking about the island, she felt more lonely than ever before. Staring at the endless, hypnotic sea, imagining all its dangers as well as acknowledging its gleaming riches, only made things worse.

It was the custom for small, interested crowds to gather in the moonlight for the return of the pearling boats, particularly when new productive sites had been found. Since she had returned, Caroline usually joined them, aching for the first sight of Luke, safely home from the sea. By the time she reached the quay that evening, the first boat had already beached, and moments later she heard the dread sound of the alarm bell tolling.

Her heart stopped, knowing what it meant. A

440

boat was missing . . . she stumbled, almost falling, and made her way to where some of the crew were clambering out of the first boat with their haul.

"What's happened? Where's my husband?" she gasped out.

Their eyes widened in terror. "Big fella shark, missus. He come try swallow up boat. We not stay—"

She shook one boy until he almost rattled. Her hands were vicelike on his arms as she tried to get more sense out of him.

"What do you mean you not stay?" she screamed above the din. "Do you mean you left Luke to—to the *shark?*"

Faintness almost overwhelmed her now, and she was conscious that other arms were holding her up. *Dear God,* she thought, *please, please send him back to me so I can tell him how much I love him . . .*

"Boss's boat tip sideways, missus," the boy said, his voice still quavering. "Jojo try to save boss, but we go. We told to go—"

She was aware of Dr. Sam's voice beside her and realized that he was the one supporting her. "It's their way, Caroline. Someone must return to tell the tale, and Luke would have impressed that on them."

She didn't want to hear any of this. All she wanted was for Luke to come back, safe and alive. It was more than she could bear to lose the man she loved to the sea. She had already lost her father . . .

She realized that many of the island women were moving away with their boys and that the waiting Europeans were moving back in silence now. She felt sick with despair. She had to fight

441

hard against the nausea while Dr. Sam tried to comfort and encourage her to have faith and hope. But it seemed as if she had stood rigidly for hours, straining her eyes against the darkening sea, before a sudden shout went up from the people still keeping vigil.

A lone boat was lurching slowly toward the shore on the long swell of the tide, and she knew that it had to be Luke's boat. But she still didn't know if he was in it or if he was dead or alive. Eventually she could make out Jojo's dark head in the boat, his arms wildly waving, but there was no way of knowing what his gestures implied.

"Hold on, my dear," she heard Doc Sam's voice say. "Your man isn't one to let go of life easily."

But the strongest man in the world wasn't a match for the most dreaded killer of the sea . . .

"It's all right! He's alive! Caroline, he's alive!"

She heard the ripple of relief run around the onlookers on the shore, and then there was wild applause as another figure was glimpsed in the bottom of the boat as it was dragged quickly ashore by willing hands. She tore away from Doc Sam and stumbled toward it as Luke heaved himself up from the floor of the boat and almost fell into her arms. She disregarded the stench of blood on him as she clung, weeping, to his chest.

"I thought you were dead!" she gasped. "And I thought I'd never have the chance to tell you how I feel."

"I thought the same, my sweet lass," she heard his ragged voice. "It seemed the wildest time to be thinking of such things, but all the while I was wrestling with that damned beast, I kept wondering why I'd wasted all this time and never told you how much I love you."

442

"Then — you *do* love me?" she stuttered, almost faint with relief and thankfulness that he was safe.

"I love you more than life itself, my darling, and I'll spend the rest of my life assuring you of the fact. And can I take it that this show of affection means something significant?"

She realized that he was teasing her, and she could hardly believe it. He must be hurt, and yet he could still tease. Her eyes blurred with tears, and she heard him answer Doc Sam's rapid questions. "It's not my blood on me, man, and I've come to no harm, except for knocking myself out on the side of the boat. Jojo must take much of the credit for tonight's success, but between us we made sure the sea has one more bloodied shark in its depths. And all I want to do now is get home and wash away the stains of this night."

But it wasn't *all* he wanted to do. From the tightening of his arms around her, Caroline knew it as surely as he spelled it out in words as they made their slow progress back to the house. They were congratulated and cheered every step of the way. The whole island would be thankful to see Luke safe, and he was also clearly seen as a conquering hero.

But to Caroline, he would always be her own special hero. Her love, her man, now and for always, she thought tremulously. And much, much later, in the secret warmth of their bedroom, Luke held her close, and the rest of the world was forgotten as their own familiar rapture began.

"I began to wonder if it would ever be like this again," he murmured into her ear. "I never felt fear in my life until I feared I would lose you, my sweet love. And then there was the agony of wondering how badly I had hurt you by my need for you. Can you forgive me for pushing you into marriage the way I did? I gave you so little choice."

"There's nothing to forgive," she whispered. "And I had made my choice long ago, only I was too blind and stubborn to admit it. Oh Luke, I wanted you so much, but I never thought you really loved me, and I do love you—so much."

She felt the exquisite urgency of his desire and responded to him instantly.

"My darling girl, I've loved you from the moment I saw you, and I'll spend the rest of my life telling you so."

Their loving reached the heights of pleasure, and she knew she would never doubt him ever again. She gloried in the miracle that he loved her, and she knew she would never tire of hearing it. Yet deep within her consciousness she seemed to hear the fleeting echo of a wise old doctor's words.

There's more ways than words for a man to tell a woman he loves her . . .

And she knew it now. Oh *yes,* she knew that now . . .

FEEL THE FIRE IN CAROL FINCH'S ROMANCES!

BELOVED BETRAYAL   (2346, $3.95)

Sabrina Spencer donned a gray wig and veiled hat before blackmailing rugged Ridge Tanner into guiding her to Fort Canby. But the costume soon became her prison—the beauty had fallen head over heels in love!

LOVE'S HIDDEN TREASURE   (2980, $4.50)

Shandra d'Evereux felt her heart throb beneath the stolen map she'd hidden in her bodice when Nolan Elliot swept her out onto the veranda. It was hard to concentrate on her mission with that wily rogue around!

MONTANA MOONFIRE   (3263, $4.95)

Just as debutante Victoria Flemming-Cassidy was about to marry an oh-so-suitable mate, the towering preacher, Dru Sullivan flung her over his shoulder and headed West! Suddenly, Tori realized she had been given the best present for a bride: a night of passion with a real man!

THUNDER'S TENDER TOUCH   (2809, $4.50)

Refined Piper Malone needed bounty-hunter, Vince Logan to recover her swindled inheritance. She thought she could coolly dismiss him after he did the job, but she never counted on the hot flood of desire she felt whenever he was near!

Available wherever paperbacks are sold, or order direct from the Publisher. Send cover price plus 50¢ per copy for mailing and handling to Zebra Books, Dept. 3956, 475 Park Avenue South, New York, N.Y. 10016. Residents of New York and Tennessee must include sales tax. DO NOT SEND CASH. For a free Zebra/Pinnacle catalog please write to the above address.

DISCOVER DEANA JAMES!

CAPTIVE ANGEL (2524, $4.50/$5.50)
Abandoned, penniless, and suddenly responsible for the biggest tobacco plantation in Colleton County, distraught Caroline Gillard had no time to dissolve into tears. By day the willowy redhead labored to exhaustion beside her slaves . . . but each night left her restless with longing for her wayward husband. She'd make the sea captain regret his betrayal until he begged her to take him back!

MASQUE OF SAPPHIRE (2885, $4.50/$5.50)
Judith Talbot-Harrow left England with a heavy heart. She was going to America to join a father she despised and a sister she distrusted. She was certainly in no mood to put up with the insulting actions of the arrogant Yankee privateer who boarded her ship, ransacked her things, then "apologized" with an indecent, brazen kiss! She vowed that someday he'd pay dearly for the liberties he had taken and the desires he had awakened.

SPEAK ONLY LOVE (3439, $4.95/$5.95)
Long ago, the shock of her mother's death had robbed Vivian Marleigh of the power of speech. Now she was being forced to marry a bitter man with brandy on his breath. But she could not say what was in her heart. It was up to the viscount to spark the fires that would melt her icy reserve.

WILD TEXAS HEART (3205, $4.95/$5.95)
Fan Breckenridge was terrified when the stranger found her near-naked and shivering beneath the Texas stars. Unable to remember who she was or what had happened, all she had in the world was the deed to a patch of land that might yield oil . . . and the fierce loving of this wildcatter who called himself Irons.

Available wherever paperbacks are sold, or order direct from the Publisher. Send cover price plus 50¢ per copy for mailing and handling to Zebra Books, Dept. 3956, 475 Park Avenue South, New York, N.Y. 10016. Residents of New York and Tennessee must include sales tax. DO NOT SEND CASH. For a free Zebra/ Pinnacle catalog please write to the above address.

PASSIONATE NIGHTS FROM

PENELOPE NERI

DESERT CAPTIVE   (2447, $3.95/$4.95)
Kidnapped from her French Foreign Legion escort, indignant Alexandria had every reason to despise her nomad prince captor. But as they traveled to his isolated mountain kingdom, she found her hate melting into desire . . .

FOREVER AND BEYOND   (3115, $4.95/$5.95)
Haunted by dreams of an Indian warrior, Kelly found his touch more than intimate—it was oddly familiar. He seemed to be calling her back to another time, to a place where they would find love again . . .

FOREVER IN HIS ARMS   (3385, $4.95/$5.95)
Whispers of war between the North and South were riding the wind the summer Jenny Delaney fell in love with Tyler Mackenzie. Time was fast running out for secret trysts and lovers' dreams, and she would have to choose between the life she held so dear and the man whose passion made her burn as brightly as the evening star . . .

MIDNIGHT CAPTIVE   (2593, $3.95/$4.95)
After a poor, ragged girlhood with her gypsy kinfolk, Krissoula knew that all she wanted from life was her share of riches. There was only one way for the penniless temptress to earn a cent: fake interest in a man, drug him, and pocket everything he had! Then the seductress met dashing Esteban and unquenchable passion seared her soul . . .

SEA JEWEL   (3013, $4.50/$5.50)
Hot-tempered Alaric had long planned the humiliation of Freya, the daughter of the most hated foe. He'd make the wench from across the ocean his lowly bedchamber slave—but he never suspected she would become the mistress of his heart, his treasured sea jewel . . .

Available wherever paperbacks are sold, or order direct from the Publisher. Send cover price plus 50¢ per copy for mailing and handling to Zebra Books, Dept. 3956, 475 Park Avenue South, New York, N.Y. 10016. Residents of New York and Tennessee must include sales tax. DO NOT SEND CASH. For a free Zebra/ Pinnacle catalog please write to the above address.

WAITING FOR A WONDERFUL ROMANCE?
READ ZEBRA'S

WANDA OWEN!

DECEPTIVE DESIRES   (2887, $4.50/$5.50)
Exquisite Tiffany Renaud loved her life as the only daughter of a
wealthy Parisian industrialist. The last thing she wanted was to
cross the ocean on a cramped and stuffy ship just to visit the un-
civilized wilds of America. Then she shared a kiss with shipping
magnate Chad Morrow that made the sails billow and the deck
spin. . .

KISS OF FIRE   (3091, $4.50/$5.50)
Born and raised in backwoods Virginia, Tawny Blair knew that
her dream of being swept off her feet by a handsome nobleman
would never come true. But when she met Lord Bart, Tawny saw
at once that reality could far surpass her fantasies. And when he
took her in his strong arms, she thrilled to the desire in his searing
caresses . . .

SAVAGE FURY   (2676, $3.95/$4.95)
Lovely Gillian Browne was secure in her quiet world on a remote
ranch in Arizona, yet she longed for romance and excitement.
Her girlish fantasies did not prepare her for the strange new feelings that assaulted her when dashing Irish sea captain Steve Laf-
ferty entered her life . . .

TEMPTING TEXAS TREASURE   (3312, $4.50/$5.50)
Mexican beauty Karita Montera aroused a fever of desire in every
redblooded man in the wild Texas Blacklands. But the sensuous
señorita had eyes only for Vincent Navarro, the wealthy cattle
rancher she'd adored since childhood—and her family's sworn enemy! His first searing caress ignited her white-hot need and soon
Karita burned to surrender to her own wanton passion . . .

*Available wherever paperbacks are sold, or order direct from the
Publisher. Send cover price plus 50¢ per copy for mailing and
handling to Zebra Books, Dept. 3956, 475 Park Avenue South,
New York, N.Y. 10016. Residents of New York and Tennessee
must include sales tax. DO NOT SEND CASH. For a free Zebra/
Pinnacle catalog please write to the above address.*